Hexene broke into a run without thinking.

Technika called to her and was quickly outpaced. The word came again, terror cutting through it like a blade. Other words came after, and these were in hissed Theban. A makeshift hex, and as soon as Hexene heard the syllables, they started a thrumming in her belly. She might not be able to reach her magic anymore, but her body knew the feel of it. She rounded the last corner between her and it, and found three maidens closing around the giant Mafaufau, chanting, one holding a doll, one a piece of chalk, the third a pouch. The terrified zombie had backed up against a wall, his arms up as though to ward them off. They looked like a trio of leopards closing in on a wounded elephant.

Praise for Unwitch Hunt

With this fun fantasy, Robinson expands the world of his City of Devils series... // Robinson leavens the mystery with a lot of humor // and a charming heroine. This adventure is sure to delight with its embrace of being oneself whether others accept it or not. — *Publishers Weekly*

Just as Jane ruled the American Southwest in *A Stitch in Crime*, Hexene Candlemas shines for *Unwitch Hunt*. — Kate Sherrod, creator of Pulp Sonnets

Justin Robinson has yet again sent one sailing out of the park, over the stands, and somewhere into the neighboring county. — A. J. Sikes, author of the Redemption trilogy

Praise for A Stitch in Crime

Robinson's tale is a treasure trove of monstrous delights and, despite Jane's gruesome origins, she proves an endearing lead. With its heady blend of noir and campy horror, this rollicking adventure doesn't disappoint. — *Publishers Weekly*

Praise for Wolfman Confidential

Robinson's writing is a delightful cross between H.P. Lovecraft and Raymond Chandler, and it revels in its oddities and dark tones. His eye for detail and entertaining side characters (a cornucopia of monsters that have overrun L.A. and often speak in tongue-in-cheek one-liners) create a delightfully rich atmosphere that the reader can plunge into. — *Publishers Weekly*

Praise for Fifty Feet of Trouble

Once again, Justin Robinson provides an engaging and entertaining romp through the world of noir Los Angeles post-monster war. He's hilarious, his characters are endearing and boy, can he weave a mystery. — Ashley Perkins, *Game Vortexer*

Praise for City of Devils

Robinson crafts a uniquely interesting world that is sure to please horror, science fiction, and mystery fans alike. — *Minneapolis Books Examiner*

CITY OF DEVILS SERIES:

City of Devils
Fifty Feet of Trouble
Wolfman Confidential
A Stitch in Crime
Unwitch Hunt

OTHER CANDLEMARK & GLEAM BOOKS BY JUSTIN ROBINSON:

Mr Blank
Get Blank

Unwitch Hunt

Justin Robinson

Candlemark & Gleam

First edition published 2022

Copyright © 2022 by Justin Robinson
All rights reserved.

Except as permitted under the U.S. Copyright Act of 1976,
no part of this book may be reproduced, distributed, or transmitted
in any form or by any means, or stored in a database or retrieval system,
without the prior written permission of the publisher.

Please respect the author's rights; don't pirate!

This is a work of fiction. Names, characters, places, and incidents either
are the product of the author's imagination or are used fictitiously.
Any resemblance to actual events, locales, or persons, living or dead,
is entirely coincidental.

For information, address
Candlemark & Gleam LLC
38 Rice St. #2, Cambridge, MA 02140
eloi@candlemarkandgleam.com

Library of Congress Cataloging-in-Publication Data
In Progress

ISBNs: 978-1-952456-07-7 (print), 978-1-952456-08-4 (digital)

Cover art and design by Athena Andreadis and Kate Sullivan

Editor: Athena Andreadis

www.candlemarkandgleam.com

For the Owl and the Turtle

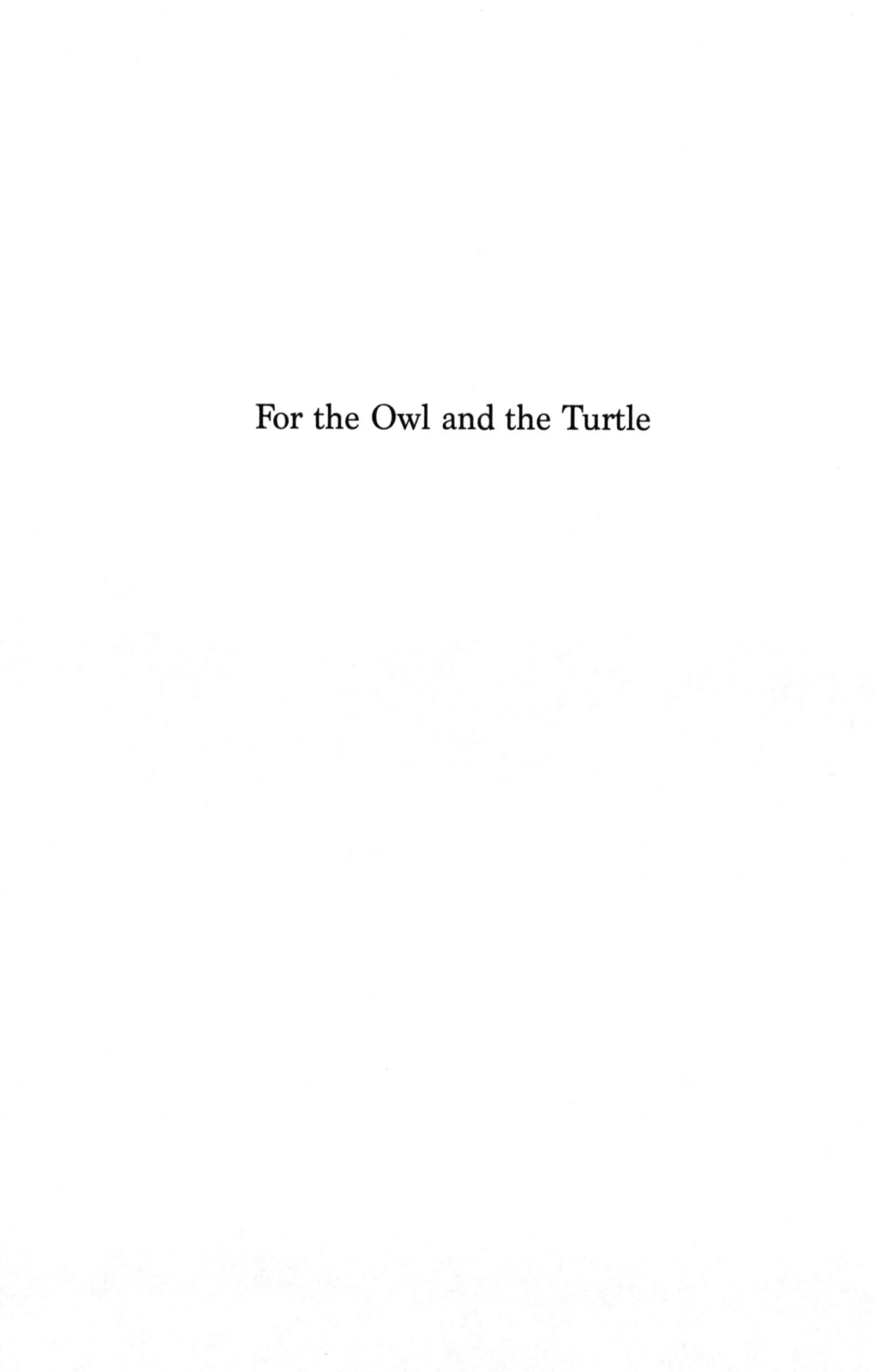

ONE

In a sane world, in a *just* world, Hexene Candlemas would be flying under her own steam, on her own broom, through her own clouds. Of course, the world was neither sane nor just. She didn't know what kind of plane she was imprisoned inside, but she didn't need to know its name to resent it. She resented the way it rattled and shook. Resented the way it stank of every monster that had ever been crammed inside. Resented the way the seats made her ass go partly numb. More than anything, resented having to be on it at all.

She couldn't fly, not anymore. Hence the cursed plane. It wasn't *actually* cursed, unfortunately. She'd lost *that* ability, too. Lost every last scrap of magic clinging to her soul, except for the one trick of being able to dissolve completely in water. She'd gotten to hang onto that one. Lucky her.

This plane was actually the second in a long day of travel. The second on this trip and the second she'd ever been on in her life. She had no idea how humans had handled this for so many years, or how monsters could handle it now. The first plane had been a huge passenger jet, thundering from Los Angeles to Santiago. From there, she'd had to switch to a smaller plane, one with twin coughing propellers, for the final journey to Las Brujas. Hexene thought the first plane had been the absolute nadir of her existence. Now, stuffed into a vehicle barely larger than its contents, she knew exactly what it felt like to be toothpaste. It was an important lesson the world kept teaching her: no matter how low one fell, there was always a lower place waiting.

The lowest place *should* have been the loss of her familiar. That was the worst thing that could happen to any witch, something her coven had warned her of as soon as she had incarnated her toad from the raw stuff of magic. Turned out there were indignities to be heaped on top of the gnawing grief. Every monster stared. Some whispered. The worst made *Oh, poor thing* faces. The Candlemas Coven were obviously witches, but what were witches doing on an airplane? Stare long enough, and the mystery would be solved. There were no familiars, no toads, or turtles, or salamanders, or songbirds, or ravens, or foxes, sitting in laps or sleeping in satchels or clutched against bosoms. Other monsters might not get *how* important familiars were, but they knew enough to note their absence.

Every time a monster made the connection, every time Hexene saw the understanding dawning in a fresh eye, she felt the loss anew. Her hand went to the empty place in her satchel and she found only an aching hole where there should have been a mildly grumpy toad. She was right back to being a kid again, little perpetually-bullied *Canela*.

Canela, for her red hair. Some witches changed colors when they turned, but Hexene came by her coppery curls naturally. They were an unruly mass on top of her head, and had been since the moment she was born. Her eyes were large, green, and usually looked like there was something nefarious going on behind them. Her face had a pugnacious cast to it, with round, freckled cheeks and an upturned nose. When she wasn't thinking about her expression, her face screwed up into a surly ball. She wasn't especially tall, and she was as skinny as a collection of reeds. She wore a dress that looked like an Amish quilt along with heavy brown leather boots. Her satchel, looking much the same as her boots, completed the ensemble, heavy with all the various magical accoutrements she could no longer use.

Unwitch Hunt

She attempted to lean back in her seat, only to be annoyed again when the thing stubbornly refused to recline. Next to her, Hermosa stared out the window. The crone's thoughts would be a mystery until she said something that would inevitably be biting. For now, though, she didn't speak a word, instead thoughtfully chewing on nothing at all. With her green skin, hunched back, and copious warts, their crone looked like a Halloween witch. Her patchwork dress was exclusively in dark colors.

Across the aisle, Hechalé hummed and knitted. Hechalé was more or less what one pictured when the word "mother" came up. She was tiny and round, with gray-streaked black hair and dark eyes. Her dress was made in a similar fashion as Hexene's—made by Hexene, in fact—and her shoes were simple slippers. Nothing seemed to touch the mother of the Candlemas Coven. Maybe it was because she still had people, so she hadn't lost everything when the familiars died. Back at LAX, before boarding the plane to Chile, Hechalé had said goodbye to her husband and her kids.

Hexene knew it would be expected of her, too, once she was officially the mother of the Candlemas Coven, to get married and have children. She didn't necessarily have to bear them—adoption was fine—but children were required. One had to embody her role in the triad, after all. In the embodiment there was power. Every time she tried to imagine the specifics, though, she found herself looking forward to skipping the mother part altogether. Being a crone sounded much more fun. She liked the idea of kids being afraid of her.

But watching Hechalé embrace Héctor and Lourdes and Francisco and Simón, Hexene felt the grip of the green-eyed monster. Not her; a different one. She didn't much relish the idea of childbirth, nor did she like the idea of having a husband around always poking his dumb nose where it didn't belong, but some of the side benefits were nice. She wouldn't turn down a small collection of people who genuinely loved her.

Hexene had said goodbye to the kids as well. She had been sort of a young, hep aunt. That had changed a bit when Francisco turned thirteen and started to look at Hexene in a way that no one outside of a Greek tragedy should look at one's aunt. They weren't technically related, but it was more than close enough to be creepy. Even if she had been interested, he was far too young. Hexene might still look to be a dewy nineteen, but she was over two decades Francisco's senior.

Hechalé's tearful goodbyes drew some gawkers. A lot of younger monsters—and a distressing amount of older ones—didn't know that witches could still make children the old-fashioned way. They weren't even the only monsters who could, but they were the ones who did it most often. It was a reminder to every other monster of one thing: witches were different.

Hexene cradled her satchel on her lap. Escuerzo, her toad, had his own pocket in there. He could ride around and see the world from relative safety, and she could reach in and pet him whenever she had the urge. Giving in to the old instinct just reminded her that he wasn't there anymore. Instead, when her questing fingers expected to find his dry, pebbly skin, they ran into something soft. It took her mind a second to recalibrate itself and remind her that Escuerzo was dead, and she was feeling a pair of dolls she'd fashioned in a fit of uncharacteristic optimism. Just in case she needed to hex the person the doll resembled. Just in case she got her magic back.

One doll was a woman in a figure-hugging red dress. The dress itself was made from satin Hexene had clipped from the original owner, who had probably gotten peeved when she'd discovered the vandalized garment. It was unavoidable; a proper hex doll needed that kind of connection. The red hair was fashioned from feathers, specifically those shed by the owner's red robin familiar. The doll was Lily Salem, the maiden of the Salem Sisters.

The other doll was a small man in a rumpled suit. His hair originally belonged to a weasel. Not *his* weasel—because he didn't have one—but anyone with eyes could see the man's totem within a few seconds of meeting him. Everything else on the doll had been stolen from the man it resembled, one Nick Moss, the last human private eye in the City of Angels.

Both hex dolls had been stuffed with a fragrant collection of herbs, cleansed in moonlight and bound with silver laces. They were ready to be used, if there was a witch around with the magic to use them. Hexene liked to think that would be her, should Nick or Lily ever need to be properly hexed, but for now, they were little more than a reminder of what she'd become. Someplace for her hand to go when she needed comfort her familiar couldn't give.

She made them right when she learned the Candlemas Coven was leaving Los Angeles. She'd been collecting the stuff from Nick gradually, and a visit to the Gloom Room, the nightclub where Lily sang with her coven, had taken care of the other. Hexene had barely been aware of her thefts. They had been more or less automatic, a compulsion she didn't want to examine too keenly.

She found out why when she actually stitched the hex dolls together. That sort of action practically demanded a mind sharpened to a knife edge. As she made the dolls resemble as closely as possible the weasel man and the robin woman, the reason she was compelled to do so was revealed in glorious Technicolor: these were her only two friends in the world.

That was sad. Even ignoring the fact that one was only barely a witch and the other was a sweaty little man perpetually on the verge of a nervous collapse, there were only two of them. Hexene's first impulse was a mental protest: *That can't be right.* She started listing acquaintances, one by one, and quickly realized every last one was a client. In a more charitable mood, she might have added the rest of Lily's coven in there, but even though Hyacinth and Verbena weren't traditional examples of their roles, there was enough of a barrier to make Hexene think of them as elders. And she was pretty sure she was older than both of them. So that left only two people in the world who saw her as something other than a provider of spells and hexes. Nick and Lily. Lily and Nick. Two friends in one of the biggest cities in the world. Now all she had left of them were two useless hex dolls. Her hand closed over the pocket, clutching them together.

She glanced around the cabin of the plane for the hundredth time, noting all of those who'd chosen to come to the city of witches. No actual witches, of course. They would be flying on their own personal airline—on broomsticks or in mortars or in some other device properly covered in flying ointment and inscribed with the correct spells. Instead, she was in this horrifying rattling tube with gremlins, robots, balam, ghouls, and, she noted with reflexive disgust, zombies. Hexene didn't have anything against zombies specifically, but she preferred them at arm's length. Being surrounded by their moans of "Brains" now reminded her of how far she'd fallen.

The one stewardess, an invisible woman whose disembodied uniform curved in such a way to suggest that in the event of a water landing she might be the most effective floatation device available, announced they were beginning their descent into Esbat Airport. Hexene could barely hear her over the chugging engines. Her stomach seized. Not because she was scared of landing—though the idea that this plane *could* land was farfetched—but because she was *there*. In La Ciudad de la Reina de las Brujas, a city made by witches. Once, she had thought of it as the home of her heart, but now it was forbidding, a club she no longer had the password to enter. A club filled with her people—or, rather, those who should be, but were now as far away from her as she was from human.

Of course, it was also the only place in the world she might get her magic back.

She felt Hechalé's motherly comfort on her and she turned, finding the other witch smiling in that way all mothers did. The one that said everything was going to be fine and don't you feel faintly silly for worrying over nothing? "Don't worry, sweetheart," Hechalé said in Spanish. "Everything will be sorted out soon enough."

"You never told me what we had to do." Spanish was Hexene's first language, too, and though she spoke English with no accent anyone could identify, she was slightly more comfortable with her original tongue.

"It's not important," Hechalé said.

"What do you mean, it's not important? Our magic, our familiars, are the most important thing there is!"

The mother smiled sadly. "I was a maiden once, too, and I thought that way."

The sound Hexene made was halfway between a groan and a growl. Now the smile was infuriating rather than comforting, and it hadn't changed one iota. "It *is* important, otherwise we'd still be back in LA."

"You miss your boyfriend? The little weasel man?"

"He's not my boyfriend!" Hexene snapped, but her hand closed around the pocket. She wasn't sure which doll she clutched.

"It's all right, sweetheart. You'll be home soon enough. And who knows, Hermosa has been hinting that she might like to *move beyond* soon." Hechalé delivered the euphemism in a stage whisper and with a superstitious look to either side.

"I can hear you," Hermosa grunted.

"Of course you can," the mother soothed. "Your hearing is as good as it ever was." Hechalé frowned, then found the thread she'd been pulling earlier. "As I was saying, you might need a husband sooner than you think. While your boyfriend might not be to my taste, one assumes everything is working...you know, in his pants."

Hexene might have been less horrified had Hechalé doused her with a bucket of water. "I have no—!"

"Oh, calm down. I know you don't have any personal experience in the matter. Otherwise more than one of our hexes would have failed."

"Please stop speaking."

"I know. It's embarrassing to hear your coven's mother talk about this, but it's a practical concern. You should have heard Hermosa when I first brought Héctor home. She was keeping track of my moon and tried to schedule the lovemaking so I would conceive."

"Virgin save me."

"That's what I thought too, but what does the Virgin know about that, eh?" Hechalé waggled her eyebrows, then composed herself. "This was before your time, you understand. Our old crone was looking to move beyond, and we hadn't found you yet. You do not know how happy we were when we saw your pretty red hair."

Hexene sighed. "Yes, I do."

But the mother wasn't listening. "Only redhead in Guerrero Negro! Only redhead in all of Baja."

Hexene shook her head. That was patently untrue. Her father and brothers had hair as coppery as hers and her mother's blonde hair had been strawberry in her youth. Hell of a thing for a fisherman's family. They burned bright red every summer before getting a thick enough layer of freckles to see them through the fall.

"And you had already started playing at hexes, hadn't you? If we had left you alone, you would have been your little village's hedge witch in no time. The point is...what was the point?"

"I haven't the foggiest."

"Aha! The relationship of every maiden and mother is difficult, for different reasons. You're going to be a mother someday, and it isn't too early to start looking for a man. So long as *looking* is all you do."

As she felt her face do its best to catch fire, Hexene looked at the options in front of her. She could start a fight over a hypothetical or she could get to an even more salient point. "What does it matter if I'm a mother or not if we don't have our magic?"

Hechalé sighed. "Being a witch is more than just magic, sweetheart. We are the Many-Faced Goddess made manifest. Embodying our roles isn't just important, it's what it means to be a woman."

"Virgins, mothers, or crones? Those are the only options?"

Hechalé's eyes hardened for a split second, then turned gooey. "We are going to get our magic back, Hexene. We will walk in the grace of the Goddess once again, I promise. It will just take some time and effort. Then maybe you'll be in a better mood and we can talk about our future as a coven and your future with the weasel man. Or someone better looking. Pretty girl like you shouldn't settle."

Hexene turned her attention to the back of the seat in front of her. She wasn't certain she could look at Hechalé without screaming, and she imagined that screaming was frowned on inside this ridiculous contraption. She reflexively reached into her satchel, fingertips searching for the warty, leathery skin of Escuerzo, but he was dead, if that word even applied to familiars. *Gone* might be a better one.

And Hexene's powers—all the powers of the Candlemas Coven—were gone with him.

Two

Hexene got her first look at her destination as she peered out of the tiny window by her seat. La Ciudad de la Reina de Las Brujas, or just Las Brujas if one was in a hurry, sprouted from the harsh wasteland of the Atacama Desert, a place no human would ever want to live in if they could help it. Hexene had never set eyes on it before; she'd just heard of it from other witches. No one talked about when it had been built exactly, but it was already hundreds of years old when it went public at the end of the last decade. Now the whole world knew about the witch capital, such as it was. It was a city without a country, without a government, but nonetheless one of the most important in the world. The revelation of its existence caused quite a few sleepless nights around the world—which was exactly how the witches liked it.

Stark against the brilliant sands of the desert, the city itself was formed from black basalt, pulled from the earth and sculpted into discrete buildings. To Hexene, the place looked jumbled, buildings growing out of one another, some crammed right up against their neighbor, with precious few vacant lots or plazas. Other structures crowned weathered trees, their desert-bred trunks gnarled. Towers rose up at irregular intervals, topped with minarets or domes or what looked like giant cuckoo clocks. Splashes of color came from the odd flag or pennon, as well as irregular spots of green. She silently hated the witches who filled the sky over their city, going busily about their errands with the freedom Hexene no longer had.

A neighborhood with perfectly squared-off corners separated the airport from the rest of the city. The buildings there were dull metal, the architecture perversely brutalist. Far taller than anything else in town, they cast looming shadows over the desert. The streets there were wide, and all at right angles. To Hexene's eyes, each block appeared to be precisely the same length.

"That must be Cogtown," Hechalé mused. Crones might be scarier, but no one could be as judgmental as a mother without actually saying anything outright.

"What is it?" Hexene asked.

"Robots," muttered Hermosa.

"Robots," confirmed Hechalé sadly. "I had heard they started to move in. The last time we were here, there wasn't a single robot."

"Didn't even exist yet. Better that way."

"Mmm."

Hexene ignored the mother and crone's discussion. The more she thought about robots in Las Brujas, the more it made sense. Robots liked rain about as much as witches did.

"Robots aren't the only ones, looks like," Hexene murmured as she watched a gremlin flivver, looking at bit like a secondhand pulp rocketship, zoom over Cogtown.

"It's not just our place anymore. The world is bigger. We helped make it that way."

Hermosa grunted in distaste. "Miss the old days."

"You always do."

They bantered as they rose from their seats and made their way down the metal staircase and onto the tarmac. Fingers of a deliciously dry wind raked through Hexene's explosion of curls. The sky was flat blue, almost painted onto reality, and it felt as though if she stood on her tiptoes, she could reach out and touch it. It was mere background for the wonder of the city beneath.

A crew of zombies unloaded the baggage from the bottom of the plane. No other planes were landing; it seemed like as much as Las Brujas was a place for more than just witches, it still didn't have too much in the way of air traffic—at least, of the commercial passenger variety. Esbat Airport had only the one terminal for people, but there was a much larger one some distance away that looked more like a warehouse.

Heat washed up off the ground as Hexene followed the rest of her coven into the terminal. The building was oppressively modern, echoing the machined blocks of Cogtown. Glittering in the late afternoon sun, it somehow managed to be both bright and foreboding. It was a bit like the Hollywoodland sign in that way. Thankfully, there was no indication that the airport would shoot off into the sky with brightly-colored explosions. So it wasn't *exactly* like the Hollywoodland Sign.

Inside, the atmosphere wasn't exactly welcoming, but it stopped well short of the forbidding exterior. The architecture continued along the same nightmarishly geometric, robotic lines, but the decor said this was a place of witches. Runed carpets stretched from one wall to the other. While any witch could take one look and know the runes were nothing special—banishing of dirt, aroma of elderberries, that kind of thing—visitors might think they were more sinister and mind their Ps and Qs. The art on the walls was a provocation: glamorous paintings of brooms, of pestles and mortars, of stools, of wardrobes, and in one particularly striking painting, a four-poster bed, and all in flight. Certainly no airplanes; those were for the benighted monsters who were scarcely more than humans in that regard. Hexene had once looked down her nose at the various contraptions the others used, from the most modern jet aircraft to a cobbled-together gremlin flivver. None of it had the simple elegance of her broom. Or its handling and acceleration. But mostly it was the elegance.

A line of monsters snaked back from a single desk, blocking the way to the baggage claim area and the terminal's exit. Hexene recognized the other people from her flight, swallowing the annoyance that accompanied accepting what had just happened as *her* flight. A single witch held court behind the desk, speaking to each of the passengers in turn, stamping a passport, and writing something down in a heavy, leather-bound ledger in front of her. At the end of the conversation, the rook on the desk would fish a small amulet from a wooden box on one end, hop over, and hand it to the monster. Two beefy zombies flanked the witch, both dressed smartly in black, watching the line with milky eyes. Something was off about the way they held their mouths, as if there was something clutched in there, like chewing gum they didn't chew.

The witch herself was a plump, smiling young woman with wavy red hair and glowing cheeks dotted with freckles. She fixed each monster at her desk with keen focus. Her clothes were rather plain, nothing more than a black dress and a matching shawl and pointy hat. Instead, it was her jewelry that drew attention: silver bangles tinkled on her wrists; several necklaces, each with a different pendant or talisman, rested on her ample chest. Rings clung to her fingers, and tasteful teardrops set with precious stones hung from her ears. She even wore silver combs and clamps in her hair, pinning it into a braided chignon. Half the jewelry looked to have a magical purpose. The rest was just shiny.

When the last of the monsters between the Candlemas Coven and the desk made its way to baggage claim, clutching an amulet in its tentacles, the witch turned her attention to the new arrivals. She frowned immediately, but quickly banished it under a layer of polite camaraderie.

"Ladies, you don't need to wait. This line isn't for us." She spoke Theban with an Irish lilt that was nearly as sparkling as the jewelry she wore. "You can just fly in wherever you like."

Then that focus she used on every arrival took over and she saw something else in them. Saw what they were missing. Hexene squirmed under the attention, wishing she could go back to when the other witch thought they were normal. A flash of horror and disgust washed over the maiden's features, but she hid it just as quickly as her initial puzzlement.

Hexene's hand went to the pocket in her satchel where Escuerzo should have been. She felt only the hex dolls.

"No, dear. We can't," said Hechalé.

"I see," said the witch. Even the rook looked at them with pity. Hexene peered at the ledger in front of the maiden and saw that it was filled with names, like a hotel guestbook. The witch was using a red ink that Hexene knew had to be at least half blood.

"It's a small problem," said Hechalé, with a glance at Hexene. "We're going to sort it out while we're here."

"Do you mind my asking what happened?"

"Mad scientist."

"Oh," said the maiden. "They *can* be trouble. What are your names?" Hechalé gave them. "The Candlemas Coven?"

"You've heard of us?" asked Hexene, annoyed at her own neediness. There had been a time when she would consider recognition to be her due rather than a lovely surprise.

"Oh, of course. I keep track of as many of us as I can." She smiled. "Call it a hobby."

"And you are?" Hechalé asked.

"I'm sorry. Used to dealing with the menfolk. Cora Crow, pleased to make your acquaintance." As friendly as she was, the maiden didn't offer to shake hands. She noted their names in her ledger in efficient calligraphy. "Welcome to Las Brujas, and good luck on your quest."

The zombies behind Cora never moved and never made a sound. Hexene had never seen zombies so disciplined, but as she looked around the airport at the other zombies who worked there, carrying bags or maintaining the aircraft, she saw that these two were far from the exception. All the zombies moved with the precision of robots. Stiff, even for the dead.

When they had barely gone ten steps from Cora's desk, Hermosa muttered the most unflattering description of Cora it was possible to make. It was enough to make Hexene trip over an imaginary fold in the carpet.

"My Goddess!" Hechalé exclaimed. "What has gotten into you?"

Hermosa didn't answer. She just chewed on that phantom bit of grit that got lodged in every old person's mouth. "You need to keep your mouth shut. Until the Many-Faced Goddess returns our magic to us, we aren't the Candlemas Coven anymore. We can't afford to make new enemies. We need friends!"

"Friends? You see where *friends* get us," the crone grumbled.

Hexene was inclined to agree. She only had the two, and they were both thousands of miles away, and had probably already forgotten her.

"Is this about the raccoon incident?" Hechalé demanded. Hermosa offered a noncommittal grunt and a shrug. "You and Serafina need to make peace over that. We can't nurse every petty little grudge in our lives. Especially not anymore."

"You tell her that. Ain't me holding the grudge."

"You two are impossible," Hechalé said.

"I didn't say anything," Hexene protested.

"You were *thinking* it. You forget that I can tell." The worst part was Hechalé was entirely correct.

The airport was not busy. Only a single passenger plane appeared to be waiting to depart, the passengers—mostly human, but with a few robots and some other monsters—lined up patiently to board. Hexene imagined that it was the plane she had just flown on, going back and forth from Las Brujas to Santiago in an endless cycle. The only other plane, visible through the wide windows, was stout and olive green, parked over by the other building. An antlike line of zombies marched in and out of its open back, hauling out cargo crates and loading them onto a pair of flatbeds.

Hexene looked over her shoulder at the rook hopping back and forth on Cora's desk. In that split second, she thought Hermosa's description had been overly kind.

Outside, a wide avenue separated the airport from the adjacent Cogtown. The vehicles on the street were of two types. The first weren't quite cars, but close to them, designed by robots and sparking with electricity as they hummed this way and that. The second were rickshaws, mostly pulled by zombies, though Hexene saw a single headless horseman at the front of a spectral rickshaw that managed to be the saddest thing she'd ever witnessed. Most of the zombies were well dressed, some in uniforms that called to mind bellhops, and some in semi-formal clothes that made them look like children from the end of the last century. One of these latter held up a sign with CANDLEMAS written neatly on it.

Hechalé led the way over, smiling as she got close. The zombie was young, with gray-green skin and milky eyes. His lanky arms poked out of a crisp yellow short-sleeved dress shirt, and his knobby knees were bare under his tight shorts. His shoes were heavy and buckled. Much like Cora Crow's zombies, this one looked like he had a wad of chewing gum in his mouth that he refused to do anything about.

"We're the Candlemas Coven," Hechalé said.

The zombie didn't say anything. Hexene would have expected a perfunctory "Brains." Not that anyone knew what zombies meant when they said it, but they said it all the same. This one said nothing, gesturing to the rickshaw before sliding the sign behind the cushions.

"I didn't think they would be sending us a ride," said Hechalé.

"Least they could do," Hermosa said, pulling herself into the seat.

"Who...?" Hexene asked.

"Old friends," said Hechalé.

"This Serafina person?"

"You'll see."

Hexene shook her head. There was too much mystery around this trip, but she would put up with irritation and intrigue if it got her magic back. She'd put up with a lot for that. She followed Hechalé into the rickshaw. The seat was nice enough, with fat black cushions under and behind her, and a running board to set her feet on. A sunshade stretched up over the back. Hexene was grateful; normally she didn't mind the heat, but this city was the inside of an oven.

The silent zombie stepped between the two poles of the rickshaw, took them in hand, and began a quick trot west into the city. The streets in Cogtown were laid out in a perfect grid. As the zombie approached every intersection, he stopped, looked both ways, waited for traffic, and then started up again at the same speed. To Hexene, he seemed less like a zombie and more like a toy train who could only move along its tracks.

Hexene took in Cogtown as they passed through it. The neighborhood's art deco towers were impressive, rivaling anything back home. The largest was a looming edifice whose hungry shadows vaguely suggested a dystopian future. After staring at it, and the traffic outside, she figured that it was a hotel. Robots of every shape and size trundled down Cogtown's precisely measured streets.

The border between Cogtown and the rest of Las Brujas was a series of winding walls punctuated by narrow alleys. Crossing into Las Brujas proper—and Hexene was already thinking in those terms—was a different world. The razor-straight streets were now meandering serpents. The terrain was no longer flat either, the streets rising and falling like petrified sea swells. The buildings were of no uniform size or type, and some featured turrets or rooms like hanging lanterns poking out over the streets. Others formed complete bridges over the alley-like roads, lights inside speaking to habitation. The architecture was *almost* recognizable, looking to Hexene's eyes as perhaps a bit like Medieval European, then French Colonial, but purposefully divorced from a perfect human aesthetic. Everything was formed from black basalt, the color coming from gardens, a few trees, window boxes, flags, and pennons. Most of the properties were surrounded by rock walls, protection hexes worked into the stone.

That wasn't the only thing the walls said. Graffiti, done in chalk, spidered over the rocks here and there. The most common was the simple and enigmatic MALLEUS SPEAKS—often, but not always, accompanied by XX. The latter appeared on its own from time to time as well, small and defiant.

"What does that mean?" Hexene finally asked, pointing at the hundredth swatch of graffiti.

"Some fool," Hermosa said.

Hechalé nodded sadly. "Perils of opening our home to other kinds."

Hexene frowned but didn't say anything. Didn't answer her question, and she wasn't used to this kind of insularity from the rest of her coven. They were never gadflies, but Los Angeles had all kinds, and they'd never shown any overt prejudice.

The rickshaw continued its endless trek through the labyrinthine streets. Hexene noted that not only were the streets not laid out according to any kind of rational plan, they also seemed to be actively working against quick travel. The rickshaw's ultimate direction appeared to be mostly west, but it looped and doubled back so many times it was hard to tell. The streets were never very wide, either, ranging from a little broader than the rickshaw to being too narrow for them to traverse. As though to taunt them, periodically a witch would zip by overhead, going wherever she wanted to without worrying about the maze. Pedestrians were mostly zombies along with the occasional human, both of whom deferentially hugged the nearest wall when the rickshaw passed.

The rickshaw finally stopped in front of what might have been a French Colonial house if separate wings had been stretched like hot cheese and connected with open-air staircases. Pillars stood around the whole structure, some supporting the roof, others going nowhere. A winding staircase led up from the street, through the basalt wall, and to the front door. A few window boxes added a bit of green to the oppressive exterior.

"Oh, it's lovely," said Hechalé.

Hexene didn't think it was bad, but "lovely" was a description she confined to architecture that reminded her either of Guerrero Negro or Los Angeles. The Candlemas Coven piled out of the rickshaw, and one by one went up the steps, Hechalé first and Hexene last. The door opened when they hit the top, revealing a smiling mother.

"Hermosa, Hechalé," she exclaimed, beaming. "It's so good to see you!"

Hechalé embraced the other mother. Hermosa merely grunted.

"Evangeline, I've missed you. Where is your family?" Hechalé asked. They spoke Theban. Hexene spoke the witch tongue when casting spells and hexes. Using it conversationally was going to be a challenge, but she could already tell she would get a ton of practice.

"In their quarters," Evangeline said. "We wanted this time to be for us. This must be Hexene," and then conspiratorially to Hechalé, "So pretty!"

"Enh," said Hermosa.

Hechalé ignored her. "Hexene, this is an old friend of ours, Evangeline Arcane."

Evangeline's skin was dark brown, her smile wide and bright. She wore colorful robes and a matching turban, which concealed whatever hair she had. She was a bit taller than Hexene, and thus the entire Candlemas Coven, with a powerful frame. She grasped Hexene's arms lightly and beamed at her. "*Very* pretty. I imagine you have more than one suitor trying to turn you into a mother before your time." She had a musical accent; almost French but not quite. A black cat leaned on one of Evangeline's thick legs and regarded Hexene with bright green eyes.

Hexene felt her cheeks growing hot, and her thoughts turned to the two hex dolls in her satchel. Her brain didn't supply her with anything to say back.

"She has more than enough time for that later. Is the rest of the coven in?" Hechalé asked.

"We were in the kitchen, preparing a proper welcome." She gestured behind her. A short hall featured a staircase and a large open area leading into a dining room.

"And Serafina is all right with this?"

"I couldn't get—" Evangeline stopped speaking when two more figures appeared in the archway of the dining room. The crone was a gnomish woman. Moles grew over her face as though they were at war with her features over who would stay and who would go. Her eyes were small but keen, and she grimaced through broken and missing teeth. Her skin was a greenish brown, like an old stump encrusted with lichen. She wore a voluminous black gown that made her look a bit like a grouchy ottoman. A large black dog with eyes like lanterns sat beside her.

The maiden was gorgeous. Her skin was lighter than the others', dusted with brown freckles. Her hair was a mass of loose red-brown curls shorter and more stylish than Hexene's. Her eyes were just as green as the cat's. She was taller than Hexene, with robust curves hugged by a black dress. If Evangeline was happy to see them, the maiden was positively ecstatic. A black serpent coiled around her arm, head poised next to hers.

"Welcome!" the maiden said. "I've heard so much about all of you."

"Thank you all for your hospitality," said Hechalé.

"How are you with Theban?" Evangeline asked.

"It has been several years since we used it outside of ritual."

"Spanish, then?"

"Please," said Hechalé. Hexene sighed gratefully, but quickly caught herself. She didn't want to admit weakness to anyone, but found herself especially reluctant to do it in front of the maiden.

"Spanish it is." The maiden surged forward, embracing first Hechalé, then Hermosa—who grunted in irritation, but returned the hug— before arriving at Hexene. "I'm Angelique Arcane," she said. Her hair smelled like jasmine.

"Hexene Candlemas."

"I can't wait to get to know you," Angelique said. Her accent was similar to Evangeline's, but softer and sweeter. Hexene smiled, and faintly wondered what Angelique wanted from her.

"Our crone is Serafina Arcane," Evangeline supplied.

Hexene mentally nodded and once again wondered what in the thousand names of the Goddess "the raccoon incident" could be. Serafina grunted and lurched back into the dining room. After a moment, Hermosa followed. Both Hechalé and Evangeline held their breath, eyes following the lurching passage into the dining room. Hexene found herself watching too, unsure if she wanted the two crones to embrace or hit each other. Instead, they promptly sat at opposite ends of the table and stared at each other in menacing camaraderie. Hexene couldn't help but be a little disappointed. Maybe the beef would surface later.

Evangeline finally sucked in a relieved breath before turning to Hechalé and Hexene. "You must be hungry. We made some toad wort..." Evangeline trailed off as she made the connection every monster did who looked at the Candlemas witches for any length of time. "Your familiars," she whispered. Then, "That's why you came. Why didn't you tell me?"

Even Serafina started, glancing first at Hermosa, as though her fellow crone could tell her it wasn't so, then at the two witches in the doorway. Angelique was who Hexene watched; the maiden's opinion was suddenly very important. Hexene saw the shadow of disgust darken Angelique's face, but then it was replaced by something else. Sadness, maybe...but not quite.

Hechalé nodded. "I didn't want to worry you."

"Worry me? That should be the last thing on your mind."

"We're here to reconnect with the Goddess," said Hexene. "Incarnate new familiars."

Evangeline frowned. "You know how to do that?"

Hexene turned to Hechalé and nodded, prompting the mother to silence their doubts—and the roiling fear in Hexene's belly. Hechalé blanched. "No, we don't."

"No one knows how to do that," grunted Serafina from the other room. "Never been done."

"Of course it has," Hechalé soothed. "There are legends of—"

"Legends?" Hexene screeched. Everyone jumped. "You said we could be witches again. That it wouldn't be a problem."

"It's not a problem," Hechalé replied instantly, automatically.

"Not a problem? You lied! You said you knew how to do this!"

"I never said that exactly. We're in Las Brujas, Hexene. The combined wisdom of every witch since the Great Hag herself is right here. There's nothing we could experience that some witch somewhere hasn't already faced...Hexene!"

Hexene was already running, out the door and into the gathering evening.

THREE

Hexene could still cry. That had confused her when she'd first been turned, because water was caustic to witches. She learned that tears weren't water; they were *tears*. It made sense in the way that didn't really, which was how one knew it was magic. The general rule was to treat the literal figuratively and the figurative literally, and then throw some eye of newt at it..

That didn't mean she *liked* to cry. She hadn't ever cried much even back when she was human. She had learned from a young age that crying at a problem never made it go away, but punching it sometimes did. Of course, there was nothing to punch here, and without her magic she didn't think she would be able to anyway. That made the hot ball of frustration steadily expand in her belly. She didn't think she could hold it inside, but at the same time there was no way to release it. So she cried, and got angry with herself for crying, which only made her cry some more.

She wasn't sure where she was going. Las Brujas, though her ancestral home, was alien. She barely registered the black basalt walls surrounding individual buildings, and the maze of alleys that made up the city. Occasionally she bumped into a human or zombie, and they always froze, the humans apologizing, the zombies either silent or muttering their single word. She ignored them all, too intent on her own misery.

Eventually she found herself pressed against one of the walls, curled in on herself, every muscle tensed to breaking. She was trembling all over, like a leaf just before a heavy storm.

"Hexene?" It could have been a minute after she stopped running or an hour. Time didn't have much meaning when all she could feel was the frustrating horror taking root in the void where her familiar used to be. She knew if she somehow found a way to let it out, the only thing that would be left was wet despair.

"Hexene?" the voice asked again. It was Angelique. Hexene didn't respond, mostly because she didn't know how. She felt the witch—*other witch*, she thought with keen self-hatred—slide down the wall to sit next to her. Angelique was quiet. Hexene felt something moving against her and she realized that it was the snake, finding somewhere else to perch on its partner. Somewhere it didn't have to touch Hexene. "They think that because we're maidens, they can get away with not telling us the whole truth," Angelique said finally.

Hexene wiped her eyes on one sleeve. She felt a persistent buzz in the back of her mind, like a hive of paper wasps. Night had fallen. She could actually see most of the stars, as Las Brujas wasn't even half as bright as Los Angeles. The illumination here largely came from lanterns and candles, though the east side of the sky—the part nearer Cogtown—was as murky as that back home. The air had grown colder, too, the heat of the day vanishing quickly in the bone-dry atmosphere.

"They lie," Hexene said.

Angelique nodded. "Even if they don't always see it that way. Either they're trying to save our feelings or they think they know better. They always have a reason they can justify to themselves."

"Yeah."

Angelique wore a big black witch's hat. Hexene liked the way it looked on her. Despite their popularity, Hexene herself had never owned one. Now it would be a grotesque lie to even think of putting one on.

"What happened?" Angelique asked.

Hexene didn't have to ask what she meant. She gave the short version. "Our familiars were kidnapped by a mad scientist who used them to make a new kind of monster."

"I don't know what I was expecting to hear."

Hexene shrugged. "It sounds a little strange when I just sort of *say* it like that, but that's what happened."

"What happened to the mad scientist?"

"He got arrested. He's probably in jail now, but I don't know."

"That's something, I guess."

"Would have preferred a good curse," Hexene grumbled.

"I could handle that for you," said Angelique.

The ball of frustration shrank, if only a little. "I'd like to do it myself."

"Is that what you'd do? If you got your magic back tomorrow?"

Hexene thought about it. "Maybe the second or third thing."

"Does your coven hide a lot of things from you?"

"Nothing this big. But then, there's never been anything this big to hide before."

"Of course. I'm sorry, I wasn't thinking."

"What else could there be?" Hexene shrugged. She felt the frustration swelling again.

"I don't know what you're going through," Angelique said.

"It's like there's a hole," Hexene started, then swallowed. "But not a hole, because it's got hard borders that hurt. So that whenever I think about magic, or I try to use it, it just aches, like I'm worrying at a cut that's not healed yet."

Angelique shook her head. "That sounds awful. And the Goddess?"

A bolt of ice shot through Hexene. A confession lurked there, inside, one she had never made. Maybe it was the moment, or maybe it was Angelique, but she said it: "I don't know if I believe in the Goddess." It was admittedly harder to be an atheist when one could work miracles.

"Oh? Where do you think our powers come from?"

"I don't know," Hexene replied. "It's not that I don't think there's *something*, but calling it a Goddess might be overstating. The idea that it has wants or thinks in any way that we could understand feels wrong somehow."

"I suppose it doesn't really matter when you get right down to it. If the magic works."

"Only it doesn't for me."

"Not right now," Angelique said calmly.

Hexene turned to the witch, finding her already staring back at her. No, not *at* her but *into* her. "You think it can be done?"

"Maybe. But it doesn't matter what I think. This is Las Brujas. We have the Baba Yaga Memorial Library here, just across town. Every witch worth her hexes will tell you that all of our wisdom, going back to the Great Hag herself, is in that building. If there's information on how you can incarnate new familiars, it's there."

Hexene snorted. "So you agree with them."

"No," said Angelique, her voice turning hard. "I think that your coven was treating you like a child, and I think that happens a lot with maidens. I think they should have told you that no one had done it before you came here. I think they should have let you make the decision on your own, even if you need a whole coven before you can speak to the Goddess and make another familiar. But I also think that you shouldn't let what they did get in the way of what you can do."

Hexene found herself nodding. Supposedly, maidens were very convincing. Monsters, humans, they all said the same thing, although *alluring* was the adjective they usually used. Hexene always assumed that it was less that she was convincing and more that the person she was speaking to was willing to fool themselves into agreeing if it meant Hexene would keep talking. It was difficult to say, since as a maiden herself, Hexene had only ever experienced it once as a human: when Hechalé, a maiden then, had pitched Hexene on becoming a witch. Hexene couldn't really be sure how much of her own excitement had been because she was being hit with a maiden's aura or how much fun becoming a witch sounded. Now, with Angelique maybe, Hexene was again. She certainly *wanted* to believe Angelique. Not believing her hurt even more than the hole.

"All right," she said.

Angelique grinned, got to her feet, and held out a hand. Hexene allowed herself to be helped up. The serpent coiled over Angelique's arm, tickling Hexene's wrist with its tongue.

"What's your familiar's name?" Hexene asked.

"Danbala," Angelique said. "He's a bit full of himself."

"He's impressive."

"Oh, don't you start. Pretty soon he'll be preening."

The snake did look to be basking in the praise. He reared up a bit on Angelique's arm and turned. A glint of golden light, coming from one of the lanterns on a building across the alley, caught his black scales. For a moment, it looked like moonlight shimmering on water.

"Too late," Angelique said, shaking her head with a chuckle. "Come on, let's get home. You have to be hungry."

Hexene's stomach groaned. "Apparently very hungry."

Angelique laughed. "Well, good. We didn't cook all that food for nothing." She led Hexene around a bend in the alley. A broom leaned up against the wall there, not far from one of the ubiquitous XX chalk marks.

"What does that mean?" Hexene asked, tipping her head at it.

Angelique snorted. "Some silliness. Come on, get on." She threw her leg over the broom and waited. Hexene got on behind her and wrapped an arm around Angelique's middle. She had been flying by broomstick for over a decade, but never as a passenger. She thought about the last ride she'd given to someone. It was Nick Moss, as it happened, up to Mulholland, a serpentine road running over the backs of LA's money. She'd thought it was funny and a little sad—her opinion of Nick as a whole, for the most part—when he'd frantically clutched her. She fought the urge now as the broom rose into the sky and Hexene had the horrible sensation of being completely under someone else's power.

And it was *cold*. Hexene's teeth chattered as she clung to Angelique. Flight had never been cold before, but then, she had her magic. She'd belonged to the sky. Now, this was another way to remind her of how much she had changed.

Las Brujas spun below her, but how much was the broom changing direction and how much was a sudden onset of vertigo, Hexene couldn't tell. From above, it became obvious just how labyrinthine the witch city really was. The alleyways obeyed no logic, and appeared to be there only begrudgingly. Cogtown blazed with electricity, spotlights spearing into the sky by the hotel Hexene had passed earlier. Only one other place was bright with artificial light: a hilltop on the south side of town.

"What's that?" Hexene called out over the wind, her voice quavering with the frigid air.

"The Château Rocheverte-La-Lucé," Angelique called back, injecting an eyeroll into her tone. "It's where the one mad scientist in town lives."

"You have a mad scientist here?"

"He's like an ambassador," Angelique said. "Don't worry about him. He's better behaved than most." *Surrounded by witches, he better be,* Hexene thought balefully.

The sky was far from clear, with witches zipping this way and that on a variety of conveyances. An amazonian maiden zoomed past on a full wardrobe—though perhaps ironically, she was completely naked. As she moved, the doors flopped open and closed, and Hexene could swear that daylight blazed from inside.

The trip was short, even though Hexene felt like she had run for a good distance to reach wherever Angelique had found her. She gave up trying to trace her route from overhead; the snaking alleyways actively resented any navigation. Angelique turned her broom about, flew a short distance, and soon was descending on a multi-tiered house that looked far different from the air. The witch set down on a large flat space on the rooftop, stopping only far enough from the ground that their feet didn't quite touch.

"Here we are," said Angelique.

"Thanks," Hexene said, dismounting carefully. She stumbled as she hit the landing pad, taking a few staggering steps before she caught herself. "Your own landing pad."

"Everyone has one. Otherwise, how would you get anywhere?" Angelique went over to a rack standing at the edge and placed her broom on the lowest level. Two other brooms were already waiting there.

"LA isn't built with witches in mind."

"That's a shame."

Hexene paused to take in the shadowy cityscape. Behind her, Cogtown glowed with machine lights. To her left, the mad scientist's home was a lone beacon. Ahead, Las Brujas was velvet black, punctuated by flickering stars. It was quiet, too, with none of the persistent din of traffic. Give monsters a city of their own and they turned it into a bedroom community. She thought she might like it here, though she had no idea what she would do with her time. Hex slingers weren't much needed in a city of witches. Did they even have jobs the way other monsters would understand them? Or had they shed that along with the need to be like anyone else?

"It's something, isn't it?" Hexene found Angelique smiling at her.

"I'm not used to this place."

"No, it's nice to see someone experiencing it for the first time. I've lived here most of my life, so I take it for granted."

"Where are you from originally?"

"Outside of New Orleans."

"So we could be speaking English," Hexene said in that language.

"I am out of practice," said Angelique.

"It sounds fine to me."

"French Creole in the house, Spanish in mixed company, and Theban when it's for witches' ears only." She switched back to Spanish, clearly more comfortable there.

"I haven't spoken Theban other than for spells since Hermosa taught me," Hexene said.

"Well, it comes back pretty quickly, or so I'm told. Our blood understands it."

"That's a relief."

"You're going to need it," said Angelique, as she made it to the edge of the platform. There, a spiral staircase descended directly down into another room. Angelique's tone implied a surprise, but Hexene refused to demand an answer. She was going to reclaim a little bit of power, even if it was ultimately petty.

Besides, she had to concentrate on her balance. The staircase stood over a second-story rooftop, but it would have been a short tumble to the flagstones surrounding the outer edge of the Arcane compound. Hexene followed Angelique through the ceiling and found what would be a foyer in a human house. Cloaks hung from hooks in the wall; a wardrobe sat in one corner. The bottom of the staircase even featured a welcome mat. Small, woven pieces of art decorated the walls.

"It's through here," Angelique said, gesturing with a twitch of her head. A door led into a hallway. Hexene found that it led into a walkway overlooking the dining room she had seen earlier. A thick rug muffled their steps and a chandelier alight with candles illuminated the room. Below, the other four witches sat at the table. It didn't look like Hermosa and Serafina had started anything since Hexene had been gone.

"We're back," Angelique called.

Hechalé looked up, worry in her eyes. "Oh, good. Are you hungry, Hexene?" Hexene nodded.

"Maidens," grumbled Serafina, shaking her head. Hermosa grunted in agreement.

"Now that you're here, we'll fetch dinner," Evangeline said with faint disapproval. Instead of going anywhere, she rang a bell.

A burly zombie emerged from the kitchen carrying a deep pot, the top covered in a pie crust vaguely sculpted into the shape of a dragon. Hechalé had a habit of overfeeding anyone who would allow her to; apparently that was a shared trait among mothers. None of the witches acknowledged the zombie, and he never spoke the only word he knew. He, too, looked to be holding something in his mouth. The pot made an impressive clunk as he set it down before shambling back into the kitchen.

Hexene found her seat, next to Hechalé and across from Angelique. The two crones barely acknowledged the maidens' presence, mostly staring with distant hostility at whatever caught their gaze.

"I wanted to make you something special," said Evangeline. "The filling will be a pleasant surprise."

Evangeline's cat hopped up on the table. Serafina's black dog sat by her. Evangeline cut thick slices from the pie. It was entirely dough all the way through, dotted with mushrooms and other bits of unidentified plant matter. It smelled as pungently as an apothecary's drawer.

"Eat up," said Evangeline to Hexene. "You're much too skinny."

"I've been telling her that," said Hechalé with smug approval.

"I'll need my strength if we're going to do something no witch has ever done," said Hexene, a touch of venom running through her voice.

Hechalé started, then smiled. "Good."

"And you shouldn't go to a Sabbat on an empty stomach," said Evangeline.

Hexene's head snapped around. "A Sabbat?"

FOUR

Hexene knew she shouldn't be surprised by the announcement of a Sabbat. It was, after all, the last few hours of the month of Mayu, and at midnight it would be the first of Aš, reckoning by the Theban calendar. Witches preferred their Sabbats at the first of the month. Still, it was hard to get the fractious witches of LA to show up to one, and the Candlemas Coven had stopped trying years ago. On another day she might be excited, but here it was another chance to be stared at. Pitied.

They would arrive by broomstick, since there was apparently no other way to get around Las Brujas. Each witch climbed up behind her counterpart from the other coven. While Danbala had no trouble, merely wrapping himself around Angelique's neck and shoulders like a muscular scarf, the cat and dog paced with consternation before figuring out where they could sit. In front of their witches, as it turned out. The cat had an easier time, but the dog was far more game.

They rose into a sky ruled by a full moon. Other witches swarmed through it, too, casting shadows on the velvet. They were all headed for the very center of Las Brujas, a place Hexene later learned was called, appropriately enough, the Stone Forest. It indeed appeared to be a forest, but an artificial one, sculpted from the same black basalt as the rest of the city. The level of detail was stunning, her eyes picking out new wonders as they neared, every time a splash of flame twitched in a new direction. The trees were intricately sculpted, complete with individual leaves, stone vines winding around them and copses of rock mushrooms amongst the basalt roots.

In the center of the forest, their destination awaited: an amphitheater built on the top of a small hill, blazing with firelight. At first, Hexene assumed the light had to be coming from torches, but the source was in fact more candles than she had ever seen in one place, set on the amphitheater's stones like clusters of golden barnacles. Flags flapped on posts spaced evenly around the rim, each displaying a spider, the patron of Aš, and thus this Sabbat.

The witches, on their variety of vehicles with their menagerie of familiars, gathered inside. As they arrived, they found seats and dismounted, or else continued to hover. There were no tunnels or paths leading in, the way there would be for a human-built amphitheater; the only access was from above. The stage in the center was ringed with concentric loops of seating. Witch culture was supposed to be egalitarian, and so, Hexene supposed, the layout was intended to reflect that. Based on how the maidens were treated within their covens, though, she doubted the pretensions.

The witches themselves were of every ethnic group across the world. Most dressed in the prevailing witch fashion, which meant black dresses, pointy hats, and often cloaks. A sizable portion was skyclad—that is to say, naked—which was the traditional way to attend a Sabbat. Others wore the costumes of their homelands, and a smattering looked to be wearing whatever happened when they stood too near an exploding closet.

The Arcane Adepts swept in, taking spots down near the stage at the bottom. Hexene withered. She felt the attention of the other witches on her, and a furtive glance around confirmed her worst fears. They were staring, and whispering, pointing at the familiars that weren't there. Once the lack of familiars was confirmed, the expressions curled into disgust. A few maidens gaped in amazement, as though Hexene were one of Barnum's freaks. They might as well have been the bullies from her hometown, calling her *Canela*, teasing her for her red hair or worse. Hexene clenched her fists, though using them productively was wishful thinking.

The murmurs swelled around them. Somehow, Hechalé and Hermosa ignored the talking. Both sat as straight as they ever did, watching the empty space in the center of the amphitheater. Hexene sank into herself, memories pinballing from place to place in her mind.

The Sabbat opened with a traditional invocation to the spider, spoken in unison by the assemblage. Hexene didn't see a cue to start, and followed along as best she could in halting Theban. The patrons of each month were close to saints in the witch mythology, the most common familiar types as emissaries to the Many-Faced Goddess. Aš marked the transition from summer to autumn, giving way from the warmth of Mayu. Customarily, Aš was a time for a witch to concentrate on her connections to others. Hexene had very few of these.

When the invocation was finished, and the witches went silent, a heavy clanking echoed over the amphitheater. It didn't quite sound machine-like, as there was no coughing engine or humming power plant, but it was definitely artificial, metal clashing on metal. Then a wood-and-brass dragon, flapping on wings of canvas stretched between a copper frame, crested the top of the amphitheater, swooped low, and landed in the center of the stage. As it came to a halt, it fidgeted like a real creature, flexing first one talon, then the other, and stretching its long neck. The way its glass eyes caught the light, it nearly looked alive. A large key in its back rotated slowly.

A man dismounted from a saddle on its back. He was dressed in archaic fashions, like Ben Franklin. Unlike Franklin, he was tall, and though he had a bit of a belly, his limbs were long and lean. He looked to be in his forties or fifties, but Hexene found it hard to tell, especially with the curled wig perched on his head. His clothes were mostly green, with a few white accents here and there. A smaller version of himself perched on his shoulders like a gargoyle, complete with batlike wings and a pointed tail. None of the other witches were acting like this was unusual in the slightest.

"Who is that?" she whispered to Angelique.

"Count Inflamel. That mad scientist I was telling you about."

Hexene wondered if there were ambassadors from all the other new countries, and if Las Brujas had sent covens to them as well. She tried to picture life on the ghost flotilla of Palatine or on the back of the leviathan Raja Makara, and found she couldn't. As big as LA was, as much variety as there was among the monster populace, it was provincial in its way. Human.

"My esteemed hosts and fellow primes, I once again bid you fond greetings from your brothers in Atomstadt." The Count spoke Spanish with the lisping accent of central Spain, and he was doing it through another accent that wasn't quite British but lurched close to it here and there. "Our peoples have long been two corners of a triangle, and traditional allies. We have collaborated on a number of grand undertakings, including the creation of the first monster, the humble zombie. Tonight I am honored to once again reach out the hand of friendship to the great capital of the witches."

Count Inflamel didn't *look* mad. Then again, not every mad scientist was cackling at full volume while trying to end the world with giant crabs. If they had been, they would have been ferreted out and burned a lot more often than they were. They only came out of the shadows because by 1945, they couldn't hide any longer. After all, what non-mad scientist would have come up with the atomic bomb?

After setting eyes on Count Inflamel, Hexene's initial hostility cooled somewhat. He looked like he had nothing in common with Uriah Bluddengutz, the mad scientist responsible for her present predicament. The Count had a genteel Old World manner; Bluddengutz was a gauche creation of the modern world.

"I have received word from the Grand Conjecture, and we wish to confirm the special relationship between our two polities. To that end, we want to offer you a far more effective system of water distribution than you presently employ."

The Sabbat broke into fearful murmuring. A witch couldn't make a potion, tend an herb garden, or scry without *some* water. She also couldn't painfully dissolve without it either. Hexene had no idea how they brought water to the middle of the Atacama Desert, and she'd been too preoccupied to wonder.

A regal African witch stood up and boomed, "Water is death! We don't need meddling over it!" Shouts of agreement chased her comment.

The Count nodded. "I understand your trepidation, but this would place the water under your command. No longer would you need zombies to carry it back and forth. No longer would you have to maintain basement cisterns. Your humans would thank you for their easier access."

"Our humans are grateful for what they have," said a gnarled green crone beneath a bear skin. She spoke with a harsh Russian accent.

"Atomstadt merely wishes to make our friendship clear."

The witch who stood now was a maiden, and Hexene watched as her coven looked on in approval. All three were skyclad. They were seated in the very front row, and as soon as the woman moved, the entire Sabbat went silent. She stepped up onto the stage, between the Count and his clockwork dragon. Her red hair fell in ringlets to frame her face. A sleek black cat padded next to her, and when she stopped, it sat as though it expected a group of Egyptians to start worshipping it at any moment.

"Your Excellency," she said in a musical Mediterranean accent, "we need no assurances from Atomstadt to affirm our affections. We are pleased to consider our special relationship to be ironclad. We are grateful your people wished to perform this favor, but we humbly decline. We witches are old-fashioned, and we've grown accustomed to our ways. And what would our poor zombies do if we put them out of work?"

The Count opened his mouth to protest, but shut it when she took another step toward him. Hexene had seen that look on a man's face many times. It was love, or close to it. A maiden's aura did that to them, whether they wanted it to or not. Since this particular maiden was in the altogether, Inflamel did his best not to look directly at her. Hexene, for the thousandth time, decided she'd much rather have a crone's aura of fear.

"I hadn't considered the zombies," the Count admitted.

"And why would you? They are often more seen than heard. Was there anything else Atomstadt wished of us on our holy night?"

"No, that was the entirety."

"Then would you excuse us? We have much business to discuss. It is Aš now, and as ever we turn our attentions to the world at large."

"Of course, of course." The Count turned and bowed to the four directions, the homunculus on his shoulders doing the same. "Thank you, daughters, sisters, mothers, and grandmothers. I am forever grateful for the time I am given."

Count Inflamel walked to his dragon, gave the key a few twists, and climbed into the saddle. The dragon took two loping steps, then flung itself into the sky, beating its coppery wings. Soon, it was up and over the wall of the amphitheater and gone. The other two witches in the impressive maiden's coven, the mother with an owl on her shoulder, the crone a spider, joined their maiden on the stage. All three were strikingly beautiful in their way.

"Now," said the maiden in Theban, "we can truly begin."

"Who are they?" whispered Hexene.

"The Moirai," Angelique returned. She named crone, mother, and maiden: "Morta, Decuma, and Nona. They're Harvesters." Hexene didn't ask for an explanation of that. It sounded like a whole conversation.

The Moirai started to speak, switching off between the members of the coven. At first, it looked like this was done at random, but soon Hexene could see it was for a larger purpose. The maiden spoke when they wanted to persuade, the mother when they wanted to comfort, and the crone when they wanted to frighten. They spoke about seeding more witches in the halls of governments across the world and made reference to the Imbolc Investigators, who were currently helping Congressman Akhenaten run roughshod over the government in the States. Hexene tried to listen, but found her mind wandering. She wasn't a political animal.

She wasn't sure *what* she was. She'd been slinging hexes in Hollywood for something to do. It made her money and got her out of the shop, but it wasn't really a calling. Even so, she would have given anything to go back to it, just because it would mean she had her magic. Her familiar.

The Moirai weren't the last coven to speak, but they were clearly the most important. Hexene spent the remainder of the time doing her best not to stare pugnaciously back at the maidens still staring at her.

Five

As the Sabbat ended, Hexene couldn't wait to get out of there. More than one maiden looked like she wanted to come over and talk to Hexene about her lack of familiar. That was even worse than them avoiding her. Fortunately, Angelique was just as eager to leave, and hustled back to her broom and was airborne almost before the last echoes of witch business died. The sky over the amphitheater was chaos as it filled with various flying implements. Several came close to colliding, but none actually did. The Arcane Adepts flew the Candlemas Coven back to the house, but as the others descended and dismounted, Angelique stayed floating..

"We're not tired!" she called down. "I'm going to show Hexene around!"

Evangeline waved. "Don't stay out too late!" Angelique nodded, then turned and rolled her eyes at Hexene.

"Where are we going?" Hexene asked.

"A maiden bar, you'll love it. It's in the French Quarter."

"Oh," said Hexene. "Where is the French Quarter?"

Angelique pointed to a section of town that was more or less invisible in the gathered dark, save for a few twinkling lights. It looked close, but Hexene had trouble judging. "Just over there."

"Where are we now?"

"The Caribbean Quarter," Angelique said, as though it were the most obvious thing in the world.

"How many quarters are there?"

"More than four. As many as there are places a witch can come from."

"So there's a Mexican Quarter?"

"Of course. It's…" Angelique pointed to the northeast, sweeping her finger from the city center to the border. "Over there, across town. Now, do you want to talk or do you want some of the best tinctures you've ever tasted?"

Hexene found herself nodding eagerly. She had never been one for tinctures before—she usually went for Shirley Temples—but she had magic then and so had other ways to entertain herself. Now, it sounded like a good way to forget. "Let's do that."

"Thought so."

Angelique spurred her broom north. Cogtown, to the east, looked like an electric sunrise. Hexene wondered what the robotic denizens thought of the metropolis of witches next door. They must be fine with it to have settled here, but she couldn't imagine such a relationship would be loving. Witches had more in common with the nature-oriented monsters, but then again, those tended to like rain.

Angelique's broom swept low over the dark rooftops. The architecture here was similar to the place Hexene now knew was the Caribbean Quarter, though to her untrained eye, it skewed a little older. It still had that nightmare quality of being distended, as though the city had been softened by flame and then stretched. The avenues were just as narrow, but from time to time she saw a lantern bobbing down one of them, marking the passage of…something. She was surprised by the tingle of fear that followed the lights. She wasn't used to fearing the unknown, but then, she used to be a real witch.

Without summoning the memory, she felt the bag enveloping her head on the awful day Escuerzo had been taken. She'd gone down to a beach to do a hex deal, and something had grabbed her from behind, strong as a gorilla and foul as a slaughterhouse. After the bag, her vision went white. And when she woke up, head splitting, Escuerzo was gone. She replayed the moment again and again, trying to see where she went wrong. The toad had *ribbit*ed just before the bag came down, and she knew it was a danger *ribbit*, but she had reacted too slowly. And suffered the consequences. They both had.

She sucked in air, forcing herself to see the here and now. Escuerzo was gone and there was nothing she could do about it. If she defied the odds and reforged her connection, then her familiar would be different. Maybe a toad, maybe not.

Angelique alighted on a flat space on one of the rooftops, a landing pad far larger than most. The roof was bigger too, featuring several arched rooftops at different angles, some above, some below the landing pad. A sign stood atop the tallest one, the letters blazing with trapped flame slithering up and down the curves, naming this place LE CHAPERON ROUGE. The staircase descended from the landing pad down the front of the building, its railing picked out against the dark with candles.

Angelique and Hexene dismounted, and Angelique added her broom to the customary rack off to the side. Other flying devices were stored here as well, including a large mortar and pestle, a few stools, and an old pitchfork. The last, Hexene thought, was in exceptionally poor taste.

"You'll love this place," Angelique said again. "A place for maidens to be ourselves."

"They don't allow in mothers and crones?"

"Oh, nothing like that. They're allowed, but why would they want to come here? They have their own places."

"Where they do their own things?"

"Exactly."

Hexene smirked. "A club where mothers can get together and crochet."

"Do you crochet?" Angelique asked with unexpected excitement. "I crochet!"

UNWITCH HUNT

"No." Hexene couldn't possibly emphasize enough that she did not.

"Oh," said Angelique, unable to hide her disappointment. "Well, there's none of that stuff here. Music, tinctures, and plenty of witches just like you to talk to."

Hexene nodded, trying not to dwell on the fact that there were no witches like her. The only redhead in Guerrero Negro, the only witch who couldn't work magic. She was Canela again. "What else is there to do in town?"

"Some witches like to go to the scries in the American Quarter, but..." Angelique made a face. "The Menagerie isn't too far from here. There's the Hanging Gardens in the Yoruba Quarter. Ix Chel Plaza...and more besides, but come on. Let's get something to drink."

Hexene didn't ask what the scries were—she didn't want to admit not knowing—but the others sounded nice.

The building looked a bit like a medieval French manor house, if the majority of its guests came from the roof. Towers and windows gave plenty of places for thick darkness to pool. The staircase went down to an alcove, where a zombie stood just outside the door. Hexene didn't get the perfunctory "Brains" here either. Several other zombies loitered in the shadows not far off. Their silence was eerie. Angelique never registered their presence. Hexene noted that each one had the characteristic chewing gum bulge in its cheek, and each wore a necklace like the ones Cora Crow had passed out at the airport.

Hexene followed Angelique inside the bar and found a place that would be called either cramped or cozy, depending on how charitable one was feeling at the time. Small tables crowded the center of the room, each with a crystal ball in the center, some filled with moving images, others pink-blue and smoky. Most of the tables had one or more witches around them, and they came from every culture on Earth. While red hair was inordinately represented, a good amount of the witches present had hair as black as crow feathers, and all of them had the glowing, unlined skin of maidens. Some leaned together and spoke in low tones, others drank their tinctures, and still others watched the stage at the other end of the room. Considering how many wore the fashionable pointy hats, the whole club looked like a collection of black, bobbing traffic cones.

The bar dominating the right side of the room looked like something out of an apothecary's shop. A selection of bottles lined the walls—Hexene saw labels in Spanish advertising different kinds of tequila, and a few in English for Kentucky bourbon and the like. Nick and Lily both drank whiskey, but Hexene never figured out if they did it because they liked it, or just because it was expected from private snoops and torch singers.

But the selection of liquor was absolutely dwarfed by what surrounded it. Jars and jars of everything from toadstools, to pickled newts, to black blood of the Earth, to Powder of Ibn Ghazi, and so forth and so on. Everything one would need to mix up a potion, or, judging from the hooch, a tincture to knock a witch off her broom. The woman behind the bar had her fire-engine-red hair up in a poodle clip with a small peaked witch's hat pinned to it. She mixed tinctures and slid them down the bar or handed them to one of three zombie waiters who silently plied the room. Her familiar, a large black rat, collected tips from the customers and trundled them back to drop into a glass flagon.

The stage was lit by shielded lamps along the front edge and lanterns on either side. A witch was onstage, but she was dressed in an unflattering business suit, her auburn hair pinned down under a fedora, her eyes behind lensless horn-rimmed glasses. Next to her, her monkey familiar was dressed identically, mimicking her every movement. She spoke without a microphone; Hexene guessed there was a hex involved to give her voice some volume.

"I tell you," the witch onstage said, in an accent that was an exaggerated and aggressive approximation of how American movie stars spoke. "It's tough doing business. Every day you come into the office, and all the work you did is right back on your desk!"

The crowd laughed, and a giggle forced its way out of Hexene. The witch's impression was perfect; humans used to sound exactly like that.

Now, it was more vampires and the like, but the impression still worked.

"Come on," Angelique said, leading Hexene to an empty table near the back. No witches looked their way, and for that, Hexene was grateful. The walls were covered in small paintings, every one of a maiden. They ranged from severe depictions of magical explorers to stuff that would never have been seen outside of a locker door in the States.

A zombie sidled up to the table. "What do you want to drink?" Angelique asked.

"I don't usually drink."

"Now's the time to start." Angelique flashed a grin.

Hexene's stomach roiled, but she managed to smile back. "I don't even know the choices."

"I've got it," Angelique said, sizing Hexene up. "What would you want? A Corpse Reviver No. 4? A Clock Stopper? An Alley Cat?" She snapped her fingers. "An Eve's Delight." She turned her attention on the zombie. "Two." The zombie scrawled the order on his pad and shambled to the bar.

"What's an Eve's Delight?" Hexene asked.

"It's delicious. You'll love it." Angelique looked like she was toying with a question. Then she spoke it. "Why don't you drink?"

"No one to drink with."

"That's not the case anymore. In Las Brujas, you have witches everywhere who understand you."

"Who look at me like a freak."

"No one is looking now," Angelique said.

Hexene shook it off. She didn't want to talk about the task ahead of her. She wanted to talk about something, anything else.

"I tell you," said the witch onstage, "my wife. I don't know why I'm the one in the office when she's the one spending all the money!"

The zombie returned and silently laid two tinctures on the table, each in a high, fluted glass. A mandrake root curled around a broom-shaped toothpick as a garnish. Angelique dropped a pair of thin copper coins decorated with snakes on the table. The zombie pocketed them and returned to his slow orbit around the bar.

"What's with the zombies here?" Hexene asked.

Angelique sipped her tincture. "What do you mean?"

"Where I'm from, they're constantly yakking. Brains this and brains that."

"Oh, they do that down here, too. They just can't talk with the hex scrolls in their mouths."

Hexene couldn't hide her horror. "You're controlling them?"

"The ones who work for us," said Angelique. "Why wouldn't we?"

"Because they're people."

Angelique chuckled and like everything else, she did it so prettily, Hexene was ready to forgive her anything. "They're *zombies*, Hexene. Why do you think we made them in the first place? Besides, what would a zombie do with free will?"

"That's for them to decide."

"What do they do back in Hollywood?"

She shrugged. "Janitors, bus drivers, waiters..."

"The same thing they do here," Angelique said, "and I bet where you're from, they can be fired at any time."

"I suppose." Hexene only had secondhand knowledge of what actual jobs were like. It all came from her clients trying to make small talk she was generally uninterested in.

"Here, we'd never put our zombies out in the cold. We give them all they could need and all they have to do is a little work in return. It's easy. Besides," her tone turned dark, "you should see what they do without the proper guidance."

Hexene frowned. "What do they do?"

Angelique swept the idea away with a hand. "It's not like they don't have a choice. We don't kick zombies out of Las Brujas. We're not cruel; they can renew their amulets without the hoops other monsters have to jump through. They can stick to the Catacombs all they want."

"The Catacombs?"

"Try your tincture," Angelique prompted.

Hexene looked down at the liquid dubiously. It was mostly green, veined with distinct lines of red and gold. She brought it to her lips and took an experimental sip. It tasted a bit like a nightmare that unexpectedly transformed halfway through into a restful dream about petting a cat. It was also a mite salty; she was pretty sure that was the death cap. Like any liquid, it burned a little, though this was a cleansing burn.

"What do you think?"

Hexene tried to tell her, but immediately burped. A perfect bubble containing the image of a forest floated out of her mouth and rose to the ceiling before popping with the faint sound of wind through new leaves.

"Good, then," said Angelique. She took a sip of her own, but didn't follow it up with a belch. "The Catacombs are below the city. They go down to the reservoir."

"Are there houses down there? Apartments?"

"Who knows?" Angelique said. "They must like it down there, otherwise all they'd have to do to live somewhere else is get in good with a witch. We all have work that needs to be done."

Hexene was about to push a little further when the witch on stage said, "Thank you for your kind attention! I'm going home to my nuclear family to read a newspaper!" She waved and disappeared between the red velvet curtains, the monkey following.

A black-haired witch dressed like a magician's apprentice stepped through the curtains with a theatrical flourish, and, in German-accented Spanish, said, "Let's have another round of applause for Bill Jones of Wichita, Kansas!" The crowd broke into fresh cheers. Apparently, Bill Jones was popular.

"Now, we have a special guest tonight. He's also from the States, but he hails from the swamps of Florida. Please give a warm welcome to His Supreme Greatness, Lord Hammersmith!"

The witch applauded before stepping back and holding open the curtain. A gremlin hobbled in from the back, hauling a massive trunk behind him. A ring of long white hair circled the base of his skull and hung to the middle of his back in frizzy waves. He wore a red bowtie, his Crow-given amulet, and nothing else.

"Evening," he hissed. He opened the trunk up and removed a cartoonishly large sledgehammer. A single witch hooted and clapped. The gremlin grinned, raised an eyebrow, and set it aside. "Want to talk... vampires." The gremlin straightened up and waggled his scaly eyebrows. "Hello, pretty lady." Then he took a step to the left, adopted a haughty posture and said, "Go 'way, gremlin!" He held up a claw, and in his normal voice said, "Just minute." He withdrew a perfume bottle garishly labeled "AB+" and sprayed it behind his ears. "How 'bout now?" he asked with a leer. He got a few laughs, but none as big as Bill Jones had.

"So tell me about yourself," Angelique said, finished with the gremlin on stage.

"Like what?" Hexene couldn't think of anything offhand that someone might want to know.

"What do you do in LA?"

"Sling hexes. Fix the weather. The usual."

Angelique shook her head. "Nothing else?"

"What would there be?" Hexene frowned. She was honestly curious as to the answer.

"Is there anybody special?"

Hexene's mind went immediately to her two hex dolls, but she fought the urge to reach for them. She *certainly* never pictured either Nick or Lily in her mind's eye. "No!" she said, scandalized. "I'm a maiden!"

"Not all maidens are *maidens*."

"If you want the power, you are."

"And you want the power."

"Of course. What else is there?"

"But you don't have the power," Angelique said, "so you're free. Is there someone?"

Hexene shook her head. "You told me before not to give up."

Unwitch Hunt

"I'm saying there could be a consolation prize. Your mother and your crone can't stop you from doing whatever you want with whomever you want."

Hexene coughed, staring into her drink. "I haven't been thinking about that."

"Maybe you should start. We probably don't have the variety you had back home, but nearly every mother in the city has a family. Sons who might be interested in helping you pass the time."

"I don't want their sons."

"They have daughters, too."

"That's not the point."

Angelique shrugged. "If you don't like humans, monsters come in from all over. They stay over in Cogtown."

Hexene shook her head. She found she couldn't look anywhere else other than the tincture. "Are you doing that?" she finally asked.

"Wouldn't you like to know?" Angelique said, and Hexene heard the smirk in her voice. But there was a softness to the teasing, as though the question got to something real. Angelique paused, and then, her tone once again merely friendly: "A friend of mine is here. You'll like her."

"Angelique! I'm not—"

"Oh, not like that. She's a friend."

Hexene turned, and found a stocky woman painfully skirting the tables while leaning heavily on a cane. Hexene couldn't tell if her hair was gray, blonde, or something in between. Her face was round and inviting, and not heavily lined. A black bat clung to her pointed hat, squeaking with dismay whenever she took an especially lurching step.

"*She's* a maiden?" Hexene said. If this witch was a maiden, Hexene was a martian.

"No, she's a friend. Like I said, they let mothers and even crones in here. They just generally don't really want to come."

The new arrival finally managed to reach their table, panting like a werewolf in summer. She said something in exasperated French.

"In Spanish please, for Hexene's sake," Angelique said.

"I'm sorry," said the new witch, busying herself with sitting down. She rattled the chair around to get some space, giving a few irritated glances to the nearby tables for having the temerity to exist where she wanted to be. She sounded American, and she looked like she had come from hearty Midwestern stock.

"Hexene Candlemas, this is my friend, Petunia Pendulum."

"It's nice to meet you," said Petunia. "I'm sorry. This is just a bit later than I like to be out. And a bit louder than I like anywhere." She cast a baleful look at the stage, where Lord Hammersmith was in the process of pulverizing a balam idol with the sledgehammer.

"Likewise," said Hexene in English.

Petunia brightened. "You speak English!"

"I'm from LA. Well, not originally, but that's where I live."

"Tinseltown, huh?" Her accent was definitely Midwestern. The vowels were flatter than the dustbowl. "And you came all the way out here. I suppose we all need to do a pilgrimage to the motherland."

"Or just move in," Angelique retorted. She sighed. "It feels weird to speak English again. Serafina and Evangeline don't like it. Mostly because they have maybe ten words between them."

"Hechalé and Hermosa don't speak it either. They never bothered to learn. Hermosa thought that if someone wanted Candlemas help, they could ask in Spanish."

Angelique laughs. "Sounds like a crone to me."

"Oh yeah," Hexene sighed, then turned to Petunia. "What about you? Does your coven speak English?"

Petunia's expression turned dark. "They...did," she said.

Hexene winced. "I'm sorry, I didn't know."

"I should have said something," Angelique apologized.

"It's okay," Petunia said, in a way that made it obvious that not only was it not, but never would be. "It's what happens when you try to fly in a storm. A storm *I* told them was coming." Her bat squeaked sadly.

"That's terrible," Hexene said. She'd been caught in a storm once. She probably would have died had someone not been there to shield her. As it was, she still remembered the small, burning points where the raindrops had dissolved her skin. Look closely enough, and the scars lingered.

"Let's talk about something else," Angelique said.

A zombie approached the table, and Petunia sent him away with a request for herbal tea. That was normally Hexene's drink. The burn helped wake her up in the morning.

"Um...I was wondering about Harvesters?"

Angelique rolled her eyes. "It's a political thing. The short version is that they think no other country should be running without our input."

"That doesn't sound terrible," Hexene ventured. As monsters went, it was her opinion that witches were the most sensible.

"Las Brujas is best left alone," Angelique said. "We'll keep talking to Atomstadt and Elphame for the sake of the old ties, but other than that, the world isn't for us. The humans made it, the monsters tweaked it, and it's theirs. We have our home, and it needs to stay that way. You know what the Harvesters call us? Worms."

"That does sound unnecessarily mean."

Angelique gave a vindicated nod. "All because we think we should tend to our own gardens."

"Politics," said Petunia in a voice dripping with disgust. She gave Angelique a stern look, quickly evaporating as she turned to Hexene. "Hexene, dear, tell me more about yourself. You're a maiden?"

Hexene hesitated, then nodded, then dove into explaining what had happened to her. She didn't want Petunia to figure it out on her own; better to do it all at once. Predictably, an expression of loathing washed over the mother's face. Then she flicked a questioning glance at Angelique.

"Hexene is going to be spending all her time in the library until she finds the way to incarnate a new familiar," Angelique said. Then, cutting off Petunia, "Which is something that is possible."

"Oh," said Petunia. "Good, good. And you, Hexene, do you have a boyfriend?"

"No!" Hexene snapped. "Why does everyone ask that?"

Petunia flushed red. Angelique laughed. "Because we know how to deal with stress here."

Hexene suddenly found her tincture of vital interest. It was half finished, and she was feeling it. The room swayed a bit, and she saw falling leaves on the edges of her vision. The gremlin on stage wrapped up his act to applause, some enthusiastic, most perfunctory, and the magician's assistant came out on stage again. She thanked everyone and promised a band after a half-hour break. The hubbub of conversation replaced the stage sounds, a welcome relief after a stretch of a gremlin detailing various inventions, then smashing things with a giant hammer.

Hexene let herself fade into the background as Angelique and Petunia talked. She just wanted to stay anonymous, keep the witches in this place from noticing her, noticing that she wasn't like everyone else. Every time her mind wandered off the path she wanted, into the shadowed places of her current situation, she lifted the tincture to her lips. Before long, the glass was empty. The zombie silently brought a new one. She only looked up when she felt the conversation die.

Petunia and Angelique were looking over Hexene's head, at the door. A group of maidens had come in, and they cruised to the bar like sharks. They wore the customary black gowns, hats, and cloaks, but were distinguished by a patch on their cloaks, and another sewn onto the tops of their sleeves. After some dedicated staring and squinting, Hexene made it out as a coat of arms, the four quadrants filled with a traditional voodoo doll, a two-masted pirate ship, a stylized sea turtle, and manacles with a broken chain.

"Who are they?" Hexene asked.

"Police," said Petunia.

"Las Brujas has police?"

"We have El Cuerpo de Barrenderas Policía Occulta. They're not police because technically they don't report to anyone. Not even each other."

"Oh," said Hexene. "I didn't know we had laws."

"We don't." Angelique said. "Not officially, anyway. Las Barrenderas are here to keep things from getting out of hand."

"They're here to do whatever a bunch of maidens without any strong guidance want to do," Petunia said.

Angelique conceded the point with a cock of her head and a single nod. "By that insignia, they're from the Caribbean Ward," she said. "Our local girls."

"Do you know them?"

"Oh, Goddess, no," Angelique said. "The best thing to do with Barrenderas is to stay out of their way."

The old Hexene found herself wanting to stand in the way of these women. She wasn't fond of cops as a professional courtesy, and being from the land of the LAPD, it was hard to think of the police as anything but the biggest and best-armed gang in town. But she was the new, powerless Hexene. Barely a witch, and certainly no match for those four maidens at the bar, all of whom looked like they were spoiling for a fight. Hexene turned back to her drink.

"Good idea," said Angelique. "No reason to let them ruin a good evening."

Six

Hexene woke up with cotton in her mouth, aching eyes, and burning sparkles in her head. The night had gone on far longer than she intended, only ending when the witches in Le Chaperon Rouge finally spotted her, and she convinced Angelique to leave. At least, that's what spotty memory told her. Propping herself up on one arm, she took in the room. When she'd come home last night, it had been too dark to see and she wasn't in much condition to look anyway. Her hand reflexively went to the place on her abdomen where Escuerzo used to nurse from her, and tensed when it came down over her witch's teat with no suckling toad in between.

She blinked in the sunlight and found it flooding in through two improperly curtained windows. Last night's bed was a sofa that probably would have been more comfortable if her head wasn't hammering like artillery. She realized then that Hermosa was across the room, sitting up in a large bed and glowering at her. "You're up," she said. "Thought you were going to sleep through the day."

"What time is it?" Hexene croaked.

"Sun's almost all the way up."

Hexene groaned and fell back into the couch. She'd been asleep for less than an hour. The thumping in her skull beat time with her heartbeat as she stared at the ceiling, where the black basalt had been scalloped into baroque designs. The door creaked open.

"She's awake," grunted Hermosa.

"Oh good," said Hechalé. "I didn't want to wake her. You know how she gets."

"How do I get?" Hexene demanded, and then regretted it.

"Like that. Now eat, get clean, and we're going. We have a lot of work ahead of us."

"Right," said Hexene. "What am I supposed to—"

A wooden tray plopped down from somewhere above, landing across her lap. Hechalé loomed into her vision. "Go on now."

Hexene struggled into a sitting position, finding that the tray held a plate of food and a cup of tea. The tea was pungent, forcibly assaulting her senses, just the way she liked it. It wasn't truly tea if it didn't fight back. The food was a mixture of mushrooms, peppers, pears, and garlic along with thick slices of bread. The more she ate, the more her headache subsided. It wouldn't go away entirely; like any mother, Hechalé could trivially heal a hangover with a meal, but she wasn't going to let her maiden off the hook completely.

While she ate, Hermosa got out of bed and lurched from the room. Hechalé cleaned up, making the bed she and the crone had shared, and straightening up a room that didn't need it.

When Hexene had eaten everything on the tray and satisfied herself there was nothing else hiding on it or beneath it, she got off the couch with difficulty, and at a gesture from Hechalé, found her way to the bathroom. She was mildly interested to see what one of those looked like in a city built by her people. Bathrooms could be dangerous places for those who had bad reactions to water.

Superficially, it looked a lot like a bathroom back home. The tub was part of the floor, decorated with reliefs of what Hexene imagined were witches in the Caribbean, doing a lot of dancing and boiling some potion or other in cauldrons. She found everything she needed to bathe, except for one thing. She wasn't going to leave out used oil, especially when that oil contained her top layer of skin. She lifted the aluminum lid of what looked like a garbage can and found a pink lump sitting at the bottom.

"Bonjour extrêmement!" said the lump.

"Uh...hi. Do you speak English? O Español?"

"I do!" the lump said in English. "Are you going to feed me?"

"Feed you?"

"Oh yes, with tasty oil and pumice and ashes and skin and I will feast and know you."

"Oh," said Hexene. "I suppose so."

"Happy days are here again!"

Hexene stared at the blob. So this was the solution witches here had landed on. Runes had been worked into the sides and lid of the creature's home. Hexes, most likely, to keep it there. This looked to be the second kind of monster witches had enslaved in their utopia, but at least this one seemed more or less happy.

She pulled her dress over her head and hung it on a hook behind the door. She felt a momentary flash of modesty, at being naked in front of a blob, but that was easy to get past. Turning into a monster did something to everyone's minds. She only knew it firsthand by what becoming a witch did to her, but she knew *something* happened to everyone else, and blobs were among the most changed. They hardly seemed to perceive time and space the way others did. The thought of this one seeing her naked body and thinking of her as anything other than food was remote.

Satisfied, she stepped into the tub and found the jar of ash. She covered herself until she was gray from head to toe. Then she opened the olive oil and massaged it into her skin. When she had worked everything into a slate-colored paste, she plucked a strigil from its rack and carefully scraped the stuff off. It came with a layer of her skin, leaving her pink and glowing. Each scrape she dropped onto the blob, who consumed it happily and asked for more, in between telling her about different novelty shops in cities across the globe. When Hexene was finished, she did feel far more capable of facing the day. She pulled her dress back on and paused at the door.

"Are you going to be okay?" she asked the blob.

"Oh, wonderful!" it said, voice muffled inside the can.

Hexene shrugged and went out. She pulled on her thick socks and old brown leather boots. She was slightly surprised she'd had the presence of mind to take them off last night. Or, more accurately, a little over an hour ago.

"Finally," said Hermosa.

"Oh, good. You're so pretty when you clean up," said a beaming Hechalé.

"Thanks," Hexene said in monotone. The Candlemas Coven went downstairs. Hexene, who had only seen this part of the house in the dark and while brutalized by tinctures, took a few turns to get her bearings. They found their way to the dining room, where a meal was in full swing, enjoyed by all three Arcane Adepts as well as a white-haired man and several people well into their middle age. Zombies waited on everyone silently, serving breakfast and taking away empty plates.

"So good to see you," said Evangeline. "Please, sit down, there's enough for everyone."

"No time," grunted Hermosa. Serafina grunted back at her, holding a cloth parcel tied with string. Hermosa accepted it and whatever noise she made might have well meant *thank you*.

"We're sorry," said Hechalé. "We want to get started as soon as we can. There is no time like the present. But...is this François?"

"Yes, it is," the white-haired man said, standing only with difficulty. "It has been a long time."

"Oh, François, you're as young as the day we saw you last," Hechalé lied, going around the table to embrace him. She held him gingerly, quite aware of how delicate the old man was. "And this can't be Samuel!"

The younger man—though younger only by comparison—sitting next to François got up, smiling. What hair he had was iron gray, and back home he would be well past retirement age. "It is. You look exactly the same."

"I'll save you time," Evangeline said, pointing to her other three children in order of age. "Monique, Cassandra, and little Raoul."

Little Raoul looked old enough to run a law firm and complain about his back. Hexene nodded politely to each one, but Little Raoul was the only one to step around the table and take her hand. She saw the same look in his eyes that she'd seen in Inflamel's at the Sabbat. Hechalé did the hard work of gushing over everyone and commenting how good they all looked while they deflected, pointing out their obvious aging. Hexene merely smiled distantly as Hermosa sidled over to Serafina. Soon the two crones were muttering at each other and making the clattering rock sounds that was their version of laughter. Hexene watched them, bemused. Whatever bad blood had existed before looked well and truly gone. The raccoon incident must have been overblown. She made a mental note to ask what it was.

"We should be leaving," Hechalé finally said.

"All right," said Evangeline, not entirely hiding her disapproval. "Give us a moment and we'll give you a ride." Angelique was already dabbing at her lips and half-rising. She had to have as little sleep as Hexene after just as much drinking, yet she looked like a spring flower.

"No, thank you," said Hechalé. "We'd like to get there under our own steam."

Serafina scoffed.

"I know you haven't been here in a long time, but remember, it takes all day to walk across town," said Evangeline.

"They could use the Catacombs," Angelique pointed out. "We'll send Torpe as a guide. Torpe?"

The zombie who had given them the rickshaw ride from the airport emerged from the kitchen and stood silently as the Adepts gave him instructions. He never gave any indication that he understood or would obey, but none of the witches seemed to expect one.

"Will you at least be home for dinner?"

"We will," said Hechalé, and then smiled at the humans. "And I will get to hear all about your wonderful lives when I do."

Unwitch Hunt

The humans were quick to brush it off, and none of them spoke over a murmur. Little Raoul kept watching Hexene whenever he thought she wasn't looking. Angelique was watching her as well. When their eyes met, Angelique shot her a grin. Hexene gave her a wan smile, but her thoughts were already with the Catacombs. The one place in the city without witches sounded like the most appealing thing in the world to her.

Seven

Torpe walked like a marionette operated by a distracted puppeteer. On the few occasions he paused, he partially collapsed in on himself, every joint holding another up like a pile of sticks that was done with the exhausting charade of being a person. He lurched outside and the Candlemas Coven followed, into a day that was already heating up.

Torpe followed the alleyway, and Hexene was lost after his first turn. After a few more, in which he looped around several lots, he stepped up to what looked like yet another fold in the rock. When he moved between its edges, Hexene realized it was, in fact, a passage. When right on top of it, she found a small alcove with three steps leading down, and then the opening of the passageway itself. A few of the human passersby paused to stare as the witches went underground.

The air instantly changed from the bleak, open-air oven into the cool embrace of a cave. Moisture that wouldn't have bothered her back in Los Angeles now felt like a rash on her skin. The tunnel before her snaked into the rock. The slope was gentle, but it was definitely descending. Light came from candles or open bowls of flaming oil and the occasional lantern blazing in alcoves. Unlike the rest of the non-Cogtown parts of the city, these alcoves weren't sculpted by magic; the scars of chisels could clearly be traced on the rock surface. Footsteps echoed from deeper in, and distance was hard to determine.

As the tunnel leveled off, they came to the first construction in the Catacombs, though "construction" implied craft and forethought that weren't in evidence. A line of railroad tracks followed the tunnel in, though on even casual inspection it was obvious these were far from professional grade. The rails themselves were composed of many different pieces of metal, hammered ungracefully into shape. The sleepers were irregular scraps of wood cut or stapled into rough uniformity.

A repurposed mine cart sat waiting at the edge. A zombie, his shirtless torso showing off reedy and rotten muscle, stood on a rickety wooden platform bolted to the cart's surface. One side of the cart had been taken off, now serving as a ramp that led into the cart itself. Seats, made from old fruit boxes, were bolted to the floor inside.

"Cerebros," said the cartman.

Torpe never responded, instead handing over a coin. The cartman shook it, then dropped it into a wooden cigar box at his feet where it rattled against a few others. He waved to the cart, as if to say "Be my guest." It, of course, came out as "Cerebros."

Hexene took her seat and found that the box was only secured to the floor in the loosest sense of the term. The cartman pulled the gangway up, and it became a fourth wall for the cart, albeit one made of wood rather than metal. When the cart got going, it was with a bone-rattling rumble. Hexene felt like she was being shaken to pieces. The cart got up to a good clip, wind blowing her wild curls all around her face until, frustrated, she tied them back. The cartman controlled his contraption with a simple handbrake, though he never gave the impression he was completely in control of much of anything. The journey across town to the library involved three different cart rides, and though each cart and track had clearly been cobbled together with whatever was around at the time, they were more or less identical.

It took Hexene until the second one to calm down enough to take in the sights. Many other tunnels, most chiseled rather than sculpted, shunted off their pathway. Hexene guessed they were sticking to the main thoroughfare, such that it was. Judging by the number of side passages, there were miles and miles of tunnels down here.

From time to time, they passed other zombies. Some were walking around on errands, while others were sitting in front of shanties. Sometimes they called out "Brains" or "Cerebros" or "Opolo." Even though they stared, Hexene found it comforting that they were there at all. As she passed more and more, she saw that the zombies who spoke were usually dressed in ripped clothes or even just filthy rags. The silent ones wore clothes that had been pressed and laundered. All of them wore amulets, no matter how shabbily they were dressed.

The dampness was uncomfortable, and made Hexene more than a little nervous. Soon water beaded on the walls and ceilings of the tunnels, perilously close to dripping. Were it not for the coolness of the surroundings, the Catacombs would have felt like the gullet of a giant worm.

More of the now-familiar graffiti spidered across the walls. MALLEUS SPEAKS and sometimes MALLEUS HEARS and MALLEUS SEES, usually with the accompanying XX. These were done in a variety of hands. There had been many messengers for this particular missive, it seemed. She finally got an answer to her question about the identity of the mysterious Malleus when she saw the first poster.

Along the short walk from the first cart to the second, it was stuck to a wall bleeding moisture. It was a wanted poster written in Spanish, like something from the Old West. It read: "WANTED: Information leading to the capture of the terrorist MALLEUS. REWARD!" The picture was a silhouette, the head cocked at a slight angle, the way zombies sometimes stood. Someone had come later and defaced the poster, drawing the XX over the mouth area of the shadow. An angry line crossed out "terrorist" and substituted "HERO" in jagged letters. Now that she had something to look for, Hexene saw several more posters during their trip, each one vandalized in a different way. The reward was never specified.

She tried to square the posters with what Angelique had told her about Las Barrenderas. None of the posters carried an insignia like she'd seen on the Barrenderas who had come into Le Chaperon Rouge. Maybe they were the work of Las Barrenderas, or maybe they came from some witch who had a personal beef with Malleus. It was dizzying. As much as government was generally pointless, she did miss having one convenient source for at least half her problems.

The third cart came to a stop, and the cartman pushed the gangway down. Torpe led the way, but instead of finding a deeper tunnel as he had each time before, he chose one sloping upward. Soon, she could see daylight up ahead. The candles and lanterns gave way to real sunlight, peering into the mouth of the tunnel. Despite the three long cart rides, the path they had taken was labyrinthine. She could remember the various landmarks—a piece of exceptionally crafted graffiti, an imaginatively vandalized Malleus poster, a shanty covered with a distinctive sailcloth—but the thought of actually traversing the Catacombs without a guide was daunting. She wondered how the local witches did it before realizing they likely never did at all. That was what flight was for.

As if to prove it, as soon as they stepped outside, a witch in a mortar, steering with her pestle, soared overhead. Hexene sighed.

Torpe continued his shamble, walking up the few stairs to the alley proper, then through this new neighborhood. Hexene wasn't quite sure which quarter this was, but a lot of the witches above were using mortars and pestles. The houses were a bit simpler, looking like mud-and-thatch huts, and many sported giant, taloned legs. Some were standing on them, others had them folded up as though the houses were roosting. A few towers topped with onion domes poked at the sky.

"Are we in the Russian Quarter?" Hexene asked.

"Where do you think?" Hermosa grumped.

"Yes, sweetheart," said Hechalé. "As though the library would be anywhere else. It's right up here."

Just as she finished the sentence, the alley the witches were traversing turned and opened into a large plaza. Later, she would learn its name: Grandmother Square. On three sides, the buildings were considerably grander than in other parts of the quarter, looking like czarist manors looming up from the ground. In the center was a statue of a house on chicken legs, a hideous crone standing out front. The statue was black, like everything here, but in the crevices it shone with the green of moss or lichen. It was the first thing Hexene had seen that looked alive by accident. Hexene didn't have to be told that this was a statue of Baba Yaga herself.

Beyond was the library itself. A building that resembled a thousand houses, huts, hovels, hermitages, hideouts, and havens, all crammed together in the skeleton of a colossal beast and cast in black basalt, rose majestically at the other end of the square. Outside of Cogtown, it was the largest building Hexene had seen so far in Las Brujas, dwarfing even the amphitheater in the middle of the Stone Forest. She stared in awe. It was the repository of all the wisdom the witches had managed to gain and keep over their long history. Perhaps the single most important building in the world.

No one walked in the square other than them. Witches landed on the wide landing pad on the central roof of the library, then made their way down and inside, never touching the ground. As the Candlemas Coven approached this holy site, a sign carved into one of the huge ribs poking at the sky informed them in Theban that this was the BABA YAGA MEMORIAL LIBRARY OF SPELLS AND HEXES. Even reading the Great Hag's name gave Hexene a chill. She wasn't a goddess, or even an avatar of the Many-Faced Goddess, but she was the greatest witch who had ever lived. Hexene refused to believe Baba Yaga would have lost her familiar to something so vulgar as a mad scientist's experiment. She would know a way out, and if she knew, that secret would be in here. Somewhere.

Though the front entrance looked like a small cottage, as they neared it soon became obvious that it was far bigger than it initially appeared. The front door was sized for an ogre, though considering the wards etched in the ebon surface, it was unlikely an ogre would get his hand back if he touched it.

UNWITCH HUNT

Any remaining artifice trying to insist that this was a cottage in the woods vanished as soon as they were on the other side of the doors. The walls were black, the ceilings vaulted. Tapestries hung on either wall, with depictions of the Great Hag in her native Siberia. At the far end, an owlish woman bustled to and fro behind a desk. An even more owlish owl perched on the shelves behind her. Hexene figured the woman was one of the librarians. She wondered how many there were. Witch culture would suggest a single coven running the place, but the library was far too big and important to entrust to a mere three women. As for the librarian, she could have been maiden, mother, or crone. It was impossible to tell.

The librarian squinted at them, and after a moment, registered the lack of familiars. "I'm sorry, ladies," she said in Russian-accented Spanish, "the library is for witches only."

"We are witches," Hechalé said, matter-of-factly in Theban. "Our familiars were killed."

The librarian's face went slack with horror, then curdled to disgust. Even the owl looked horrified. "Oh! I've never...what are you doing here?"

"We're going to find a way to incarnate new familiars," Hexene said, shocked when the words came out much louder than she intended. The echoes bounded around the room.

"Well...keep it down, then," said the librarian. It was clear she'd wanted to say far more, but she couldn't. Whatever Hexene and the others were, they were something like witches and they had a right to be in the library.

The central wing, which looked like it had been the original body of the library, simply *felt* Russian. And ancient. The chamber was wide and vaulted, with shelves and racks on every wall and in rows along the room. Hexene saw very few books; most of what was present was bones. Entire grimoires had been etched into the bones of cave bears, wolves, and even humans. Some were on complete skeletons, articulated like they would be in a museum. Others were on fragmentary bones resting in nooks or hanging on hooks.

"Go on," said Hermosa. "I'll look here. Don't need you two hens looking over my shoulder."

Hexene looked to Hechalé, who nodded. "Come on, sweetheart. We'll cover more ground this way."

Hexene wanted to stay in a wing decorated in a Mexican style. Ancient Mayan and Aztec stelae stood between bookshelves of Spanish codices. It felt like home more than anywhere else she had seen so far. It would have been nice if the friends who had let the Candlemas Coven stay with them had been in the Mexican Quarter. She even would have settled for the American Quarter. Hexene was about to volunteer to hunt through the old codices for what they needed, but when she turned to Hechalé, the mother's face had gone dreamy and nostalgic.

"I spent a lot of my maidenhood here," she said, going to the shelves.

Hexene sighed and kept moving. She passed through a vast room where the spells had been written on the skins of exotic animals, and another where living fish had been bred and enchanted with the proper scales, another where the words were formed on the papery wings of moths. She stopped in what she eventually determined was a German-sourced wing, judging by the commentary on the various grimoires, and the name above the door: TOTENKINDER. She couldn't read German, but anyone who'd been in the States during World War II could recognize the shape of it.

She might have stopped there because it appealed to her childhood. While the walls were sculpted into a forest scene, the grimoires themselves were on baked goods. Old, stale baked goods, sure, but every single one had come from an oven somewhere. Petrified candy and even frosting still clung to some of the magical pastries. Hexene handled them with care and winced when tiny crumbs came off them. Stale or not, before long her hands smelled of cinnamon and gingerbread. As side effects of magical knowledge went, it was better than one's shadow developing a mind of its own, or chicken eggs hatching snakes. She plucked the tablets off the shelves one at a time and brought them back to a carrel in a quiet corner to study.

Much of what she found on the baked tablets were hexes, inscribed, of course, in Theban. Useful in her old life, but now useless. Most of what witches chose to write down was the practical aspect of what they were. Spells and hexes would keep witches alive in a world that emphatically didn't want them.

That wasn't to say she found nothing. Sifting through the grimoires, she soon found that the notes in between the spells themselves were far more important. Much like cookbooks might include anecdotes about how the author encountered the cuisine or ingredients in question, these would have similar stories surrounding the spells. Hexene was never getting a full story, but instead bits and pieces that were constantly referencing other bits and pieces that might or might not be in this wing, or even exist.

She found many references to Baba Yaga, though it took Hexene some time to figure out that roughly half of them were about her, as they called her the Three-in-One, or in the original Theban, the Heqatun. Hexene came across the term early in the day, and by afternoon, one of the writers finally connected that nickname to Baba Yaga, leaving Hexene to wonder how much she had managed to ignore when she dismissed it as useless. She supposed it *was* useless. After all, *she* wasn't Baba Yaga. She was just trying to do something no other witch had done. Although according to a lot of these anecdotes, the impossible was the Great Hag's stock in trade.

No one had ever been powerful—or stupid—enough to kill Baba Yaga's familiar. Or, if they had, Hexene could find no mention of it. Late in the afternoon, she did finally manage to find a reference to a witch who had lost her familiar. Most of it was of the "oh, poor thing" vein, filtered through the sensibilities of a medieval German witch, which was about as sympathetic and nurturing as that description implied. It mentioned in passing that she vanished into the east, but what that meant beyond going on a trip wasn't expanded upon. It could have been metaphorical for all Hexene knew. Witches loved their cardinal directions.

Hexene read until her eyes crossed and her sinuses were covered in a thin layer of atomized gingerbread. She put aside the baked tablet and rubbed her eyes, then winced and teared up when she realized she'd just candied her eyeballs. She cursed under her breath and brought her fist down on the table, hard. The pain felt better, if only because it had some company.

"Oh sweetheart, you look exhausted." Hechalé stood at the mouth of the row where her carrel sat. The mother's expression was a pantomime of maternal compassion, but it worked on a deep place inside Hexene the maiden resented.

"I didn't find anything useful."

"It's all right, love. There's always tomorrow."

"How many tomorrows?"

"We have as many as we want," said Hechalé. "The Arcane Adepts are old friends. They love having us as guests."

Hexene sighed. She couldn't imagine immortality without her powers. But perhaps more to the point, she couldn't imagine *Hermosa* being immortal without her magic. The crone would likely move beyond as soon as she cottoned to the fact that this search was a waste of time. And then who was going to join a coven where the crone and mother had no familiars? Soon enough, Hexene would be in the same boat as Petunia Pendulum. She snorted. *Maybe I should start a coven with her.*

Hechalé frowned. "What's so funny?"

"Nothing," Hexene said, then before she could stop it, "other than this whole situation."

"You're tired," Hechalé reaffirmed. "Let's go have some pie."

Hexene shook her head, but followed the mother anyway. They found Hermosa clutching a human femur in her hands, turning it over and over as her rheumy eyes followed the looping Theban script. "Bah!" she decided, and threw it away.

With the reflexes of a mother, Hechalé caught the bone before it clattered into the black stone floor. "Hermosa! What are you thinking?"

"Useless bone. All the useless bones! Stupid little maidens prattling on about flying and spells and potions."

"So you found nothing, too," Hexene said.

"Perceptive one, aren't you?"

Hexene had the urge to punch the crone. She resisted, mostly because Hechalé stepped between them. "Mm, I think you could use some pie too. I swear, I don't know what you two would do without me."

Hermosa's grunt implied she might like to find out, and Hexene found herself agreeing. The rest of her coven had swiftly become the two most obnoxious people she had ever met.

Hechalé replaced the bone on an empty hook, and the witches left the library, finding Torpe waiting for them. The sun had set, and dark had covered Las Brujas. In the gloom, the shadow of Baba Yaga loomed large, seemingly ready to step off her pedestal. Hexene wouldn't have minded that; maybe the Great Hag would have something to tell her. More likely, she would have just eaten the three of them. They weren't mortals, but without their witchcraft, they were close enough for hag dinner.

The trip felt quicker this time, passing places that sparked memories. This time around, many of the shanties they passed were inhabited. Some zombies sat on old boxes out in front of ragged tents, watching the witches go by. Sometimes, Hexene saw sullen hate in their eyes; mostly it was just exhaustion. These spoke, saying what she assumed meant "Brains" in a dozen different languages.

Torpe brought them inside and into the kitchen. They sat down in a little alcove, and the other house zombies served them cold pie from the previous night. The other two witches didn't seem to mind, but Hexene still disliked the silent zombies waiting on them hand and foot. She was as tense as an overtuned guitar string.

"I'll tell you this," Hechalé said, "that library is everything I imagined and more. So much wisdom in one place!"

"None of what we actually need," muttered Hexene, shoveling another forkful of pie into her mouth. After the long day, the food made her body remember that it was in fact ravenous. She was on pace to swallow the entire serving like she imagined Angelique's familiar would do to a rat.

Hermosa grunted, perhaps in agreement.

"You two," sighed the mother. "It was one day. One day hunting through the biggest library in the world. Did you think we were going to find the secret in *one day*?"

"I don't think we'll ever find it," Hexene said, and immediately regretted it. Wanting to believe was so seductive, but that was the problem with belief. Belief wasn't something to be decided. It was there, or it wasn't.

"I need you to look on the bright side."

"There is no bright side."

Hechalé slammed the table with her palm. "Then pretend!" she shouted.

Hexene jumped. She might have let that disarm her, but her anger was already a brewing storm. "Pretend? Why would I want to do that? Just so you don't get sad?"

"So you do your best research! And so you don't pick me apart with your constant whining!"

"Whining?" Hexene demanded. She found herself standing up, unable to remember the actual motion of doing so. She was out of the alcove and waving a finger at the mother, who was also now standing. Hechalé was short, but she was formidable as a battleship, especially now. "You think I'm overreacting to losing our familiars?"

"You're not helping! And you're ignoring the most important part, aren't you?"

"And what's that?"

The danger was there, just ahead of them. Hexene saw it in the conversation. Saw the words that hadn't been spoken yet, but everyone knew could be. The only problem was, once they were spoken, everything changed. Couldn't sign your name in the Devil's Book and cross it out later. Hechalé might have held back at another time. All the other times.

"Who was the first familiar taken?"

Hermosa watched them both silently, apparently content to let this play out. Hexene swallowed. The answer to Hechalé's question, of course, was Escuerzo, her toad. Speaking that aloud was impossible. Better to talk through riveted steel.

Hechalé answered for her: "Your toad! And when was he taken? When you were out selling hexes!"

"It wasn't my fault," Hexene said, her voice brittle.

"No? Selling hexes you don't need to? Meeting those kinds of people?"

"It wasn't my client!" she said, but there was no conviction behind the words.

Hechalé knew she had drawn blood here. "Doesn't matter, does it? You get our familiars taken and all I want from you is a little sunshine and you can't even give that!"

Hexene ran. Again. She couldn't face this, all those words she'd thought coming from the mouth of her mother. She wasn't going to break entirely in the kitchen. That would have been too much, especially if Hechalé comforted her, as Hexene knew the mother would. So she ran, brushing past Evangeline Arcane, just come into the kitchen, and upstairs. Hexene couldn't bear to be in the same room as the coven, so she planted herself in the hall outside, beneath one of the tables, and quivered in anger and frustration. At some point, she slept.

Eight

Hexene didn't remember her dream. She seldom did; they were nearly always forgotten five minutes after she woke up. The only thing that lingered was a feeling, but here, even that was gone, banished in the white-hot sizzle of her own flesh. Hexene's eyes snapped open in an instant and she was staring at her left arm, where thick, greasy streams of whitish smoke rose through the patchwork fabric of her dress..

She was momentarily transfixed, even as the agony blinded every other part of her. Finally, she cursed, and that helped a little. Hexene could turn the air blue in three languages, and she proceeded to do just that. That was when she took in the rest of her surroundings. She was in the hall outside the guest room, apparently having fallen asleep slumped beneath the table in the hall. Through the open door, she could see zombies standing over the bed where Hermosa and Hechalé slept, as well as the sofa where she was supposed to be. Thick smoke rose from Hermosa's side of the bed.

Hechalé sat bolt upright. "What's going—" The rest was a high, keening scream as the zombie by the bed threw a bucket of water into her face. The scream turned to smoke along with the rest of her, in front of Hexene's horrified eyes. It was only then that she saw the zombie in front of her. He looked just as surprised to see her as she was to see him. He might have been tall or average-sized, but from her perspective, he was as big as the statue of Baba Yaga in Grandmother Square. He clutched a bucket, water sloshing over the sides.

Later, what Hexene would remember most strongly was his mouth. It was stitched shut.

He recovered, pulling back the bucket to give her a fatal dousing. Hexene wasn't going to let him. She sprang upward, palms flat on the underside of the table. It would make a decent battering ram, and on the off chance she could sap the zombie on the head with it, she'd do to him what he was trying to do to her. The table hit him somewhere, but she never got the satisfying *crack* that said he would be mulch come sunrise.

The zombie fell back against the wall, knocking the tapestries off it. His bucket fell, water sloshing over the floor. Hexene cursed again, recoiling in horror from the spreading pool. The zombies emerged from the bedroom, one carrying a full bucket. *They brought extra,* Hexene thought with exhausted clarity, *of course they did.*

The zombie she had hit with the table was struggling to get to his feet. Another pushed past the armed one, ready to grab Hexene. *To hold me down,* she realized, and a cold wet feeling in her guts, worse even than the burning in her arm, gripped her. She wanted to fight these three, show them the price of attacking a witch. But there was no magic to call, no hex to sling. For all she knew, the Arcane Adepts were already dead, collecting on the ceiling like cigarette smoke. She had only herself, and she could do nothing.

So she ran. She hated herself for it, but it was all she could do. She ran down the hall, and down the stairs, hitting the door and stumbling out into the night. The zombies followed, the maddening tread of their feet as steady as a heartbeat. Hexene barely saw a thing. She had only impressions, of the deep shadows of Las Brujas at night, of the wonderfully dry air, of the burning of her arm.

She came to reasoning thought as she stopped in front of the entrance to the Catacombs Torpe had used to guide them to the library. Zombies were down there. Legions of them, some obviously with a hatred toward witches that hadn't been seen on earth for centuries. But on the surface, Las Brujas was a maze that she couldn't hope to navigate, filled with witches who thought of her only as a freak. Hexene looked both ways, and both pathways led into the dark. Possibly to dead ends. She wouldn't know until she found herself at one, the zombies closing in with their fatal water. Behind her, the steps of the zombies grew louder. They were behind a single bend, ready to kill.

She made the only choice she could, mad as it was on the face of it. She plunged into the Catacombs. Her arm burned from the water, worsening in the damp air. She clutched at her dress, above the wet part, grabbed the fabric and tore. Her quilted dress gave, and the sleeve, from mid-bicep down, came off. She'd heard the phase "blessed relief" but never understood it until this moment. She dropped the soaking cloth; it wasn't going to kill her but it was like holding a pan fresh from the oven. Angry red streaks marred her forearm where the water had done its horrible work. There would be time to worry about that later.

Hexene ran deeper into the Catacombs, past the cart tracks. She had no money for a fare, and she wasn't going to trust a zombie. In the back of her mind, she thought of making it to the library. Zombies wouldn't be allowed in there, and even a half-witch could be safe. But that was a long trip she couldn't make without the carts. Her legs were heavy, her muscles sore, her will drained. The echoing footsteps grew louder. Closer? Maybe. In the Catacombs, it was hard to tell, and Hexene's shredded mind wasn't able to make those kinds of calculations. Only the stark terror of being consigned to the water. To melt. To be nothing.

Her breath burned. She imagined the moisture in the air getting into her lungs, dissolving them in threads of gray. The fear was turning into hysteria. If she let herself fall into that spiral, she'd be easy prey. She concentrated: she could deal with water rationally. It wasn't like an evil eye charm, where she'd have to flee in panic. A bolt of terror hit her at the thought of one of those, but she shifted into the mere threat of hideous death and felt a bit better. She could approach this rationally.

She couldn't fight. It grated on her, but it was true. She couldn't run. The Catacombs were too big and there was no way she knew them better than the zombies. That left a final option: hide. Far from her favorite, but it would have to do. At least she was relatively small. Zombies peeked perfunctorily from their shanties, uninterested in the fleeing witch. Either they'd seen it before, or even novelty wasn't a reason to get up. She never paused, looking only long enough at each little tent or pile of belongings to figure if there was a place to fold herself up in or if there was a zombie around.

She glanced down a passage off to her left. The smooth walls of the tunnel she was in gave way to the irregular hand-dug ones. At the end, she spotted a small pile of things: a few crates, a piece of sailcloth, a small pot over the remains of a fire. It was dark down there, the only light from a few candles melted to the crates. She saw no zombie lurking around, either. There wouldn't be a better spot.

She ran for it. The footsteps behind her thudded in inexorable rhythm. She found a place, behind the crates and under the sailcloth, and wedged herself behind it. The wall of the tunnel was just behind her, the rock cool on her back. She pulled a crate closer. The flame on the candle wobbled and she blew it out, leaving only one more candle out of reach. She wrapped her dress around her like a blanket and waited. She could see the mouth of the tunnel through a thin strip between the crates. Her water wounds throbbed in time with her heartbeat.

She waited, heart thundering in her chest. The view was hardly good. She saw mostly leaping shadows out beyond the flickering candlelight. The footsteps echoed, louder and louder, erasing the distance between impact and echo. It was right on top of her. Shadows loomed. She shrank, but it was too late to run. The crate moved aside, and Hexene braced herself to die.

Nine

"Mafaufau," said a voice above her like the closing of a tomb. Hexene lunged at the figure, ready to rip into him with her nails and teeth if necessary. If she was going to die, she was going to make her killer remember he had been in a fight. Iron vises caught her wrists and held her, quite easily, off the ground. Her wounded arm burned with the new contact, though the pain was distant compared to the white-hot agony of before. She kicked frantically, but her legs didn't do much more than flail.

"Mafaufau," said the figure again.

She blinked, and it hit her: the zombies who had murdered her coven had sewn-shut mouths. She gaped at the giant holding her, the fight vanishing from her in an instant. The zombie reacted to her sudden calming. The vises lowered and released. The blunt-fingered hands that had held her were as big as her forearms.

The figure in front of her was enormous in a way she thought was exclusively reserved for pachyderms and cliffsides. He took up pretty much the entire tunnel, and even then he was stooping. She couldn't see his features clearly, but he carried the not-unpleasant scent of freshly turned earth.

"Mafaufau," he said again.

"Please," she whispered.

Then, behind them, the echoing footsteps stopped. Behind the eclipse, shadows reached along the walls. The gargantuan zombie turned. The candlelight caught his arms, a faded brown partly covered in pretty geometric tattoos. He was wearing an old undershirt stretched over a broad back and rotund belly. Long, curly hair fell to his shoulders. In places his skin looked like a moth-eaten sweater.

"Mmmph," said one of the zombies at the mouth of the tunnel.

"Mafaufau," rumbled the zombie in front of Hexene. His bulk blocked the tunnel almost completely. Hexene peeked between his legs, hiding her entire body behind one of them. The zombies were mostly shadow, but in flickers of light, she saw the stitched-up mouths. One of them still carried a sloshing bucket.

The lead zombie shook his head, and the others followed suit. Hexene's protector never moved. He might as well have been a landmass. The zombies exchanged glances, made a few more muffled noises through the stitches, and shambled away. When the last echoes of her pursuers died, the elephantine zombie turned. Hexene, the fear bleeding away somewhat, could now take her rescuer's face in by the light of the candles. His features were cherubic, even if some of his full cheeks and lips had been eaten away, and his nose was receding alarmingly. For a zombie, though, Hexene liked the looks of him. His eyes, covered in death's cataract, seemed like they saw just fine. An amulet hung tight against his barrel-like neck.

"Mafaufau," he said.

"Thank you," Hexene managed.

"Mafaufau."

"I'm Hexene." She touched her breast. She almost added *Candlemas*, but didn't see the point. Her coven was dead. The grief of that was behind a dam, and she knew if she started pulling bricks, it would drown her.

"Mafaufau."

"It's nice to meet you." Hexene wished she could ask him some questions, but she was pretty sure she knew what the answer would be. It was the first time she had ever really spoken to a zombie, and she wasn't certain what to say. Especially when this one had saved her life.

Mafaufau—she knew it wasn't his name, but it was nice, and she would remember it—looked over his shoulder, as though to make certain the other zombies were gone. He turned back to her and pointed over her head, at the tunnel partly blocked by his makeshift camp.

"Mafaufau," he told her on no uncertain terms.

She nodded. "Is there...I should find some Barrenderas, right? Are they over there?"

"Mafaufau," he said, and pointed again, this time really jabbing the air.

"Thank you," she said again. It wasn't enough, not nearly enough, but it would have to do. Whatever Mafaufau's reasons for doing what he did, they were his own. Hexene could respect that. Still waters ran deep, and he would keep her out of them.

She nodded once again, and went the way Mafaufau told her to. She imagined once she got to the surface, the first witch she found would direct her to wherever it was Las Barrenderas hung around. Felt wrong going to the police, but at least these weren't proper police. That's how Angelique made it sound. She described them more as a militia, and Hexene could square her feelings with that. Besides, at least two, and maybe as many as five witches had been murdered tonight. Something had to be done.

Hexene followed the tunnel, trusting that it would lead her to the surface. *Get out of the Catacombs*, Mafaufau seemed to be saying, *this is our place, not yours*. She couldn't agree more—but without her ability to fly, the surface of Las Brujas wasn't hers either.

The layout of the Catacombs wasn't as perversely difficult as the surface, but it was far from direct or intuitive. The tunnels snaked around without warning, split into twos and threes, and occasionally even looped back on themselves. The oddest twists and turns were found in the tunnels that had the clearest signs of digging, where the scars of chisels marked every wall. Eventually, though, with her feet aching, Hexene made it to the surface. She would have thought it would be well into the following day, but the sky was only just beginning to lighten. The night had gone on forever. Hard not to see some magic there, but that was always the way of the world.

Emerging into the growing dawn, Hexene took two steps out onto the curving streets of Las Brujas. She couldn't tell where she was, as none of the black, toffee-stretched buildings around her looked at all familiar. They all had a look like giant gingerbread houses, with candy accents sculpted from black basalt. The closest thing to compare was a MALLEUS SPEAKS scrawled not far from the Catacombs exit. She guessed the Caribbean Quarter was somewhere to the east, and the sun was rising in that direction, so she picked that path down the alley. *Just like the witch in the story*, she thought. *Hope I don't vanish there.*

She rounded one of the bends in the alleys, and the zombies were just *there*. She couldn't begin to guess how they'd found her, let alone ended up in front of her. But they were impossible to mistake—the three spidery figures, one still carrying the sloshing bucket, were as burned onto her brain as the streaks on her arm. One pointed at her with a bony finger and said, "Mmmph!"

That was enough for the other two, and instantly all three were shambling after her. Hexene bolted, but the night's terror and exertion were finally catching up to her. She knew she wasn't going to be able to keep ahead of them for long. The Catacombs were a dead end. Just another place to get cornered while zombies apathetically watched her melt. She ran without a larger plan, heading for the rising sun when she could. She didn't spare her breath for a shout. She wasn't sure she could; her lungs burned almost as much as her arm. She didn't think any witches would help her anyway. They might even see what the zombies were trying to do as a mercy. *At least she doesn't have to live without her familiar*, they'd say, shaking their heads and clucking their tongues.

Then the town fell away. She blinked, coming up short. The alley opened up into the wide boulevard between Las Brujas proper and its black sheep suburb, Cogtown. The brutalist towers of the robot-built enclave stood tall against the rising sun. Here, every corner was a right angle, every street straight and level. She threw a glance over her shoulder; her pursuers were somewhere behind her, hidden by twists and turns, but they'd figure out where she'd gone easy enough. Now it was about raw speed.

She gathered what wind she had left and bolted. A robot shaped like an irate washing machine beeped at her as she pushed past. With the dry air racing through her hair, she could almost pretend she was flying. Almost.

"Mmmph!" she heard behind her.

There was no way to redouble her efforts; she was already sprinting full out. Her breath burned in and out of her lungs. There should be smoke spitting from her mouth. She should be eating herself alive to run this way. That's what she imagined. She would run herself into oblivion. At least then the zombies wouldn't get the satisfaction of her death.

The tallest building in Cogtown called her. Maybe it was the promise of lots of places to hide, or maybe it had its own gravity. It didn't matter. She turned down a street—the sign called it Lovelace Avenue—and ran for it. In huge, industrial nightmare letters, the building she was running for proclaimed itself the HOTEL METROPOLE.

The hotel itself was a cluster of towers, joined by skybridges. Smaller buildings surrounded these, looking like a bunch of little kid towers hanging around with the grown-ups. The arrangement of the structures didn't immediately look symmetrical to Hexene, and she wondered if there was more construction on the way, or if the architect was perverse for a robot.

She glanced over her shoulder and saw her pursuers. In the open ground, she had the advantage. No zombie could ever run her down. At least, not until she was a crone. She found herself grinning, probably madly: *There's no way I'll make it to cronehood like this.*

The grounds of the Hotel Metropole were surrounded by a low wall built out of sandstone bricks that Hexene guessed were uniform down to the atom. She easily scrambled over it, falling down in a heap on the other side. The sun was climbing in the sky, the pools of shadow beginning to dry up. The grounds were laid out in swooping, geometric pathways between statues of robots and buildings that increased in size the closer they got to the center of the compound. Hexene saw the symmetry now: the Hotel Metropole was laid out like a spiral, drawing the visitor to the central tower as though they were caught in a whirlpool.

Hexene wasn't about to let herself get bullied by some architecture. There were places to hide. There were always places to hide. The small outbuildings reminded her of the fishermen's shacks in Guerrero Negro, the ones just over the dunes from the bay. She had spent more time than she cared to remember sneaking in and out of those. She could almost smell the salt air as a memory flooded in of cramming herself beneath the raised floor of a shack, pressing herself into the cool earth. She lay there, motionless, watching Gordo's feet, and the feet of whichever of the boys he wasn't beating on that day, go by. Waiting until they vanished in search of less slippery prey. She might have thanked Gordo for that training, but she'd much rather curse him. Curse him in the human languages, so he'd know he was a pig, then curse him in Theban to make him act like it.

In the present, she raced to a single-story shed on the outskirts of the compound, close enough to be handy yet far enough from the wall she'd jumped to give her some cover. It stood in the shade of a statue that looked a bit like an angry robot kraken, but she wasn't an art critic. The door to the shed was locked, but the window wasn't. She slithered through it, finding that her old skills at evasion hadn't deserted her completely. Nothing caught; there were no hanging nails or splintery wood like there would be in a human structure. This shed was built to machine-perfection. It was cool inside, but Hexene could tell the thing would be an oven by the afternoon. The price of being built by robots, she supposed. Still, she shut the window and threw the latch.

The interior was gloomy but, for a shed, spacious. A family could have lived comfortably in the single room, if they moved out the various tools and spare parts that hung from the walls and stocked the shelves. It was organized here, but not *as* organized as she'd imagined it would be. A few tools looked to be out of place, a few piles a bit scattered. Hexene didn't dwell on it; she had far more important things to keep track of. She peeked over the windowsill, waiting for the zombies to come into view. If they did.

Until a voice behind her croaked, "Help me."

TEN

Hexene whirled. She didn't register what the voice was saying at first, merely that there was a voice and that meant danger. Only when it spoke again did she process what the speaker wanted.

"Be quiet," Hexene hissed. "I'll help, but be *quiet*."

The voice fell silent. It had spoken passable Spanish, and it had done it in an accent Hexene could only identify as German because it sounded like the bad guys in World War II pictures. She imagined Nick would have been the one to ask for anything more specific than merely "German." He'd known Germans, as much as you knew anyone you'd shot at and had shot at you. She reflexively reached for the hex dolls, but only then realized she didn't have her satchel with her. It was back at the Arcane Adepts' house. Not that the contents would do her any good in her present state.

She peeked up over the sill one more time and caught sight of one of her pursuers. He was far off, across the grounds and heading in the direction of the main tower, and was soon out of view. Hexene silently wished him godspeed. She turned and peered into the dark of the shed.

A light, deeper inside, dyed a bit of the darkness green. Hexene crept between the shelves, careful not to run into any. She could just imagine evading the zombies this long only to summon them with a vaudevillian pratfall. As she went deeper into the shed, the sense of disorganization increased until it gave up on the pretense of being anything but a giant mess. A pile of old parts stood in her way, and it took her some time to move it piece by silent piece before she could access the back of the shed.

What she found was gruesome. Or possibly not. In the moment, Hexene wasn't entirely sure how to feel. Initially, the horror hit her with solid force, but dispersed when she didn't see blood or guts. Only she *did*; just not in the way she was expecting. The sight was as much of a journey as the trip through the Catacombs.

On a workbench pushed against the far wall of the shed was a robot. She had been completely disassembled, though, by someone with a keen attention to detail—or possibly a keen sadism. Every joint had been separated, and all of them trailed cords and wires. Her skin was copper and the faint green glow came from her eyes. Her head was the only thing that looked at all active; cords from the severed neck—Hexene's mind gave up terms like *jugular* and *carotid*—were plugged into a small generator.

"Good morning," said the robot.

"Hi," said Hexene, unsure of what else to say in this situation. "How did you know it was morning?"

"My internal timepiece functions. And I can see daylight through the window."

"Oh."

The robot spoke without moving her lips, even though she had them. She looked like an art deco statue of a pinup girl. "Can you help me?" the robot prompted.

"Help you do what?"

"Put me together." The robot's voice was emotionless, but Hexene heard the irritation. She couldn't tell if it was there, or if her mind simply put it there.

"I'm not a mechanic," said Hexene.

"I know that. By appearances, you are a witch, maiden-class. But you have hands, no?"

Hexene held them up to demonstrate. "I have hands."

"Two more than I have at present. I will tell you what must be done. You need only do what I tell you."

"I can do that." Hexene approached the workbench, looking over the parts of the robot. "What's your name?"

"Technika," said the robot.

"I'm Hexene."

"I did not ask. First, find my torso."

Technika continued to issue orders, and Hexene followed them. She didn't know what she was doing, beyond connecting wires and securing bolts. She wasn't an expert, but it looked to her like Technika had been carefully disassembled rather than smashed apart. That probably meant something, but Hexene wasn't a detective either, and she was doing her best not to think about the circumstances of her arrival. The idea that the zombies could backtrack and find her in this place with no easy exit was a chilling one.

"What are you doing here?" asked Technika, almost as though she could read Hexene's mind.

"I was chased. Some zombies are trying to kill me."

"They have water, then?" Hexene nodded. "I see. Do you think they are likely to find you?"

"I hope not."

"Then I should be watching the door. Perhaps you would apply a hex trap for them. Fetch some dirt from outside. Turn it into powder. Then make your little symbols."

Hexene stopped what she was doing and looked into the robot's face. She was slightly annoyed that said face was entirely immobile, because the expression, at least with those words, felt like polite condescension. "Is that what you think powers hexes? Dirt?"

"Of course. I have seen the witches take dirt and turn it into spells. Go on." Technika, who by now had a torso and one-and-a-half arms attached, waved Hexene over to the door of the shed.

The maiden sighed. "You need more than dirt. It has to be special dusts and powders."

"Dirt."

"And it doesn't matter anyway. I can't do that kind of thing anymore."

"You are not a very good witch. I understand. A competent witch would have already cursed the zombies pursuing her and would have no need to hide here. I suppose I should be grateful for your incompetence."

"I am a very good witch!" Hexene snapped. Then, quieter, "I *was* a very good witch."

"I am afraid I do not understand. You are still a witch if you fear the destructive power of water."

Hexene shook her head. "I am. Or not. I'm something. But I lost the ability to work any kind of magic when my familiar died."

"Ah yes, the pets your kind attach such significance to. We have had to make allowances at the Hotel Metropole for those witches who wish to stay. Animals are unconcerned with the disposition of both urine and feces."

While Hexene had always thought of Escuerzo as exceptionally tidy for a toad, he would occasionally go wherever he liked. "You work at the Hotel Metropole?"

"The present status of my employment is uncertain, though enough time has passed that it is unlikely I have been retained. I am the former concierge of that establishment."

"How long have you been here?"

"Four months. I can give you a more precise determination if you like."

"Four months. That's awful. What happened?"

"A gremlin," said the robot. Her voice was largely monotone, carrying only a hint of a lilt that, like her expression, could imply just about anything. Here, though, her voice evened out and deepened. Mechanical rage, but rage nonetheless. "His name is Baron Sweettooth, but most know him as Slick. It is my understanding that he is famous outside of this city for his various confections."

Hexene nodded. She knew him, or of Sweettooth Confections at least. He sold sugar in solid form, but dyed it the colors of the rainbow. Turned out no one ever went broke trying to sell sugar. He was maybe most famous for Bebop Cola, a drink that was so sweet it could pucker Hexene's mouth from twenty paces. "I've heard of his company. I didn't really think of him at all."

"That is best. He is a worm. He comes here because there is no real law."

"What about Las Barrenderas?"

"You are newly arrived."

"Yeah, I am."

"There is no law here. Las Barrenderas enforce order, and that is not the same thing. Similarly, they do not come to Cogtown. We are left to our own devices. Whatever justice one can afford, one gets."

"And a cola magnate can afford more justice than a concierge."

"Indeed," said Technika. "When he disassembled me and secreted me away in this oubliette, I assumed I would be spending the rest of my existence in this degraded state."

"Oh. I'm glad to help, I guess," said Hexene. The robot was brusque and rude, but she was willing to talk, and she hadn't shown any pity for the lack of a familiar. It was oddly refreshing.

"Yes." Technika paused, and when she spoke, it was the first time she had been at all halting in her speech. "I am grateful for the misfortune that led you here."

Hexene got back to work, reattaching Technika's right forearm, and then going to work on her abdomen, hips, and finally legs. "Can I ask you something?"

"I do not see a method of stopping you, short of physical harm."

"Right. Why did Slick do this to you?"

There was a click, and a rasping, inhuman voice came from Technika. "Want you, want you. Mine, mine!"

Hexene jumped. "What was that?"

In the voice Hexene had become accustomed to, Technika said, "That is him. A recording."

Hexene shuddered. "Don't do that. I can barely understand gremlin chatter anyway."

"He wished me to be his romantic partner."

Hexene blinked. "Can...can you do that?" There was no indication that Technika had the proper parts.

"I am quite capable of being a romantic partner, depending on the needs of the individual. I have an extensive knowledge of cinema, I speak three languages, and I have the capacity to appreciate sunsets. The issue was that I do not wish to be *his* romantic partner. I told him this, many times. He would not accept such an answer. He attempted to purchase my company. He attempted to compel my company. Finally, he would take no more refusals and he abducted me. If I would not submit to what he required, I would not be allowed to exist in a free state."

Hexene wished this was the first time she'd heard of something like this. Back when she'd had her magic, sometimes a woman would come to the Candlemas Coven, or even just her, and ask for vengeance for such an outrage. Hexene never charged for that kind of work. She found herself hoping Technika would ask for such help, though she was unsure of what she could do. She'd figure something out.

When Hexene had attached the last piece of Technika—her right foot, as it happened—the robot nodded. She picked up the amulet that had been sitting on the table next to her disassembled body and hung it around her neck. "Thank you, Hexene. I have a gremlin to kill." She took a single step, then crashed into a shelf, falling to the floor with a hideous racket. "Perhaps not," said Technika, lying facedown on the floor.

"What happened?" Hexene demanded, her voice turning to a frantic hiss as she pictured the zombies bursting in through the door. She thought she was going to have a robot to help her out. Sure, a robot was just as weak against water as she, but two was better than one in a fight.

"In my former state, my power requirements were drastically reduced, but they were not entirely eliminated. I believed I had enough in my reserves to carry out my plan, but that is demonstrably not the case. Perhaps you would render further assistance?"

Hexene sighed, but had already made up her mind. She gripped Technika by the smooth metal of her shoulders and attempted to haul the robot up onto her feet. She might as well have tried shotputting an anvil. "I can't carry you."

"Of course you cannot. You cannot weigh more than 45 kilograms. I weigh more than 120."

"You could have mentioned that before I nearly wrenched my back."

"I thought it would be obvious after you had handled my various parts."

"I didn't add them together!" Hexene glanced at the door again. The noise hadn't summoned the zombies. Or maybe they just hadn't arrived yet.

"There is a wheelbarrow in the southwest corner."

Hexene stepped over the fallen robot and the various debris pieces the act of her falling had strewn around the floor. The wheelbarrow was right where Technika had said it was; Hexene imagined the robot had plenty of time to assess her surroundings in maddening detail. She pulled it away from the wall and wheeled it over to the fallen robot.

"Can you get up?" she asked.

"With some assistance. Can you find a lever?"

Hexene returned to the place where the wheelbarrow had been stored and pulled a shovel off the wall. "Will this do?"

"I can only see the floor in front of me," Technika said. "So, perhaps."

Hexene smacked the robot in the back with the shovel. "What do you think now?"

"Was that a shovel?"

"Yes." Hexene hit her again. That felt good at least.

"It should do."

Hexene pushed the blade underneath Technika's abdomen. The shovel made a cacophonous shriek on the concrete floor. She didn't bother looking at the door this time; either the zombies were going to burst in at this point or they weren't. She was beginning to think she'd successfully lost them. When the shovel was good and wedged under the robot, Hexene pressed down on the handle. Nothing moved. She put more weight on it, and really put her back into it. Nothing. She stood back, then shrugged to herself. She stepped on the handle, first one foot, and then the other, wobbling to keep her balance and pressing a hand against a handy shelf. The robot shifted, groaned. She got her newly reassembled arms under her and pushed off. With effort and a lot of profanity, the two of them finally managed to dump Technika in the bed of the wheelbarrow.

Hexene slumped against the wall to get her breath back. The exertion throbbed in the fresh burns along her arm, but other than that, she felt good. She was exhausted, but it was a good kind of enervation.

"So, where do you want to go?" she asked, mostly to be asking something.

"Take me to my domicile," Technika said. "I have a battery there, attached to the Cogtown power grid. I will be able to replenish my reserves."

"Please tell me you live nearby."

"Of course. It would be inefficient to live a considerable distance from one's place of employment."

"Right, of course." Hexene was able to move the wheelbarrow if she leaned her entire weight on one end. The key was keeping the back stands off the ground. If she failed, she wasn't sure she could get the whole thing tilted once again. She wrestled Technika out of the shed with difficulty, then pushed off toward the street running along the backside of the Hotel Metropole, which she learned later was Babbage Boulevard. The walls enclosing the false garden ended as soon as the largest towers began to sprout. She looked around for the zombies, but saw nothing. The foot traffic here got around primarily on artificial limbs.

"Did you refuse a zombie's offer of romantic partnership?" Technika asked.

"What?" Hexene squinted at the late afternoon shadows between the towers.

"The zombies who were pursuing you. Did you refuse a demand for romantic partnership?"

"Oh. No. I don't know why they were coming for me." Hexene told the story in broad strokes, trying to keep her distance from the emotions involved in Hechalé and Hermosa's deaths. That was difficult, as she remembered the final thing she'd said to the mother. They were never going to make up. That was how things had ended between them.

"You were targeted by Los Silenciosos," said Technika after Hexene fell quiet. Though she spoke in Spanish, Hexene heard the capital letters with *Los Silenciosos* the same way she did with *Las Barrenderas*.

"How do you know that?"

"If you see a zombie whose mouth has been sewn shut, that zombie is affiliated with Los Silenciosos."

"I don't know who they are or why they would attack my coven."

"That is a good point. Despite what the witches claim, evidence does not exist that ties Los Silenciosos with acts of violence like the encounter you describe. Perhaps they are changing their tactics."

"Who are they?"

"They are an organization of zombies, united behind a leader called Malleus. Their demands are related to labor, both conditions and compensation. I cannot tell you more than that, as I do not pay attention. The concerns of zombies are not mine."

Hexene nodded, "Are they related to what's going on in Cuba right now?"

"Perhaps. I have not seen any evidence that ties the two together, but a zombie-led revolution has been of concern to more than one of the Metropole's guests."

Hexene supposed there didn't have to be a direct connection for the two to be related. The Metropole's guests weren't the only ones panicking about the zombies in Cuba. Hexene didn't keep up on the news much, but the revolution had gone from a joke to a problem when the zombies took Havana. The Malleus graffiti had been on her mind since her arrival, and now it was at least partly explained. Why Los Silenciosos would want her dead...she shook her head. It had to be the Adepts. They were the true target, and the Candlemas Coven had been in the wrong place at the wrong time. That was worse than some elaborate conspiracy: a pointless quirk of fate that destroyed her future and killed her mother and crone.

"I don't think they were there for my coven," Hexene said.

"Yes, considering your recent arrival, a case of mistaken identity is a likely hypothesis. Then we need fear only Slick in our present endeavor."

"What? How?"

"He lives in the penthouse suite of the central tower above. Why did you think he kept me where he did?"

"I didn't think about it!" Hexene hissed, as though that would help.

"Indeed. He wished to keep me close in my degraded state. Sometimes he would enter the shed to see if I had softened in my stance. I had not. Though..."

"It was getting harder."

"No," said Technika. Hexene wasn't much of a lie detector, but it was hard to miss that one. She put her back into it and wheeled the robot out onto the wide avenues of Cogtown. The robot pedestrians came in every shape and size. Many people remarked on the mutability of goblins, but they couldn't hold a candle to robots. There were certainly some recognizable types, but there were also those who conformed to no particular aesthetic. Hexene envied their variety, though she didn't see much point in being a thinking, feeling Sherman tank.

She didn't see a single zombie, though. Not the ones chasing her or any others. Robots, apparently, did the bulk of their manual labor themselves. Here, at least, it would be far easier to notice her pursuers sneaking up on her. Hexene pushed Technika along the boulevard and turned a corner at Al-Jazari Street.

"It is the second house from the corner," the robot said. There was no other distinguishing feature Technika could have offered. The houses along Al-Jazari, just like in the rest of the enclave that Hexene had seen, were entirely uniform, metal cubes of precisely the same size, sitting in the middle of square lots also the same size, with the same metal "cactus" in each front yard. They looked like the idea of houses rather than the real thing.

As Hexene put some distance between them and the Hotel Metropole, her heart slowed. Slick and the zombies all seemed to have their eyes turned elsewhere for the moment. A bit of long-overdue luck there. Something was going to catch up with her, though—and it turned out not to be zombies, but the fatigue and hunger from a long day. It wasn't the couch in the guest room of the Adepts' house that beckoned, though; it was her bed back home in Los Angeles.

The coven lived behind their little shop, each with a room of her own—Hechalé sharing hers with her family—along with the kitchen and the living room. It wasn't a lot of space, especially for a coven with the reputation of Candlemas, but it was theirs. Hexene's room was cozy, with a single window looking out onto Hollywood. She might have preferred something a little higher up, but it would do. She'd grown up in a one-room shack. Not hearing the night sounds of a whole family was still a bit of a luxury for her. Her bed was soft and covered in a quilt that looked a lot like her dress. She imagined being there now, with a belly full of cake, and falling into that blissfully welcoming bed. Sleep would come quickly, and any dreams would be forgotten.

Instead, she was directly under the punishing desert sun, wheeling around three hundred pounds of robot. The roads, at least, were as smooth as glass, with nary a pothole to be seen. She might have liked a downward slope, but this was definitely a beggars and choosers situation.

She turned the ninety-degree corner and wheeled Technika to the ruler-straight walkway. "Do you have a key?" Technika held up a hand and a small bar with an ornate end extended from her index finger. "Okay, good."

They'd only made it halfway up the walk when the door opened to reveal a robot. Its face was a collection of flashing lights, the mouth a speaker. Its head and body were cubes, and its arms and legs were pinchers mounted on the end of cables.

"What is the purpose of your arrival here?" the robot asked.

"This is my place of residence," said Technika.

"Negative. I obtained this residence 2,576.4 hours ago."

Technika was silent for a moment, her thought processes invisible behind her immobile face. Then: "What was the disposition of the items located within?"

"All assets of the previous occupant were liquidated."

Hexene wasn't certain if that was literal or not. She was leaning toward yes.

"Would you allow me to connect to your battery?" Technika asked.

"Negative," said the robot. "The status of your connector ports is unknown."

"I would surrender to an inspection."

The robot took two steps backward and slammed the door. Hexene cursed and kicked the wheelbarrow. Pain exploded through her foot and she spent the next minute hopping around, futilely cursing every aspect of her situation, even the self-inflicted parts.

"That was foolish," Technika observed.

"Yeah, thanks," said Hexene. She put her foot down and found she could limp around without too much trouble. She wanted to kick the wheelbarrow again for starting this whole thing, but managed to stop herself. Barely.

"I need you to remain functional," said Technika. "I cannot walk on my own, so you are walking for both of us."

"Figured that out. That's why everything hurts." Hexene groaned in frustration and sat down. Rubbing her toe was easier.

"What are you doing?"

"Resting," snapped the maiden. "Why, what do you want to do?"

"I confess that I am at a loss for next steps."

"What about public charging stations? You have those, right?"

"Of course."

"How about that?"

"Do you have any money?"

"No."

"Nor I."

"We could panhandle?"

"You wish to avail yourself of the sympathy of robots?"

Hexene scrunched up her face with a frustrated growl. It would be easier getting a killer clown to an opera. She stared across the street at a house that was identical to the one behind her. "Las Barrenderas," she said finally.

"What of them?"

"They'll protect us, right?"

"The actions of Las Barrenderas are impossible to predict with certainty, but they are likely to protect you."

"It's the only thing I can think of. What's the nearest...precinct?"

"They call them Wards."

"They would."

"The German Ward is not far from the Cogtown border," Technika said. "Travel south two blocks to Hollerith Street. To the west, it will terminate on the edge of the German Quarter. The German Ward of Las Barrenderas is not far beyond."

"Now all we have to do is make sure we don't run into any zombies or gremlins," muttered Hexene.

"Such a plan is nearly always advisable."

Eleven

None of this was any fun. Hexene had to lean her entire weight against the wheelbarrow to keep it propped up on the wheel, and couldn't slow down no matter how much she wanted to. If the wheelbarrow fell flat, she was pretty sure she wouldn't be able to heave it up again. Her bruised toe complained the whole way. As promised, the arrow-straight Hollerith Street turned into a nameless, winding alley as soon as it hit Las Brujas proper, and Hexene cursed every witch who even thought about city planning.

It would have been so easy to haul Technika around on a broom. Sure, the robot would have sacrificed a little dignity, but the travel would have been quick. Certainly preferable to the slow bleed of being pushed around in a wheelbarrow by an exhausted woman. Or, Hexene reflected, with enough preparation she could have summoned a lightning bolt from the sky and recharged Technika with that. Such a gross display of power had its appeal.

But no, she was left to navigate alleys that had as much planning and stability behind them as a winter sea. The alleys twisted, turned, and doubled back and if Hexene didn't know better, she'd say that was the intent. She spotted several entrances into the Catacombs, but went past them. She was going to give zombies of any stripe a wide berth.

Which was easy. She didn't see a single one in these alleys. Not in Cogtown, not in the German Quarter. As it turned out, she had been in the German Quarter before. All around her, the houses, all of which looked like they were made of black gingerbread, were quiet. No zombie servants loitered outside or cared for the small gardens. A few lights glowed in windows, but there was no sign of the second most common monster in Las Brujas.

The most common, though, was everywhere. Witches zoomed by overhead, visible in the dying light of the evening mostly as persistent movement. It set Hexene on edge. Something was wrong. She couldn't put a precise name to it, but she felt it in the air, like a blade about to be drawn.

She found the German Ward after what felt like hours. It looked like several small cottages piled on top of one another by a massive and not particularly careful toddler. The cross-hatched windows glowed with light. Fortunately, it was set in a slight recess, and where the wall parted, a stone path led right to the front door. The wheelbarrow was going at a good clip by the bottom, and Hexene steered it into the doorjamb, where it clanked and rebounded.

"I am not entirely immune to impacts," Technika informed her.

Hexene would have liked to still have the shovel just to test that remark, but she wasn't sure she could swing it with much conviction after the trip through the city. Even the hunger gnawing away in her belly did little more than join the angry aches that chewed on the rest of her body. She collapsed onto the front stoop and cradled her head in her hands. She made a mental note to stand up at some point, but was already coming to terms with the fact that such things were far easier said than done.

"Ho, maiden," said a voice in Theban. The accent was clipped and reminded Hexene of war movies.

She looked up and craned her head around. The aches that had been put to fitful sleep woke up with howls. Standing in the doorway were three figures. Maidens, by the looks of them, two sporting red hair and one black. Their complexions made milk look positively swarthy. They wore black, two in gowns, one in pants, with cloaks over the top. Two wore conical hats. Patches at their shoulders and on their cloaks told the tale here. The four-part coat of arms held a collection of candy, a gnarled black tree, a loom with golden thread, and a winding line of rats.

The black-haired one repeated her greeting. A large, black rat sat on her shoulders, its little paws on its zaftig hips.

"Ho, maidens," Hexene said. She wasn't confident enough in her Theban to use it with strangers, so she switched to Spanish. "This is the German Ward of Las Barrenderas, isn't it?"

"It is," said the black-haired one. One of the two redheads leaned against the doorframe, looking Technika over with contemptuous amusement. An orange cat sat at her feet, insouciantly licking his genitals. "Did you transport this robot in a wheelbarrow?"

"Yes," said Hexene. "She's starving. Do you have a generator or a battery or—" She stopped talking because the witches had burst into laughter.

"Oh, that's funny," said the other redhead. Her hair was cut short, and looked a bit like the ruff of feathers on the back of her hawk's head. When she laughed, the hawk cried out and though Hexene couldn't prove it, the tone felt mocking.

"Why aren't you..." the black-haired one trailed off, then, "Where's your familiar?"

The others noticed the lack, and their expressions fell somewhere on the continuum between scandalized and confused. A witch didn't go anywhere without her familiar, and Hexene was getting the impression that hiding it away was a taboo.

"I don't have one," she said, the shame nearly eating her words.

"Don't have one?" said Hawk, as though there was just no way to square that circle.

"But you're a witch," said Cat. "Or are you just one of those humans who dresses like us?"

"No," said Rat. "She's a witch. I can smell it on her."

"No such thing as a witch without a familiar," said Hawk.

"Maybe she's an unwitch, then," said Cat, and the others laughed.

"Please," said Hexene. "I need help. My name is Hexene Candlemas."

"Nice try," said Cat.

Rat peered at her. "No. Look at her. You, unwitch, what was your familiar before you lost it?"

"A toad," Hexene said, swallowing. "His name is...was Escuerzo."

"You see? It *is* her."

Hawk's eyes widened in surprise. "*Hexene*," she said, then switched to murmured German with her two companions. Recognition bloomed in Cat's face.

"Isn't she supposed to be dead?" Cat blurted in Theban.

"I was attacked," Hexene told them.

"She's supposed to be dead," said Hawk.

"Does she look dead?" said Rat.

"Half," said Cat, shrugging. "Serves her right for what she let happen to that adorable toad."

Hexene jumped in her skin. *How the hell did she know Escuerzo was adorable? Because he was. That wasn't debatable.* "Three zombies were in the house. They had buckets of water," she said instead, resolving to get to the bottom of the rest later.

"They killed your mother and your crone, we know," Rat said. "We thought they got you too."

Hexene shook her head. "I ran."

"Smart," said Rat, "especially since you can't fight back the way you are."

Hexene had a crystalline image of what would happen if she punched Rat in the face. That teutonic nose of hers would be the first to go. A nice little pop, and then it'd be a real gusher. Hexene would have bet good money on that. She felt her hands clenching of their own accord, and took a deep, shuddering breath.

"I'll go tell the Arcane Adepts that their houseguest is still with us. Maybe they'll come and fetch you," Hawk said. She leaned through the door and grabbed a broom. Within moments, she was airborne, her hawk familiar flapping along with her.

"They're alive?" Hexene gasped.

"Of course they're alive," snapped Rat. Her familiar shook his head sadly, and Hexene imagined she saw disappointment in his beady black eyes. "They reported your whole coven dead."

Hexene shook her head in disbelief.

"Don't worry," said Cat with a smirk, "we'll track down those corpses who did it."

"Los Silenciosos," Hexene said. "Their mouths were sewn shut."

Rat and Cat exchanged a weary look. "Of course it was them. If there's trouble in this town, you can trace it back to their warrens."

"Hey!" Rat said.

"No offense," said Cat.

Rat shot Cat a glare. "Wait here," she said to Hexene. "We'll see what the Adepts want to do with you."

"Can we go inside?"

Both witches looked positively nauseated. "No. Witches only. Now if you'll excuse us, we should look into getting some justice for two dead witches."

"Or unwitches," Cat said.

They both retrieved brooms from inside. When they moved past Hexene, they were careful not to touch her, as though her present state were contagious. Then they rose into the dark sky to join the other witches going to and fro.

"The hunt will produce quarry," Technika said.

"How do you know?"

"It does not take murder to drive witches in this place to hunt zombies. It is self-evident that this is what drives them now."

"Does this happen often?"

"Without specific parameters, it is difficult for me to specify that it is often. It happens with some regularity, though this effort appears to be more intensive than most."

Hexene glanced through the open door into the inviting warmth of the Ward. She wasn't precisely cold, more tired and afraid, and she wanted to find a place to sit where she didn't feel hunted. The gateway in front of her leading out into the alley could be darkened by a trio of zombies at any time. The worst part was the feeling that as obnoxious as those three maidens had been, she'd felt much safer when they had been around. Hexene briefly considered going inside and rubbing whatever awful familiarless cooties she had all over their Ward. She stopped herself. She needed them, as distasteful as that was. Antagonizing whatever passed for the local law probably wasn't the best idea.

She sat down next to the wheelbarrow, leaning against the cool metal. Technika's arms and legs dangled over the side. Hexene watched the mouth of the pathway, but nothing passed. The alleys were completely free of pedestrian traffic. She wasn't certain how long she and Technika had been sitting in silence when she heard the faint rushing sound of a witch grow louder than the general susurrus of the present air traffic. Two silhouettes descended into the light of the Ward House. One was Hawk, her familiar perched elegantly on the back of her broom. The other was Angelique Arcane.

Hexene stood, feeling the relieved grin stretching her face. Angelique's expression split the difference between concern and relief. She landed, embracing Hexene tightly. Danbala slithered between them.

"Hexene! I was so worried!" Angelique exclaimed.

"I'm okay. I barely got out, but I'm okay."

"Thank every face of the Goddess. We found the spots of water, and we saw the smoke, but...it's hard to tell. I'm so sorry about Hechalé and Hermosa."

The acknowledgment of it brought the feelings back in force, building them up into a wave. The strength of the embrace, the safety of her presence, broke that same wave. Hexene found herself sobbing for the deaths of her mother and her crone, and hating that she was doing it in front of a Barrendera. Angelique held her and whispered comforting nonsense in her ear, eventually falling into soft French.

Hexene took hold of her emotions quickly. Anger was always a closer friend than sadness or fear. She could work with anger. There was a direction, and here it led to revenge. She sniffed, and broke reluctantly from Angelique, wiping the tears away with a balled fist.

"Done?" asked Hawk, and Hexene again fought the very real urge to punch her. "So here's the unwitch. Do whatever you want with her."

Angelique turned. "Show her some kindness." Hawk sniffed, but she did flinch slightly at the steel in Angelique's tone. Angelique waited for Hawk to take a swing. The Barrendera smartly chose to get on her broom and leave before things came to blows. Angelique turned back to Hexene and offered a wan smile. "I'm sorry about her."

Hexene shrugged. "I'm getting used to it," she lied. "Where were you? When the zombies attacked?"

"On the other side of the house. By the time we heard anything, the zombies were gone, and all that was left...you know."

Hexene swallowed, picturing the smoke that had been her coven rising to the ceiling.

"I am pleased you have located someone willing to offer some form of assistance, but if I might make my presence known and state my own needs, I would be most grateful."

Angelique jumped, apparently noticing the robot in the wheelbarrow for the first time. Hexene realized that Hawk had never mentioned Technika. As abrasive as the robot had been, that thoughtless disrespect brought the banked anger back up to a simmer.

"This is Technika," Hexene said by way of explanation. "She needs help."

"She should find help in Cogtown," Angelique whispered, drawing Hexene away from the robot.

Unwitch Hunt

"We tried that. She's not going to get it there." Hexene explained what had happened in the quickest possible terms.

"Fine," Angelique said. "We can probably find a way to give her some electricity. Just keep her away from Serafina and Evangeline. They still don't like that we have to live next to robots. I don't know what they'd do if they found out they were living with one."

Angelique removed a tiny jar from a pocket on her dress and opened it, revealing a small amount of flying ointment. She applied the blue-gray grease to the wheelbarrow, and pretty soon it was floating. It would be a temporary enchantment, but would serve long enough to get them home. She never once spoke to Technika, and the robot herself might as well have been deactivated.

"Hang onto it," she said to Hexene.

Hexene mounted the broom behind Angelique, wrapping one arm around the maiden and clutching the wheelbarrow with the other. It felt like it was bobbing on water.

"You're going to be all right," Hexene said to Technika.

"As long as I am not dropped." Hexene had to admit, Technika was right.

Angelique rose only high enough to clear the rooftops, and so Hexene could see the alleys of Las Brujas quite well. No one walked them, but numerous witches flew along the winding avenues, barely skimming the surfaces. As they flew closer to the Caribbean Quarter, the activity increased. Evidence of violence started to appear: scattered garbage, hexes etched into stone, burn marks. A human form slumped against a wall, a pentagram behind it. All around, candles guttered, stuck to the floor of the alley and the wall behind. Scrawled in Theban on the wall behind the figure was MALLEUS SAYS NOTHING.

A chill wriggled through Hexene's body. The dead zombie was wearing a dress; her attackers were in pants. It wasn't the same one, and after what Technika had said, she didn't think the witches of Las Brujas were going to be discerning.

TWELVE

Hexene had been horribly right. Over the course of the following month, she couldn't leave the house without passing zombies who had been hexed to death, their bodies left to mummify in the Chilean sun. The hex the witches invariably used was awful, first trapping the unfortunate zombie in a binding star, then popping its skull. Hexene had never seen that particular curse before, but apparently down here it was common knowledge. None of the zombies she passed was one of her attackers, and she checked every last one. Only one even had the stitched-up mouth of Los Silenciosos, and she was obviously a woman. The witches who killed her hadn't cared.

Vengeance was good, even necessary. But it had to be precise; vengeance without precision was mere brutality. Witches were supposed to be above that. *We're primes*, she thought, *the original monsters*. But it wasn't like sidhe and mad scientists were known for being exact with their vendettas either.

When they first returned to the Adepts' house, Hexene tried to go back to the room she had used before. Weird stains marred the bed, something evil caked to the side and dripping down onto the floor. The last little bits of Hermosa and Hechalé. Angelique promised she would get the zombies in to clean, but Hexene kept seeing her mother falling into smoke as the water did its awful work. Her burns itched. She couldn't sleep in there.

Angelique put Hexene and Technika in an attic nook near the back of the house. They couldn't be more out of the way without leaving entirely. A small, circular window overlooked a narrow alley and the rooftops of the southern edge of the Caribbean Quarter. The room was unconscionably stuffy in the daytime, but at night, with the window open, it was almost bearable. Hexene slept fitfully on a tiny cot. Angelique fashioned a crude charger for Technika; a simple ward with a curse of lightning. If Technika placed her palm on the center, the ward could charge her, although Technika complained it didn't do so very well. It took the edge off the hunger and gave her the strength to move around, but she wasn't, as she put it, "optimal."

The zombie servants never ventured outdoors. They scurried around the house as quickly as their shambling gaits would allow, and they did whatever was asked of them with a desperate speed.

It took Hexene a week to return to the library. It felt pointless, but she kept hearing what she'd said to Hechalé the night she had been murdered. The first week, those words were too heavy to move out from under. After that, they spurred Hexene out the door to *do something*. It might well be pointless, but it wasn't sitting in a stuffy room with a motionless robot whose body crawled with lightning.

Angelique was waiting for her on the first night Hexene came home from the library. Her smile lit up her entire face, and if Hexene was being honest, most of the house. "You were at the library," she said.

Hexene nodded. The futility of the day was heavy on her shoulders, but the sight of Angelique made it lighten just a bit. "Not that it helped."

"There's always tomorrow," Angelique said. "I'm glad you're working to get your magic back."

"I need to do something. Otherwise I'll scream."

Angelique stood up and put her hand on Hexene's arm. Danbala slithered away from the contact to wrap himself loosely around his mistress's neck. "Have you decided what you'll do when you get it back?"

Hexene's chuckle was bitter. "When?"

"When," Angelique said more firmly.

"I don't know. Even then, I'd be a witch without a coven."

"You could look for a new coven," Angelique said. "There have to be some witches who are looking."

"For a maiden who got her coven's familiars killed."

"You could find someone."

Hexene wanted to believe her. It would be so easy. But she couldn't. She shook her head. "No. I don't think I'll ever have another coven."

Angelique pulled her into a soft hug. Hexene found herself pillowing her head on the other maiden's shoulder. "I'm sorry you feel that way. Good luck in the library. If anyone can do what you're trying to do, it will be a Candlemas."

It took Serafina and Evangeline another week to learn Technika was in the house. They hinted that she should go, but didn't say anything directly about it. As for Hexene, Evangeline kept offering hugs and a sympathetic ear. She apologized several times for being unable to stop the attack. Serafina just avoided her. Hexene preferred that. She'd rather be alone with her grief and guilt, or at least as alone as being with Technika was.

Evangeline was supportive of Hexene's trips to the library. The first day she left her room, the mother had nearly clapped. On subsequent trips, she sent Hexene out with a sack lunch every day. Sometimes there were even notes in Theban inside with messages like *I am proud of you!* Those just made Hexene feel worse. What had she done to be proud of?

Evangeline also gave her some money to get around, though hardly much of it. Hexene learned that there were two forms of commonly accepted currency in the city. The first were witch coins called favors, which any witch could mint. They had a common exchange value, but could be redeemed from the issuing witch for a hex. Although the favors were allegedly of equal value, everyone knew that ones from certain covens like the Moirai carried more value. In practice, redeeming a favor didn't happen very often, but it was the reason that only witches were allowed to give and receive them. The zombies took Chilean pesos. One peso for a cart trip, and Evangeline was only too happy to give Hexene enough for her commute.

It wasn't the only thing she learned over the course of the month. She got to know the city's geography, learning that it was roughly shaped like a melty flower. Some Quarters extended from the Stone Forest at the center, while others sprouted alongside those like petals. She largely kept to the Adepts' home or the library. The only places the eyes stayed off her.

Hexene lost track of time. Days were spent in the library in research, with lunch in the shadow of the Baba Yaga statue. At night, she would return home and have a conversation with Technika, who claimed to be marshaling her strength for a showdown with Slick. Technika never got into details, and after a week Hexene came to the conclusion that Technika was scared of the gremlin. Hexene would have offered sympathy, but she knew that acknowledging it would be worse than simply playing along. So instead they talked movies. They were both fans, and Technika never tired of Hexene's stories of spotting celebrities. Out of consideration for the robot, Hexene never explained why she was a welcome sight on movie lots. Technika didn't need to know how many of her favorite stars had hex habits.

Hexene hadn't even realized a month had gone by until Angelique came to collect her for the Ettu Sabbat. Hexene didn't want to attend *any* Sabbat, but of all the ones to have, Ettu was the worst. She couldn't very well say no, though, and rode on the back of Angelique's broom into the amphitheater where the flags were now marked with bats. The Ettu Sabbat opened first with the invocation to the bat, then pivoted to a remembrance of every witch who had died in the previous year. Most were crones who had chosen to move beyond, but soon they read the names of Hechalé and Hermosa Candlemas. Hexene felt the weight of the stares of the Sabbat gathering when their names were read. The pity coming from them was a lead anchor around her neck.

Hexene stayed still until they were finished. Later, she refused Angelique's offer to go to Le Chaperon Rouge for Samhain celebrations.

She went to her room instead and tried not to think of her mother and crone.

The following morning when Hexene rose, she found that Technika, instead of kneeling with her palm lightly touching the wall, was standing by the window.

"What is it?" Hexene mumbled.

"Hexene. I did not wish to wake you. I know your fragile flesh requires extensive time to be unconscious."

It was lucky for the both of them that there was nothing in the small room that would make a convenient smacking device. "Well, I'm up now. What is it?"

Technika pointed to the sky visible outside the window. "He knows."

Hexene joined Technika at the window and saw what she was pointing at in the lightening desert sky. A gremlin flivver, built like a pulp rocketship, zoomed over the city. Hexene had already seen it once, on her first day there. The vehicle was objectively ridiculous, with its fire-engine-red skin and gleaming chrome fins, but now it carried menace.

"Slick?"

"Yes," said Technika. "He has apparently noticed that I am missing. He hunts for me."

"What do you want to do?"

"I do not know."

"It's time you came up with a plan," Hexene told her, putting one hand on the robot's copper shoulder.

"And you will assist?"

"Sure. What else am I going to do?"

"Regain your magic, exact revenge on those zombies, return to the United States—"

"That was a rhetorical question."

"Oh."

Hexene waited, and once she was certain the robot wasn't getting it, she said, "I'll help."

Unwitch Hunt

"Thank you," Technika said. "I do not know what a witch without her magic can do, but you are better than nothing."

"Don't make me rethink this."

Hexene left Technika to her thoughts. She bathed quickly, picked up her lunch and money from the table by the door where they waited for her, and went out.

The streets were still perversely quiet. As she walked, Hexene saw more evidence of crimes against the local zombies. Hexes, candles, and even the occasional corpse marked a city still in the grips of violence. From time to time, Slick's flivver burned overhead, scattering the flocks of witches.

Hexene ducked into the nearest entryway into the Catacombs. It had become an old friend by now. At first, she was terrified of encountering the assassins, but she never did. Still, she never deviated from her three cart rides, and walked quickly between them. No need to tempt fate.

The opening of the tunnel was plastered with posters, all in Spanish, demanding the surrender of the murderers of the Candlemas Coven. THREE MURDERS, THREE MURDERERS, proclaimed the posters. They had gone up the first night, and no one had bothered to correct them; Hexene was still listed among the dead. Might as well be. She wasn't a true witch. She was an unwitch, like the three Barrenderas at the German Ward had called her. The witches of Las Brujas didn't care one way or the other. Dead, Hexene had value. She was an excuse to go after the zombies. Alive, she was at best an embarrassment.

The posters petered out before long. Hexene imagined the witches getting spooked as they descended into the Catacombs. They looked down on the zombies, even hated them, but they had to trust them with the water. Hexene took her cart rides, her regular cartmen giving no indication they recognized her.

In the library, she refused to wither under the librarian's judgmental eye. She went back into the wing with the candy codices, hunting for more information on the previous unwitches who had "returned to the east." Being a witch had never been this much work. There had been lessons, of course, right when she was turned, but mostly it was about doing what Hechalé and Hermosa did. Now she had to work for it, without even knowing if what she wanted could be achieved at all.

After lunch, instead of returning to stale gingerbread, she headed to the bone room. The bones hung on hooks in the walls and on free-standing displays of black iron. They hung at various angles, looping, spiraling Theban script catching the lantern light. The bones were of all shapes and sizes, including heavy tusks that could only have come from mammoths, thick chest-plates from an extinct scavenger, and curved teeth the size of her scarred forearm.

She looked for the story of Baba Yaga. Like any witch, she felt some kinship to the Great Hag. In some legends, Baba Yaga was the first, the prime of primes. In other legends, she was simply one of the greatest of the early witches. Hexene tended to believe the latter. Witchcraft was a part of the world everywhere, discovered as women learned what power they could wield. The true creative energy, distinct from the scientist's power of definition. Hexene imagined that it rose everywhere more or less at the same time.

Finding stories of the Great Hag was about as difficult as finding something about Jesus in a Christian bookstore. Finding any one story that agreed with the others, well, that actually *was* a challenge. The most common were stories of the Hag going about her business in the woods, living in her hut with chicken legs, cursing or eating wanderers as she saw fit. Sounded like the life to Hexene, though she'd have to quit the vegetarianism in favor of good old-fashioned cannibalism if she really wanted to get into the spirit of the thing. In some of the stories, though, Baba Yaga was described as a trio of sisters. At first, Hexene thought she was reading the Theban wrong, as the language tended to confuse three and one. But soon it was obvious that this very confusion was the intent. She was still puzzling over it when she emerged from the library at the end of the day.

She returned home following the same route as always, her thoughts back with Baba Yaga. She begged off dinner, but Evangeline insisted on sending her to her room with a full plate. Typical mother. Hexene climbed the stairs to the attic to find Technika kneeling by the mouth of the staircase, her eyes glowing green in the dark.

"You scared me," Hexene accused, putting a hand over her heart.

The robot didn't apologize. She merely said, "I have formulated a plan against the gremlin."

Thirteen

By design, Hexene didn't get out much. Every day, she took the Catacombs to the library and back again, avoiding any contact with witches who might stare. A day spent hiding with her nose buried in books, codices, baked goods, bones, wings, and so on, kept her privacy intact. The end result was that she still didn't know Las Brujas well. So she and Technika picked Le Chaperon Rouge to talk, since it was the only place Hexene knew that wasn't in the Adepts' home.

At street level, Le Chaperon Rouge loomed, but it was never intended to be seen from that angle for more than a few moments. Proper patrons would descend the steps from the landing pad on top and go right in. From down here, it had some Gothic grandeur, though the weird angles made it seem like something from a bad dream.

No zombies loitered out front. Barely a block away, one of the alley walls had been defaced. Hexes surrounded an old tag of MALLEUS SPEAKS. The Theban words, scrawled in a jagged hand, promised that Malleus would be meeting the wrong end of a death curse soon enough.

As Hexene approached the door, she readied herself to explain why she was bringing a robot in, but the zombie doorman was nowhere to be seen. The club inside was packed, maidens squashed shoulder-to-shoulder from the

Unwitch Hunt

bar to the tables. It was a minor miracle that Hexene found a free barstool against the wall. The robot stood next to her, and Hexene realized she'd never seen Technika sit down. Kneel, sure, but kneeling wasn't something one did in bars as far as Hexene knew. This could be one of the hidden costs of a metal butt, she imagined. A few of the patrons noticed the robot, but no one did more than wrinkle her nose. Usually their eyes slid off Technika to land on Hexene, and then there were whispers and surreptitious pointing. She felt herself clenching, and hid behind her robot friend.

Onstage, a pleasantly round maiden strummed a mandolin and sang in Portuguese. Hexene got maybe one word in ten, and they were all "rainbow." The bartender leaned over to Hexene, and only then made eye contact. Recognition flitted behind her eyes and she caught herself, giving Hexene a small smile. "What would you like?" she asked in Theban.

Hexene sighed in relief, then recovered. The bartender's scent, like exotic toadstools washed over her. "I don't know," she said. "I don't really drink very much."

The bartender smiled and touched the little witch's cap pinned to her poodle bob. "I'll surprise you," she said. The accent was American, and sounded East Coast to Hexene. She pulled a bottle of tequila from the shelf behind her, then a clear mason jar, an old alchemist's flask, and a clay pot, dumping bits of powder into a mortar. She ground it all up and dissolved it in the tequila. She stirred the whole thing with a tiny colonial broom and slid it over to Hexene, the broom still in the drink like a straw. "It's a Bruja Ha," she said with a wink.

Hexene held it in her hands. The amber liquid had a sparkle to it she could only see out of the corner of her eye. Just over the top, the air wavered like a heat shimmer, but it wasn't especially warm.

"Now that you have your intoxicant," Technika said, and trailed off, her attention going to three maidens working their way through the crowd with their attention glued on Hexene. "Do you know these?"

Hexene shook her head. The first of the maidens made it next to her, her hopeful expression mirrored on the face of the opossum on her shoulder. "Excuse me? You're Hexene—"

"What would you like?" the bartender asked loudly, pulling the attention to her.

"I'm sorry, we were just—"

"She was just telling me how she came here for a nice, quiet date," the bartender said, nodding at Technika.

Shock washed over the features of all three maidens, swiftly followed by a realization. "Ohhhhhh," said the lead one. "I understand."

"Why don't you ladies go have a seat and I'll bring you a round on the house?"

The maidens nodded, and one reached out to Hexene. "Stay strong," she said, nodding.

"Okay?" Hexene said. When the maidens were gone, she turned to the bartender. "Thanks."

"Think nothing of it," the bartender said, switching to English. "After what you've been through…glad you're moving on is all."

"Moving on?" Hexene blurted. The bartender gave her an encouraging smile and a nod as she moved off to take care of her other customers. "What the hell is going on?" Hexene said.

"Can I relay the particulars of my plan?" Technika asked.

Hexene turned halfway on her stool to face the robot, and shrugged. "Sure."

"As Slick no doubt knows I am not where he left me, any plan will have to assume he is aware I am missing."

"It follows," Hexene said. She sipped the Bruja Ha. It tasted like molten desert night and the feeling of coming into a party and knowing everyone. She was beginning to think she had been missing out by not drinking. Nick and Lily would be happy when they finally saw her again. If they ever did.

"You will contact Slick—"

"How? I haven't seen a telephone since I got here." Not hearing the infernal racket of the ringing had been an unexpected blessing.

"The only telephones in Las Brujas are in Cogtown," Technika explained. "Witches do not like them, and many robots do not need them, so they are rare. Thus, we are not using them. You will instead use a letter to be delivered anonymously to Slick's suite in the Hotel Metropole. We will instruct him to communicate via a letter dropped at a location of our choosing, which he will mark with chalk when he has delivered said communication. You will tell Slick that you have subdued me and wish to return me to him in exchange for a monetary reward."

The prospect of money wouldn't have annoyed her in LA. She had been paid quite well for her hex slinging. Now, she resented the need for it, if she was ever going to restart any kind of life. "What will we do with the reward?"

"We will split it evenly as partners in a venture. We will arrange a meeting, and he will want it to be in his suite. This is acceptable, as he is unlikely to agree to meet anywhere else. You will deliver me in a state that appears deactivated to him."

"And then?"

"Do you wish me to explain how I intend to kill him?"

Hexene coughed as the Bruja Ha abruptly leapt down her windpipe. "No, no. That's fine." She didn't remember the point she was about to raise, because as she turned her head, she watched Angelique come in with Petunia and a maiden Hexene didn't know. This one looked like she might be fifteen at the most, all round-faced and gangly-limbed. Hexene caught Angelique's eye and the other maiden started, then recovered from her surprise long enough to wave. She and her companions sat down at a recently vacated table rather than coming over. Hexene turned back to the bar, wondering if she should be offended or not.

"I thought she was pretending when it came to her affection for you. I am pleased to see my perceptions are reliable."

"Thanks," Hexene snapped, and quickly downed the rest of her drink. It hit her hard, making her want to watch a sunset through a stand of saguaros. Out of the corner of her eye, she saw giant ants marching under a pink sky.

"Want another?" asked the bartender, who was either just suddenly there, or the drink was stronger than Hexene thought.

"Oh, I don't..." she realized she didn't have money.

"The maiden over there," the bartender pointed at Angelique, "said your drinks are on her. So you want another?"

"Why not?" Hexene said. The bartender smiled and built another Bruja Ha, sliding it across the moisture rings left by the last round. A group of maidens called her over to the other end of the bar.

"It is my distinct shame that I moved too slowly to provide a drink."

The voice was behind and to Hexene's left. The accent wriggled through too many vowels to pin down, and that was before the slurring from a night of drinking came in. She turned away from Technika to the speaker and found a man that, if pressed, she would have to admit was handsome. He looked a bit like Tyrone Power, but his skin was a deep bronze, and he sported a pencil-thin mustache. His hair looked like it had been styled in a pompadour at the beginning of the night but had since come unraveled, some of the glossy black tresses beginning to reassert their natural curl. He was dressed in most of a tuxedo, and looked to Hexene like a nightclub singer who'd lost a fight with the evening. He regarded her with tawny green eyes that could almost focus on her.

"What?" she said.

"Forgive my intrusion. I wished to introduce myself to this vision in red, and this vision in copper, and I..." he broke off, gaze dropping to the half-consumed tincture in his hand. "What am I doing?"

"What?" Now she actually wanted to know.

"I am a foolish balam. There is no spark here. Look at you. You are apple-cheeked and bright. You are the woman the man wishes he could grow up next to, and watch friendship blossom into love. And yet I am blank. I feel nothing for you." He turned to Technika. "And you, a steely portrait of womanhood from the distant shores of the twenty-first century. A woman for whom the act of love would be a defiant exploration, and only one both brave and generous could unlock the secrets in your clockwork bosom."

"If I were to kill him, do you think any would care?" Technika asked.

"I...don't know," Hexene said. The robot took a step toward the balam, who was still staring at his drink.

"No, no," said Hexene, putting a hand on Technika's shoulder. She stopped, but that was more about politeness than the illusion that Hexene could hope to control her companion.

"Ladies, I apologize to the depths of my rotten soul," he said, apparently never noticing how close he'd come to death. "While I pray you might again find the revelry I have crudely interrupted, I know the night: she cannot be caught once she slips through your fingers."

The balam slunk off through the crowd. Hexene saw him lean against a wall and gaze tearfully at his drink. The bartender had only just noticed and started over, but stopped when the balam left them alone.

"It seems you are a popular target for conversation," said Technika.

Hexene shrugged. "At least that time was different."

"I am pleased I was never afflicted with an obsession with novelty. Perhaps that is why I was rebuilt as a robot."

"I'm beginning to think it wasn't that far a journey for you."

"Thank you, Hexene. You are most kind."

Fourteen

Hexene watched the hapless balam repeat his performance several more times before she left Le Chaperon Rouge. It took him two approaches and two blubbering retreats before Hexene realized he should be changing. She should see some fur, or claws or something. When they were aroused, balam turned into jaguars, and they could be turned on with a look, a bit of spicy dialogue, or by quietly reading explanations of the local tax code. She used to have a client who bought hexes from her specifically so he *wouldn't* change in the middle of his workday. But this fella? Nothing. And he was unmistakably a balam. No other monster could simultaneously look that good and like they were in the middle of a weeklong bender.

Conversation with Technika was sparse. The robot was mostly interested in her plan for revenge, and if Hexene was going to be honest with herself, so was she. She might not have a personal beef with Slick, but there was enough crone in her to want to set things straight. Besides, it was a good way to avoid thinking about her lost magic and dead coven. Helping kill a soft drink magnate was an achievable goal. So they hashed out a few more details in lulls of conversation, and Hexene petulantly drank another Bruja Ha, sticking Angelique with the tab.

They left the witch club deep into the night. Angelique was still at her table with Petunia and the other maiden, but even she didn't notice when Hexene left. The one person in the bar Hexene actually wanted to look her way and she never did. Hexene didn't blame her.

The winding alleys of Las Brujas were completely clear. Even the skies had quieted somewhat, though the odd shadowy shape still streaked by. Some paused, and Hexene felt eyes on her, but that was over in seconds. No doubt the witches paused, thinking who else would be walking the streets but a zombie. Instead, they would find a maiden and a robot, who for some reason were walking rather than flying. Hexene had the feeling Technika would have been harassed on her own, but having a witch around, or the next best thing, was enough. No one got close enough to see the empty place where there should have been a familiar. She could just feel it. The walk was pleasant enough; she had come to learn the twisting route well.

"Mafaufau!" The voice echoed around the corners of the alleys, yanking Hexene out of her woolgathering.

Hexene broke into a run without thinking. Technika called to her and was quickly outpaced. The word came again, terror cutting through it like a blade. Other words came after, and these were in hissed Theban. A makeshift hex, and as soon as Hexene heard the syllables, they started a thrumming in her belly. She might not be able to reach her magic anymore, but her body knew the feel of it. She rounded the last corner between her and it, and found three maidens closing around the giant Mafaufau, chanting, one holding a doll, one a piece of chalk, the third a pouch. The terrified zombie had backed up against a wall, his arms up as though to ward them off. They looked like a trio of leopards closing in on a wounded elephant.

The maiden with the pouch poured a handful of powder into her right hand, then blew it at Mafaufau. The hapless zombie tried to shield his eyes and bellowed his one word. The one with the chalk darted in as Mafaufau was blinded and drew two quick marks on the wall: the beginning of one of their pentagrams. Hexene felt the building spell like a live wire, crackling with hurt.

"Stop that at once!" Hexene shouted in what she hoped was authoritative Theban.

When all four participants in the violent drama stopped what they were doing to stare, Hexene realized she had no idea what to do. She hadn't planned on that working. As Mafaufau stared at her, confusion in his milky eyes, she had the sense that he was wondering the same thing she was: *What next?*

"We've cornered a corpse, sister," said the witch with the doll. A clear bottle of water hung from her belt on a leather thong, a pufferfish flitting about inside.

"Want to help?" asked the one with the powder. A monkey stood on her shoulder, nodding and chittering.

No story came. No reason to stop them from their awful sport. Hexene's mind went in circles, and didn't spit out a single thing. The longer she waited, the sooner they might recognize her. It was a minor miracle, it seemed, they hadn't yet. "That's my zombie," Hexene blurted.

The three maidens paused, each one exchanging a confused glance with her familiar. The pufferfish, monkey, and chicken didn't know either.

"So what's he doing out after dark?" demanded the maiden with the chicken and the chalk.

"He can go where he likes," Hexene said, and as she said it, she knew exactly how it was going to sound to the three maidens.

They laughed. "Oh, can he?" mocked Pufferfish.

Hexene paused, unsure of what to do. The three maidens weren't wearing any Barrenderas livery, at least. Hexene straightened up to her full height. It wasn't impressive, especially next to the giant in the alley, but it was all she had. "Yes," she said. "He goes where he likes and any who try to stop him have to deal with me."

Now the look that the maidens exchanged was with each other. They weren't afraid, not yet, but they were on the edge of being concerned. They put their backs to Mafaufau and squared their shoulders at Hexene.

"Mafaufau?" the zombie asked softly. Hexene nodded to him.

"So you'd have us believe that you are willing to fight the three of us in order to protect that?" said Monkey, jerking her thumb over her shoulder at Mafaufau.

"I'm willing to do a lot of things to you," said Hexene. "For *him*."

"The hex we're putting on him works on witches too," said Chicken.

"Yeah? Well..." Hexene reached into her satchel and grabbed the first two things she found inside. One was the Nick Moss doll, the other was a bottle of Essence of Goblin. Even when she had her magic, the only thing she could have done with that would be to make Nick have the uncontrollable urge to spout doggerel poetry. That might have been fun, but it was hardly useful in this context.

The other witches flinched. Not much, but enough to let Hexene know they were wary. "What are you going to do with that?" asked Pufferfish, mostly in challenge.

Hexene directed an imploring look at Mafaufau. *Run*, she thought at him, but it wasn't like he could hear that. She thought it harder as she started to ramble through a threat. "I'm going to put the worst hex there is on you. I'm going to turn you into the...slime...on...a...salamander's ass!" She yanked the cork out of the bottle with her teeth and got a noseful of Essence of Goblin, which smelled like a mildewy log in the middle of a winter's glade. The Nick doll in her hand seemed to beg her to come up with something better than what she was going with. She wanted to tell him that in their association, she'd seen much the same care and attention to detail from him when it came to planning.

Behind her, lightning popped and a drumroll of thunder rattled up the alley. "Aha! The power comes to me!" she exclaimed, hoping that what she thought was happening actually was.

The witches took a step away from Hexene and Mafaufau, casting fearful eyes at the powerless maiden. The monkey brought its hands up to shield its eyes.

"Hellfire of the skies, heed my prayer," Hexene intoned, in nothing that had ever been any kind of spell, "transmute mine enemies. Make of them the lowest slime of the lowest beast!" In Theban, even nonsense sounded good. She backed it up by shaking some of the Essence on the ground in front of her. She pulled a vial of powdered ogre tusk from the satchel and emptied a bit in her hand before tossing it around her in pinches. "Show them the price for those who cross the Crossroads Witch!"

A leg of lightning stepped past Hexene's right side like the limb of a gargantuan spider. Another traced the alley wall. Based on the flashes that hurled her shadow in moments ahead of her, she imagined there were more of these bolts haloing her. The three maidens had seen enough and they fled, grabbing brooms and mounting them as they zipped up into the sky.

"Oh no," said Technika behind Hexene, followed immediately by an awful crash.

Hexene spun around and saw the robot collapsed facedown in the alley. "Technika! Are you all right?" She ran to the robot's side.

"Assisting your ruse depleted my stores of energy," Technika said into the ground.

Hexene tried to picture carrying Technika, or even turning her over. "Maybe there's a wheelbarrow around here somewhere."

"Mafaufau." The zombie was next to Hexene. To move that quietly, he was light on his feet both for a zombie and for someone that large. He pointed at Technika and said his word again.

"Can you?" Hexene asked.

"Mafaufau." He picked the robot up as easily as if she were an empty sack and slung her over one shoulder.

"Hexene? What is going on?" Technika asked.

"This is a...friend of mine, I guess. Mafaufau, this is Technika."

"Mafaufau."

"What is your friend doing?" Technika asked.

"Carrying you, apparently. Thank you," she said to the zombie.

"Mafaufau."

"You too, Technika, thanks."

"I was curious as to why you and the zombie did not kill the lot of them when you had them at bay, but you do not seem to be fond of that solution."

"Not especially."

"Your squeamish nature renders my ultimate plan in peril."

"I'm not going to stop you when that time comes."

"I should hope not."

They arrived at the home of the Arcane Adepts without further incident. Hexene thanked Mafaufau again, and he said his one word to her, transferring the robot to the house zombies before lumbering off, presumably to his home in the Catacombs. It took three of them to lug Technika back up to the attic. When they were back in their room, even the persistent snap and buzz of Technika's recharging at the ward wasn't enough to keep Hexene awake.

Fifteen

Without discussing it, Evangeline started providing Hexene with some of the witch coins, the favors of the Arcane Adepts. Not many, but enough for what she required to enact Technika's plan. She needed a ticket to the Scryline Theater. Technika, though she had never been, suggested it. The theater was one of the popular destinations for the tourists who had come through the Hotel Metropole, and was apparently one of the favorite pastimes for the local witches as well. Angelique called the scries trash, but that just made Hexene more guiltily interested.

The American Quarter wasn't far from the Adepts' house. Hexene initially thought it would make her homesick, but it only reminded her of the endless tracks of suburban housing that went up right at the end of the Day War before the Night got started in earnest. Here, every witch had a boxy little home with a boxy little lawn and for some reason, a driveway. The only part that did make her the tiniest bit homesick was the Scryline—and as the largest building in the Quarter, and the second largest she'd seen in Las Brujas proper thus far, that did count for something.

From the outside, it looked like the Grauman's Chinese Theatre distorted through the lens of a bad mince pie nightmare. The courtyard out front featured statues, but of no one Hexene could identify. From a distance, she just assumed they were stars, like Imogen Verity or Turner Coates, or at least one of their most famous characters. Instead, she found a man in a business suit and hat, carrying a briefcase. Another was a woman in a housedress, vacuuming. One was a woman swimming, reaching for an abalone shell on the base. There were many more, and all similarly mundane, if geographically diverse. The statues carried the unmistakable sense that anyone viewing them should not only know who they were but be impressed that a bronze representation was right there. To Hexene, they looked like they could be any John or Jane Doe.

At the box office, a mother paused her knitting long enough to sell her a ticket. "Any room you like, love," she said sweetly, "although I think the new Deirdre Troutman is starting again soon."

"All right," Hexene said. She had no clue as to who Deirdre Troutman was and she liked to think she followed the pictures at least somewhat well.

A bored maiden took her ticket and waved her in, barely acknowledging her. A crone worked the concession stand, rubbing her green hands together and occasionally sucking the one tooth still in her head. She sold some regular candy, like malt balls, M&Ms, and Hot Tamales, but most of the display was given over to the witch palate. Candied toadstools, straws packed with a mix of flavored sugar and different essences, and the like. Hexene noted that the soda fountain carried Bebop Cola and a few other of Sweettooth Confections' offerings.

The crone cackled as Hexene approached. "Finally put some meat on those skinny bones, dearie?" Hexene bought a Baby Ruth, while the crone gave her an up-and-down look like she was wondering how Hexene might taste after spending a little time in the oven.

Inside, the stone walls featured reliefs in a fake Chinese style. Heavy curtains marked different hallways, and down each were doors into different rooms, each sporting a different rune. She poked her head into the first room, which was marked with the symbol for Venus, and for a moment was convinced she was dreaming.

The room could almost have been a movie theater back in the States, but instead of clean rows, there were small groupings of three seats in semicircles around small tables. The screen was a massive mirror, tilted at an angle to reflect the mouth of the cauldron beneath. Scrying was a crone's purview, so Hexene had never paid all that much attention to it. As a maiden, she was supposed to be more interested in the beguiling arts anyway. Still, she recognized the roiling smoke at the borders of the mirror, as well as the faint gloss given by the scrying potion boiling away inside the cauldron. That's not what surprised her.

The surprising thing was that it was Nick Moss on the screen.

She'd know him anywhere. He was relatively short for a man, and he had the furry face and keen eyes of a perpetually nervous weasel. He wore a rumpled suit with a ridiculous bowtie, and though she was certain he'd shaved that morning, he was already working on a new beard. He was sitting in a police interrogation room, across from a pair of mugs who had to be the wolfmen of the LAPD. One was older, with graying hair, a florid complexion, and eye-searing taste in fashion; the other was younger, hairier, and meaner. Nick frowned at a file open on the table in front of him. Hexene had watched Nick think many times, watched that brow crinkle up, and it always put her in mind of a weasel trying to deal with an exceptionally smart rabbit. Nick was lost in thought while the two wolfmen argued over the wisdom of putting the human on the case.

Hexene couldn't help herself. She leaned down to the nearest maiden and whispered, "Excuse me. What's this?"

The maiden looked up with some irritation. Her familiar, a raven, croaked in annoyance.

"The new Nick Moss. It just came out."

"The new what?"

"Nick Moss. He's a private eye in Los Angeles. Only human doing it!"

Hexene blinked. "I know that. But why are you watching him?"

"Why am I watching Nick Moss?" the maiden scoffed. "He's a dreamboat!"

"Him?"

The maiden's expression turned stormy. The other two maidens with her were looking up at Hexene now, as annoyed with the interloper as the first. Then one of them pointed at her, her expression shocked. Her familiar, an opossum, looked up from its M&Ms, blinked and pointed too, with its tail. "Wait. It's her!"

"Her who?" Raven snapped.

"Are you Hexene Candlemas?" Opossum asked.

"What?" Hexene sputtered.

"Yeah! That's Hexene! Remember? From the whole ape caper?"

"That's not Hexene," said the other, her octopus familiar congealing sullenly at the bottom of a bottle. "Hexene is much prettier."

"Thanks?" Hexene said hesitantly, thoroughly baffled now.

"No, she has to be Hexene," said Opossum. "What were you thinking?! Nick was coming to tell you he loved you! You could have stayed with him!"

Hexene felt her face growing hot. "I didn't want to...that's not what he was..." Other witches had begun craning their heads around, at first to shush them, and then to make the same horrifying realization.

Raven shook her head, halfway between disappointed and enraged. "You broke his heart."

"I didn't. I'm not...! You're all mistaken, and he smells like egg salad and panic, so—" Hexene turned and marched out of the room with as much dignity as she could muster. None of the witches pursued. She spent several minutes gathering herself in the hall and hoping no one noticed her. She thought of all the maidens who'd stared at or approached her over the past month, of the bartender at Le Chaperon Rouge who seemed to know so much about her. Eventually she'd stop shuddering, but it wasn't going to be anytime soon.

She took a deep breath and slipped back into the room. She didn't know what kind of rotten luck had compelled her to pick this theater for the dead drop. *The same luck that got my familiar killed*, she supposed. This time, she avoided recognition by lurking at an empty table near the back, and putting her head in her hands whenever someone passed by. While her red curls might make her stand out nearly anywhere else, in Las Brujas they were hardly noteworthy. She tried to avoid watching Nick's story on the screen, but there wasn't anything else to do, and she still possessed the human instinct to stare at vehicular accidents.

Hexene soon learned that what they were seeing wasn't an uninterrupted stream of a person's life. Someone had cherry-picked what she judged to be the best parts and spliced them all together in a more-or-less coherent story. After a couple hours, it looped back again to the start. Witches, and a few others, filed in and out at more or less random times. Nick's story went from his hiring by the LAPD to a nighttime trip to a club in Hollywood. Hexene couldn't believe it; Nick didn't like being outdoors in the late afternoon, and here he was in a nightclub, and dressed like a clown no less. Her hand found the doll in her satchel. *Sorry, Nick. Wish I could help.*

No matter how engrossed in Nick's story she got—and she would never confess to being more than mildly curious—she kept an eye on the drop. The room was lined with alcoves, and a softly lit bust of some relatively unremarkable person sat in each one. The drop was in the one closest to the door on the right-hand side, outfitted with a woman wearing a poodle clip and a rope of pearls around her neck.

Hexene and Technika had composed the letter together even though Hexene's head was still pounding from her indulgence at Le Chaperon Rouge the night before. The following day—today—she had delivered it to the Hotel Metropole without a hitch. All that remained to be seen was whether or not Slick took the bait. Hexene was ready to wait all day; she had a thick slice of the previous night's pie in her satchel for when she got hungrier than her candy bar could handle.

In the old days, she could have delegated this job to her familiar. Escuerzo was never as mobile as some other familiars, but he was inconspicuous. And poisonous, but that had never really come up. Even ignoring Escuerzo's practical applications, she would have liked him to have been there when she discovered Nick was some kind of matinee idol here. Someone had to appreciate how stupid that was. Only Escuerzo was dead, and his drawn-out murder had been *entertainment* to a chunk of the populace of this city.

About halfway through the second showing of Nick's terrible night, the door opened. Hexene, already slumped in her seat, glanced up casually, expecting another trio of maidens to enter. Nick seemed more popular with maidens than anyone else, though he did have a table of crones in the front who cackled whenever he opened his mouth. Instead of a witch, though, the monster entering could only be a robot.

The creature was taller than a man, and looked like someone had gotten the bright idea to cross a salt shaker with a tank. It trundled over to the drop, ignoring the few annoyed looks it got, and planted an envelope behind the bust. Then, with a flash of light, it burned a hole in the bust's chin. After that, it turned and left.

Hexene waited for a good bit before she got up, plucked the envelope from behind the bust, and stuffed it into her satchel. She walked home, both to save a few pesos and because the route was fairly simple as ground routes in Las Brujas went. She was almost able to navigate the winding alleys with something approaching ease these days, as long as she stuck to the Quarters she was most familiar with. She passed multiple hexing sites, including one in which the mummified body of the unfortunate was still slumped against the wall. Packs of witches, mostly maidens, constantly cruised overhead like sharks, shields with a dizzying array of heraldry flapping on their cloaks. She thought of Mafaufau as she walked, hoping that he had found someplace safe to hide out for the time being. Probably somewhere deep in the Catacombs.

Hexene opened the front door into the Adepts' home and almost ran into Little Raoul. The middle-aged man smiled wistfully at her. "Hello, Hexene." He spoke Spanish quite well, even better than his parents.

"Hi, Raoul," she said. He stepped aside for her and she went to her room. At first, Raoul had given her the impression of a masher, but now he just seemed sad. It didn't quite feel like pity, though that was there too. Whenever he looked at her, which was often, he always seemed to be thinking of something else. She climbed into the attic room and found Technika kneeling by the ward, her palm pressed into the center, lightning playing over her copper body.

"I have the letter," Hexene said, loud enough to be heard over the hair-raising crackle.

Technika pulled her hand from the ward; the room was suddenly silent and far darker. She turned her head all the way around. Hexene had finally gotten used to that. "What did it say?"

Hexene held it up. "I thought you would want to read it with me."

"If you like."

Hexene pulled herself up onto the floor and crossed her legs. She opened the envelope and brought out the single sheet of paper. In a childlike scrawl, the message read: WISH TO ACQUIRE OFFER. $25,000 AMERICAN. BRING TO SUITE. EXCHANGE. MORNING. 5 ETTU.

5 Ettu was the day after tomorrow. "The plan continues apace," Technika said.

"One thing," Hexene said. "It wasn't Slick who came to the drop. It was a robot, looking like a salt shaker but angrier."

"Salt shakers cannot display emotions of any kind."

Hexene couldn't stop the grunt of frustration that forced its way out of her. "Do you know who I'm talking about?"

"Erg and Ohm. They are Slick's bodyguards. We will need a way to incapacitate them."

"You could have warned me!"

"I just did. I believed you might have discovered a way to regain the power you have lost by now, but I was incorrect. Fortunately, there are other ways to effectively inhibit robots."

"You're talking about the fears," Hexene said, not quite believing what she was hearing. Even talking about using the fears was a taboo.

"Robots do not feel fear," Technika said, "but yes. We will be utilizing such. If we are to take revenge against Slick, we cannot be squeamish. Luckily for you, I know where one can find such things."

"How?"

"I was the concierge at the Hotel Metropole. I must be able to assist guests. Tomorrow, we will see El Mirón."

Sixteen

The Mexican Quarter was one of the largest and oldest Quarters in the city, extending from the Stone Forest until it butted right up against the northeastern corner of Cogtown. Their destination was close to the border, and so Technika led Hexene into Cogtown, where they walked along Vaucanson Street, which paralleled the collection of walls between Cogtown and Las Brujas proper. Though Las Brujas twisted and turned, Vaucanson ran as straight as all of the other robot-designed thoroughfares. The result was a wall that rippled and warped along its western edge, sometimes creating deep pockets of sidewalk, and in other places obliterating it utterly. Technika kept her attention on the sky, no doubt hunting for Slick's flivver, and Hexene could hardly blame her.

Ahead, the basalt wall disappeared into the vibrant colors of the Atacama Desert. Beyond the bounds of Las Brujas the landscape looked like another world, but to Hexene it was at least a comfortable one. The dry air was a balm on her skin, and though she could stand it being a bit cooler, even the heat here lent her energy rather than taking it.

The walls were decorated with a combination of Aztec and more modern Mexican art. Just the sight of it made Hexene feel a bit more at home. Of course, that meant she was already looking over her shoulder for a bully calling her Canela the moment she and Technika walked in.

Technika passed the bulk of the neighborhood, only dipping into the final alleyway leading inside. The streets here had a cobbled look, reminding her yet more of home. Guerrero Negro had a few paved roads, though where she had lived, in a fisherman's shack a short walk from the shore, it scarcely resembled this place. The buildings were mostly in the Spanish style, but more than one step pyramid loomed over neighboring haciendas.

Technika seemed to know exactly where she was going. Hexene imagined it had something to do with her robotic mind. She didn't have the first clue as to how robots actually functioned. The nice thing about Technika was that Hexene never had to guess about what the robot was feeling. Ironically, she had no artifice.

Technika led Hexene down an alley, turning a few times before coming to an opening in the wall. Just beyond, tables had been set out beneath white awnings. On the tables was a variety of groceries, some on ice, others just on the surface. A smiling maiden watched over everything, though her familiar, an eagle with a singularly grouchy expression, was much less inviting. Behind her, an indoor market opened up, the front entrance buttressed with columns sculpted into brightly-painted feathered serpents.

The maiden greeted Technika and Hexene with a smile and a nod. Her skin was brown, her hair a deep red. She wore a bodice laced tight and a full traditional skirt. When Hexene was younger, she'd had one of those outfits, made by her grandmother—abuela Quinn, not abuela Foley—for use on holidays. It had been worn and altered from when Hexene was six until she turned sixteen, when she abruptly refused to wear anything she didn't make herself. That was when she had first tried to craft one of her quilt dresses, simply because it didn't look like anything she had ever seen in Guerrero Negro. This maiden, though, looked entirely comfortable in the costume, because for her it wasn't one.

Technika marched past the maiden and her produce into the shade of the building beyond. It opened up into a market, and in here were bags of candy, boxes of cereal, cans of soup. Some of the labels were in English, others in Spanish, and yet more in languages Hexene didn't know. A mother sat behind a counter, her face round and kind. A pink salamander with a mane of gills swam in a small fishbowl in front of her. The walls were covered in vivid murals of desert and jungle landscapes.

"Good afternoon," said the mother in English.

Hexene tried to hide her dismay. She looked white, she supposed she *was* white, but she didn't feel that way. She responded in Spanish. "Good afternoon."

"Your Spanish is good. American, aren't you?"

"Mexican. I lived in the States for a long while."

The mother nodded, opening her mouth to say something, then stopped herself. Her expression darkened as her eyes darted around. "Where is your familiar?"

Hexene had no response. Technika kept walking to the back of the shop, and so Hexene followed her lead. Thankfully, the mother didn't follow. The doorway in front of them was dark, tendrils of mist reaching from its borders. As they crossed the threshold, the temperature dropped like a cannonball in a lake. A thin sheen of frost covered the walls and floor. Theban marks were etched beneath the rime, but the spell was one Hexene didn't know. Carcasses of animals hung from hooks in the ceiling, while cuts of meat, whole fish and lobster, as well as piles of shrimp and scallops sat out on freezing tables.

A crone, her features severe yet striking, lurked in the corner wearing a bloodstained apron, heavy blades hanging from her belt. An ocelot sat at attention by her feet. The crone chuckled, and it sounded like gravel being shaken. "Keep going. Don't want what I got."

Hexene didn't, in point of fact. She wondered if the crone had known that the way crones seemed to know things, or if she could tell from the way Hexene avoided looking at the gory carcasses. She didn't grow up a vegetarian; being that picky as a kid wouldn't have worked. Fish and the like were a lot less gross than these dead animals. At that point, one might as well just eat a person. Skip to the real thing, the way the Great Hag had done. No need to fool around with pigs and cows who couldn't even defend themselves.

In the cold, Hexene scratched at the water scars on her arm. They had healed for the most part, but she didn't think the red streaks were ever going to disappear entirely.

Technika ignored the carcasses too, navigating through them and to a doorway in the back of the room nearly hidden by hanging meat. The temperature rocketed back to where it was before the meat locker. This chamber was far smaller than the others, barely large enough for both Technika and Hexene. A few candles, stuck to small ledges on the walls, provided a bit of illumination, revealing melting stalagmites of corpses of candles past.

"What is your pleasure?" asked a rasping voice, speaking Spanish in some kind of sibilant accent Hexene couldn't identify.

The eyes appeared gradually in the shadows in front of them, growing larger and larger, or perhaps closer and closer, until they were the size of hubcaps on a coupe. They glowed slightly, though not enough to actually shed any light, and they were cleanly defined between the glowing white and vertical black pupils, with no irises between. Hexene realized she was in the presence of a bogeyman, but the name had pretty much already given that away.

"El Mirón?" she asked, just to be sure.

"You know any other bogeys around offering you the moon, pretty? For a price, of course, for a price."

"Greetings," said Technika. "We wish to acquire no less than one but no more than three optical illusions."

The bogeyman's eyes went from oblong to circular, and his pupils followed suit. "*You* want optical illusions? No, no. Don't tell me. Whatever you two lovebirds get up to is none of El Mirón's business. I only provide the car; no need to see how you drive."

"It's not—" Hexene started.

El Mirón's eyes returned to their former catlike shape. "Did I ask? No, I did not. You see how this works, pretty? You ask for something and I provide. Then you pay me. We part from one another happy that we have met but with no need to speak further. For example, I see that you are a witch, but do I see a familiar? No."

"What do you know about that?" Hexene demanded, the rage red.

"Nothing, nothing at all. And what I do not know will go with me into the grave. Because, you see, I do not *care*. Do you understand, pretty?"

"Stop calling me pretty."

"Why? You *are* pretty, and I don't know your name."

"It's Hex—"

"Ah ah ah," scolded the bogeyman, and Hexene thought she saw the shadow of a finger waggling in her face. "I don't want to know. However, you are a customer, so if you wish a different mode of address, I will provide. And I do so without request for any additional moneys."

"Call me Canela," she blurted without thinking.

"Canela it is. Yes, yes, I like that. Now, you can get anything from El Mirón, anything at all. Except flashlights, for I am no fool. For optical illusions, I will ask but one dram and sixteen pesos."

Hexene was about to protest. "Dram" was the name for the smallest denomination of favor, but it was not to be given to anyone who was not a witch. Technika broke in, "Done."

"Wonderful. I suppose you already know not to look at the illusions, don't you, Goldie?"

Technika ignored him, turning to Hexene. She grumbled, but removed the seventeen coins from her satchel. The dram had a picture of a snake on it—a depiction of Angelique's familiar, struck on the mint the Arcane Adepts kept in their cellar. The higher-value coins had cats and dogs on them.

"In the bowl, please," El Mirón said. Hexene barely made out a rough clay bowl at her feet. She knelt and dropped the coins inside with a clatter.

"Ah yes, that sounds right. I am pleased you didn't try to short me," the bogeyman said. "She that does gets nothing at all. *You*, my dear Canela, get this."

Hexene didn't see where they came from. They were just suddenly *there*, in front of her, fluttering to the floor like fallen leaves. She snatched the objects out of the air, inspecting them. One was an M.C. Escher print on a battered postcard. Nick had one just like it. The other two were small cards each showing a horseshoe that started with two prongs but ended with three. They would do. She shoved them in her satchel. "Thank you," Hexene said to the bogeyman.

"The money is all the thanks I need."

Hexene left the room, chased by the sound of claws sifting through coins.

Seventeen

Transporting the crate was harder than Hexene had expected. She'd figured it wouldn't be any more difficult than the trip across town in the wheelbarrow, but somehow it was. Hexene should have known that adding a bulky wooden crate on top of Technika's already substantial body weight would make her harder to move, but she wasn't used to problems like this. She was a witch; logistics were something that happened to other people.

The Adepts' zombie servants had provided the crate. Zombies had a lot of them, it seemed. Technika explained it: many zombies arrived in them simply because shipping was cheaper than an airline ticket. When they had put it out in front of the Adepts' place, it had taken only a bit of modification to make one wall collapsible with a single hit from the robot. Then Technika climbed in. Hexene knew it was far outside of her abilities to do anything other than curse it for existing. Instead, she asked Torpe to find someone willing to carry it for the meager payment she could offer. Turned out the payment wasn't the problem; it was finding a zombie willing to be out on the streets. Eventually they did, and the zombie lashed the crate to a dolly and pushed it while muttering "Cerebros" the whole time.

He left her in the lobby of the Hotel Metropole, pocketing his money with a vaguely thankful "Cerebros" and slinking off into the relatively safe streets of Cogtown. Hexene's heart boomed in her chest, but she was calmer this visit to the hotel than the last one. Her burn itched beneath the repaired sleeve of her dress, but she resisted the urge to scratch it. She kept feeling the bag come over her head, when she was taken on the beach. She knew it was just nerves, just her mind. But knowing something and *knowing* something were two different things.

The Hotel Metropole was just as impressive inside as out. Art deco columns, sculpted into angular and genderless figures, supported the ceiling. The floors were as smooth, no doubt to accommodate the hotel's many wheeled guests. The only things that looked at all soft were leather cushions on the small couches that lined the lobby. The walls were decorated with intricate tiles creating squares and angled lines, connecting in perfectly symmetrical patterns. The concierge bore no small resemblance to Technika, though she looked like she was made of pewter. Her immobile face was locked into an expression of expectant interest.

"Good afternoon and welcome to the Hotel Metropole," she said in German-accented Spanish.

"Slick's suite. He's expecting me."

"Slick?" inquired the robot. "We have no guest by that name."

Hexene sighed, searching her memory for the gremlin's proper name. "Baron Sweettooth. Call his room."

Something about the way the robot reached for the telephone conveyed a whole lifetime's worth of annoyance. "And who shall I say you are?"

"Just tell him I have his delivery."

"Good afternoon, sir," the concierge said into the telephone, "I have a young woman in the lobby who claims to have a delivery for you. Oh? As you wish, sir." She hung up the phone and said, "He requested that you be sent right up."

Hexene gestured at the crate, still darkening the main doorway. "I'll need some help."

The concierge arranged for a robot to assist her. Hexene had no idea if this creature was originally a human or not. It was difficult to imagine how it could have been. The robot was low to the ground and trundled along on four heavy wheels, while forklift arms carried the crate. Hexene would have assumed it to be some kind of device, but it beeped and booped apparently at random. If she didn't know better, she would think it was humming under whatever it had in place of breath.

It guided her to the service elevator just off the main lobby. On her own, she would have missed it entirely; the silvery walls just kind of opened up, the seams concealed in the art deco design. The robot trundled in, plugged into the panel on the wall, and the elevator started to climb. The higher they went, the louder Hexene's heart pounded. She was certain the robot would be able to hear her before long. She closed her eyes, tried to calm herself, but it wasn't working. She was walking into a gremlin's lair without her magic. They had a plan, but no plan survived contact with a gremlin. She wasn't sure if that was a saying, but it should be.

No, she told herself, Technika knows this gremlin. *She made the plan. Slick has no idea what's coming for him.* And all Hexene's role involved was talking. That was it. Even if she'd still had her magic, she didn't have to cast a single spell, throw a single hex. Her hand wormed its way into her satchel and rested on the Nick and Lily dolls. Her heart started to slow, or maybe that was her imagination.

The service doors opened into a wide hall. While the architecture here was the same as the lobby, it had been softened with certain touches. Oriental rugs lay on the floors, Christmas decorations sat on antique end tables, and the artwork was exclusively large prints of corporate ads, most from Sweettooth Confections. Doors stood closed along the hall, which terminated in a pair of ogre-sized double doors. These opened as soon as Hexene got her bearings.

Beyond was a plush living room with wide, arcing white couches at war with the angular walls and regular almost-human columns. A table sat in the middle of the room, its centerpiece a huge bowl of candy. One wall was entirely windows, looking out over Cogtown and the Atacama Desert to the south. By the looks of the glass, it was heavily tinted, keeping out the rays of sunlight that would have turned its gremlin occupant into a pile of popping goo.

The gremlin in question stood in front of the couches. Snow-white hair, slicked down with copious oil, crowned his scaly green head. His red eyes glittered, and his three-fingered talons clutched at one another. He wore a white suit tailored to his diminutive frame. He might have almost been dashing if Hexene didn't already know the sordid tale of what he'd done to Technika.

"Stay," the gremlin rasped. Hexene suppressed a shudder as she heard the voice in person for the first time.

Erg and Ohm, the two robot bodyguards, rolled into view on either side of the doorway. Some of their limbs looked distinctly dangerous, and these were pointed in her general direction. Each had their amulet tied around one appendage or another. Both robots were faintly ridiculous in their menace, which somehow ended up making them more frightening. Hexene would have hesitated going up against them when she had her magic, let alone now. This was, of course, the point of bodyguards: if they looked scary enough, they never had to actually do their job. She hoped they'd feel differently about their employer once he was no longer alive enough to pay them.

One of them rolled up to her. "Stand fast!" it shrieked at her, its voice made up of escalating tones over an English accent. Its single limb patted her down. When it was finished, it screeched, "Unarmed! Unarmed!"

"Come, come," Slick rasped, beckoning them with one oversized claw.

Hexene walked with as much confidence as she could muster directly into the gremlin's lair. The robot carrying the crate chugged along behind her, setting it down inside the room, then falling still. After a few seconds, it beeped—angrily, Hexene thought—and knocked the crate onto its side. Hexene nearly cried out in dismay, but that would have betrayed the plan. Whether or not it was the porter's intent or merely the cruel laws of the universe, the crate was now resting on its collapsible wall. She turned to call after the robot, but it was already retreating down the hallway they came from.

"Sit, sit," rasped Slick, gesturing to the couch.

"Your parcel..."

"Not fragile," he said. "I know."

Hexene obeyed, folding her hands in her lap to keep them from shaking. She kept glancing at the crate, wondering what Technika could be thinking. She would be staring at the collapsible wall, now pinned by her own substantial bodyweight and the floor.

A huge machine stood against one of the walls, hidden from the hallway. Banks of flashing lights and reels of tape covered the front; it looked like a picture of one of the old, human-style computers from before mad scientists, brainiacs, and the like had turned them into the modern sleek and practical devices. Slick worked a few of the knobs, then hit a switch.

"Welcome to my home," the machine boomed. "Would you like a cocktail?"

Slick turned and gestured to a small bar cart sitting by the floor-to-ceiling windows.

"No, thank you. I'm fine." Hexene tapped the crate with her boot.

Slick nodded, turning back to the machine. More fiddling, and then he hit the same switch. "Please tell me how you came into possession of my merchandise."

Technika was a hard person to like. She was cold, she was humorless, she might even be a little psychotic, but she was a person, so Hexene bristled at Slick's choice of noun. The two tank salt shakers were behind her now; she felt them as sure as a bee probing her hair for the flower it was certain was in there. Any second now, and she'd feel the bag—

She cleared her throat, tapping the crate again. "I was visiting a friend in Cogtown, and I saw her escaping from the shed. She was low on power, exhausted, so she was easy enough to hex. Once I got her home, I talked to her and learned about you. I thought the president of Sweettooth Confections would have some deep pockets."

Slick laughed. It sounded like sandpaper on a phonograph. He made his machine talk for him. "You know who I am. What do I call you?"

Hexene stuttered out the first thing that came to mind. "Lily Moss."

"Miss Moss," the gremlin rasped, using his own voice, then laughed. "Miss Moss." Hexene had to admit, it wasn't a bad handle. Sounded like something a sea hag might use, especially one of the ones who preferred the swamps.

The gremlin worked the machine again. "A service deserves a reward."

One of the robots rolled over. Two small arms on its trunk held a briefcase, which it set on the table in front of Hexene. Tipped with pincers, they were good enough to click the case open and reveal the cash within.

"$25,000. I trust American currency is to your liking?" Slick's machine asked.

Hexene stared at the money. She'd seen that much in her life, but never all at once, and never for something as simple as all this. She tapped the crate a third time.

"Acceptable?" the gremlin prompted. She nodded.

"Of course, there is one more matter," the machine said.

The doors boomed shut behind her, and one of the robots parked itself right at the seam. Slick hopped up and down, rubbing his hands with glee. Hexene stood up in time to see the other robot moving to the corner behind her, where two barrels sat.

"What's going on? We had a deal!" Now her heart felt like it was going to bust through her ribcage. She had no hex to reach for and no way to make it land anyway. She was nailed to the spot; there was nowhere to run and her friend was trapped by a single stupid stroke of terrible luck. The robot picked up one of the barrels and moved around the couch, between it and the table.

Slick laughed, then worked his machine. "We had a deal, but you were cheating me. I had you followed from the Scryline. I saw you with *her*." As the machine spoke the pronoun, a snarl rippled over Slick's reptilian lips. The hatred burned in his eyes but froze Hexene's blood. "So you're going to get what your kind always should."

The robot set one of the barrels down in front of Hexene. With one hand, it pulled the lid from the barrel. Water sloshed up over the sides.

Hexene saw no way out.

Eighteen

The gremlin climbed up on the couch opposite Hexene, grinning and clapping. The robot's arms shifted, leveling what might have been a weapon at the unwitch. A bolt of fear shot through Hexene's body and she rode it. She was going to die, so she might as well make it on her terms.

She fell back on the couch. As soon as she moved, one of the robot's arms flashed, making a hideous whirring sound. A couch cushion exploded to her left, hurling a snowfall of scorched stuffing into the air. Hexene stomped one of her heavily booted feet against the side of the wooden barrel. A wave sloshed over the side, and the robot retreated a few feet.

"Hydrate! Hydrate!" it howled. The arm that Hexene had determined to be a gun adjusted its aim. Hexene didn't look down the barrel; she knew it would hypnotize her. She had to move.

She slammed the barrel again, and this time the wood showed some give. Encouraged, she pushed against the barrel with all her strength. More water splashed out over the far side. She stared at the lip, and would have liked in that moment, to have someone to pray to. Someone who might have listened. But that's not the way the world worked. There was no one to depend on. It was up to Hexene and Hexene alone.

"Kill bimbo!" rasped Slick, pointing at Hexene as though he could mean anyone else. He didn't look angry, though. He still sported a huge grin, and periodically a serpentine tongue emerged to caress his yellow teeth.

She felt the water, a living, hungry thing in the barrel. If she let up the pressure, it would right itself, and then who knew what. *Vomit death all over me*, she thought. She planted another foot into the side of the barrel and pushed, her body coming off the couch, with only her shoulders bearing her weight.

That was what saved her. The motorized palooka's gat went off again, that whirring sound like a whole hive of wasps through a ham radio. A hot geyser exploded under Hexene's lower back, and she yelped as burning stuffing slapped and fountained all around her. Maybe that was what pulled out the extra bit of strength she needed. The barrel went over, splashing water all over the floor.

"Oh yes!" hissed Slick.

"Hydrate! Hydrate!" The robot's tonal voice carried real panic, but not for very long. The water sloshed up over the apron of its body in an angry wave. Sparks and smoke erupted underneath, along with the stench of burned plastic. The robot continued to issue its warning of hydration as its voice grew progressively slower and deeper. Its retreat slowed, too, and pretty soon, it was obvious it was coasting until it came to a stop against the floor-to-ceiling window with a sad tap. All of its limbs went as limp as they were able, mostly pointing in the general direction of the floor.

The telltale whir started up behind her and Hexene leapt from the couch, over the deadly layer of water, and onto the crate. Almost instantly, she leapt again; this time, the explosion showered her with burning splinters. She landed on the other side of the couch, next to Slick, and hoped she wasn't actively on fire.

"Die, bimbo!" Slick hissed, and lunged at her.

Hexene could still throw a punch. It wasn't the best angle, but she had learned where and how to hit someone where it hurt when she was five years old. It had taken only one unanswered bully before her father showed her the proper method of balling up her fist and making a fella wish he'd picked easier prey. She'd put her own research into that punch over the years, whenever she couldn't hide, and later, when she'd lost the desire to. And here, now, that punch might not have won her any prizefights, but it did the job.

Slick ran right into her fist like he thought it might look good coming out of the back of his head. She felt something give in his mean little face. He fell onto the couch, dazed, his nose a smear of busted-up tissue. Green blood decorated Hexene's knuckles, along with a little bit of red where her skin had split with the impact. It had been a long time since she'd skinned her knuckles and it felt good. Sure, the gremlin weighed about as much as a terrier, but she'd been the one to erase his higher functions for a second.

"Protect! Protect!" proclaimed the other robot. It sounded just like its dead pal. She didn't know if she'd killed Erg or Ohm, but she was just going to call this one Ohm for the sake of convenience.

The crate was burning, a column of choking gray smoke throttling the room. Ohm was a shimmering haze beyond it, but the smoke couldn't block the clashing dirge of the robot's gat. Hexene lunged forward on the couch, wrapping her fingers around the shattered wood. The robot drew closer.

"Terminate! Terminate!" it howled.

Hexene was on her feet, balanced on the couch, and she ripped the lid upward. With a shriek, the nails gave up their grip and the lid fell over, splashing on the sodden rug. The whirring grew. Hexene tensed, ready to hurl herself away.

Technika sat up in the crate, holding a picture in her hand like a cop badging his way into a crime scene. The other robot rolled to a stop, lights flashing.

"Impossible! Impossible!" repeated the stymied robot.

Technika got to her feet. "Where is Slick?" she demanded.

Hexene turned to where the dazed gremlin had been on the couch, but all that was left was a spattering of green blood. "He was right here!" A door slammed, somewhere deeper in the suite. It was hard to tell. The fire on the crate was guttering, but that had barely stifled the strangling smoke. Hexene pointed to the other door. "Over there, I think!"

Technika pulled herself out of the crate and paused as she saw the water soaking the floor. "This was unexpected."

"There was a lot that was unexpected. I should have had the pictures, for one. They didn't search me all that well."

"No," Technika said. "I could not allow you to do that to them. If we are to use such tools, they must be used by me." As she spoke, the robot gingerly made her way to the couch, then she and Hexene went over the back, which hadn't been reached by the water.

"Didn't you hear me kicking the crate?" Hexene asked.

"Of course. I did not know the origin of the taps. I was waiting for the crate to be moved for my convenient egress."

"Yeah, that would have been nice," Hexene muttered.

Technika struck the door they found with her palm and it obediently swung open, revealing a hall. The end terminated in a spiral staircase, and by now, Hexene knew what they were looking at. The roar of a rocket engine fading rapidly into the sky confirmed it.

Technika moved faster than Hexene had ever seen her. She made a horrible beeping sound as she went. Involuntarily, Hexene guessed, though she wasn't going to ask. The robot rushed up the stars, Hexene at her heels, emerging on the suite's private landing pad in time to see the back end of Slick's distinctive flivver blasting into the clear blue. The tone coming from Technika reached an awful crescendo. Hexene clapped her hands over her ears until the robot stopped.

They stood under an awning that flapped in the hot breeze coming off the desert, on the circular metal platform.

"We will need to calculate another approach," said Technika.

"Yeah, I was thinking something similar," Hexene lied.

Nineteen

Hexene readied herself for another round with the surviving robot, but when she and Technika made it back to the suite's central room, Ohm was gone. Hexene wasn't about to kick against that little slice of luck. She and Technika opened up the service elevator, and the former concierge of the hotel was more than capable of making the car work with another key hidden in a finger.

After attempting an illicit trade like that and killing a robot in the process, Hexene half expected security to be waiting for them in the lobby, but the elevator doors opened up on the same peaceful, cavernous room as before. She and Technika walked quickly to the exit, and from there back to Las Brujas proper. Hexene kept her eyes on the sky, and she imagined Technika was doing the same. From time to time, she caught sight of Slick's designer flivver. It didn't look like he was going anywhere in particular, opting instead to orbit the city. She imagined he was giving them time to clear out before he would return—either with the cavalry, or to fortify his suite like a castle, complete with a moat full of cola and candy-coated cannons.

Hexene felt a lot safer when they were in the winding alleys of the German Quarter. She knew the route fairly well from her time going to and fro, passing from the German, skirting the edge of the French, then finding the Caribbean Quarter. The Adepts' house was a short walk from there. It still took five times as long as comparable travel in any other city. Knowing the way at all was a small triumph, but that was the only kind she'd get.

They went in through the gate, then around the side of the house to the kitchen entrance. The kitchen was stuffed with heavy scents of spices, and only one of the house zombies was attending the oven. She flinched when the door opened, but never said a word and left the room soon after. Hexene wasn't keen to talk to the Adepts or to Evangeline's family. She cocked her head and listened for them, but heard nothing. She opened up the breadbasket and sliced off a fist-sized hunk, sighing happily as she ate.

"I should return to recharge as well," Technika said.

Hexene nodded, but a knock at the kitchen door stopped her from talking. It was heavy but soft, the sound of a large fist trying to make little sound and only partially succeeding. She went to the door and paused, hoping whoever it was would go away. The knock came again, faster this time, a little desperate. She opened the door.

"Mafaufau," Mafaufau said, panic in his milky eyes. Fear looked wrong on the massive zombie, but he was too big to see past, so there could have been anything out there.

"Come in," Hexene said, stepping aside.

The zombie squeezed in, and though the kitchen was fairly large, he couldn't move around it without bumping something. He stepped out of the doorway, and Hexene peered out.

"Mafaufau!" he hissed.

A squadron of witches passed overhead on broomsticks. Hexene waited until they were past to shut the door. She wasn't going to draw them in with any sudden movement. *Just a maiden closing a door*, she thought at them, *no need to investigate*. She stayed by the door, listening.

The pots and pans hanging from the ceiling clashed. "Mafaufau," the zombie apologized.

Hexene turned, and Mafaufau was holding two of the pots in his massive mitts, trying to keep everything from clashing together. "What's going on?" Hexene asked.

"He will merely say 'Mafaufau'," Technika pointed out. Hexene shot Technika an obscene gesture. "Is that a new hex?" Technika inquired.

"Mafaufau," said the zombie, releasing the pans to point skyward. It was obvious what he meant by that.

"You need a place to hide out," said Hexene.

"Mafaufau."

"Of course," Hexene responded to what she assumed he very well might have been saying.

"He will not fit in our room," Technika said. "*We* barely fit in our room."

"Is there a basement here?"

"To whom is that question addressed?" Hexene cursed at the robot. "I do not see how that will assist."

The maiden ignored her companion, and after a search through the kitchen, found stairs in the pantry leading down into the earth. A lantern hung by the doorway; she lit it. She never thought she was going to miss electricity so much. Any witch worth her hexes could make some light if she had the time and the right tools. Everyone else in Las Brujas simply had to make do with what the witches allowed.

Hexene took the wooden stairs down. The walls were close and the ceiling low enough that Mafaufau had to hunch over; his shoulders scraped along both walls. Wooden shelves holding jars and pots of food and spices extended past the golden fingers of light. A mint for coins took up one corner. The walls were, like everything else, single pieces of black basalt. Dust was light, but the air was damp. It wouldn't have bothered Hexene normally, but after the blissful aridity of Las Brujas, a faint burn crept into her lungs. She found out why: a cistern partway filled with water sat in the far corner.

"How's this?" she asked.

"Mafaufau," said Mafaufau.

"I believe that is the best we will get," Technika said. She stood on the stairs, not bothering to come all the way into the cellar.

Mafaufau nodded, lumbering to the corner opposite the stairs. He carefully settled his bulk into the space there and nodded again, apparently satisfied. "Mafaufau."

"Good," Hexene said. "We're upstairs in the attic, but we'll come down to check on you..."

She trailed off as Mafaufau looked to his left at the stairs, his milky eyes widening. "Mafaufau!"

Hexene frowned, raising the lantern high and peering into the dark to see what the zombie had spotted. Technika took a step up the stairs, getting out of the maiden's way. And then, Hexene saw it. The space underneath the stairs had been used for storage, a combination of old barrels and some empty burlap sacks. One of the lids of the barrels wasn't on flush, and poking out of it was a gray-green hand.

"Maf—"

"I see it," Hexene said, her voice dropping to a whisper.

"As do I," Technika said. "Perhaps as I am the most physically capable, I should..." Hexene stepped off the stairs and approached the hand. She set the lantern down nearby and pulled the lid of the barrel aside. "...allow you to do whatever it is you were going to do anyway," Technika finished.

"Mafaufau," said the zombie, beginning the process of rising to his feet. Hexene picked up the lantern as the other two monsters crowded around her. The flickering light pushed the shadows away from the person in the barrel. It was a zombie, face frozen in a cry of agony or, more accurately, of agonized "Brains!" The back of his skull looked like a shattered clay pot.

"Mafaufau," said Mafaufau in horror.

Hexene was inclined to agree. But beyond the initial shock, which was waning faster than perhaps was healthy, she was coming to an awful realization.

"I know this bastard," Hexene whispered.

"Can you be certain?" Technika asked. "A witch's recall is often imperfect."

"You don't forget the face of a monster who tries to kill you," Hexene said. "This was one of the three zombies who came for my coven."

"Mafaufau," said the zombie in apparent agreement.

"Only..." Hexene pointed to the small circular scars around the zombie's lips. "His lips were sewn shut."

"Yes, you said as much, which would indicate affiliation with Los Silenciosos."

"Mafaufau."

"Why would someone cut his lips open like that?"

"There is no rational reason," Technika said.

"A desecration?" Hexene hazarded, looking to Mafaufau.

"Mafaufau," he said, shrugging.

Hexene's finger hovered over the papery lips, as though that would illuminate anything further. The light glinted off the necklace resting on the zombie's sunken chest. Without hesitation, Hexene grabbed it and, with a yank, pulled it from his neck. The head lolled grotesquely forward, but Hexene barely noticed. This zombie had killed her coven; he wasn't worth much.

"I saw these given out at the airport. You both have them," Hexene asked, holding it up. It was a simple charm, depicting a crow in flight. Mafaufau's huge hand went reflexively to his.

"Some call them 'crow collars'," Technika said. "Think of them as passports. This city is for witches, and any who wish to reside here requires the permission of the populace."

"But there's no government to provide permission."

"One does not need a government to pick and choose one's residents," Technika said. "The maiden who distributes these at the airport is a member of the coven who has taken it upon themselves to regulate the non-witch population of Las Brujas."

"The other witches just let them do it?"

"I am not privy to any disagreements."

"Mafaufau."

Technika went on: "Any non-witch who wishes to spend time in this city, even in Cogtown, needs to place her name in the ledgers of the Crow Sisterhood. In exchange, she will receive one of these necklaces, denoting her right to be here. This shall be renewed every year, and can be revoked at any time and for any reason."

"It hasn't seemed to help the zombies."

"Rights for the minority only exist when the majority has the will to enforce them."

Hexene knew that was true. Back in LA, you only had to look at how the human populace was treated. She might have ignored that, had it not been for her friendship with Nick. Hexene turned the charm over in her hand. A few symbols were etched into the copper surface, but unfortunately none were in Theban. "They're personalized?" she asked hopefully.

"They are," Technika confirmed. "They serve as identification if Las Barrenderas wish to confirm an identity with the Crow Sisterhood."

"Then we could take this to the Crows and they'll tell us who this zombie is."

"It would stand to reason."

Hexene shoved the charm into her satchel. She paused, staring at the zombie in the barrel. She wanted to tell Angelique. This had to be the work of Evangeline, or more likely Serafina. Crones were known for cruel vengeance. But why hadn't they told her when it happened? Angelique undoubtedly would have, had she known. Hexene put the lid back on the barrel, careful to allow the zombie's fingers to protrude as they had before. She replaced the sacks as well, doing her best to recreate the scene as it had been when she first saw it.

"We should probably go see the Crow Sisterhood now."

"Mafaufau," Mafaufau said, shaking his head.

"We'll take the Catacombs," Hexene promised. "You can guide us through them, right?"

"Mafaufau," he said, the tone uncertain.

"The witches who were after you will have moved on," Hexene said.

Mafaufau raised an eyebrow. "Mafaufau," he said flatly.

"We won't be aboveground long enough for them to see us."

"Mafaufau," he sighed, glancing superstitiously at the ceiling and shaking his head. Still, he gestured toward the door in a very clear *After you*.

Technika, Hexene, and Mafaufau climbed the stairs and crept to the kitchen door. Hexene cracked it open and looked upward. A few witches soared by on some errand or another and she realized she had no idea what Mafaufau's pursuers actually looked like. She couldn't even recall if they were in Las Barrenderas livery.

"All clear," she said, and she might have been right. Besides, whoever they were, the witches were looking for a zombie, not a zombie, a robot, and an unwitch. She slunk out, among the black columns of the witches' stone garden. They circled the house, the whole time looking up at the air traffic. Even Technika did it, though Hexene imagined the robot was more concerned with a specific gremlin flivver than anyone on a broomstick. They moved quickly to the nearest entrance to the Catacombs and Hexene let out a long sigh.

"Mafaufau," said the zombie, lumbering to the fore and leading them down the tunnel.

Twenty

It was early evening by the time Hexene and company emerged from the Catacombs in the Hibernian Quarter. Located just to the south of the Russian Quarter, this neighborhood felt remote to Hexene. It might have been the sight of the consuming black of the desert night out to the west, or it could have been the smaller houses on lots that were as large as anywhere else in the city. The Irish witches appeared to like their elbow room and their gardening; the splashes of green weren't limited to window boxes.

Most of the lots contained three distinct buildings as opposed to the sprawling manses of the other Quarters. Most were shaped like large brick beehives, and they all had some of the same stretching nightmare qualities as the rest of the city. Invariably, one of the three was larger than the others, and Hexene expected this to be the home of the mother, with room for her family. One was always situated near the front gate, and one was always nearly hidden in the back, often brooding on a small rise.

Mafaufau stopped before a short gate made of petrified wood. Lanterns lit either side and hung from the eaves of the structures beyond. Hexene saw that these weren't quite individual cottages like the others nearby, but were connected by long, sloping hallways, forming a loose triangle. To the

Unwitch Hunt

north, Slick's flivver zoomed over the city, Technika's glowing green eyes following it.

"Mafaufau," he said, gesturing to the gate.

Hexene nodded, swinging the gate open and going up the walkway. She knocked at the wooden door and waited. The door opened, revealing a slender zombie. She said nothing, obviously holding something in her mouth.

"Good evening," Hexene said. She thought it was best to be polite. "We would like to see the Crow Sisterhood."

The zombie looked them over and stepped aside, gesturing to a small bench in the foyer. The cottage beyond was bigger than it looked, though Hexene suspected cunning use of space rather than any magic. Still, it was nearly filled to overflowing. Bookcases were stuffed with tomes and codices, each with scraps of paper protruding like meat from an overfilled sandwich. More books and papers formed stacks around the room, and though it looked at first glance to be haphazard, Hexene was willing to guess there was a method behind the apparent chaos. Somewhere beyond it all, visible as a dancing glow, a fire burned in a hearth. Most of the furniture was covered in books and papers, with only a few places to sit, and that would be after navigating the labyrinth.

The zombie gestured with one finger, pointing at the bench again. Hexene took the meaning, but didn't sit down. Her companions couldn't; in fact, poor Mafaufau could only barely fit inside.

"It is as I recall," Technika said.

The zombie returned with Cora Crow, the maiden Hexene recognized from the airport, and another witch. This was obviously a mother, her raven-black hair streaked prettily with gray. She was slender, her black dress clinging to her figure. Her familiar was nearly identical to Cora's, though a bit larger. Both birds watched the three arrivals with glass-bright eyes.

As the mother set eyes on Hexene, her face exploded in a sweet smile, and she began to speak in rapid-fire gibberish. Hexene blinked in confusion, and, in Spanish said, "I'm sorry, I don't understand."

Then it was the mother's turn to look shocked. She too switched to Spanish, speaking it with an Irish lilt. "I'm the one who is sorry," she said. "I took one look at you and assumed you spoke Irish."

"My grandparents came from there," Hexene said apologetically. "All four of them."

"Then you should learn the language!" the mother said with good humor. "But I'm getting ahead of myself. I'm Morrigan Crow, mother of the Crow Sisterhood. This is our maiden, Cora."

"We've met," Hexene said of Cora. "It's nice to see you."

"I remember you," said Cora. "You remember, Morrigan. The one I told you about." The maiden nodded significantly at the conspicuous absence of a familiar anywhere on Hexene.

Understanding dawned on Morrigan's face. "Oh, you poor dear. You poor, poor dear."

"I heard you were dead, along with the rest of your coven," Cora said.

"Cora!" Morrigan scolded.

The maiden shrugged. "She's not. It means I have to update our records."

"I'm not," Hexene agreed. "The rest of my coven is." Cora had the good grace to look ashamed.

"That is awful," Morrigan said. "Where are my manners? Would you like something? Tea, perhaps? The offer goes for your companions as well, though I'm afraid we don't have anything for robots."

"I would love some tea."

"Mafaufau," said the zombie eagerly.

"Delgada, would you fetch some tea from the kitchen?" Morrigan asked, and the zombie shuffled off. "What should I call your friends?"

"Technika, and we've been calling him Mafaufau."

"Mafaufau," said Morrigan. "That's lovely. Just lovely. Well, Mafaufau, if you would be kind enough to stay where you are, I would appreciate it. I don't think there is room enough in our home for you. Hexene, if you and Technika would come this way?" Morrigan indicated a path through the various piles that snaked through the room and arrived at a pair of fat chairs, sitting next to one another. Morrigan sat down opposite them, and Hexene had no idea what the mother was sitting on. It looked like several stacks of paper, but it appeared to have arms. Hexene sat, while Technika stayed standing behind her. When Cora saw the seat wasn't going to be taken, she plopped down next to Hexene. The rook on her shoulder hopped to the back of the chair and croaked contentedly.

"Now, what can we do for you?"

"I wanted you to identify one of the amulets you pass out at the airport."

"Whose?"

"One of Los Silenciosos." Hexene held out the necklace she had been clutching since the cellar. Their eyes widened. Morrigan took the amulet gingerly, as though it still possessed the ill will of its former owner.

Delgada the zombie returned, the tea set clinking softly on a tray. She set it down on a stack of books that didn't wobble in the slightest. Hexene didn't see any obvious hex symbols, but she began to feel, on the edge of sensing, the persistent hum of them. Witches had their ways of keeping organized.

Morrigan set the charm down and poured the tea into the ceramic cups, each one decorated with the silhouettes of a flock of birds. The tea was thick, and brimming with enough leaves and twigs to start several birds' nests. Morrigan handed a cup to Hexene, then one to Cora before pouring one for herself. Finally, she poured one more and handed it to Delgada, who brought it to Mafaufau. The tea smelled bitter, but had a sweet, fruity taste. Hexene recognized deadly nightshade, her favorite.

Morrigan looked her up and down, and the raven on her chair did the same, clucking in its bird throat. "Cora spoke of you when she returned home," said Morrigan, switching to Theban.

Hexene felt a momentary stab of guilt over locking Technika and Mafaufau out of the conversation, but this felt private. "I suppose I am a curiosity."

"Nothing like that," Morrigan said. "She said your coven was without familiars."

Hexene nodded. "That is true. They were killed by a mad scientist."

"Mad scientists. I suppose we put up with them as fellow primes, but one would think we could get along quite well without them."

"That would be a fun topic to raise at the Sabbat next Aš," said Cora.

Morrigan scowled at Cora. "I didn't mean as policy, merely as a lament for the modern state of things. Back when they were mere alchemists, rooting around in the earth for gold, they were more palatable. Now it's gliomaigh adamhacha this and ga bháis that." She shook her head. "And you see where it all leads, to a witch cruelly cut off from the Grandmother of us all." She shook her head again, turning her attention back to Hexene. "I imagine your coven was here in an attempt to reforge your bond to the Many-Faced Goddess?"

"Do you know of a way to do that?"

Morrigan sipped at her tea. "I have a memory, I think. Something from a lecture, or a story? There was a witch coven like yours who lost their familiars. I want to say it was to crusaders passing through the Black Forest on the way to...no, that's not right. Was it the Inquisition?"

"It doesn't matter how the familiars were killed," Cora said.

"Doesn't matter? Familiars are our sacred link! Without them, what are we but—"

"Not because of that," Cora said patiently. Her rook hopped onto her hand and she stroked its feathers gently. Hexene had never envied anyone more in her life. "For Hexene. It doesn't matter how the familiar died, it just matters how the witches found new ones."

Morrigan scowled again, but nodded. "Context *is* important," she insisted, "but I suppose I can let it go for now. It is absolutely maddening in the meantime. I wish I could recall who told the story to me first." She snapped her fingers, then looked at Cora. The two of them said it at the same time: "Ravenna."

"What's that?"

"Our crone. Whatever I know, she knows more." Without being asked, both familiars hopped into the air and flapped off down a hallway. "I don't know why I didn't think of it before," Morrigan said.

"Because Ravenna likes company about as much as she likes robots," Cora said.

Morrigan shot her another glare. She recovered and painted on a smile for Hexene, then switched to Spanish. "In the meantime, let's have a look at that charm." The mother picked it up and peered at the etched surface. Cora got up, leaning over her mother's shoulder to look at the designs on the back. "Zombie. Renewed four times."

"So he's been here for four years?"

"Four full years. He was due to be renewed again in a little over a month." Morrigan looked around, squinting at the piles of paper and books all around her. "Let's see, let's see," she mumbled. She dipped the necklace into her tea, then pulled it out, whispering to it in Theban. Tea clung to the outside of the charm in a thin gelatinous layer. Morrigan spun the charm between her fingers, back and forth, back and forth, winding the thong up, letting it unwind and wind again. Then, softly, she blew against the charm itself. The tea fluttered off of it in tiny droplets, tapping on some distant surface.

"Over here," Cora said, slinking between the piles before arriving at one. She knelt and pulled out a codex from the stack. Only magic could have kept the whole thing from tumbling down. She opened up the leather cover and leafed through the pages.

"Give it to me."

"I can find it," Cora said. "It's a renewal, not an arrival."

"It will be faster if you give it to me. I have my own system."

Cora gave Hexene a long-suffering look, and for a moment, Hexene felt like a real maiden again, commiserating over the demands of mothers and crones. But then the feeling was gone, dissolving as Cora flinched subtly away when she returned to her seat.

"Here it is," Morrigan said, checking a piece of paper against what was carved on the charm. "Mort d'Arthur, émigré from France. Had I known he was one of Los Silenciosos, I would never have renewed his residency, I can assure you."

"Is there an address?"

"No. It doesn't look like he was affiliated with any coven. Not surprising considering who he fell in with."

"You don't know where the zombies here live?"

Morrigan blinked. "Why would we? If a household keeps zombies, we might keep track of them as a courtesy or a safety measure. We can't let zombies wander off. They could hurt themselves." She lowered her voice and switched to conspiratorial Theban. "No brains, you know."

Hexene didn't know what to say to that. She would have been less surprised if Morrigan had tossed a live grenade on the table. "Uh...okay. But other zombies?"

"Find their way to the Catacombs. There are miles and miles of tunnels down there. We only excavated the ones necessary to access the reservoir, and of course built the reservoir itself. Once zombies started coming here in large numbers, they added to the tunnels. Every now and again, an enterprising maiden gets it in her head to map them."

"Sometimes she doesn't come back," said Cora.

"And the rest of the time, she realizes it was a foolish task to begin with," said a new voice in Theban, cracking with age.

"Ravenna," said Morrigan, standing up. Cora did the same. Hexene followed suit, turning to face the new arrival.

She looked a bit like a small, angry tree that got that way by clinging to a cold clifftop long enough to have all its leaves stripped from it. Hexene wasn't certain the new witch was wearing a dress, or if she were clothed entirely in various-sized shawls. She leaned heavily on a gnarled staff, where a distinctly aging jackdaw perched. The other two familiars flapped in behind her, landing on the shoulder and head of their respective witches.

"Understand you wanted me. Some kind of question. The birds weren't clear," Ravenna said.

"Ravenna, this is Hexene Candlemas." Hexene gave a little curtsy, and immediately felt silly about it.

"So it is. Now, why was it I heard the Candlemas Coven was dead?"

"Most of the coven is dead," Hexene said. "I'm all that's left."

"Hmph," Ravenna said, raising an impressed eyebrow. "Very well, then. Tell me how much of what else I've heard is true or not." Hexene related the quick version of what happened, and Ravenna nodded along. "Sounds very close. Only a matter of time before those troublemakers started killing us. Unfortunate, because it only ends up hurting the good ones."

Morrigan nodded sadly. "Ours are afraid to go out, poor things."

Hexene refrained from pointing out just who the zombies were afraid of. An argument with the Crow Sisterhood wasn't going to help her case.

Ravenna settled down on another stack of papers with a sigh. "Well, sit down, Hexene Candlemas. You answered my questions, and it's only fair I answer yours. What did you want?"

"She wanted—" Morrigan started.

"Your name's Hexene Candlemas, eh? And here I've been calling you Morrigan Crow this whole time like an idiot. Didn't know I was an idiot."

Morrigan swallowed. "You're not an idiot."

"And you," said Ravenna to Cora. "Wipe that stupid grin off your face before I do it for you."

Cora concentrated on her tea.

"Now, *Hexene Candlemas*, what can I tell you?"

"You know what happened to my familiar?"

"I heard a bit from Cora, and my eyes still work enough to tell me you don't have one."

"He was killed, along with the others from my coven. We came here to reconnect with the Many-Faced Goddess."

"You want to incarnate a new familiar," said Ravenna.

"Have you heard of that?"

Ravenna settled back, frowning into the memory. "There are stories. Ones I wish I remembered better than I do, I'm afraid. The stories about witches losing their familiars are horrible. We don't like to think of them, and so we hear them once and lock them away."

"Or you tell them around a campfire," Cora said, and then flinched.

"Or that," Ravenna agreed. "It's not something I revisit. My first piece of advice would be to take yourself to the library. You know the one. The Great Hag stands watch outside it."

"I know it."

"Good. If you had come here asking without even trying to look for yourself, you wouldn't be worth helping. Don't think any help would take for a witch like that, if you follow."

"I'm not a witch. Others have been calling me unwitch."

"Unwitch," said the crone, tasting the word. "Not a bad descriptor, but not quite right either. I suppose you're as much of a witch as you believe yourself to be. It's all moot, though, without your familiar. Without the conduit to the Many-Faced Goddess."

Hexene nodded. "I miss him."

Ravenna's eyes went soft. For a moment, she was beautiful. "I know you do. And he's gone. The next familiar you make will be a different being with a different heart."

"So it's possible."

Ravenna shrugged. "We're witches. But you aren't here for some cheer, are you? Let me see if I can remember the old story. Best I can do, I'm afraid."

Hexene nodded eagerly. "Please."

"Settle down. This is in another age, you understand. Year? I don't remember. Nobody does. Talk to a scholar, and he'll tell you Rome had fallen, but that's not true, at least not the way he'll mean it."

"I thought it was crusaders," Morrigan put in.

Ravenna shook her head. "Weren't even knights, the way you're thinking. Doesn't much matter, there have been crusaders of one kind or another forever, and the only thing in common is they hate our kind, which is where I'm getting to. Now this coven, the ones in our story, they were somewhere in what we'd call Europe now, and they were doing what our kind *should* be doing. They were looking after their little tribe, making sure the children were born, the hunts were successful, and the crops got enough rain. And, sure, once in a while cursing another tribe that got too close. Really sounds like the dream, right?"

Hexene found herself nodding. That did sound nice. A little tribe of her own to look after, especially if they left her alone socially out of fear, sounded lovely.

"So back then, everything was fine until one tribe or another decided they were better than the tribe next door and they'd go a-conquering. And what do you know? Soon as you get to the next tribe over, turns out they're as bad or worse than the tribe you just conquered. So they'd keep going and going until they got stopped. And stories will tell you that it was some heroic man who said 'No more' and fought them at a battle of such-and-such river or so-and-so bridge. But that's not the truth. It was always plague. Plague is our world's little way of solving war." Ravenna nodded to herself.

"Because of a witch curse," Cora said, halfway between a statement and a question.

"Maybe," Ravenna said. "Sometimes a witch will get things going, but plague's been there for us forever. Worst thing that could happen to this world is if someone figures out a cure."

"There wasn't a plague in World War II."

"Not *yet*," Ravenna said, "but those maniac mad scientists and their doomsday bombs...can't always wait, you understand. Now where was I? Getting me off track with dumb questions, the lot of you. Right! So one day, another tribe comes in and takes over. Puts all the men to the sword, or spear maybe. And before the witches could do anything, they go ahead and kill all the familiars too."

"Christians," said Morrigan, nodding.

"Who knows?" Ravenna asked. "Oh sure, Christians don't care for us, but that was an excuse. The ones who don't like us were going to do what they did anyway and think up a reason why later. Point is, it doesn't matter. Three witches, no familiars. They didn't really have a tribe to look after anymore either, so they went east."

"They just walked away?" Cora protested.

"Sure! Why not?"

"There was some sneaking involved," Morrigan assured the maiden.

"If that makes everyone feel better, they went on tiptoes in the dead of a moonless night," Ravenna said. "Point is, they got away. And they got Hecate's problem."

"Hexene."

"That's what I said. Got her problem: no familiar. So they start going to our holy sites, and it was at a Temple of Kali...no, it was the Gorgon Island..." Ravenna trailed off, trying to think, then she waved her hand. "Doesn't matter. What does matter is what we are, and that's what the coven remembered. The whole idea of our three roles giving us power. So the maiden became the archetypical maiden, the mother the archetypical mother, and so forth."

"And they reforged familiars?" Hexene asked.

"No. Not yet. They went back west to the tribe that had killed theirs. The chieftain laughed at them, and he was going to order them killed, but that was the moment the coven truly forged the connection. They became one with the Many-Faced Goddess for an instant. And when they were done, all the invading tribe was dead. They had new familiars, too, in a different shape than they used to. Can't remember what they were. Could have been they had sea cucumbers before and had kangaroos now. Doesn't matter."

"What does that mean?" Hexene said.

"What does what mean? I said a lot."

"Becoming one with the Many-Faced Goddess."

Ravenna shrugged. "How should I know? I only barely remember the damned story."

TWENTY-ONE

Hexene, Technika, and Mafaufau trudged through the winding corridors of the Catacombs on the long walk back to the Caribbean Quarter. The tunnels were quiet, and they only came upon zombies rarely. Tents and shacks along the way were empty.

"We need to discuss our next move," Hexene said.

"Indeed," Technika said. "Did you think we should use the kitchen at the Arcane Adepts' home?"

Hexene groaned. "Mafaufau, can you take us to Le Chaperon Rouge?"

"Mafaufau," he said, and at the next split in the tunnel, took the opposite fork from the one leading to the Caribbean Quarter. They surfaced not long after, only a few bends away from the maiden club. The skies were clear. Slick must have finally returned home.

"Eventually, I'm going to find at least one other bar," Hexene said.

"I know names," Technika said, "though I do not know how well they are truly liked."

"What did you know about Le Chaperon Rouge?"

"I recommended it to those visitors who wished to meet maidens. There were a great many of those, but sometimes they did not return to their rooms."

Hexene nodded in approval. The outside of the bar was still quiet, with none of the lineup of zombies. The door was open, a susurrus of conversation and the clink of glass filtering out into the night. A moment after Hexene stepped inside, the bartender flicked a hand. "Your zombie stays outside!"

Hexene stopped in her tracks, completely poleaxed by the command. The bartender recognized Hexene. "I'm sorry. We don't allow zombies in here. He has to wait outside." Hexene turned and saw Mafaufau looming just outside the entrance, staring at her. She wasn't sure what she saw in his milky glare, if it was fear or anger. She'd believe either. "Now, what can I get you?" the bartender asked.

Hexene just shook her head and went back outside. Mafaufau had found a shadow pooling in one of the folds of the wall. It was big enough to fit two other zombies, but it couldn't quite shroud him. Hexene leaned on the wall next to him.

"Mafaufau," he said.

"Sorry," she muttered. "Don't know why I thought it was a good idea to take you into a room full of witches."

"Intoxicated witches," Technika clarified.

"Thanks, Technika."

"True communication requires both clarity and precision."

Hexene sighed. She had been hoping to discuss this with a tincture in hand. And talking to that bartender had been fun, too. She'd seemed so nice before, though that was before Hexene realized why the bartender seemed to know her.

"How are we supposed to find two zombies in an entire city?" she mused aloud.

"In the middle of a pogrom, no less."

Hexene shuddered, casting a guilty glance at Mafaufau. The massive zombie had turned his back, and a scratching sound came from the wall. "What are you doing?" she asked him.

He sighed. "Mafaufau." He stepped aside, gesturing at the wall. A looping, jagged scrawl decorated it now.

Hexene squinted at it. She couldn't make heads or tails of the writing. "Did you write this?" she asked.

"Mafaufau!" He nodded, brandishing a bit of chalk. She had no idea where he got it, but chalk was pretty easy to come by in a city of witches.

"Can you read this?" she asked Technika.

The robot looked at it. "I am unable. I am similarly unable to determine if that is due to language or penmanship."

"I think that's a D," Hexene said hopefully.

"I can find d'Arthur's connections," said a familiar voice right at Hexene's shoulder.

Hexene's heart jumped and she spun, ready to deck the intruder. The balam from the other night stood there, swaying slightly. His tux was just as artfully undone, and he held a tincture in one hand. Drunk or not, he had approached totally silently.

"Who is d'Arthur?" asked the balam.

Hexene looked at Mafaufau, who was just as nonplussed as she, then to Technika. "Should I kill him?" the robot asked.

"Kill him? Why?"

"He knows too much."

"Don't kill him!"

"No one will mind. It is not as though he is a witch."

The balam either ignored the conversation or didn't hear. "Is d'Arthur a friend, perhaps?" He blinked, then focused on Hexene. "I know you, do I not? Your beauty is not one I should forget. You look like a girl with whom one would play baseball, until the day she flowered, and then love would be carried on the wings of the bumblebee for a single, stolen kiss."

"What are you talking about?" Hexene asked, half angry and half confused.

"I confess, I know no longer." He gestured at her. "I feel nothing. Nothing!"

"How were you able to decipher those words?" Technika asked.

"And nothing for you, though you've the beauty of a skyscraper, or perhaps a bridge. Ah yes, to travel upon you, to open such vistas to my innocent eyes—"

Hexene slapped him. "Answer the question."

"It is Samoan."

"What?"

"The language written there in the unsteady, yet gloriously masculine hand."

"You read Samoan?"

"Of course. My aunt's cousin is Samoan, and so the language, she sits upon my tongue with the ease of an old lover."

Hexene stared at the balam for what felt like several minutes. Then she turned to Mafaufau. "You speak Samoan?"

"Mafaufau."

"That will be the answer to everything," Technika said.

"Of course you can write," Hexene muttered. She had seen zombies write before—the waiter at this very club. She had just never *thought* of it before.

Mafaufau turned and wrote on the wall. "No one asks," read the balam. "A true tragedy. He did not write that last, it is but my own opinion. Now, who is this d'Arthur? What is going on?"

"Who are you?" Hexene demanded.

"Forgive me. I am deep into my cups once again, for that is the only place I can find solace. My name is Amir Noire. I am balam. Or, I *was* balam, but my body will no longer change, so it is more like I am a man. Yet what is a man who cannot turn into a jaguar? Is he even a man?"

"Yes," Technika said.

"You are too kind."

"I merely state facts."

Amir wiped a tear away. "I am pleased to finally meet one who will listen, who can offer comfort upon her steely bosom."

"What are you doing here?" Hexene asked.

"I told you. I cannot change. So I come here, because where are there women of such desirability? Those who would coax forth the jaguar within?"

Hexene shook her head, wondering if Amir never thought about what a bunch of witches would do to him if he suddenly changed in the middle of a room full of them.

"Maidens," said Technika. "If there is one reason the tourists come."

"No, not the maidens. It is the mothers I desire, with their fertile curves and hair kissed with snow, their bodies accustomed to love yet too often denied. Surrounded by such loveliness, I could not help but change. Yet here I am, locked in this form, drinking away my misery."

"Then why aren't you in a mother bar?"

"They kick me out."

Hexene shook her head. "All right, but what I meant earlier was, why are you *here*? As in standing there."

"I have learned many things in my travels. One of them is this: a group of unusual formation yet pleasing to the eye is always ready for adventure. And I thought, perhaps, this would be the adventure that could claim my body, or perhaps my soul."

"Uh huh."

Mafaufau turned back to the wall and kept writing. "We go to where Los Silenciosos gather," Amir read. Then he raised his drink. "I am thrilled to assist in any way that I can."

"You are not invited," Technika informed him.

"Nonsense," said Amir. "How else will you communicate with your mountainous friend?"

"Mafaufau."

"You see? He agrees."

"He has a point," Hexene allowed.

"Alternately, we could glean all Mafaufau knows now, then I can dispose of this balam. He cannot change. He poses no threat," Technika said.

"No. He's coming."

"Would that were true," Amir said wistfully. Technika beeped, which somehow managed to carry the same feeling as a disgusted sigh.

Mafaufau started writing. Amir translated as quickly as he could. "Los Silenciosos gather in certain places in the Catacombs." The balam broke from the reading. "Los Silenciosos? I have seen posters about them. They are the anarchists, no?"

Mafaufau shook his head and wrote. "Malleus brought them together. They are against zombies being controlled with hexes. They stitch their mouths shut so witches can't control them."

Hexene shuddered. It made a certain amount of morbid sense.

"Aha!" Amir said. "And this d'Arthur, besides being a Frenchman, is one of these Silenciosos. I see now. Yes, this is a good adventure we have found ourselves upon."

Hexene shook her head, then turned her attention back to the zombie. "I'm sorry. Do you have a name? A real one?"

The scratch of chalk was the only sound, other than the laughter and conversation from inside. He stepped away, his hands quivering. "No. The change was frightening. I did not want a name. But I have one now," Amir read, then wiped away a tear.

"Mafaufau," said the zombie.

"It is a lovely name," Amir assured him. "Were I in your place, I might have chosen it."

Twenty-Two

This was the longest trip into the Catacombs Hexene had ever taken, though admittedly she usually stuck to her library commute. They walked for so long that Hexene was certain the sun must have risen outside, but in the underground world below Las Brujas, the sun hardly mattered. It was perpetually night down there. The only light came from lanterns and candles, punctuating the sticky gloom with splashes of gold.

Mafaufau left the smooth tunnels behind quickly. Those were the ones planned by the witches, sculpted from the earth by powerful magic. Modified here and there, certainly, with alcoves chipped away by industrious hands, but witch-made nonetheless. Instead, Mafaufau took the group into the tunnels that were entirely built. The chisel marks on the walls looked like teeth. These tunnels weren't uniform and efficient. These weren't meant solely as a route to and from the reservoir. These thickened and thinned, and were veined by innumerable smaller tunnels. Some sported hand- and footholds to climb up and down.

"I have never been so deep in these Catacombs," Amir said.

"There would be no reason," said Technika.

"Wonder how much the witches know about what's down here," Hexene mused.

"Mafaufau," the zombie muttered.

The graffiti grew more common. The bulk was in Spanish, but English and Portuguese were heavily represented, and Hexene recognized a dozen languages besides. She imagined it all said more or less the same thing, since no matter the language, "Malleus" was never translated. XX wasn't either, no matter what script surrounded it. The posters were similarly far more common down here. Every single one had been defaced. Many simply had the XX marking. Others featured the now-familiar MALLEUS SPEAKS or one of its variations.

As they departed the planned tunnels, zombies grew more plentiful too. They glared in open suspicion at the group, and it was Hexene they focused on. She fought the urge to wither under their hate, hiding in the pretense she still had her magic. In the old days, she would have looked for an excuse to punch them in the nose. Instead, she found herself moving into Mafaufau's looming shadow.

The sign was made to look like one of the flashing electric numbers on Sunset Boulevard, but its glittering lights were provided by open flames, mirrored to intensity. The flickering helped create an illusion of the kind of glitz that would be seen in a human city, but there was no pattern to it. Good enough, because the sign said "BRAINS."

Beyond the sign were the walls of a structure, or as close as it got down here. No one panel matched any of the others. Some of it was formed from the sides of crates, with stamps like FRAGILE still visible in fading ink. Others were pieces of aluminum. Hexene wasn't certain how they kept from collapsing, but they did, marking off this section of BRAINS from the rest of the tunnel.

The zombie at the door wasn't as big as Mafaufau, and Hexene was pretty sure that anyone bigger would need a license plate. Both eyes had rotted out of his skull, but he was staring at them just the same with the open pits of his eye sockets. The skin on his head was peeling away like old paint on weathered siding, and his beard might have been made of moss. His clothes were simple and heavily stained and repaired.

"Moz-geé," said the bouncer, standing up and putting his palm out to stop them.

"Mafaufau," said the zombie.

"Moz-geé," said the other one.

They continued to argue like this for a time, until finally Mafaufau nudged Hexene forward. He gestured to her, and she got what he was saying. *Look. No familiar.*

Finally, the other zombie nodded, but it was begrudging. He stepped aside, muttering "Moz-geé," as they passed.

The club was lit with oil lamps and candles, burning at irregular distances and giving more than enough room for shadows to pool. Everything had been scavenged. The bar was made out of old crates. No items of furniture matched any others. Zombies were everywhere, leaning up against the ramshackle bar or gathered around rickety tables. A stage that looked like it could collapse at any second stood against one wall, lit at floor level by what Hexene assumed were candles. The zombie onstage wore a slinky dress, and in the shuddering light bathing her, it almost looked like it was in good condition. Her arms were bare and missing skin down to the bone in a few places. She still had lips, though. Probably needed those for the singing she was doing.

Brains brains braaaaaiiinnns
Brains brains braaaaaiiinnns
Brains brains brains
Brains brains brains
Brains brains braaaaaiiinnns
Brrrrraaaaaaaaaiiiiiiiiiinnnnnns

Hexene imagined the meaning was as impassioned as her attitude. She felt like the ex-woman was singing about loss, but then, she only had the one word. The audience, a bunch of zombies dressed for day labor, sure seemed to appreciate it. They bobbed their rotting heads, taking sips from cloudy cocktails that were nauseatingly chunky.

Mafaufau guided the group to the darkest corner of this place, and since it consisted almost entirely of dark corners, that was no mean feat. There they found a standing table, made from an indifferently cut-up piece of aluminum.

"Mafaufau," he said, holding up his hands as though to keep them there before lumbering off into the crowd.

"He wants us to stay here," Amir said.

"We figured that out," Hexene said.

"Good. Shall I get us some drinks? Ah, a foolish question. If we are in a bar, how do we not sample the wares, eh?" Amir snaked his way to the bar. He caught a fair share of looks, but never reacted. The balam seemed equally at ease everywhere.

"It would have been far simpler had I killed him," Technika said.

"Save it for Slick."

"I would like that very much," Technika replied, "but I have been diverted."

"We know where he is. Should we ask Amir and Mafaufau if they want to come help you take revenge on the gremlin too?"

"He knows we are coming. We need a different approach."

"I'll keep thinking about my thing, and you keep thinking about your thing."

"Whose things are we discussing?" Amir asked, sliding three aluminum cups onto the table and moving two of them in front of Technika and Hexene.

"I do not imbibe liquids," Technika said.

"Apologies," he said, taking it back. "I will save it for Mafaufau, should he require refreshment when he returns."

Hexene lifted the drink. Macaroni chunks of brain floated in the briny liquid. She set it down. "You can have this one too."

"Lucky me!" Amir swigged deeply from the cocktail. "Ah, it is lovely. A certain meaty, brainy taste."

"You are tasting the brains," Technika said.

"So I am! I don't taste any kuru...they must be calf brains. I wonder if that is indeed what they are." He swirled the liquid in the glass. "And gin. I think this is gin. So tell me, why are we searching for this d'Arthur fellow? I know he is one of Los Silenciosos, yet I cannot fathom why such a motley band would seek to speak to one of them, let alone a specific one."

"Mort d'Arthur and his two friends killed the mother and crone of my coven," Hexene said.

Amir gasped, putting the drink down and taking Hexene's hands in hers. "That is horrible. Do you perhaps need a strong, yet sensitive shoulder to weep upon?"

"No," she said flatly.

"I understand. You are strong and independent." Amir snapped his fingers. "You are of the Candlemas Coven then?"

"You've heard."

"Indeed I have. It is a topic of conversation among the witches at Le Chaperon Rouge. Some of them seem to know you from the scries as well, but I do not know the particulars. Other than that you were romantically entangled with a handsome man until you broke his heart."

"He's not handsome."

"Is this why you broke his heart?"

"I didn't..." Hexene took a deep breath. "What are the other witches saying?"

"There are many who wish to even the score, as they say. There is much talk of that, far more than the identities of they who were so tragically murdered. They also say Hexene Candlemas was a fool to leave her beau behind in Los Angeles."

Hexene pictured breaking every last cauldron in the Scryline. It didn't help. Amir savored the drink once again. "While I find the witch palate superior to the zombie in most elements, I must admit to an increasing affection for this cocktail. I will have to discuss its recipe with the bartender."

"He will only tell you brains," said Technika.

"Ah, but the *way* he will say it!" Amir laughed. "So, this is an expedition of revenge then? We are seeking this d'Arthur to bring him some form of justice?"

Hexene looked at Technika to find the robot was looking at her. Her still expression was impossible to read. "No. He's already been dealt with."

By one of the Adepts, clearly, though she had imagined they would have mentioned it to her, or offered to let her help. Hexene still didn't know what to think of that—she hoped the other two zombies would have answers.

Amir's eyes widened. "I misjudged you two then!"

"Not by us," Hexene said quickly. "He had two friends, though. They're all with Los Silenciosos, so I thought if we could find them, we could talk."

"What do you wish to discuss with them?"

"Why they did what they did," Hexene said. "Something feels wrong."

Amir frowned. "I will admit that I have fallen into investigations once or twice. Usually I am the one being investigated in some manner or another. I fear that my mien is often misinterpreted."

"I cannot imagine how," Technika monotoned.

"You are too kind. As it transpires, I often find myself romantically entangled with someone in the midst of a life-changing crime. I am not involved, of course. I seek only to explore a world of delicate love."

"Before you change into a killer jungle cat," Hexene said.

"That is not my fault," he said. "It would be like blaming you for brewing potions."

"I don't have my magic," she snapped.

Amir started. "This is far more complex than it initially appeared," he said. "You have no magic and you were targeted for assassination. Are these related?"

"No," Hexene said immediately, but the thought had grabbed her and wasn't letting go. To witches, she was at best an object of pity, and at worst a plague-carrying pariah. "No," she said more firmly. "There's no way a witch would use water on another witch."

"Do you say that because it is true," asked Technika, "or because you wish it to be so?"

"Ah, that is a pertinent query," said Amir, nodding as he chewed on a rubbery bit of gin-soaked brain. "To use a weakness points to a diseased mind."

"It is merely a matter of time," Technika said. "Murder carries with it a desire for efficiency."

Amir turned to Technika, a stark look of horror washing over his face. "Efficiency?"

"Indeed. When seeking to kill someone, it is beneficial to choose the means that will accomplish the deed with the most celerity."

"But then we will be having at one another willy-nilly!" Amir protested.

"I am not advocating it," Technika said, "merely pointing out its inevitability. Eventually, someone will want someone else dead and choose the most efficient way to go about it, which is our weaknesses. Humans have already done it for thousands of years, though their weaknesses are more prosaic. Pointed metal and such."

Anyone using a weakness was a taboo, but that didn't mean it didn't happen—after all, they had just deployed a fear themselves, as queasy as that thought made Hexene. Slick had made the attempt earlier on her and it had cost him a bodyguard, but that was interspecies conflict and a matter of self-preservation. There was an extra layer of depravity when it came to using one's own weakness to kill one's own kind. It was a form of cannibalism.

"I suppose I should be grateful that the weakness of my people is not known for its tractability," Amir said. He was referring to the fact that common house cats could kill a balam with a single swipe of their claws.

"How are you able to be in this city? There are cats everywhere," Hexene said.

"There are fewer than you would imagine. Certainly, a cat is a common form for a familiar to take, but that is but a tiny percentage of the familiars out there. And then, because so many familiars are rats and mice and songbirds, no one wants any *real* cats in this city." Amir shrugged. "And there is the matter as to whether a cat familiar is defined as a true cat when it comes to killing. It is not something I have ever thought to test. Perhaps I will later." He gulped down the last of his drink, then picked up the one that had been Technika's.

Hexene shook her head. "I don't think the assassination attempt and my loss of magic are connected. I hope they aren't. What I do know is that there are two zombies who can tell us for certain."

Amir nodded, "Yes, this is good."

"I concur with your analysis," Technika said.

Hexene sighed. "Now we just have to find a particular pair of zombies in an entire city."

"I did not expect there to be so many when I came here. I simply thought that there would be mothers in plenty to tempt me from my malaise, but every other face I behold is missing its nose." Amir looked around the room. "Perhaps a year ago, I would not have minded. I would have found some of these zombies to be irresistible. But now, I see only the papery skin, the dripping sores, the curdled blood, and it does not inflame me as once it did."

"That is truly tragic," Technika said.

Amir nodded sadly. Hexene scanned the room and found Mafaufau easily, still circulating from group to group. He was the biggest zombie in the room by a significant margin, and more of them were watching him than watching Hexene's group.

"I think I shall concentrate on the good, though," Amir said. "I foresee many excellent opportunities to be killed in a grand adventure."

"Your optimism is bracing."

"Did you lose your magic in this place?"

It took Hexene a moment to realize Amir was addressing her. "No, back home. We came here to get it back."

"And shortly after your arrival, three of Los Silenciosos attempted to murder your coven and succeeded for two of you. I see now. And now you and your robot love are united in a single purpose."

"Why does everyone...she's not my love."

"I cannot feel love," Technika stated.

Amir gasped. "Say it is not so, my steely angel."

"I am a robot. I feel neither love nor hate." Hexene snorted. "You disagree with my assessment of my own emotional ability?" Technika asked.

"You hate Slick."

"Who is Slick?" Amir asked.

"That is not your concern," Technika said. Then to Hexene: "I have good reason."

"Maybe you need a reason to love someone," Hexene said.

"Aha! Our maiden is a secret romantic! Yes, look how the sun kisses her apple cheeks even indoors! She thinks of a specific special one! Perhaps this unfortunate she left behind in the City of the Angels!"

"If I had my magic, I would hex you here and now."

Amir thoughtfully chewed on some brains. "Then I count myself luckier than most."

"Mafaufau," said the zombie. He was remarkably light on his feet, but then, Hexene was distracted. Images of Nick and Lily kept flashing through her head, as well as all the reasons she *didn't* miss either one of them.

"Any luck, my mountainous friend?" Amir asked.

"Mafaufau." Mafaufau shook his head.

Hexene cursed. "Any other ideas?" Mafaufau shrugged.

"Perhaps a night of sleep," Amir said. "I often find that my dreams solve problems my waking mind cannot begin to unravel."

"I do not dream," said Technika.

"Then you will sit quietly while I dream for the both of us," Amir said, putting down the empty glass and picking up the one meant for Hexene.

He obliterated the cocktail in a single long swallow, and was soon chewing a wad of brains like a zombie in the Major Leagues.

Hexene wanted to kick and shout, but Amir was right. Rest wasn't the worst thing in the world. She followed Mafaufau out the door of BRAINS. Because the zombie was so big, she didn't see what was going on in front of him. Out of nowhere, he collapsed like a felled tree. She barely had a chance to focus on the figures beyond before an evil eye charm was in her face. She screamed, and an old sack thumped down over her head.

Twenty-Three

Just like that, she was back to the moment Escuerzo was taken from her. That sack might as well have been a time machine. She even smelled that milky gorilla stink, and beyond that, the salt of the ocean. Worst of all, though, was the sudden panicked hope that this meant her familiar was still alive. She could move faster this time, and she could get him back.

No. She was beneath Las Brujas. It was a *different* sack. A *different* hijacking. Someone else was kidnapping her, but this time she had so much less to lose.

The assailants were completely silent, which gave away who they likely were. As soon as Hexene made the connection, whatever calm she had regained from escaping the past promptly fled right out the window. She strained to hear the telltale slosh of water, but the maddening wash of blood in her ears drowned everything else out. Strong hands bound her wrists together behind her back, then gripped her by the shoulder, frogmarching her into the darkness of the Catacombs. As ways to die went, this wouldn't have been her choice.

What if they're taking us to the reservoir? The thought leaped into her head like oil jumping from a frying pan. She turned to bolt, but a hard fist planted itself in her guts. Her breath left her all at once, leaving behind a yawning ache that tried to swallow her up. She felt herself be lifted off the ground, and folded in half over the hurt. She gasped, and when the air finally returned to her head, she realized she had been slung over a shoulder. From the smell of him—rot and mildew—it was a zombie. So that settled that.

The journey was a long one. They were descending; she could tell that much. She couldn't see through the weave of the bag. It had smelled like old onions at first, but that was barely discernible under the dank basement odor of the zombie. From time to time, she heard Technika start to say something in German and then make a *bzzt* before falling silent. Mafaufau and Amir never said a word, though she could swear she heard someone snoring.

When the zombie threw her off his shoulder, she tensed for a splash. Instead, she received a welcome explosion of pain across her back. It was a chair. An old ladder-back chair. She felt her hands being untied from each other and secured to the back. More clanging said they were doing something to Technika. The snoring turned to a snort before fading back into the contented sawing.

The bag came off her head. The light was dim—just a few candles guttering in alcoves, perched on hillocks of old wax—but Hexene still had to squint. Her companions were next to her, Mafaufau and Amir in chairs, Technika secured to a board. Mafaufau was awake; Amir's chin was on his chest and he was snoring blissfully. His cocktail was sitting on the floor between his feet. Hexene blinked, thinking maybe she had imagined it. No, it was still there, half-finished.

They were in a cavern that could have almost been natural. The walls were wet, and drips echoed throughout. *Tap tap tap*, each one the sound of pain. Hexene fought the urge to flinch every time. She wasn't going to show weakness. She couldn't.

The air was as thick as gazpacho and twice as cold. Crates loomed in shadowy stacks all around the sides of the room. Zombies were everywhere, dressed in old military fatigues, but with no rank or insignia. Most had berets perched on their rotting heads. Every one of them sported a stitched-up mouth. They were armed, too. Hexene relaxed when she saw the pistols on their hips. Bullets could kill her, and they definitely hurt, but water was worse. That was when one of the zombies, one with an eyeball hanging out of his head, shifted, and the light caught the gun. She saw blue plastic. It was a water pistol. They all were.

Hexene reflexively jolted against her bonds. The chair bounced a little, but that was it. She was tied tightly, and the chair was heavy wood. She looked over at Mafaufau. His was metal, and he didn't look like he was going anywhere. He shook his head, as though to confirm her thought.

A zombie stepped out of the darkness in front of them. He wasn't especially tall, and he was lean like most zombies. While their frames looked rotten, though, his looked hungry. A mane of black hair poked out from under his beret, and the remnants of a beard clung to his chin. He was missing patches of skin over his cheeks and forehead, and his complexion was decidedly green. His most distinctive feature was the sutures through his lips, forming twin Xs.

"Malleus," Hexene said. The zombie regarded her dispassionately.

Amir snorted and came to. "Malleus? Where?" He focused on the zombie in front of them. "Aha. You must be Malleus. For you could be no one else. Good evening...or perhaps good morning. I have lost track of the time, I am afraid. I am Amir Noire, and I am pleased to meet you."

Malleus stared at Amir, then pointedly looked from him to Hexene, and settled on the unwitch. He held up a metal object in his hand that looked a bit like a tiny stapler. He squeezed it, and a soft clicking echoed through the room.

"Morse code," Technika said. Hexene jumped. She didn't know the robot had woken up from her trance.

"Do you know Morse code?"

"Of course," said Technika and Amir in unison. Then, with chivalrous grace, Amir went on, "Please, you translate for our witch. And if I could trouble one of you ladies or gentlemen to give me a sip from my drink? I am parched."

"Malleus said, 'Why are a witch, a robot, a zombie, and a balam looking for Los Silenciosos?'"

"I'm not looking for Los Silenciosos in general," Hexene said. "I'm looking for two specific members who knew Mort d'Arthur."

Malleus clicked. Technika translated, her voice completely devoid of emotion. "Who is Mort d'Arthur?"

"One of Los Silenciosos. He probably went missing in the last week or so."

Malleus looked to first one zombie, then another, then back to Hexene. "There is no Silencioso by that name."

Hexene searched Malleus's face. It was impossible to tell if the zombie was lying. Zombies were hard to read at the best of times—after all, who can tell if "Brains" is a lie or not—but with the stitched-up mouth and a poker face worthy of a South Seas idol, Malleus was not just a closed book, but one wrapped in tape and chains. Hexene swallowed; the persistent drip gently echoing through the chamber reminded her of the danger. She couldn't be far from the reservoir, to say nothing of the water pistols in the room all around her. She needed to test the zombie leader.

"Not anymore. I found his body."

She flinched when several zombies skinned their pistols and pointed the dripping barrels at her. Malleus held up the hand with the clicker, his ring finger and pinkie splayed as though to say "Stop."

"You found a dead zombie," Technika translated.

Hexene nodded. "I took his identification to the Crow Sisterhood. They said his name was Mort d'Arthur, and his mouth was stitched shut, just like yours. I haven't been in Las Brujas long, but I've been here long enough to know what that means."

Malleus paused again. Everything the zombie leader did was deliberate. It wasn't the usual disconnect she saw in the physicality of zombies, where they looked like they were operating their bodies at a remove, like marionettes. Malleus considered every little thing he did. That, at least, made Hexene's heart slow. If he intended to kill her, it wouldn't be out of sudden anger.

"There is no Mort d'Arthur affiliated with Los Silenciosos. I believe that you saw a dead zombie. I believe he had our mark." Malleus touched the stitches on his lips. Then he looked to the other zombies, and though Technika continued to translate, the words were obviously for them rather than Hexene. "No Barrendera would come to us with that story. She would think of something better, and she would have twenty of her sisters in wait who would have descended upon us by now."

Hexene let out a breath. She should have guessed that was what Malleus was afraid of. Las Barrenderas had been among the most enthusiastic of those persecuting the zombies.

"Who are you?" Malleus asked.

"Hexene Candlemas."

The zombies didn't murmur. Their shock was expressed through the shuffling of their feet over stone as they shifted their posture. Even Malleus's normally impassive eyes widened a little. "Again, something no one would lie about. I have heard a rumor, that you are without your magic. Is this true?"

Hexene inhaled. Lie, and break whatever trust she built. Tell the truth, and let this zombie know she was powerless. "It's true."

Malleus's shoulders relaxed. It would have been imperceptible had Hexene not been entirely focused on him. He was the architect of her fate, and as near as she could tell, one of the most powerful people in Las Brujas. "So you believe this Mort d'Arthur and two others killed your coven. You seek revenge?"

"I don't know. Maybe? Something is wrong about all of this, and I don't know what, exactly. If I could talk to the zombies who were there, maybe I could find out what."

"I will tell you this. No matter what the witches may tell you, Los Silenciosos had nothing to do with the murder of your coven. I didn't order it. We aren't killers."

"You carry water," Hexene said.

"We have to be able to defend ourselves. Witches can hex us at any time. The threat of water is all we have, but it is intended only as threat."

Hexene didn't believe him, but this wasn't an argument she particularly wanted to have, especially in her present circumstances. "What about finding the others?"

"I don't give zombies to the witches."

"But if we were able to find the zombies who did it, we could tell everyone that Los Silenciosos had nothing to do with it. This whole thing would end."

The corners of Malleus's eyes crinkled. After consideration, Hexene determined this to be a laugh. "Nothing will stop this," he said. Hexene was about to protest, but Malleus clicked his device again. Technika translated. "But perhaps it will delay it for a time. Eshu Ibará knows everyone," Malleus said to Hexene as a zombie shambled from the room. "She will know who this d'Arthur was and where he laid his head at night."

"Thanks," Hexene said.

For the first time, Malleus looked surprised. His hand quivered a bit, and he clicked out, "You're welcome."

"Would you untie us?"

Malleus gestured to the other zombies. Hexene didn't flinch as the scrape of their tread closed in. Their silence was eerie, but she was growing used to it. Hands yanked roughly at her bonds. The ropes fell away, and Hexene cradled her hands in her lap.

"Mafaufau," said Mafaufau.

"I must agree," said Amir. "Ah, my drink."

Hexene was about to say something, but shrank under the persistent gaze of Malleus. The zombie leader watched his captives with faint interest and, Hexene thought, judgment. Amir showed no concern, leaning back in his chair, crossing his legs as though he were entertaining at a nightclub's corner table, and sipping at the cocktail that had somehow made the journey unscathed.

"This is a nice place you have here," Amir said to Malleus, nodding in approval. "I have not toured the Catacombs extensively, but there appears to be many miles down here."

Malleus simply stared.

"It is a strategic masterstroke," Technika said. "Control the water, control the city. Or, at least, that would be how it would work if this were a human city. Witches can survive long enough without for reprisals to exact a heavy cost."

"They wouldn't endanger their human families," Hexene said.

"No?" Technika asked. "If that were true, do you not think Los Silenciosos would be in a better position?"

Hexene turned in horror to Malleus. He merely stared. Before she could think of anything to say, the zombie who had left lurched back in, another zombie behind him.

She was nearly doll-like in size and proportion, her skin a deep gray-green. She didn't appear to have any eyes, or any skin on her face above her mouth. She was just a staring skull. Sparse dreadlocks covered the back of her head. She wore an old dress that probably started life as a flour sack; it was a beloved flour sack, though, and showed evidence of numerous repairs. She clutched a heavy book to her chest, and Hexene would be willing to bet it weighed more than she did. Like everyone else, her mouth had been stitched shut with a pair of Xs.

Malleus gestured to her, and then to Hexene. An American zombie, or at least one without the stitches, would have added a "Brains," in there somewhere. Hexene took the hint and explained to Eshu what she was after. The other zombie nodded at the names and beckoned into the dark corridor beyond.

"Thank you," Hexene said again to Malleus as she moved past him. The collection of Los Silenciosos all stared at the interlopers. She gave them a smile and a nod. They didn't return either one.

Malleus clicked, and Technika translated. "You're welcome. Take care of yourself. Las Brujas is a dangerous place for those without magic."

"So it is," Amir agreed, nodding wistfully. As he passed, he handed Malleus the now-empty tumbler.

"Mafaufau," said Mafaufau.

Eshu Ibará shuffled into the throatlike corridor. She was ghostly in her silence. Hexene remembered herself as a child, a human child. She would have been wearing a dress stitched together from a flour sack herself. Unless it was Sunday, of course. Then she would be wearing the one from the store, which was either too big or too small depending on whether she was growing into or out of it. But *that* Hexene—or, more accurately, Maria Foley, or even the hated Canela—the one who barely wore the shoes she had, would have been dressed like Eshu. Hexene wondered what Canela Foley would have thought of this. Of being in an underground labyrinth filled with monsters, and only afraid because she was half the monster she should be.

She walked in Mafaufau's shadow. The massive zombie was as quiet as Los Silenciosos, but there was no menace in him. He reminded her a bit of the whales who had come every year to the bay by her home. She had liked to sit up on the dune and watch the calves being pushed to the surface for their first breath. Amazing that something fifteen feet long could be cute. Now, the idea of staying that close to the water made her distinctly uncomfortable. Not long ago, she had been trapped beneath the ocean in a mad scientist's undersea lair. That would be enough to make anyone leery of the ocean, let alone someone who would dissolve in a tidepool. As much as she liked to linger in the memories of her youth, she didn't miss the sea.

Maria Foley, and Canela for that matter, would have been thrilled to have companions like Mafaufau and Technika. Amir she could take or leave, but he did seem like fun from time to time. Maria would want her magic back above everything else, assuming she knew she had it to begin with. She would want a familiar to bridge the gap between herself and the goddess that every culture on Earth had worshiped by a different name. She would want to work her hexes again. The answers, everyone said, had to be in the Baba Yaga Memorial Library of Spells and Hexes. *Had* to be.

But it was the largest library on the planet. She was looking for a needle in a stack of needles in the middle of a needle factory on Free Needle Day.

Was revenge, or whatever it was that she sought out of d'Arthur's friends, a distraction or a more noble calling? Something was wrong. She could feel that, especially now, in the quiet places between her footsteps. Find what was wrong, and maybe she would know what anything meant. This mystery, perhaps, was solvable in a way that her magical predicament wasn't.

The Catacombs wound their way through the dark. In the flickering lantern shadows, she glimpsed entire shantytowns in the darkness. They passed other gathering places as well—cafés built from scrap, chessboards like those in a park, even a small puppet stage where a play undoubtedly called *Brains* was unfolding. The walls of the Catacombs here were decorated, with the defaced wanted posters and the usual graffiti, yes, but also true art. Some painted on the walls directly, others in poster form, stuck on the sweating surface.

Eshu took them through a cramped corridor. Some of the zombies lived in tents, like Okies fleeing the dustbowl. Others had built shacks. Some only had a damp blanket on the ground on which to sleep. This tunnel looked to Hexene like the Catacombs' equivalent of a residential area. Eshu stopped in front of a ragged tent and pointed. The front flaps were open, one secured to the side, the other hanging free. No one was inside.

"Who lives here?" Hexene asked, then felt like an idiot.

Eshu opened the massive book she clutched, flipping the brown pages. Hexene saw scribbles of ink, though they riffled past too quickly to read. Eshu paused on one page and pointed with a bony finger. Hexene leaned close, trying to make out the words by the dim light of a nearby candle. The spidery script read *Fallow Graves & Flaco Calavera*. Hexene thought of the records of the Crow Sisterhood. It would probably offend everyone involved if Hexene brought up that comparison to either side.

"These were Mort d'Arthur's friends?" Hexene asked. "They lived here?"

Eshu nodded, her empty eye sockets betraying nothing.

"It has a certain charm," Amir said. "I have slept in many worse places."

"I would expect nothing less," Technika said.

Hexene ignored them and crawled into the tent. It stank. She hadn't recalled her attackers smelling particularly awful. Maybe once they aired out, it wasn't so bad. Here, where they evidently slept, they were allowed to marinate in their stench and nurture it into a mighty stink that colonized the nostrils.

There wasn't much left in the tent, either, assuming they'd had much in the first place. An old tin can and a wool blanket encrusted with rubbery bits of what Hexene guessed was half-decayed flesh formed the entirety of the prior occupants' remaining possessions. Hexene sifted through the blanket, though moving it hurled plumes of stench into the close air, along with two small pieces of paper, fluttering to the floor like moths. The first was a single dog-eared photo, forgotten when Graves and Calavera left. Hexene turned it over and knew instantly where Calavera was.

The second was even more damning, though for a different reason. This was a small strip of paper with a hex carefully printed out along it. Hexene recognized it because it was the first and most effective hex any witch learned. The evil eye, so important to witchcraft that a charm built around warding it off actually frightened witches themselves. All the hex did was visit bad luck on the recipient, but that bad luck depended entirely on the environment. Bad luck in a room full of pillows? Not too dangerous. Bad luck in a city full of witches that wants you dead for rotting? Considerably worse.

Hexene reflexively reached for her satchel, but it was gone. She remembered that she had left it behind at the beginning of her day, for the meeting with Slick, and had never grabbed it from the house during her brief return. She wanted to draw a line through the symbols, just in case the hex decided to latch onto her for carrying it around. She grumbled to herself and slipped it into her boot. She emerged from the tent clutching the photo. Eshu Ibará was already gone.

"Aha, what did you find?" Amir asked. "Your face is radiant with discovery, like a young man who has just learned about breasts."

Hexene started in shock, shook it off, and handed the photo over. She turned to Mafaufau. "That zombie club you took us to earlier, is it still open?"

"Mafaufau." The massive zombie shook his head.

"Even the dead must sleep," Technika intoned.

Amir raised the photo overhead. "I know this woman! She was singing to the torches!"

"Torch singing," Hexene corrected.

"This is what I said. We saw her at the club earlier and...yes, I am caught up now." Amir handed the photo back to Hexene.

The photo showed the singer in the middle of a set, crooning her sad song of "Brains" to a rapturous audience. Hexene pointed at the corner, where a smudge had obliterated a bit of the detail. "A kiss mark," she said, though she was unsure if it was from lipstick or some lip that had come detached. She'd seen the Salem Sisters kiss photos of themselves for fans. On the other side, in an unsteady scrawl: *Flaco, mi corazón.*

"You are certain?" Technika asked.

Hexene was about to assert, but Amir broke in. "Oh yes, Hexene is correct. I know the shape of any lips I have ever beheld, and these belong to the sweetly decaying singer."

"Where is Eshu?" Hexene asked.

"She left," Technika said. "I trust you are not going to ask if she said anything."

"I guess not." Hexene sighed. The club was closed, and her lead was gone. Abruptly, the weight of the day came crashing down on her shoulders. She needed sleep. Perhaps not a full night—or probably day at this point—but a little bit of time in oblivion. Even thinking about it made her yawn.

"A capital idea," Amir said. "Allow me to welcome you to my room in Cogtown. It is no Hotel Metropole, but it is something. Enough for the four of us to sleep the sleep of the just."

"I will not be setting foot in Cogtown," Technika stated.

"I don't like the idea of staying with the Arcane Adepts," Hexene said, "but it's not like we have options."

"They do not know we found d'Arthur's body. So long as you maintain the ruse, we will be safe."

"As you wish. What of you, my massive friend? Do you slumber in the jungle with your boon companion?"

"Mafaufau."

"Excellent."

TWENTY-FOUR

Amir insisted upon escorting Hexene and Technika back to the Caribbean Quarter even though it was a bit out of his way. Hexene wasn't going to object, especially since that meant Mafaufau would be coming too. With the two assassins still in the wind, she felt much safer with the massive zombie next to her, even if the guilt at the prospect of him being forced to traverse the distance between the Arcane Adepts' home and Cogtown nagged. Besides, her boots felt like they were full of lead.

The sun was high in the sky by the time they emerged from the Catacombs. Hexene had no idea how long it had been, but she had walked from one end of Las Brujas to the other at least once. The streets, though, were fairly quiet. Even the skies were relatively clear. It felt like a lull in the persistent storm that had been wracking the city since the attack on the Candlemas Coven.

At the gate of the Adepts' house, they made plans to meet with Mafaufau and Amir that night. The zombie and the balam slunk off down the alley. Hexene winced as she noted the enormous zombie doing his best to stay within the shadows of the walls on either side. Mafaufau couldn't properly hide anywhere; his best hope was relying on the fact that most zombies weren't nearly so large. He could easily be mistaken for a golem, meat or clay.

She let herself in through the front door. She almost followed Technika up the stairs, but it had been a long day and Hexene was ravenous. "I'm going to get something to eat," she whispered.

"If you judge that such is required," said the robot, continuing to their room.

Hexene made her way to the kitchen door. She was exhausted, and she bumped into the dining room table more than once along the way. In her mind, she played the day's events over and over, from their botched ambush of Slick all the way to the meeting with Malleus and Los Silenciosos. The whole thing was a briar patch, and she was stuck in it.

She was lost in thought and later she guessed that's why she didn't hear them at first. Once in the room, though, the sounds surrounded her. She didn't get a good look at the cause, but she saw enough for her mind to fill in the blanks with some salacious additions. Angelique Arcane was on the kitchen counter with a man.

Hexene gasped involuntarily. "I'm sorry!" she exclaimed. What she remembered most were both of their faces, eyes wide in shock and maybe a little terror. Hexene didn't stick around, retreating through the door into the dining room. She couldn't decide if she should flee somewhere, or if she should stay there and try to process what she'd seen. On the other side, she could clearly hear Angelique and her beau exchanging desperate whispers and the struggles of fixing their clothes by the light of a few candles. *How did I not hear them moaning?* she scolded herself. In her mind, the moaning was already at full-throated levels and heading for full arias.

The door opened behind her, and Hexene jumped. "I'm sorry," Hexene repeated. "I didn't mean to barge in. I was hungry, and—"

"It's all right, Hexene," Angelique said in a near-whisper. She was a bit disheveled, but if Hexene hadn't just seen what she'd just seen, she would have assumed the other witch had just encountered unusually high winds while flying. Her familiar somehow also managed to look flustered, despite being a snake. "I thought everyone was in bed."

"Why weren't you?" Hexene blurted. Angelique snorted an involuntary laugh, and Hexene felt her cheeks growing hot. "That's not what I meant."

"Yes, it is," Angelique said. "I understand. I can't take Rodrigo to my room. Someone would see."

Hexene nearly reminded her that someone *did* see, but thought better of it. She was pleased her composure was returning by bits and pieces. "That makes sense."

Angelique touched Hexene on the arm and implored, "You won't tell anyone, will you?"

"No, of course not."

"Trust a fellow maiden," said Angelique, flashing her brilliant smile. "I suppose I don't have to tell you what Evangeline and Serafina would do if they found out."

"Is he still in there?"

Angelique giggled. "No, he left. The kitchen entrance is a useful thing, don't you think?"

"How long have you been..." Hexene couldn't think of a word that felt comfortable, so she just nodded at the kitchen.

"Over a year," she said.

"It's kind of risky isn't it? Just for sex?"

A slump came into Angelique's shoulders, and a light flashed in her eyes. Hexene knew the posture: it was the one right before a thrown punch. "I love him," she said simply, the words heavy with truth.

Hexene found herself gaping. She shook her head. "I'm sorry, I had no idea."

"Why would you?"

"I don't know. It just never really entered my mind."

Angelique appraised her. "I think it has."

An image of the two hex dolls flashed in front of Hexene's mind's eye. "It hasn't!"

"I bet if Serafina and Evangeline could trade me for you, they would.."

"Not like this. Do you not like being a maiden?"

"I loved it. For the first fifteen years, at least. You're made to live in this unchanging state. Like you're under glass."

The image of Evangeline's elderly husband and her gray-haired children popped into Hexene's mind. Raoul's wistful sadness had been palpable. "You want to be a mother."

Angelique shrugged, and in that moment she looked entirely unguarded. "Serafina and Evangeline would never allow it."

"Can't you tell them you're in love?"

Angelique barked a bitter laugh. "I have. Not with Rodrigo. There were others before him. Cheng, Bobby, Jacques..." a gesture implied more. "They're not ready. Serafina doesn't want to move beyond, Evangeline doesn't want to be a crone. So here I am, sneaking what I can until Rodrigo gets so old that looking at him hurts."

"I'm so sorry."

"For listening to me prattle on? I wish I could be like you. The perfect maiden."

Hexene snorted. "Other than the fact that I have no familiar and no magic."

"It's temporary," Angelique said, though there wasn't much conviction behind it. "Is that where you were? At the library all night?"

"Uh huh," Hexene said, but it came out in two uncertain fragments. She pounced on the end with a distraction. "Say, do you know a Mort d'Arthur, Flaco Calavera, or Fallow Graves?"

"Those don't sound like witch names."

"Zombies," Hexene said.

Angelique waved it off airily. "I can't tell zombies apart."

"Oh."

Angelique leaned in, and with a conspiratorial whisper, "Are those the names of the zombies who killed Hechalé and Hermosa?"

Hexene found herself nodding. "Yeah."

"So you're a detective now?" Angelique asked, then broke into her winsome smile. "Probably why you were such a good witch. So you're hunting for the zombies that killed your coven, huh? A little revenge?"

"Yeah," Hexene said. It might even be true.

"Well, there's no guarantee they're even still alive," Angelique said. "Every witch in this city is looking to get even for you." If Angelique had been behind d'Arthur's death—and Hexene doubted she was—she would have admitted it here.

Hexene pulled the hex from her boot. "I think I was beaten to it."

Angelique's eyes widened. "Let me see that." Hexene handed it over, watching the other maiden closely. She inspected the hex. "Can't be," she whispered, shaking her head.

"What?" Hexene asked. The glimmer of recognition in Angelique's eyes was impossible to miss, but Hexene wasn't sure where it led yet.

Angelique turned it over, displaying the evil eye to Hexene. "This is Serafina's handwriting."

Twenty-Five

Hexene stared up at the ceiling in her attic room. Technika's shadow stuttered and danced with the persistent flash of lightning from the ward. Hexene had learned how to sleep with that in the background, but that wasn't what kept her up. It was what Angelique said.

Serafina's writing.

It wasn't that Hexene was surprised. Hiding d'Arthur's corpse wasn't exactly something that screamed innocence. She wanted to believe the Adepts, or at least Angelique, were blameless. She hadn't been certain what she was looking for while hunting down Graves and Calavera, but she had held out some hope that it didn't lead to betrayal.

Whatever Serafina had hoped to gain from the deaths of the other two Candlemas witches hadn't extended to Hexene; she had been living in their home for over a month since then, and they'd had ample time to send up another group of zombies to finish the job. They wouldn't even have to change their armament. The reservoir would do just fine for both Hexene and her robotic bodyguard-of-sorts. Something else was happening, but Hexene couldn't see what. In Las Brujas, the beefs could go back to the old country, whichever one you cared to name. Hechalé had mentioned a beef between the two crones back when the Candlemas Coven had moved in, but that looked buried. It had to be, right?

Hexene wasn't much more than an unwitch anymore and now she was looking at the possibility of fighting more than half a coven. One look at their familiars said who would have the advantage. It didn't matter if she had a gun-shy robot, a gentle zombie, and a broken balam on her side. They weren't the most intimidating of posses anyway.

Hexene got up. The lightning stopped, a single bolt finishing the trek up Technika's arm before sizzling into nothing as it reached her heart. "Where are you going?"

"To clean up," Hexene said. "I need to think."

"What must you ponder that you cannot here?"

"I don't know who to trust."

"There is no one to trust in this city," Technika said.

"What about you? I can't trust you?"

Technika's expression was blank, as always. "I do not want you dead."

"So that's one person."

"Perhaps I have an overly optimistic view of what trust entails."

"I've been thinking of you as too optimistic," Hexene agreed, making her way down the stairs. A moment later, the scratch and hum of lightning started up again.

Hexene found her way to the bathroom. She sat on the lip of the tub, kicking her feet in the air. On impulse, she lifted the lid on the small container where the blob lived.

"Hello extremely!" said the blob. "Do you have something wonderful for me to eat?" Hexene looked down at the simple nightgown she was wearing; it had been a gift from Evangeline when she'd noticed Hexene slept in her dress. She shrugged and tore a bit of lace off the end, tossing it onto the blob. It stuck to the pink gelatinous surface before slowly sinking. "Oh, that is lovely! I can taste your sorrow!"

"Can I ask you something?"

"Oh, I wish you would! I love questions!"

"What do you think of the Arcane Adepts?"

"Who?"

"The witches you live with?"

"I live with witches?"

Hexene stared at the blob in disbelief. The bit of lace inside it steadily fizzed away into nothingness. "Yeah, you live in their bathroom."

"Oh. That explains it! Mmm, do you have any more of that delicious lace? You taste like an autumn sky!"

Hexene dropped another piece of lace on the poor creature and shut the lid. She left the bathroom and ran right into Evangeline's son Raoul. He looked exhausted; the bags under his eyes had bags.

"Hello, Hexene," he said.

"Hi, Raoul." She started to walk away, then stopped. "Do you mind my asking how old you are?"

"I am no spring chicken. I turned forty-seven last Sua," the man said, naming the second month of the Theban calendar.

"Forty-seven. You're not married?"

He shrugged. "I thought one day I would marry a maiden and help her transition to motherhood. But my mother...she never found a good match for me."

Hexene nodded slowly. "And when you and your wife had children, Evangeline would be encouraged to cronehood."

"I suppose," he said. "My mother is still young and she has many good years of being a mother ahead of her."

Hexene thought of Samuel, Raoul's oldest sibling, who had to be at least sixty. She briefly wondered what the lot of them would think if they knew what Angelique was up to. So many of them wanting to move on and not being allowed to. It was a slow-motion tragedy. "Many years," she agreed without much conviction. She turned to go.

"Hexene? Might I ask *you* something?"

"Sure."

"Have you thought of becoming a mother?"

She shrugged. "Not very much."

"I suppose you have time, too."

She frowned at him and walked down the hallway until she heard the bathroom door shut. It was almost on impulse, but she couldn't stop herself now. She sprinted as quietly as she could on bare feet for the staircase. She paused at the top, cocking her head, listening for the tread of a person or the shuffle of a zombie. She heard neither one and picked her way down the stairs. Wherever the stone was bare, it was freezing. The house, no matter how many modern trappings were lying about, would always feel faintly like a castle. She wondered if that was the goal, if the witches wanted to live in the past, or that was simply a side effect of magically creating a city from stone in the middle of the desert. Hexene had never been one for princess nonsense. She liked the climate out here, but she'd much rather have something built with wood or even stucco.

The darkness was nearly complete on the bottom floor. A simple light spell wasn't hard, but it was out of Hexene's reach. So she navigated by the looming shadows in the darkness, her steps delicate. She slipped through the dining room and into the kitchen. There, the herb smells of the most recent meal permeated every surface. Without meaning to, the image of Angelique and Rodrigo appeared when she looked at the counter where they'd been. She did her best to ignore it, finding the cellar door with difficulty. Once inside, with the scent of earth all around, she felt along the wall until she found the lantern and lit the tiny flame. It was blinding after the trip through the house. She only wanted to know one thing, and she was pretty sure she knew already.

She climbed down the stairs, then turned. The barrels and old gunnysacks lay beneath in their storage spaces. She had been right, though. Mort d'Arthur was gone.

Twenty-Six

The shanty tent smelled about as good as anything did in the Catacombs. A combination of semi-rotten people and persistent moisture was never going to produce anything that would get a perfume named after it. Amir had bribed the zombie who squatted here—an old-timer with mushrooms growing out of his face—and he'd made himself scarce. That was a common affliction, Hexene was noting, the whole mushroom gardening thing. She wondered if zombie mushrooms were any good for hexes.

Hexene, Technika, and Amir waited just inside the tent. It was made of burlap, stitched together like a meat golem whose creator wasn't too fond of him. The flaps were ostensibly closed, but they didn't really reach all the way, still affording the three of them a good view. The old-timer's stuff, what there was, crowded in the back of the tent. Amir had promised they wouldn't bother it, and Hexene had no real temptation to look. She saw only a ratty bedroll, a half-broken crate, an old skillet, and a fork. Seemed like most of the zombies in the Catacombs lived the same life. If they wanted comfort at all, they had to go topside and be hexed.

Hell of a choice, Hexene thought.

On the way into the Catacombs, Amir had spotted a poster stuck to one of the winding rock walls. MISSING ROBOT, it said, a drawing of

Technika below the words. Then, along the bottom: LOST & CONFUSED, *Please help my girlfriend find home. Find Baron Sweettooth at the Hotel Metropole.*

"What is this?" Amir had asked.

Technika shrank when she saw it. "It is nothing."

Amir, admirably, let his further questions go with a frown. Hexene should have known Slick wasn't going to give up. Powerful monsters weren't used to hearing the word no, and it could move them to violence. It was a reminder that eventually she and Technika would have to do something about the gremlin, or he would no doubt escalate matters.

The three of them had made their way through the Catacombs and were now staring at the front entrance of BRAINS, that nightclub where the singer worked. They had been waiting most of the night, and it was past midnight now. Hexene's butt had gone from sore to numb in the time she'd spent sitting there. She was still exhausted, too. After discovering that d'Arthur's body was missing, sleep had been harder to find than a friendly smile. She'd finally gotten a bit in the late afternoon, waking up with a faintly baked feeling and Technika telling her it was time to meet the others.

Technika knelt by the front in nearly the same pose she used when charging herself in the hex. Amir reclined, as comfortable in such a ridiculous position as a cat. Next to him, he had a cocktail from BRAINS, and Hexene wasn't entirely certain how he'd gotten it. Only the bite-sized chunks of brain floating in the alcohol spoke to the origin of the drink.

Mafaufau was inside the club. The giant zombie was the only one of them who could go into BRAINS without being remarked upon. He would be keeping an eye on the torch singer, just in case she had another way out of the club other than the main entrance.

"We should just go in and take her," Technika said. "There is no reason for us to be so circumspect."

"I don't think that the group of us kidnapping a zombie is the best solution," said Hexene. "Won't exactly make us popular with Malleus."

"I must agree with Hexene," Amir said. "When one seeks the company of a lady or a gentleman, it is of vital import that said lady or gentleman wishes one to be there. For the dance of love must have at least two partners, else there is no true dance at all."

"This is not a matter of love," said Technika. "This is a matter of finding a known murderer's lair."

"A reasonable point. Although I think that a murderer can become a lover if one is gentle enough."

"That's not the goal here either," Hexene snapped.

Amir sighed. "Not that such plans would do much for me. The jaguar is, as you say, asleep."

Zombies went into and out of the club. The bearded bouncer sometimes said his word to them, and they said it back. The zombies belonged here. Not just in the club, but in the Catacombs as a whole. Las Brujas might have been made by and for the witches, but everything underground was truly the domain of the undead.

"I should have brought a deck of cards," Amir said. "I did not think, when I arrived in this fair city, that my cards would become my prized possession."

"You soon learned that there are no such things outside of Cogtown," agreed Technika.

Hexene frowned. "That *is* weird."

"All the games they play are with the Tarot," Amir said.

"Oh," said Hexene. "Yeah. I thought that was just my coven."

Amir sat up on an elbow and squinted at her. "When you became their maiden, they taught you card games?"

Hexene shrugged. "Of course. Don't the balam teach you anything?"

Amir lay back, making gestures with his hands that would have gotten him kicked out every school, church, and restaurant Hexene could think of. "Oh yes. You learn the secrets of pleasing the woman, of pleasing the man, of pleasing those who do not quite fit into one hole or the other."

"Is that all?" Technika deadpanned.

"Oh no. After that, one moves on to groups."

Hexene coughed. "Wait, why? Why would you possibly have to know that?"

"Know how to please a lover? I know you are a maiden, but you must have explored the secret delights of—"

"No," Hexene cut him off. "Why would you have to learn how to do any of that? As soon as you're aroused, you turn into a jaguar and try to kill everyone."

"It is true. Or it would be true if I were a balam, rather than merely a sad man who does not like cats."

"Right, so why do you learn how to please anyone if as soon as you're going to, you eat them?"

"Maul," corrected Amir. "We do not *eat*. We are not *cannibals*. We merely maul."

Hexene gestured to keep going. "Okay, fine, maul. The question still stands."

"There are stories. Legends, perhaps. Stories of balam who learn to control themselves long enough to complete the act of love before transforming. To maul."

"I have heard of balam who use hexes to prevent transformation," said Technika.

Hexene nodded. "I've supplied those."

"Then you know," Amir said. "They do not prevent transformation, they prevent *arousal*. One does not love without arousal for all participants. One must coax the juices from—"

"Stop again," Hexene pleaded. "So, you learn all this stuff just in case you can ever use it?"

Amir nodded. "One does not want to be caught unprepared."

"Wait," said the maiden. "When you're getting these lessons...*how* are you getting these lessons?"

"Lecture. There are visual aids. Dioramas in some cases."

"Don't you get..."

"Hexene is asking if arousal is not a danger during these lessons."

"Oh! Yes, very dangerous. It is not unusual for everyone present to transform. There are the most terrific fights."

Hexene shook her head. Sometimes she wondered if the witches had it to do all over again, if they would have stayed in the shadows. There was no way the world could have gotten any weirder.

"There," said Technika.

Hexene snapped out of her imagination and focused on the front door. The zombie singer was indeed emerging from the club. She was dressed in what Hexene guessed were street clothes down here: a simple dress stitched together from a few different sources. The slinky gown she had worn was probably still inside, in whatever she had for a dressing room. She shambled away, down the tunnel, and Hexene and her companions stayed perfectly still, not wanting to draw any attention as the subject of their surveillance moved past.

A moment later, Mafaufau shambled from the club. He kept a good cushion of distance between himself and the singer, pausing when he came up alongside the tent. Hexene and Amir helped Technika to her feet, moving as quietly as they all were able, and joined Mafaufau in the tunnel.

"Mafaufau," said Mafaufau.

Hexene nodded. "You're right. Everyone keep back."

"It is fine," said Amir. "I can see quite well in the dark."

"Of course you can," Hexene said.

Amir nodded. "It assists in the joys in which one must partake to bring one's partners to the heights of bliss."

"I thought it was because you are half-jaguar."

"I suppose if you want to be literal."

They followed the torch singer through the Catacombs, as far back as they could manage without losing her. Though they were a distinctive sight, they never drew more than a sullen glare and a muttered version of "Brains" in some language or another. Hexene stayed in the middle of the pack. She was the only obvious witch, and thus the only obvious target.

The singer's destination was a shack built into an alcove of a tunnel. It looked more permanent than the vast majority of settlements Hexene had seen in the Catacombs. A sign, perhaps, of money and popularity. A staircase, chiseled into the rock wall, wound up to a wooden door set into the stone. What looked like a small circular window was set right at eye level, but when they got closer, Hexene saw it was just the bottom of a Bebop Cola bottle framed with some scavenged aluminum.

"Please," said Amir, "allow me to speak with the woman."

"Why you?" Hexene demanded. "You'll just try to hit on her."

"Do any of you know her name?"

The shock hit her like a bucket of water, and the subsequent guilt was very much like the melting that would follow. "No."

"I would call her Brains," said Technika.

"Mafaufau."

"Or that."

Amir smiled. "I asked a phantom who has taken a liking to the young woman. Once I assured him that my interest was in the arena of a fan as opposed to a lover, he was most forthcoming of information regarding her." The balam leaned on the jamb and rapped gently on the door.

From inside: "Brains?"

"Miss Deth?" Amir asked. "Mona Deth?"

"Brains."

"Lovely. My name is Amir Noire, and I was wondering if I might have a word?"

"Brains?" The sound of metal scraping over stone—some kind of bar lock, Hexene learned later—came from inside the door, and then it opened, revealing a sliver of Mona Deth. The torch singer's vulnerability and rotten skin were both apparent when they were this close. As she took stock not just of Amir, but of the others, her milky eyes widened. "Brains!" she accused.

"No, no. I promise you, Miss Deth. We are not here to start any kind of trouble."

But she was staring at Hexene, trembling the whole time. "Brains!" She tried to shut the door, but Mafaufau placed one inexorable hand on it. No force the torch singer could summon would move it now.

"My name is Hexene Candlemas," Hexene began, then stopped as something in the apartment was knocked over.

"Stand aside," Technika said. She hit the door, and it slammed into Mona Deth, sending the slender singer sprawling. The space revealed inside was teetering on the edge of cozy. The walls were stone, but a few pictures had been hung there, standing alongside the odd bookshelf. The rugs weren't in the best shape, but Hexene had owned much worse. The door opened on a hallway that disappeared into the dark, and at that moment, Hexene caught sight of a skinny back shambling away at top speed.

"There!" Hexene shouted. Technika was first through the door, followed by Hexene and Amir.

Mafaufau helped Mona up with an apologetic "Mafaufau."

"Wait!" Hexene called after the fleeing zombie. "We're not here to hurt you! We just want to talk!" The words didn't stop the zombie, and Hexene figured they wouldn't have stopped her, either. Experience was a harsh teacher, and fear doubly so. They raced through the twisting hall, which ended in a clapboard door, now banging open.

"He is still running," said Amir. The two of them, maiden and jaguar man, quickly outpaced the robot. The other side of Mona's home opened onto a wide tunnel where other shacks stood at irregular intervals and at different levels, all of them shining with some kind of flickering light, from candles to campfires. The zombie, Flaco Calavera, ran down the center avenue with a queer hopping gait, as though his legs no longer could bend very far, and this was as good as it got. Still, he managed quite a clip. Hexene and Amir raced after him.

Calavera turned a corner, slipping between two shacks. A zombie sat on the porch of one, clumsily strumming a beat-up zither. Hexene turned the corner in time to see Calavera ducking into a small side tunnel up a short incline. The only light came from a burning torch set into a sconce beside it. They might as well have been a thousand years in the past. Hexene was now ahead of Amir, but only barely. As she ducked into the tunnel, the smell that greeted her was different. It wasn't the ambient rot of so many zombies being in one place, nor was it mildew, or the specific meaty scent of the mushrooms that grew wild everywhere. This was the unmistakable birthday cake odor of candles that had recently been blown out.

"Wait!" she called out.

"He is not listening," said Amir, coming up next to her.

"Amir, do you see anything?"

"Such as what?" the balam asked, the confusion audible in his voice.

"Candles, symbols on the walls and the floors."

"Yes, of course. There are—"

Hexene threw an arm in front of Amir and skidded to a stop. "Flaco, you need to stop!"

It was unlikely that the zombie heard anything over the awful din of the tunnel's ceiling collapsing.

Twenty-Seven

Hexene wasn't knocked unconscious. Her senses were simply too overwhelmed to register much of anything beyond a solid wall of cacophonic white. One moment, she was stopping Amir from charging into death and the next she was flat on her back at the mouth of the tunnel, a wasteland of rock at her feet.

Amir cradled her head, his face looming over her. His mouth was moving, but it took a little bit of time for her ears to stop ringing enough for her to hear what he was saying. "Hexene! Hexene!" Her name, as it turned out.

"I can hear you," she said, sitting up. Her head swam, but it was only a brief dip.

"What happened? How did you know?" Amir asked.

Hexene clambered to her feet while the balam hovered nearby, ready to catch her if she swooned. She was going to use every last bit of willpower not to. She wasn't the swooning type.

Mafaufau and Technika finally arrived. "Where is Calavera?" Technika asked.

"Mafaufau."

Hexene pointed. "The tunnel collapsed. It was hexed."

"How did you know? It was almost too dark for *me* to see," Amir said.

"Whoever did it had blown out the candles lighting the way. Who does that but someone who wants to hide hex marks?"

"I can think of many reasons to turn off the lights," Amir purred.

"In this context?"

"Well, no. Not in this context."

Hexene went to the mouth of the partly collapsed tunnel and grabbed a torch from the sconce. Zombies had begun to gather at the small intersection behind. They stared, muttering their single word back and forth, but none of them wanted to investigate any more closely.

Hexene went back into the tunnel, torch held high. The hex that had taken the ceiling was hastily drawn. The chalk outlines, now visible by the crackling light, were ragged and careless. The hex itself had been far from complete, too. In the moment, it had seemed like an apocalypse. Now, it looked like it was merely a layer of heavy rock jarred loose and turned into a killing rain. It might not even have done more than knock Hexene and Amir senseless, but Flaco Calavera was a zombie. Head trauma was their water.

Sure enough, they found Calavera lying facedown amid the rubble. A stone had obliterated a good half of his skull.

"Mafaufau," said Mafaufau, turning away.

Amir touched his arm. "It will be all right."

"No, it will not be," said Technika. "This zombie is dead."

Amir glared at her. "Imagine how you would feel had we happened upon a freshly watered robot."

"I would be pleased that such a stupid machine no longer troubled us."

"Have you no heart?"

"As it happens, no."

Hexene cursed. "Our one lead. Dead."

"There is still the final member of the triad. Fallow Graves," Technika said.

"And where's he?"

"Perhaps Mona knows," Amir said. Hexene nearly demanded to know who the hell Mona was before she remembered. The group at the bottom of the incline stared at Hexene and her companions. None of them moved. None said a word.

Hexene put the torch back on the sconce. She saw no buckets of water, but that didn't mean they weren't there. She couldn't stomach scampering down the damaged tunnel in some attempt to find a long way back to Mona Deth's place. That would have been admitting defeat, admitting weakness. She'd had enough of that.

Mafaufau came up next to her. She touched his leg and gave him a look. He understood, keeping pace with her rather than turning into the comfortable eclipse that had become their habit. The zombies watched the strange group pass by. Anger bled off them in sullen waves, but they didn't make a move, merely shifting away reluctantly to make room for Hexene and her group. She thought about telling them it wasn't her, but they wouldn't believe it. *She* wouldn't if she were in their position. The only ones who might have were Los Silenciosos, and despite what the witches aboveground thought, that organization was far smaller and more select than their inflated reputation implied.

The tunnel twisted away, but a small alley between a row of shacks led up to Mona Deth's now closed back door. The zombies below still watched, some from the central avenue, others from the tiny lots and front porches of their sagging shacks. Hexene had never seen a true angry mob form. Witches had stories about how they used to be, trotting them out whenever someone needed an explanation about why they had come into the light, as it were. But Hexene had seen children gather. Sometimes it was to take down a bully, but more often than not it was to hunt a person who was lower than them in the order of things. Without her magic, she might as well be Canela. She swallowed; there was no place to hide here. No familiar cool dark that still held her shape in the dirt from the last time she'd hidden there.

"They are not going to allow us to stay long without attacking," Technika pointed out.

"Oh, nonsense," Amir returned. "They are merely curious. I can't imagine there is much action here."

"In the endless tunnels beneath a city of witches?" Technika asked, and Hexene might have missed the bone-dry humor had she not gotten used to the robot.

"Mmm-hmm," Amir said guilelessly. "It is most quiet here."

Hexene knocked on the doorjamb. "Brains?" asked the voice on the other side.

"Miss Deth? I'm Hexene Candlemas. I wanted to talk to you."

"Brains!"

Amir shook his head. "May I?" Hexene nodded. He leaned onto the door, stroking it lightly with his finger. "My dear, we feel terribly about disrupting your evening. In truth, we wished only to speak to Mr. Calavera, but he has fled..." Amir stopped, shrugged, and continued, "...a long, long way away. But there is one other we wish to speak to. We will not harm anyone. We are a friend to all zombies, and if you like, I would be most pleased to be a special friend to you—"

"Amir!" hissed Hexene.

"You're right," said the balam, shaking his head. "She is beautiful, but she stirs not the jaguar inside. Miss Deth? I apologize, but I will not be attempting romance upon you."

The door opened. Mona Deth stood in the open hallway, her eyes hard as basalt. "Brains."

Amir shrugged. "It is a problem of late that—"

Hexene cut him off. "Flaco Calavera had a friend. Fallow Graves. Do you know where we could find him?"

"Brains," Mona said, with just the ghost of a headshake.

Hexene glanced down the hill. More zombies had gathered. "Can we go through here, please?"

Mona sighed. "Brains," she said, stepping aside and gesturing.

"Thank you," Hexene said. "You have a lovely home."

"In comparison," Technika said.

"Mafaufau."

"I must confess," Amir said, "I am a fan. Your voice is lovely."

"Brains," said Mona, offering a pained smile.

Hexene opened the front door and the others filed out ahead of her. The image of Flaco Calavera, his head smashed, wasn't going to leave her any time soon. She didn't know what his relationship with Mona was, what they'd meant to each other. She had to say something. "Mona? What happened to Flaco...that wasn't us. I'm looking for someone, and I'm pretty sure whoever that is, is who did it. So if you're looking for payback, I'll be getting it."

"Brains?" Mona asked, frowning. Then it dawned on her. "Brains!" She turned and shambled down the hallway to the back door. Hexene shut the front.

Twenty-Eight

As before, Mafaufau and Amir insisted on escorting Hexene and Technika to the gate of the Adepts' home. Along the way, they passed two more of Slick's posters.

"Eventually, you will explain, no?" Amir asked, gesturing at one.

"No," Technika said.

"If this Baron Sweettooth is a man whose nose I will be obliged to bloody—"

"It is none of your concern," Technika said.

"Don't worry," Hexene said to Amir.

"Mafaufau?"

"She'll tell you when she's ready," Hexene said quietly.

"Of course," Amir said. "One must coax the nectar—"

"She's not going to be ready if you keep talking like that."

Soon, they arrived at the Adepts' home and Amir and Mafaufau split off for Cogtown. Hexene was exhausted from the previous day and night, and was looking forward to a bit of rest. She didn't know where to find Graves, or if it was even possible, but she could hardly think in the state she was in. She just hoped that Calavera's corpse would let her sleep.

Two zombies murdered. It happened every day in every city across the world. No one cared about humans, sure, but humans could be turned into anything. There was potential there. Zombies had already been turned and so could be forgotten. Hexene had done it, the same as any other monster.

She wasn't a detective, but she also wasn't born yesterday. None of this was a coincidence. A witch murdered Calavera, and d'Arthur had been in a witch's cellar. She had to be crazy to walk right back into the house of the ones who probably did it and attempt to sleep, but the way she figured it, she'd be worse off if she started acting different. If they could keep tabs on her effectively enough for that collapsing tunnel gag, they'd find her wherever she ran, and she'd never see them coming. This way, she could keep an eye on them.

Or she was walking right into death. Here, without it washing at her heels, it was easy to think she might be better off if she gave in. After all, she didn't have her magic, didn't have her toad. Just a hollowed-out place inside where he should be. She found herself clenching her fists, knowing that this was what the murderer thought, too. Thought Hexene wasn't worth killing, or that she'd give into despair and take care of it herself. That alone was worth a punch in the nose.

"What is our next move?" Technika asked as they walked up the stairs.

"Didn't you want to talk it over with the others?"

"Not especially. Amir offers little of value, and Mafaufau would only tell us his name. Ours are the opinions that matter."

"Well," Hexene sighed, "I was thinking that for the time being we could probably deal with Slick. There's a chance he doesn't know about Amir and Mafaufau, and they could be just the weapons we need."

"I do not know if I wish to trust them with so sensitive an errand."

"Think about it," Hexene said. "Or else think about how we can find Graves."

"I have been devoting some energy to that conundrum. As a concierge, my occupation was assisting guests in locating whatever they required. Unfortunately, none of them ever needed to find a specific day laborer who appeared to be doing his best not to be found."

Hexene chuckled, shaking her head. "What?" Technika asked.

"No, it's just...I know someone whose job it is to find people."

"You should contact that individual."

"I'm just trying to think of what he would do. Maybe we should go back to the Scryline." Technika uttered a single long beep. Hexene didn't know if that was a yes, a no, or a defeated sigh.

Hexene went inside the house, and had to stifle a surprised squeak when Angelique grabbed her by the arm. "Hexene!" she hissed.

"What? What's going on?" Hexene's heart lurched against her ribcage, but she did her best not to show any fear.

"Hexene?" Technika asked.

The robot's face was a metal mask, her eyes featureless green lights. Experience alone let Hexene detect the faint lilt of the question in Technika's voice. The robot was asking if she should hurt Angelique. Hexene shook her head, then met Angelique's eyes. Hexene saw the same fear she was trying to hide.

"I need to talk to you," the other maiden said, her voice dropping to a whisper, "alone."

If Angelique wanted her dead, she could have just had zombies waiting on the other side of the door. The thought chilled her worse than the water, but there was some comfort there. Hexene nodded to Technika. "Yeah, it's fine. Why don't you go to our room? I'll be up in a minute." Technika beeped again, but went up the stairs.

"Come on," Angelique hissed, dragging Hexene from the foyer and through the house. Like every other building Hexene had seen in this place, the Adepts' home was a maze, and Angelique was taking her through a part where she'd never been. Hexene only then realized that she hadn't done much exploring here. She had kept to the route between her attic room, the kitchen and dining room, and the front door. Hexene had subconsciously kept this site of pain as impersonal as she could possibly make it.

Angelique finally stopped in a room that smelled strongly and pleasantly of cut wood. A half-finished wardrobe stood in one corner, tools next to it. A broom, freshly coated in flight oil, floated above a workbench. Tools of various kinds hung from stone hooks on the walls. Angelique shut the door behind them and took a deep breath.

"You nearly gave me a heart attack!" Hexene exclaimed. "The last time someone surprised me in this house, it was a bunch of zombies with water."

Angelique offered a weary smirk. "That wasn't the *last* time you were surprised here."

"I thought we weren't talking about that," Hexene said primly.

"We're not. And thank you for that. Right now, though, I really needed to talk to you, and you were out and I didn't know when you'd be back, so I just sat there waiting for you to come through the door."

"What happened? Why were you waiting for me?"

"Serafina and Evangeline were talking about you."

Hexene's blood turned to ice. She tried to keep the tremor from her voice, and mostly succeeded. She decided to play dumb. "I'm overstaying my welcome?"

"Not exactly. I was going into the conservatory, because I needed the wings of a bat...it's not important. I was going in, and they were talking, and I heard your name so I listened. I got the impression I was coming in on the end of whatever they were going on about."

"What did you catch?"

"Evangeline said something about the last Candlemas remaining. Serafina said the debt was almost paid."

"Debt? What debt?"

"I don't know! I thought you might."

"I didn't think we owed them anything. I mean, other than for letting us stay here."

"Witches always have some kind of feud. Could be from when Serafina and Hermosa were maidens for all we know."

"When we came here, Hechalé made it sound like Hermosa and Serafina had some beef in the past."

Angelique nodded. "Evangeline made some comments before you got here. 'Be nice when Hermosa gets here,' that kind of thing. Could it be that?"

Hexene shrugged. "No one can hold onto a grudge like a crone. But why now? And why wait?"

"When you're as old as Serafina, I don't think a month matters that much."

"What else did they say?"

"Nothing then. Evangeline saw me, so I came in and got what I was looking for, and pretended I hadn't heard whatever it was I heard. Serafina said they had to go take care of something, and they both left."

And went right to the cave-in, Hexene thought. With Angelique right next to her, it was difficult to think of anything beyond the path the other maiden mapped out. It made the kind of warped sense that this sort of thing had to. "Did they come back?"

Angelique nodded. "Not too long before you did."

Hexene felt like she did the night Escuerzo died. She had been at sea—literally—but once the stark terror had receded, all that was left was an empty place that she had no idea how to fill. "But why...I'm here. I'm always here."

"You haven't been here all day!" Angelique said. "It's why I scared you."

"I sleep here, though. If they wanted to do something, it's not hard to find the time."

"We don't have laws here, true. But just killing a witch under your roof? That's not going to make them popular."

"I'm not really a witch anymore."

"An unwitch, then."

"It doesn't add up. It doesn't make sense."

Angelique chuckled. "Everything a crone does is supposed to make sense now? Look, I found something for you." She ran to the workbench and rummaged below it. A moment later, she pulled out an old leather satchel, and from that, a lumpy scroll. Unrolling it revealed words tattooed across it in French. Hexene could catch some words if they were written down usually, but between the calligraphy and everything else, it was hardly recognizable.

Hexene passed her fingers over the lumps and abruptly felt sick. This was a tanned and prepared toadskin. For a split second, she was convinced the skin *was* Escuerzo, somehow transported here. *No*, she reminded herself, *Escuerzo is gone*. His body was obliterated by the mad scientist's device. There wasn't so much as a wart left of him, let alone a full hide.

"What's wrong?" Angelique asked.

"Toad," Hexene said.

"Oh? Oh!" Realization dawned on Angelique. "I wasn't thinking. I'm sorry. I found this in the library."

"*The* library?"

"*Our* library. They must have it, or something like it, in *the* library, but that doesn't matter."

"Angelique, it's in French."

"It's actually not French, I don't think. Not really."

"What made you think I could read it?"

"Oh, sorry."

Hexene stared at the bumpy skin. She wanted to touch it, to stroke the pebbly surface, but at the same time, she knew she would only feel death. This wasn't saying goodbye to her familiar, this was wallowing in his demise.

"The important part is what it says here." Angelique's slender finger traced the line of words. "It's written in verse, in a language that's mostly dead. I think it was originally spoken somewhere around Avignon, and then it wasn't usually written down. *I* can barely read it."

Hexene grabbed onto the lifeline: As long as she was annoyed, she wasn't grieving for her toad. "What does it say?"

"It says that there was a witch who regained her magic."

The bolt nearly staggered Hexene. She croaked through a suddenly dry mouth, "How?"

"A sacrifice. To the Many-Faced Goddess."

Unwitch Hunt

"There's nothing left to sacrifice," Hexene said. "Escuerzo was the only thing that I loved enough that it would be a sacrifice."

"Not like that, exactly. Don't think of it as a sacrifice for *you*, but rather one for *her*. What does the Goddess want more than anything?"

Hexene shook her head. She was coming up empty. As far as she knew, the Goddess was an abstract force given name and personality by minds too small to grapple with the alienating reality of a faceless force with ultimate power and no morality. The idea that she might *want* something was as bizarre to Hexene as learning that a table had a favorite color.

"*Witches*," Angelique said triumphantly.

"So I need to make a new coven?" There was a certain logic there. If—

"No."

"Oh. Then what?"

"You need to take the magic of other witches."

"How?"

Angelique swallowed, looking around the empty room as though spies might suddenly appear. "Kill them."

"What?"

"I know how it sounds. But look at it this way: You have two witches who murdered your coven and tried to do the same to you. Now you have not only a way to get even, you have the perfect reason. Right here." Angelique stabbed her finger onto a word scrawled across the toad's brow. Hexene barely saw the looping script. She wasn't certain how long she stared at the skin before she emerged holding a question.

"What are you doing? You're asking me to...this is your coven!"

"No," Angelique said. "They tried to kill a witch. I can't trust people like that." She took Hexene's hands in hers. They were warm, and Hexene felt herself trembling. "Besides, when it's done, you and I can form our own coven."

"Two maidens does not a coven make," she said, trying to look away, because she couldn't concentrate with the weight of Angelique's attention on her.

"I don't think it would be hard for me to transition to mother," she said, and Hexene was hit with the image of Angelique and Rodrigo again. "We can find a crone, I'm certain."

"Or I could be the crone," Hexene said thoughtfully.

"Or that." Angelique smiled.

It sounded like a wonderful idea. Not only to have a coven again, but to form one with Angelique Arcane. To have her magic and a new familiar. All it would take was violence—no, *vengeance*—and on the other side, the promise of a new life. Better than her old one.

The murder was between her and the promise of her new life. She could call it whatever she liked. Vengeance, justice, it didn't matter. She would be killing two witches. In Los Angeles, she had been a petty criminal, but she had known a few who were closer to the language of true violence. She had met the zombie enforcers for the Bellum crime organization. She had crossed paths with more than one goblin who made his money and his rhymes on threats and consequences. Hexene had always been different. She provided a simple service that happened to be illegal. What she was preparing to do now was entirely different.

"All right?" Angelique asked. Hexene found herself nodding.

Twenty-Nine

As she climbed into the attic room, Hexene's mind was like a hive of bees all buzzing for murder. Technika pulled her arm away from the ward drawn onto the wall, the last claws of lightning climbing up, scratching along the metal surface. She remained kneeling, turning her head all the way around to track Hexene as the maiden entered the room.

"You are not behaving as though you are preparing for sleep."

Hexene barely heard her. She wanted to pace around, but there wasn't much room to move, and besides, she could only stand up straight in the very center, across from their little window. Instead, she cracked her knuckles, one at a time, something she hadn't done since she was freshly turned.

"And now you are making different sounds," Technika continued.

"What?" Hexene couldn't remember what the robot had said.

"I am led to believe the other witch shared information with you that has altered the context of much that you know."

Hexene shook her head, then turned that into a nod, then back into a shake. "No. Well, yes. I don't know." The robot continued her expressionless stare, and Hexene spilled what Angelique had said.

Technika was silent, and save for the glow of her eyes, might as well have been dead. "I should preface this by saying that I understand the irony of me, who has been advocating for murder throughout our association, counseling against violence, but I would be remiss if I were to allow you to continue on your present course of action without voicing some misgivings."

Angelique's story still spun in Hexene's mind. She wanted to feel the broom under her and the sky around her, and the story put it there. "She had the scroll, and it squares with what Ravenna Crow told me."

"As you said, the scroll was in some unknown language. We do not know what it squares with, if anything."

"Are you saying she was lying?"

"I am saying we should fetch Amir to translate it and determine that it is, in fact, not instructions for how to turn a toad into a scroll."

"If I don't do it now, I'll lose my nerve."

"Perhaps that should be taken as evidence you should not do it."

"Technika, we're talking about my magic. If there's a way to get it back, I need to do it."

"You are not listening. We do not know if there is a way to get your magic back. Similarly, if there is such a way, we do not know that this is it. You have the word of one witch. All I am suggesting is obtaining additional evidence to confirm the facts of the situation."

Hexene blew out a breath she hadn't known she was holding. "You're advocating I trust Amir? I thought you hated him."

"I am beyond such prosaic emotions." Technika said imperiously. Then: "Yes, I hate him."

The laughter hit Hexene all of a sudden, the tension bleeding out through it. "And you still think I should talk to him."

"He appears more or less trustworthy and I do not believe he would maliciously mistranslate this scroll. Assuming he can understand the language."

"That's a fair assessment, I think. If anyone I've met so far would know some dead French dialect, it would be him."

"Indeed. Additionally, we do not have many translators to choose from. If you or I do not speak a language, we are forced to rely on Amir. I would regard this more as an object lesson in how far we have fallen."

"Right. Angelique had the scroll in the workroom we spoke in, so we should be able to look at it there. There's only the small matter of smuggling Amir inside. And Mafaufau."

"Why do we need Mafaufau?"

"He's one of us."

"We are an 'us' now?"

"Yeah. Three would feel better, but I can live with four."

"Had I known what witches were like, I might not have come to Las Brujas. Remain here. I will fetch the rest of us." Technika planted her hands on the floor, lifting herself off the stone. Then, with an unnatural swivel of her hips, she was on the stairs and walking down, the rest of her body twisting to face the front, joint by joint. Hexene silently wished her a quick trip to Cogtown. At least she, as a robot, wouldn't be overly harassed on the streets of the city. As soon as she left, Hexene realized that Technika hadn't voiced any concern over Slick. Was the robot valuing friendship over the awful potential of falling into the gremlin's clutches again? That was a lot more sentimentality than she would expect from Technika. Or herself.

If Evangeline and Serafina were behind it all, they had murdered Hexene's coven. And because it had taken Hexene so long to act, now they had zombie blood on their hands. Twice over, now, at least. Hexene couldn't imagine they, or any of the witches in this city, would shed any tears over a couple of dead zombies, but the other members of the Candlemas Coven, maybe. Hexene was no crusader, but what she found herself increasingly wanting to do felt like justice.

"Hexene?" The voice belonged to Little Raoul.

Hexene poked her head over the spiral staircase and found the middle-aged man at the bottom. "Yes?"

"It's time for breakfast," he said.

"Oh." Hexene looked at the window. Pink light streaked the sky. It was easy to lose track of time after a stakeout all night, and deep underground to boot. The weariness was in her bones, and her mind was as jagged as a shard of sunlight. She almost told Raoul to leave her alone, but caught the words before they left her mouth. "Coming."

Whatever was happening, she had to play along. Had to let the Arcane Adepts think she was the same Hexene, as clueless and pliable as always. She was barefoot when she went downstairs, something she would live to regret.

Raoul gave her a weary smile when she joined him on the landing. "I wasn't sure you would come."

"I'm hungry," she said simply.

They headed for the dining room, which took them through several hallways, a couple rooms, and finally to a staircase. After a few moments, Raoul asked, "How do you like Las Brujas?"

"It's different than I expected," she said diplomatically. "How do you like it?"

He shrugged. "I've never lived anywhere else."

"Do you ever think you might want to?"

"I don't know that there's still time for any of that."

"I'm sorry," she said.

"Nothing goes as you think it will," he said as they walked into the dining room.

The Adepts, and Evangeline's family, all turned to Hexene, mostly smiling in welcome. Serafina didn't, but then, it would have been far more suspicious if she had. Crones as a rule didn't smile unless they were about to enact a particularly gruesome curse on someone.

"Sorry I kept everyone waiting. I lost track of time." She sat down across from Angelique. Raoul sat next to her.

"No apology necessary," said Evangeline. "Please, eat something. You're much too thin."

The zombie servants, their mouths stuffed with hexes, brought in the food. Egg pies, fried greens, a plate of assorted cheeses, a bowl of fruit, a pot of honey, and two loaves of sweetened bread soon covered the table. The zombies then brought out pitchers of milk and tea. Serafina, as was proper, took her food first, then Evangeline, Hexene and Angelique, and finally the humans. Evangeline's cat sat on the table by its mistress, accepting food regally from her plate. Angelique's snake coiled around one of her arms, tasting the air.

As Evangeline was serving herself, she said, "You have an important task and it's no wonder that you might lose your schedule from time to time. I envy you a little bit, too. Getting to spend your days surrounded by such wisdom."

"Nothing stopping you," Serafina said. She spoke Spanish, which surprised Hexene. The cutting remark was intended for Evangeline, but the language said the crone wanted Hexene to hear it as well. Her dog barked, and the crone dropped some egg pie for it.

"I suppose not," said the miffed mother.

"Any luck yet, Hexene?" Angelique asked. Her smile was strained, her eyes hard.

"No, not yet," Hexene said. "The library is very big. It's one thing to say it has the accumulated wisdom of thousands of years of witches—it's another to try to navigate it."

"It's nice to see a maiden who reads," Serafina griped. "Don't see that too much anymore. That one just spends her time drinking with her friends."

"Weren't you a maiden once?" Angelique shot back.

"No proof of that."

"Well, if you were, you'd remember that doing that kind of thing is part of being a maiden."

"She's having her fun," Evangeline said. "Important for a maiden to sample her potions now, so when she transitions into being a mother, it's out of her system. She can concentrate on her family." She favored them with smiles, and laid a hand on her husband's leg. He looked as tired as all of his children.

"We're talking about me transitioning now?" Angelique asked, the question barbed.

Hexene did her best to eat. As hungry as she was, her anxiety kept her from tasting any of it. She had to force each mouthful down and feign as much enjoyment as she could manage.

"No, no," Evangeline said quickly. "Serafina still has some years left in her."

"More than a few."

Angelique shrugged. Hexene saw the tension in the gesture. It was too quick; no doubt she was as nervous as Hexene about sitting with these two after the murder attempt. "Then let me have my fun. When you tell me it's time, I'm sure I can find someone."

"Oh, listen to her," Serafina said. "So sure she can find a man."

Hexene nearly spat out her tea. Evangeline gave the crone a scolding look. "Our Angelique is as beautiful as the morning and you know it." She turned to Hexene. "Eat, girl, eat! You're skin and bones. It's not healthy." Hexene nodded and forced a mouthful of pie down her throat. It stuck halfway, and she gulped tea until it dislodged. She gave Evangeline a queasy smile.

"Tell me, my dear, what have you found in the library?" the mother asked.

"Yes, girl. Show our little maiden what she's missing," Serafina said.

Hexene cleared her throat, flicking a glance at Angelique. The maiden was eating, glaring at her food so she didn't glare at her coven. Hexene knew the gesture because she had done it more than once. Now, she would have given anything to be annoyed by her mother and crone.

"Well, as I said, there's a lot. I have a specific story about a witch who regained her magic. It sounds like I have to reforge a connection with the Many-Faced Goddess."

"I could have told you that," Serafina said.

"You could have saved me some time," Hexene snapped, and then caught herself.

Unwitch Hunt

Serafina stared hard at her. Hexene braced herself for a hex. Then the crone burst out into rattling laughter. "You could learn a thing or two from that one, Angelique."

"You just like her because she's a crone in a maiden's body," Angelique said sweetly.

"Angelique!" Evangeline scolded. "That's no way to talk about our guest."

"It's fine," Hexene said.

"Anything else?" Evangeline asked. "Just a connection?"

"A lot of it is sort of talked around. Losing magic isn't exactly a fun prospect for witches, so they tend to only bring it up when they absolutely have to. Most of the stories about this one witch who did it aren't actually about her. She's sort of in the background of other stories. It's a little frustrating."

"But you have found something," Evangeline exclaimed. "You should be proud of yourself."

Hexene glanced at Angelique. Maybe the other maiden knew what Hexene was going to say, because her eyes widened and she mouthed *No*. Hexene plowed ahead. "Have you talked to Las Barrenderas at all?"

"Why would we talk to them?"

"About Hechalé and Hermosa."

"Oh, yes," Evangeline cast her eyes down. It was a show, and to Hexene, it rang false. "We have, but there's not anything to report."

"Las Barrenderas," Serafina snorted. "Just a bunch of maidens running wild, doing whatever they want to do, whenever they want to do it. You want justice? You find it yourself."

Was that a challenge? "You have any ideas?"

"Whoever did it is underground now." As soon as Serafina said those words, Hexene saw Mort d'Arthur's corpse shoved under the cellar stairs, then Calavera broken in the tunnel. Literally underground.

"Why do you think they did it?"

"Why do zombies do anything?" Evangeline cut in. "They were those..." she waved her hand, trying to come up with the word.

"Los Silenciosos," Angelique said.

"You would think that a group calling themselves that would be a little quieter," Serafina muttered.

"I don't think it was them."

"Their mouths were sewn shut. You said that," Evangeline pointed out.

"Just because a zombie has his mouth sewn shut doesn't mean he's one of them. A hex could make him do that."

"Powerful hex."

"Easy enough if you already have the zombie. Take some skin, take some hair, what's he going to do?"

"Listen to her," Serafina said. Now the crone's voice was low with danger. "Telling us how to hex zombies."

"Do it a lot?" Hexene challenged.

"It's how it's done here. Suppose it's a little different back in America."

"It is."

"When you have a mummy running things, there's no end to the foolishness."

"Their president is a vampire," Evangeline corrected, but she was staring hard at Hexene. Her familiar flicked its tail back and forth.

"A vampire, even worse."

"Sweetheart," Evangeline started, and here Hexene was already finished listening, as was her custom when anyone who wasn't Hechalé started a sentence that way. "This place is how things should be."

"I don't know how you can say that to me."

"In our house, we say what we please!"

"Especially," rumbled Serafina, "to an unwitch who should be happy we haven't handed her to Las Barrenderas already."

"What?" Hexene shook her head in shock. "What did I do?"

"This whole time, none of this smelled right, girl. You know that. Much as I might like you, might think you could set an example for others, I can't shake the thought. The thought that Hechalé and Hermosa died because of you." Her familiar's growl was low and dangerous.

"That's mad. I don't have any reason to hurt my own coven."

"I said the same thing," Evangeline said, nodding sadly, "but we could be better safe than sorry. Torpe?"

Hexene didn't even have time to look around before the zombie's strong hands clamped down on her shoulders. She might know how to hit, she might even be strong for her size, but she wasn't that big, and any zombie in Las Brujas spent time doing manual labor. She felt the seconds stretch out, blood pounding in her ears. The skin of Torpe's hands was fraying like an old blanket. He was missing the nail on his left middle finger.

"It's all right, Hexene," Evangeline said. "This will be completely painless. We're going to see what you know and what you don't."

Serafina was already scribbling onto a small piece of paper, etching the Theban letters that would focus the Many-Faced Goddess's power through the crone's will. She put the quill down, peering over the table before selecting a few of the pots of spices they had recently been using as seasoning. Salt, powdered ant fungus, some eye of newt, and a little ground-up holly. She made a hill on her plate, rolled the scroll, and gently sucked the mix up into the cylinder.

"What are you doing?" Hexene demanded, unable to tear her eyes from the preparation.

"You're such a good witch," Serafina taunted, "you should know."

Hexene did know. It was the ant fungus that spoiled the game. This was a mind-control hex, but a simple one—the good stuff would take time and effort, rather than this jerry-rigged nonsense. Of course, a smart witch, a witch experienced with this stuff, could use a hex like that to gentle someone long enough to prepare the good one. Easier to slap manacles on wrists that were hogtied with twine. That was why Hexene struggled, even knowing it was futile. Torpe was no Mafaufau, but he had strength and leverage on his side.

"Calm down," Evangeline said. She still retained the aura of a mother, but now the comforting waves felt wrong. "This will be over quickly. We're just going to find out exactly what's going on here. François? Why don't you get everyone out of here."

"Mother," Raoul started.

"It's all right, love. She'll be just fine and you can get back to making eyes at her across the dinner table. Oh, don't think I didn't notice."

"Come now," said François, Evangeline's husband. Chairs scraped against the floor as the humans left the table.

Hexene turned from witch to witch to witch, landing on Angelique. The other maiden's eyes were wide. She was paralyzed as surely as Hexene was, but no zombie held her fast. Even Danbala, her snake, looked hypnotized. Angelique caught Hexene's look and finally spoke up. "Wait, what are we doing?"

"What we should have done weeks ago," Serafina said. "But someone said that this one needed time to grieve. She's had it, and now I've had it."

"I don't like it, but we owe it to Hechalé and Hermosa to know for sure."

"Open your mouth, girl," Serafina said, rising from her chair, clutching the scroll in one talon. Her dog advanced beside her, a snarl rippling its lip. "Won't hurt, won't take long."

Hexene thrashed, but Torpe held her fast. Serafina advanced while Evangeline stood on the other side of the table and shook her head sadly. Her cat licked its forepaw and passed it demurely over its ear. Angelique was a sudden blur of movement, striking like a snake. She ransacked the table, overturning more pots of spices as she frantically gathered a hex.

"Have you lost your mind?" Evangeline demanded. The cat yowled. "You're making a mess!"

But Angelique ignored her, crafting a hex, barely hung together with salted spit and Theban verbs. Serafina clamped a hand on Hexene's jaw. The edge of the scroll smashed into her closed mouth. "Open up," demanded the crone. The dog's snarl turned into barking.

Then Angelique's chair fell backward and the maiden was standing, holding her plate in front of her. She blew the dust over Serafina's face and followed it with a quick Theban incantation and a few gestures. The air between them shuddered. The dog yelped. "What do you..." the crone started, and while Hexene imagined that the rest of the sentence was supposed to be *think you're doing*, the rest of the words came out scrambled. She still caught the edges of them, attesting to how flimsy the hex was, but it would stop Serafina from finishing any hexes of her own for a short while.

"What are you doing?" Evangeline shouted.

Angelique bolted from the room, leaving the mother staring after her in confusion. Torpe still held Hexene, but Serafina had let go, babbling in the made-up language the hex had turned hers into. Hexene caught syllables here and there, the hex already giving way under the crone's iron will. The dog barked, but even that sounded backwards.

Evangeline said something to Serafina in French—there was no need to include Hexene in any further conversation. It was easy enough to figure out what, as Evangeline started around the table and Serafina held out the hex to the mother. The cat bounded over the plates and silverware, growling deep in its throat.

"I don't know what she was thinking," Evangeline said in Spanish, this time to Hexene. "I know she's taken a shine to you, but we're not going to hurt you. We're just borrowing your will for a little while. Nothing to be afraid of. You'll have everything back before you know it."

The splash froze Hexene. For a moment, she was certain she had been hit, that she would watch her body turn to smoke before her eyes. The long red scars on her arm burned in expectation of agony. She waited for the pain to explode across her, but she felt nothing outside of her scars. She kept waiting.

Serafina was right over her, one hand still clamped over Hexene's chin, the other holding the scroll out to Evangeline. The mother stared in abject horror, a scream caught just behind her teeth. Smoke rose from behind Serafina, like a fire had been lit. The smell wasn't burning wood; it was like the aftermath of a lightning strike. It was scorched air. Serafina's expression, which had been frustrated confusion over Angelique's tangled tongue hex, went slack. Her rheumy crone's eyes went wide in abject terror.

She shrieked.

The sound sliced through Hexene like a razor. The hex lost its grip on Serafina, unable to hold on through the abject need of that sound, and the scream came out exactly as she had intended. She staggered backward, her arms reaching up as though to claw something on her back. There wasn't anything there. That's what Hexene saw when Serafina turned around in the grips of her pain: a growing hollow where her back had been. It collapsed in smoking chunks, like waves eating away at a wall of sand. The smoke of Serafina's death was what smelled of ozone. The crone collapsed to her knees. The shriek continued, but it had found a new note: a keening wail that added an emotional anguish to the physical.

At the same time, her dog turned to embers. Its frantic barking turned to squeals, and those vanished as the embers floated into the air like fireflies and were gone.

Behind her was Angelique, two of the servant zombies by her side. One held a bucket out, a few drops falling from its lip. The other held a full bucket.

"Angelique, what are you doing?" The look in Evangeline's eyes was an inch from madness. Hexene knew that if she had looked into a mirror after seeing Hechalé and Hermosa die, she would have seen that same expression looking back at her.

Angelique stared at Serafina as the crone dissolved. Horror washed over the maiden's face, but also elation. What had just happened had been a culmination, but it hadn't been exactly what she had thought. She turned on Evangeline. The mother took a step back, hands up. The cat hissed, its black fur standing on end.

"No, Angelique. You can't mean this."

Hexene muttered, "No." Torpe's hands came free from Hexene's shoulder. Either his command had been fulfilled, or else this moment had overpowered his hex as well.

The maiden swallowed. "I have to," she murmured. "I've come too far not to." The snake hugged her with his coils.

"No, you haven't. There is still time to stop. We can each transition, just like you wanted. We even have a new maiden right here." Evangeline gestured to Hexene.

Angelique followed the gesture, but snapped back to Evangeline, as though she didn't want to look at the other witch. "Her? She's useless. No magic."

"She can get it back. We'll help her at the library. We'll find a way."

"No. She doesn't have any guts, either. I gave her a path. I told her what to do and she didn't do it."

"Give her a chance. Give me a chance."

"You both had your chances." Angelique nodded and the other zombie threw the bucket's worth of water all over Evangeline. The mother screamed, but that was gone too as her face crumbled inward on itself. Hexene swore she could still hear the shriek in the air long after Evangeline's head disappeared beneath the onslaught of water. Her cat turned into embers and vanished with one last yowl. Hexene knew that she would see that abomination whenever she closed her eyes.

"Torpe, hold her." Angelique's voice quavered. She wouldn't look at the discolored stain that was her crone, nor the rapidly shrinking mound that used to be her mother. The zombie's hands clamped down over Hexene's shoulders once again.

"Mala," she said to the other zombie, "fetch Las Barrenderas." Angelique locked her eyes on Hexene, a terrible emptiness yawning behind them. Hexene didn't think it had been there the whole time. It had been hollowed out when the water had done the same to the rest of her coven. "Tell them I've detained a murderer."

Thirty

To the naked eye, the pentagram didn't really look like much. A Christian might have gotten the wrong impression about it and looked frantically for someone to burn, but to anyone else, it was just a large star etched out in chalk on a floor with candles burning at each point. Completely normal under some very specialized circumstances.

Power shone through every line of the pentagram. If she shut her eyes, Hexene could still see it, burned in afterimage. Brightest at the candlepoints, but every line still gave enough light to read by—if she could read with her eyes closed. It wasn't just sight, either. A hum kept rattling at her bones, persistent in the background at most times, but never benign enough to completely forget. If she got close to one of the lines, the shuddering grew more and more violent until it threatened to shake her to pieces, like a brick building on a fault line. She didn't want to think what would happen to her if she actually tried to cross one of the chalk lines. She wasn't even sure she *could*. There was a smell, too. It was the smell of atomized magic, with just a soupçon of burnt hair.

The hair, of course, was her own. It had been pulled from her head by the first Barrenderas who had arrived with one of the killer zombies. Hexene knew it was unfair to think of the zombies that way. Made about as much sense as blaming the blade on behalf of the hand who swung it. The witches of Las Brujas had turned the local zombies into mere tools. The zombies—Graves, Calavera, and d'Arthur included—had committed murders they had no say in.

The Barrenderas who arrived to arrest her wore the sigils of the Caribbean Quarter—the traditional voodoo doll, a two-masted pirate ship, a stylized sea turtle, and manacles with a broken chain that Hexene had seen her first night at Le Chaperon Rouge. The dour maidens listened as Angelique tearfully explained that Hexene had murdered both Evangeline and Serafina. Hexene could only hiss and spit like a cat; Angelique had worked up another tangled-tongue hex, a better one this time, before the Barrenderas arrived.

Las Barrenderas nodded and hauled Hexene away, arguing amongst themselves over who had to touch the unwitch. Now that she was a murderer, any semblance of politesse was out the window. Finally, they picked one, a young woman with a hangdog face and skin like spilled milk, and she donned gloves before heaving Hexene to her feet and clapping a pair of manacles on her that buzzed like a hive of cheesed-off bees.

They dragged her off to the Caribbean Ward, a building that looked a bit like a partially melted plantation in old Saint-Domingue. Every witch they passed stared at her like she was a cockroach found hiding under the last bite of a good meal. Her captors brought her up to a tower room, where one yanked the hairs from her head while another drew the pentagram on the floor. A third sprinkled speckled powder along the lines. Hexene's hairs were long and looped in curls; they wrapped them around the candles, lighting each one. Finally, her captor hurled her into the center of the pentagram, and all the candles were stuck into their proper places. The invisible cage was secure.

The pentagram was designed to keep her right where she was. And it had done so admirably in the two days since she had been arrested. The room was about the same size as her room back in the Adepts' home, and that little irony amused her for about half a second. It even had a window, though that was too high off the ground for her to see anything beyond a thin wedge of sky. The rest was bare, and it really did look like she imagined one of those tower dungeons from medieval times would have. The pentagram took up the center of the room. It wasn't quite large enough for her to lay down and stretch out, and it wasn't against any walls, so her choices were between standing up, sitting down, and curling up in a despairing, fetal ball. She spent roughly equal amounts of time in all three configurations.

Her mind was mostly occupied with Angelique Arcane. Hexene had thought of herself as a pretty savvy person. She had, after all, slung hexes in one of the savviest cities in the world. Having misread Angelique so badly, she now had to face the fact that not only could she not see trouble coming, but she had a whole *history* of not seeing trouble coming. That was exactly how she ended up without a familiar in the first place.

Having her self-image shattered would normally have been enough to snap the rest of her, and that was *before* she had to contend with her coven being killed and the last words exchanged with her mother being hateful ones, seeing two more witches dissolved in front of her eyes, and the betrayal of someone she thought of as a friend.

To keep herself from sinking into a black place deep inside, she tried to trace what had happened. Angelique had hexed three zombies to murder the Candlemas Coven. She'd mostly succeeded. Then she bumped off first one, then two of her weapons, most likely to cover her tracks. She tried to get Hexene to go after the other two Arcane Adepts, and when Hexene hadn't immediately jumped to her bidding, had seized a moment and offed the two of them herself. It was a lot of death. And all for love.

Angelique had told her as much when Hexene caught the two of them together. She was in love, and she wanted to be a mother. She had wanted to be a mother for years, decades maybe. The Arcane Adepts hadn't let her. They had taken away love after love and eventually whatever good had been inside Angelique had broken. At some point, the monstrous act of sororicide had become a reasonable solution. The answer had been in front of Hexene more or less since the first night at Le Chaperon Rouge, barely hidden behind a few innocent questions and moments hanging in the air, missed because Angelique was so easy to listen to. So easy to believe.

Visitors came and went while Hexene was in different states. Some came by to call her an unwitch and mock her for her lack of familiar. Others just gawked. They brought her a tray of food on the morning of her second day. Hexene knew no one had spat in it, simply because no witch was foolish enough to leave her spit lying around where anyone could use it. Didn't matter that she was an unwitch; the prohibition was too strong. Not that the stale bread and rancid milk were worth eating anyway.

Her first real visitor came about halfway through the second day. A maiden like everyone else, she had dark skin and hair the color of bronze. She wore a black dress and cloak, both adorned with the heraldry of the Caribbean Ward. Her eyes were bright, nearly yellow. A large crab sat on her shoulder, its claws held high.

"Good afternoon," she said. Her Spanish was polite, and carried the same accent as Angelique's. Hexene didn't bother to respond. If there was to be bullying, Hexene knew better than to participate. She merely stared back, silently daring the other maiden to move onto the other side of the pentagram and say whatever she was going to say. This maiden, though, was reserved. "Hexene Candlemas, though you are no longer a true witch as recognized by the Many-Faced Goddess, you were once one of us. It is that former connection that brings me to you now. Tomorrow you will face a tribunal to determine the fact of your guilt."

Hexene snorted. "The *fact* of my guilt."

The maiden didn't blink. "You were captured in the house of a coven in good standing with an eyewitness to the two murders you committed. You should be pleased you're getting a trial at all."

Hexene made an obscene gesture before she could reflect, and was happy with herself. Maybe the old Hexene wasn't entirely gone.

"Lovely. Now, do you have any questions or requests?"

"Do I get a lawyer?"

"We don't have lawyers in Las Brujas. Not enough vampires here, and we like it that way. If you want someone to speak on your behalf, you can have an advocate. If you provide a name and their quarter of residence, we can bring her to you."

"It has to be a witch."

The laugh came so suddenly, up from the maiden's diaphragm, that it was clear that the comment caught her off guard. "I didn't know you were so funny."

"So that's a yes."

"Of course it is. Do you have someone?"

"No." A fleeting thought of Lily Salem ran through Hexene's mind, but she was back in LA. They weren't going to send someone to Hollywood to pick her up, and it wasn't like Lily knew how to navigate Las Brujas any better than Hexene.

"Good. That simplifies things, anyway. The trial will consist of a presentation of evidence, and you will of course be allowed to speak in your own defense. Tell your side of the story, though I can't imagine what that might be."

"That I didn't do it, that I was set up, that kind of thing."

"I wouldn't use that if I were you, but I suppose it doesn't matter in this case. In the event that you're found guilty, you will be sentenced to death by water."

Hexene shuddered. The other maiden was so casual. She thought nothing of throwing one of her own to the deep. "Sounds efficient."

"We don't have much of an occasion to use it."

"I thought Las Brujas didn't have laws."

The maiden chuckled. This one was pure calculation. "There's one law, but no one has ever needed to write it down. Witches feud all the time. Sometimes all the way to the grave. A witch who hunts multiple members of her own kind, who uses water to do it, is a rare bird indeed. It's the kind of bird that all of Las Brujas has a vested interest in removing, and so we do it. No one enjoys it, but it's a need."

"I didn't do it," Hexene murmured, mostly to herself.

"It's good that you're already accepting what has to happen. The Many-Faced Goddess lived at one time through you, and though she took back her grace, it would behoove you to make your peace with her before the dunking. Now, would you like anything specific for supper? I see you didn't eat very much bread, and your milk hasn't been touched."

"If I asked, would you get it for me?"

"Of course. What would you like?"

"Why?"

"Some of my comrades might be here for retribution, but I am here for justice, and justice does not preclude you eating an apple or drinking milk that hasn't already turned to yogurt."

Hexene thought it over. "Tea."

"Tea? Any particular kind?"

"Whatever you have here."

The maiden nodded. "I'll bring it up myself. Now, if you'll push your tray to me?"

Hexene nudged the tray to the edge of the pentagram. The hum wormed its way through her, sinking talons into her bones. She winced and retreated, watching the maiden. Hexene briefly entertained the notion of striking when she took the tray, maybe dragging her into the pentagram, but she didn't. She was too tired, and the Barrendera too quick. She grabbed the tray and disappeared down the stairs.

Hexene was slightly surprised when the other maiden returned with a pot of tea and a single cup on a tray. She placed it just inside the pentagram and stepped back, once again quickly enough that Hexene had no time to do anything. Not with everything from fatigue to despair conspiring to drag her down into the water, along with her inevitable verdict.

So she sat, cross-legged in her prison, and sipped tea, trying to think of any way to save herself.

Thirty-One

The manacles buzzed against Hexene's wrists, chafing her with their insistent magic. Her captors were thorough, or at the very least smart enough to keep her bound as soon as they took her from the pentagram. That had been easy enough, too. They simply extinguished the candles at the five points and the screen fell. Hexene took a deep breath, suddenly surfacing after having no idea she had been drowning.

"Come with me," said the maiden who had talked to her before. The crab on her shoulders beckoned with one claw.

Hexene acquiesced, and went ahead of the jailer on the way down the stairs. Other Barrenderas waited at the bottom, closing in around her. Their familiars growled, or clicked, or squawked as Hexene drew close. The witches took her through a few hallways of the Ward, then up two flights of stairs to emerge on the rooftop. Night gathered overhead, threading out long pink tendrils. The flat area of the roof featured stone racks where a number of flying devices, mostly brooms, waited. Hexene's captor gestured to a wardrobe. "Get in," she said.

The wardrobe opened its doors for Hexene like a hungry beast. The wood inside was etched with Theban protection charms, all of them glistening with flying ointment. Hexene climbed in and the other witch followed. "You will want to hang on," the witch told her, indicating a small ring on the floor nearby. Hexene sat down in the corner, her manacled arms awkwardly behind her. She wasn't going to hang on. She had been part of the sky once, and she wasn't going to let this witch treat her like she wasn't. Besides, the worst that would happen would be a fall, and she was going to be executed anyway.

"Suit yourself." The wardrobe lurched into the air. Witches on broomsticks rose up all around them. The entire flotilla then streaked over Las Brujas, heading for the Stone Forest. Dry wind buffeted Hexene from inside the wardrobe. Her bare feet were frozen. She refused to close her eyes, as though that was some kind of moral victory. It was one she would fight and win, simply because she knew she wasn't going to win anything else that night.

The trip was a quick one. Getting to the center of Las Brujas from the Caribbean Ward would have taken hours on foot, even if she had used the Catacombs. In the air, it was a trifle.

Other witches had already gathered, though there were far fewer than had been at either Sabbat. Hexene wasn't sure if she should be offended or not. The murder trial of an unwitch had to be worth something. She saw a few familiar faces: Angelique Arcane, Petunia Pendulum and the maiden who had been with them that other night at Le Chaperon Rouge, the Crow Sisterhood, and the Moirai. Friendly faces, or as close as Mafaufau, Technika, and Amir would provide, were absent. This was a place for witches. And one soon-to-be swimming unwitch. She shifted, her feet cold against the rock. Somehow, being barefoot made her feel smaller. Weaker.

Las Barrenderas fanned out along the stage behind Hexene. She felt them staring at her back. A witch had the power to turn her hatred into something tangible; these seemed like they were trying to do that without a visit to their local apothecary. Hexene stood as straight as she could manage under the attention. She knew she didn't cut an especially impressive figure, but she was going to do what she could with what she had. Not much in both cases.

Angelique was sitting with her friends, and the Crow Sisterhood were clustered in a small group as well. The Moirai were right in front of her, halfway up the riding levels. Other than the Barrenderas behind Hexene, they were the only ones standing.

The Moirai, unlike Hexene, were impressive. They looked like they could have been turning sailors into pigs thousands of years ago. All three—Morta the crone, Decuma the mother, and Nona the maiden—were skyclad, as though human ideas about modesty were too primitive for them. Nudity marked them as stodgy traditionalists, sure, but somehow managed to add to their formidable mien. Their features were uniformly bold, with large, expressive eyes, heavy brows, and beaklike noses. The maiden's hair was a deeper red than Hexene's, and fell in graceful ringlets rather than Hexene's wild curls. The mother's hair was piled on her head in black-and-silver braids. The crone's hair was snow-blind white and fell around her shoulders.

Their familiars each took dignified postures next to them. A black cat sat regally next to Nona. An owl sat on Decuma's shoulder, its talons drawing pinpricks of blood. A baseball-sized spider crawled from one of Morta's shoulders to the other.

"Hexene Candlemas," said the crone Morta. "You are here to answer for the most serious crime a witch can commit upon another. The murder of your sisters." She spoke Theban with some kind of Mediterranean accent. It sounded false to Hexene, but she suspected that was because the specific accent the witch used didn't exist anymore. The crone's aura of fear reached out with hungry claws to throttle Hexene.

"You will be allowed to speak in your defense," the mother Decuma said. Her accent was almost identical to the crone's. As she spoke, her aura reached out and Hexene felt a combination of guilt and comfort.

"We are here for the truth and the truth alone," said the maiden Nona. Hexene felt brushes of her aura now, too, and couldn't decide if she wanted to trust the maiden in her obvious lie, or if she wanted to stroke the Lily doll. She could do neither out of purely practical concerns.

"I'm innocent," Hexene said. She wasn't certain she'd said it, so she said it again, this time louder. A few of the witches in the audience started to murmur, but that stopped as soon as the Moirai crone responded.

"You will be allowed to speak *later*," Morta said.

"The congregation will hear Angelique Arcane now," said Decuma.

Petunia Pendulum and the maiden whose name Hexene didn't know helped a swaying Angelique to her feet. Hexene had lived in Hollywood until recently and had to give the other witch credit; this was a hell of a performance. She would have liked to have a little gold statue on hand to give her when this was over. Angelique nodded to her friends, feigning bravery before imparting the story of Hexene Candlemas, Unwitch Witch Hunter to the assembled witches.

"I am here," Angelique said.

"Tell your story," said Nona.

"True as you can make it," Morta said.

Angelique nodded, batting those eyes that had until recently beguiled Hexene. The congregation, even the amphitheater itself, seemed to lean closer, as though Angelique's words were some kind of blessing. The sad thing was, Hexene knew she would be right there with them if she hadn't seen Angelique do what she did.

"My name is Angelique Arcane. I am the maiden of the...Arcane Adepts." Her voice broke here, and Petunia patted her on the arm. Something about that gesture rang false. Maybe it was paranoia. Hexene shifted her attention to the black bat clinging to Petunia's tall hat. It never moved. The same as Angelique's serpent, draped over his mistress's neck like a meaty scarf. "I didn't know Hexene Candlemas or any of the Candlemas Coven. Their mother and crone knew my mother and crone. I think they all used to live here. We had heard that they—"

Morta broke in. "The Candlemas Coven?"

"Yes."

"Be clear. Always be clear. A sister's life is at stake," Decuma said.

Hexene resisted the urge to roll her eyes, but only barely.

"The Candlemas Coven had lost their magic. Evangeline—that was my mother—she told me the story on the night before the Candlemas witches arrived. Hexene, their maiden, had been slinging hexes in Los Angeles."

"Is that slang?" growled Morta.

"It means she was selling hexes to whomever would pay," said Nona. "Unsavory, but common outside of our utopia."

"Utopia?" blurted Hexene.

"Yes," said Nona in a voice that might as well have had literal icicles on it. "I suppose someone like you might find it wanting."

"Someone like me, someone like a zombie—"

"Tut!" shouted Morta. "Zombies are not at issue here. We did not ask the zombies to move here; they did that on their own. Now they complain at how they are treated? Now, Hexene Candlemas, you might have had your manners burned from you while selling the gift the Many-Faced Goddess saw fit to bestow, but here in this hallowed place, the Stone Forest of our city, you will hold your tongue."

The crone's aura, no doubt perfected over millennia, reached over Hexene like a twilight shadow. Though Hexene wanted to fight, she was suddenly hyperaware that she was the one person in the amphitheater without magic. So she quailed and hated herself for it.

"Continue," Decuma said to Angelique.

"While meeting with a client, Hexene's familiar was stolen away, and later on, the same person took the familiars of the rest of her coven. It turned out to be a mad scientist."

The murmurs started up again, the entire audience agreeing that it was evil, tragic, and totally expected. The Moirai didn't react to any of this, implying that they were as supportive as statuary was likely to be.

Angelique went on: "They were coming here, to Las Brujas, to research a way to regain their magic. My coven hosted them. They were very nice houseguests. Their mother was sweet. She helped around the house. Hexene and I became friends. Or...I thought we were friends." Petunia patted her arm. Hexene silently wished both of them death by immediate explosion.

"Then, one evening, I heard a commotion coming from the guest room where they were staying. We got down in time to see zombies rushing out the door. The Candlemas witches were gone, but there was clear..." She swallowed, looking so queasy Hexene couldn't tell if it was an act or not. "...evidence that at least two had been killed. With water."

Gasps filled the amphitheater. More than one mother swooned. Every crone present glared daggers at Hexene, and she felt the poke and prod of their auras. It was an act of will not to flee.

"At first, we thought Hexene was dead too, but she turned up at a Ward claiming she had fled from the zombies. We took her at her word then. Why wouldn't we? Things were fine for weeks and weeks. She went back to her research. But then a few nights ago, I was coming down to supper and she had two zombies with buckets filled from our own cistern. By the time I got there, she had...Evangeline was melting. I saw it, with my own eyes. Saw her melting."

Hexene thought Angelique was laying it on a little thick, but the assemblage seemed to be buying it. "Hey, any reason you didn't put a truth hex on her?" Hexene asked suddenly, nodding at Angelique.

A lot of eyes swung to her, but the ones that concerned Hexene the most were those belonging to the Moirai crone. "We don't impugn the honor of a sister in good standing. A hex slinger from the north might need a good hex to keep her tongue where it should be."

"Go ahead," challenged Hexene. She grabbed the anger, the frustration. That alone was something of a shield against the suffocating aura of fear billowing off the crone. "I'd love for you to know the truth."

"Her zombies threw the water at Serafina, and it didn't get her all at once." Angelique spoke loudly, quickly, doing what she could to cut Hexene's plea off at the base. "She half dissolved. The screaming...I can still hear it now."

"That's your conscience," Hexene called out.

"Silence!" shouted Morta.

Hexene felt herself cowering before she could recover. The words had the desired effect, though: Angelique was momentarily rattled. She made a show of collecting herself. Dabbing prettily at some tears, groping for Petunia's hand and squeezing it. Stroking the scales of her familiar, though—Hexene knew that was directed at her. A silent taunt. *Look what I can do and you never will again.* Hexene thought of the toadskin scroll and nearly cursed aloud.

"I was able to subdue her with a hex and the help of our zombies that she hadn't corrupted. I called Las Barrenderas, and they took her."

"Why?" asked Morta.

Angelique stared blankly, the shock momentarily pulling her from her theatrics. "Why did Las Barrenderas take her?"

"No, foolish girl. Why did Hexene Candlemas do this?"

"I...I...I shouldn't have said anything."

"What did you say, dear?" asked Decuma.

"I found a reference in the library. I thought it might help Hexene. It was a scroll that told some of the story of a witch who had lost her familiar but had created a new one out of the Goddess's will. She needed to make a sacrifice. I thought it would be something of Hexene's. But I think *she* thought it had to be a witch."

"This was before her coven was killed?" Angelique nodded, the very picture of innocence. Hexene would have sacrificed a great deal to kick Angelique as hard as she could. "Very well. You may sit," said Morta.

Angelique obeyed, holding Petunia's hand and putting her head on the maiden's shoulder. The maiden that Angelique had paraded in front of Hexene the instant it became obvious her powers were gone and weren't coming back easily. Hexene stared at the three of them, and saw a coven. This time she *did* curse, a muttered "Coño," as she put those three pieces together. She remembered what Angelique had told her about Petunia: her coven had all died, save her. Now Angelique's was dead, too. If this was what it looked like, the maiden's coven was in grave danger.

"Hexene Candlemas!" Morta barked.

"Huh?"

"If we aren't distracting you, we would now be willing to hear your story."

Hexene looked from face to face. She saw no sympathy until she found the moon-like face of Cora Crow. The maiden watched her with sad interest, her rook preening its mistress's red curls. Hexene swallowed her emotions because she knew they would do her no good here. Besides, she was madder than anything else. Mad at herself for losing the familiars, mad at Las Brujas for being what it was, mad at Angelique for setting this whole thing in motion. She spoke because she had no other choice, and she wanted to convince someone, even if it was just Cora Crow, that she wasn't a murderer.

"All right. I don't think it will matter much. Seems like the decision's been made. I'm an outsider. I sold our gifts. I'm an unwitch. But here it is for all of you. On the night my coven was murdered, I woke up in the middle of the attack. I watched zombies douse my mother and my crone. Watched both of them die. Then I ran, and those zombies chased me all the way to Cogtown. Later on, I found one of these same zombies, dead in the Arcane Adepts' basement."

"This corpse is still there?" Nona asked.

"Of course not," Hexene spat. "Angelique was careless to put him there at all, but she's not stupid. She's long since gotten rid of him, somewhere. Buried out in the desert for all I know. Eaten by a blob, maybe. There's one in their bathroom who could do the job. Anyway, she came to me the other day with a scroll—this was right before her coven died, but over a month after mine did, she was lying there—and told me that I needed a sacrifice to get my magic back. She was specific, though. The sacrifice had to be witches, and she suggested the rest of her coven. She told me they were the ones who killed Hechalé and Hermosa. I believed her at the time, too, because, well...look at her. You *want* to believe her."

"So you went to kill her coven."

"No. I thought about it, but a friend of mine talked me out of it. She told me that I should get a translation of the scroll before I did anything.

The scroll was in some kind of French, and I couldn't read it."

"Then you warned the Arcane Adepts," said Decuma.

"No," Hexene said, and winced. "I wasn't sure what to think yet. I didn't have the translation. The only translator I could trust was in Cogtown, and he hadn't gotten back to me."

"You trust someone in Cogtown?" growled Morta. "There wasn't a witch you could talk to?"

"Witches don't want much to do with me. Can't imagine why."

"I can think of a reason or two."

"At supper, just after I sent for the translator I mentioned, Evangeline and Serafina wanted to put a hex on me. They wanted to see what I knew about everything. I think they suspected me of being a killer. I think maybe Angelique talked to them about it, too, so the three of us would fight. Things...escalated."

"You're claiming self-defense," Decuma said.

"No. In the middle of it, Angelique stepped in. She hexed Serafina, then left. When she came back, she had two hexed zombies with water. She killed the two other Adepts and held me for Las Barrenderas." Hexene jabbed the air with her finger. "You want proof? The zombies who were used as weapons were hexed. I *can't* hex. I've lost my familiar. I have no magic."

"You have these hex scrolls?" Nona asked.

"No," Hexene admitted, "but how else am I supposed to have forced zombies?"

"Zombies don't need much forcing," Morta said. "A whole cell of their butchers is beneath our feet. Besides, a maiden has other ways of getting what she wants out of someone."

Hexene was almost insulted. "The cave-in! I almost had one of the zombies, but a witch hexed the tunnel and killed him."

"Down in the Catacombs?" Morta asked. "No. We're not so foolish to descend into that cemetery."

"I'm giving you evidence! You just have to collect it! That's all!"

Angelique was shaking her head. Not angrily, but out of pity. Hexene wished the other maiden had screeched a "You lie!" That would have been good to break her down. But Angelique was playing the crowd too well. Her quiet despair, even disappointment, in Hexene was doing the work that no amount of histrionics could.

"What motive does Angelique Arcane have?" Decuma asked.

"She doesn't want to be a maiden anymore. Her coven had her trapped. She fell in love with a man, and it was time. She couldn't wait anymore. She couldn't stand the disappointment of breaking it off with someone else she loved. She'd done it too many times. So she hatched a plan. She'd make a new coven. She would be the mother, her friend Petunia Pendulum would be the crone. And I'd be the maiden."

A few gasps echoed out over the amphitheater and eyes went to Angelique and Petunia, who held each other, utterly still.

"Only I had lost my magic. Angelique went ahead with the first part of the plan, and she gave me time. I was getting nowhere. She found another prospective maiden, and suddenly I was more useful as a way to get rid of her coven, so that's what she did."

"Have you proof?" Morta asked, her voice soft for the first time since the hearing started. Hexene looked into the crone's face, and found a glimpse of the mother she had been so long ago.

"No."

"Speculation isn't evidence," Nona said.

"I'm ready to render my verdict," Morta said.

"As am I," said Decuma.

"And I," said Nona.

"Guilty," said the crone, raising her hand. The vast majority of the audience did too.

"Innocent," said the mother. Angelique's head whipped around to her.

"Guilty," said the maiden.

Applause broke out from the audience. Seemed like the verdict was the one everyone had been hoping for.

Justin Robinson

"Hexene Candlemas, you will receive the only proper punishment for sororicide. You will be consigned to the water at dawn tomorrow. Sentence given to the Caribbean Ward to carry out as they see fit. May the Many-Faced Goddess find something useful in your essence."

Thirty-Two

Hexene slept soundly that night. She curled up inside the reactivated pentagram, knees to chest, closed her eyes, and when she opened them, sunlight was brushing the opposite wall. Impending death had calmed her, or else all the stress had caught up with her. She couldn't remember any dreams, and for that she was grateful. She couldn't imagine they would be any use to her.

She had gotten somewhat used to sleeping on the hard stone floor, and the aches and strains bothered her less. Her little tower was far away from the major thoroughfares of the building, so when she heard footsteps or conversation, it was usually people heading her way. When, maybe an hour after she opened her eyes, she began to hear low voices in the hallway below, she sat up.

It was time to go to die. Hexene wasn't going to show them—Angelique, mostly, but all the others too—that this was hurting her in the slightest. It was an annoying inconvenience at worst. Sure, she was going to be melted down into smoke, experiencing excruciating agony the whole time, but she was going to take away any semblance of satisfaction they might get from the proceedings. She thought an emphatic obscene gesture in Angelique's direction would work nicely. She wasn't sure if there was a proper way to ask if the good old-fashioned American finger would translate to the assembled witches. Maybe a Voorish Sign?

Two witches, the jailer Hexene had come to know and another who had come in more than once to insult her, climbed into the room. Their familiars, a crab and a massive centipede, each fidgeted nervously on their witch's shoulder. "Time to go," said Crab.

"First time seeing someone watered?" Hexene asked lightly, as Centipede blew out the candles.

"Stay quiet," said Crab. Too quickly, in Hexene's opinion. Something was agitating her, and making her crab click its claws restlessly.

Hexene did her best not to let her confusion show. Confusion was weakness, and weakness would lead to satisfaction somewhere. So she was quiet as Centipede clapped her in irons, the buzz of magic returning after the blessed moment of silence when the pentagram's ward went down.

"So where are we going?"

Centipede cuffed Hexene on the back of the head. Her familiar chittered. She said something in French that Hexene was pretty sure translated along the lines of "Shut up, unwitch." The blow was hard enough to send her stumbling forward a few steps. She caught her balance and whirled, but when she tried to bring up her fist to show this witch how a punch was thrown, the manacles reminded her she was bound. The rattle of the chain was a heartbreaking futility. Centipede laughed and gave her a stinging backhand across the face. Hexene staggered again, and though she felt the maiden's handprint burning on her cheek, righted herself immediately.

"Do that again, cur," she spat in Spanish.

The witch was about to oblige when Crab caught her arm. "What do you think you're doing? They're going to want her in perfect shape. Not with broken teeth and your handprints all over her face." The way the Barrendera said *they* had weight.

"You heard what she called me."

"I did. And if it were anyone else, I might not care. Do you want to answer to the Moirai?"

"The Moirai?" Hexene blurted.

Now both witches turned to Hexene. Crab's face was stony, while Centipede smirked and said, "You heard right."

Crab shoved Hexene down the hallway. She moved, wondering what the Moirai could possibly want. They had judged her, but she had gotten the impression that was where their interest ended. It could maybe be chalked up to the rarity of the crime everyone believed she committed. Witches killing other witches had been frowned upon for thousands of years. After all, when nearly the entirety of human civilization wanted something, it was generally considered poor form to offer any assistance.

After a few twists and turns, the hallway opened into the front room of the Ward. Hexene didn't see the Moirai. Instead, Mafaufau stood by the front desk where whichever Barrendera was on duty greeted any visitors to the Ward. The current one, a maiden with glasses thick enough to stop most hexes, was nervously playing with a writing quill. A scroll, fully unfurled, sat on the desk in front of her. An octopus crawled around the inside of a clear glass jug next to her. Hexene stared at Mafaufau and tried to convey *What the hell are you doing here?* with a frown. She knew the answer would only be *Mafaufau*, but it never hurt to pose the question.

"There she is," said Octopus, speaking Spanish with a heavy French accent. "Please tell the Moirai that we acquiesced to their request with all due speed."

For a moment, Hexene wondered if Mafaufau was on some kind of hex that made him look like one or all of the Moirai. Then she put it together. The scroll, the messenger, the fact that Mafaufau looked like he was holding a wad of gum in his mouth. It was a crazy plan on the face of it, but it seemed to be working. *Best to play along.*

"Now, I know your mistresses asked that Candlemas be turned over to you, but she is a dangerous criminal. A murderer. We would be happy to send a few of our number with you, just so she doesn't get away."

Mafaufau shifted, looking faintly uncomfortable. He reached out with one massive hand for Hexene, who walked to him. When he gripped her, it was soft. She instantly felt a little better, even if they were still in the Ward. Hexene did her best to look cowed, which wasn't difficult with the ghost of the handprint still burning on her face. She stared at the floor, the dusty black stone of the entryway, and tried to show everyone that they didn't need another escort. The zombie and hexed manacles were more than enough. She moved her arm, she hoped imperceptibly, against Mafaufau's hand—a nudge toward the door. Mafaufau, bless him, got the hint and turned in that direction.

"Zombie!" called the jailer. "One moment, zombie. We're not done discussing what should be done here. We want to make certain the prisoner reaches your mistresses with a minimum of complications."

Mafaufau looked down at Hexene and widened his eyes as if to say, *What now?* She shot a baffled eyebrow raise back. *Don't ask me, this is your plan!* Mafaufau guided her through the door, even as the jailer called out to him again. Her voice was plaintive, almost entirely devoid of the reflexive imperiousness witches tended to use when addressing zombies.

Hexene fought panic. He was being gentle, and that didn't sell. She flung herself toward the door and let out a strangled cry. Mafaufau paused, collected her, caught the next look, and picked her up. After a moment's hesitation, he slung her over one of his mountainous shoulders.

The front of the Ward featured a short path with long, irregular stairs leading up to the gate. On either side, a stone garden pretended that plants would grow in this dry place. The jailer called after them and Mafaufau picked up the pace. She bumped and jostled against the expansive muscle. The Barrenderas had gathered at the doorway, trying to decide what to do.

"Zombie, if you would just hold on," the witch called, but her voice was quavering. Apparently no one wanted to get in the way of a Moirai zombie. Mafaufau kept walking, his lumbering gait picking up speed like an avalanche. Hexene's stone-battered muscles complained with each heavy step. She thought they were being awfully ungrateful; as far as she was concerned, Mafaufau was the best friend she'd ever had.

UNWITCH HUNT

The maidens at the door grew smaller. Mafaufau had to be barely five steps to freedom. Four maybe. Three. And then a whooshing sound made Hexene crane her head to see the sky. Flying just overhead, the Moirai made for the landing pad on the roof of the Caribbean Ward. Hexene's heart decided at that moment that maybe it should make a break for it on its own. At least, that's what it felt like to her.

The Moirai were every bit as regal as they had been at the previous night's Sabbat. They sat side-saddle on large strigils, looking like they had just hopped off an ancient Greek urn to check in with the 20th century. They had not yet identified what was happening at the front of the Ward, and as they passed out of sight to the landing pad, they never slowed. It would take them some time to come down from the roof and they hadn't appeared to be in a hurry. Hexene held onto that hope with white knuckles.

"There they are," said the jailer, watching the unofficial leaders of Las Brujas come in for a landing.

A shape vaulted over the wall. "My love!" It was Amir, rushing for the witches at the door. The three witches gathered there—Crab, Centipede, and Octopus—all uttered some variation on "Huh?"

Amir moved with catlike grace, tripping over some rocks and then acting like that had been his intention all along. He still wore his half-undone tuxedo, and Hexene wondered two things: if he had any other clothes, or perhaps more distressingly, if he had a closet filled with half-undone tuxedos. He carried a cocktail that still had a few sips left in it, the ice clinking against the sides of the glass.

"My love, I have been too far from your side!" he called again.

The witches looked at each other, wondering who his love could possibly be. The Moirai were, for the moment, entirely forgotten. Mafaufau picked up the pace. "Wait!" Crab called.

Amir rushed to her. "Oh, my sweet rose, I have searched this fair city for you." Hexene craned her neck around; it was impossible not to watch this. She thought Amir was faking his ardor fairly well, but he broke the spell a bit when he took a sip from the cocktail.

"Who the devil are you?" Crab demanded.

"I am merely your obedient servant! I will perform any task for merely a glimmer of favor!"

"Do you know this man?" asked Centipede, somewhere between scandalized and intrigued.

"I've never seen him before! Stop that zombie! His mistresses are here!"

Centipede took two steps, calling after them; her familiar mimicked the action, chittering loudly.

"Wait, I'm sorry," Amir said. "It was not you who set my loins aflame. It was her! Yoohoo, my dear!" he called to Centipede, skipping to her side.

"What's happening?"

Hexene lost the rest because she was through the gate and down into the streets. Technika waited at the mouth of an entrance to the Catacombs. Mafaufau set Hexene down and touched her shoulder in proper greeting.

"I am pleased to see you relatively uninjured," said the robot.

"It's good to see you, too."

They made it to the entrance in time to hear huffing and puffing and the clinking of ice cubes on glass. Amir sprinted up the alley. "It's time to go! My ruse has failed! The hexes are out!" He rushed into the Catacombs. The others followed. A moment later, the shouts of pursuing witches echoed all around them.

Thirty-Three

The skies swarmed with witches and a single red flivver, fire roaring from its jet engine. For every Barrendera cloak Hexene saw flapping in the wind, there was another that had no heraldry at all. Even the informal authority wasn't needed; every witch was hunting the fugitive. And the roaring jet engines of a gremlin flivver said Slick had opportunistically joined the hunt.

She ducked back inside the Catacombs and let out a long, ragged breath. Her friends—and she was comfortable calling them that after what they'd done—crouched at this entrance into the Catacombs, somewhere deep in the Yoruba Quarter. Her entire body ached, though the places that had spent hours in contact with the stone floor at the Caribbean Ward were worse. It was difficult to massage them, what with her hands still manacled behind her back. Mafaufau couldn't break the manacles, Technika couldn't open the lock, and Amir insisted that he had never worn manacles or put them on someone else without all parties involved being enthusiastic participants. So Hexene had remained bound as she fled, and even worse, barefoot. Her feet were bruised and cut from the run, and once again she resented her boots sitting unused in the Adepts' home. Unlike her satchel, she could actually use those.

It was like the old days. She was Canela again. The bullies hadn't changed. They still wanted to hurt her for the difference they saw. Sure, they could lie to themselves, pretend there was some bigger reason behind their rage. That they had a perfectly good reason for putting pain on her. But it all came down to the difference. Red hair, a witch without her magic, both made her an outsider. Both marked her. "It's still bad," she said.

"As I said it would be," Technika told her.

"I had to see for myself."

"Mafaufau."

She nodded to the zombie. "We need to get somewhere we can hide."

"Down here," Amir said. "Miles of tunnels."

"The witches will come down here soon enough," Technika said. "When they do, it will be in force."

"If we linger close to the reservoir, it is unlikely the witches will find us."

Hexene shuddered. "No. We're not camping next to a giant lake. How would you like it if I wanted to stay in a roomful of cats? Or a house of... head trauma?"

"I see your point," Amir said, sipping at his cocktail. He was making it last. "The only other place we might be able to hide is Cogtown."

"Cogtown is not safe," Technika said. "Someone hunts us there as well."

"You two are not good at making friends."

"We made you, didn't we?" Hexene asked.

"True, but I am a drunken fool, and our zombie friend is a lost soul." He thought it over. "If not Cogtown, then where? We cannot make it through the deep desert on foot. We will be caught if we try for the airport. What does that leave?"

Outside, heels hit cobblestones all at once. It sounded like people had just leapt gently down from walls, but it was the sound of witches landing suddenly at once. One of them shouted something in a language Hexene couldn't identify, but she was pretty sure it was something like "Over there!"

"We have to move!" Hexene hissed. Technika, though she had been the only one standing, was quickly outpaced by the others on the way into the Catacombs. These upper tunnels had been devoid of zombies ever since the persecutions had started what felt like a lifetime ago. The garbage left behind was wilted and mashed into the floor. Candles had long ago burned down into wax stalagmites. Torches weren't lit; lanterns were dark. Amir, with his longer strides and keen night vision, quickly took the lead, with Hexene, Mafaufau, and finally Technika following behind.

"Where are we going?" Amir stage-whispered.

"Away from here!" Hexene shot back.

"Ah yes, the first choice of flight." Amir sipped at his cocktail while running.

Voices filled the tunnel behind them. It was impossible to tell how many witches were in pursuit. Their voices, indecipherable to Hexene, bounded over the walls.

"I never thought I would be sad to hear the music of Koyraboro Senni," Amir said wistfully.

"You speak their language, too?"

"Of course. My great-uncle on my mother's side is Fula, and he spoke so—"

"I get it, you speak every language."

Amir shrugged sadly, which was no mean feat while running and holding a cocktail. "I do not speak the language of love."

"Mafaufau," said Mafaufau, plucking a lantern from one of the alcoves.

"He's right. We should be running more," Hexene said.

Amir took them down the first twist he could find, then another, always going deeper. Hexene would have liked to have taken one of the carts, now abandoned, but it would be far too loud. She had no doubt witches would be waiting for them on the other side. Though the voices behind them grew softer, new voices always appeared ahead or down a side tunnel. Without fail, Amir identified their language, the pursuers speaking Mongolian, French Creole, Tatar, Irish Gaelic, Cree, Nahuatl, and of course French and Spanish. From time to time, Hexene picked out a little Theban, usually a variation on "Have you seen her?" by groups whose paths had crossed.

Voices reverberated from both sides. Hexene felt like a cornered rat, and the cats were ready to dine. Mafaufau grabbed her shoulder. "Mafaufau," he said. She could tell he meant it. He looked up the tunnel and back. "Mafaufau," he said again.

"Yes, this is very interesting," Amir said. "Perhaps we should move."

Hexene stared into the zombie's milky eyes and nodded. "That's not what he's saying. He has an idea."

"What idea?" Technika said.

"Well, we could get him to write it on the wall," Hexene said, "or we could just trust him. I say we trust him."

"Mafaufau," Mafaufau said firmly.

"Of course, my friend," Amir said.

"A dissenting vote here counts for nothing," Technika said.

"Mafaufau," said the zombie. He pulled a book of matches from his pocket and ignited one, then lit the lantern. He glanced around one last time and headed resolutely for the voices that sounded far closer. Hexene nearly panicked, almost overrode the vote. She thought of every witch who had spoken of zombies in the last couple months. They didn't even really have brains anymore, just an empty skull that their creator had cleaned out. She held her tongue. Mafaufau lived down here. He knew Las Brujas better than anyone, and he could think just fine. He'd proven his loyalty, his bravery, and his resourcefulness. Brains or no.

They moved more slowly now, with Mafaufau in the lead. He paused at a turn and took them down a tunnel, then made a swift turn again, going down a passage Hexene might have otherwise missed. This one bore the marks of chisels in the stone walls. Mafaufau's bulk hid most of the light from her, fingers of gold reaching around his massive form. Though he was slower than Hexene or Amir, his knowledge of the Catacombs made them cover more ground. He was going down passageway after passageway, many that were small enough to miss on first glance, heading inexorably in a single direction. As they moved, the voices petered out behind. Soon, only stray echoes reached them. Mafaufau stayed away from the major thoroughfares; these were the alleys in a city of alleys.

Hexene was exhausted. Her arms ached in their unnatural position. She found herself stumbling every few steps as she ran, barking her knees more than once on the stone floor. She always got up, shrugging off the help of Amir and Technika. She was going to do it herself. At least this one part.

"Mafaufau," said the zombie, stopping. It had been hours, maybe most of the day. Hexene couldn't tell if she was more hungry or tired, but either way, she wanted to collapse where she stood. They had found a chamber, with only a single path leading to it. A circular door made of petrified wood was partially open at the other side.

"This is it? We're here?"

"Mafaufau."

"Where is here?" Technika asked.

Mafaufau patted his pockets and shrugged. "Mafaufau."

Amir shook his head. "I have no chalk either."

"All of my stuff is at the Adepts' house," Hexene said.

Mafaufau gestured at the door. "Mafaufau."

Hexene stared at the door. With how much they had moved, they could be anywhere beneath the city. The Catacombs might not be a literal labyrinth, but they functioned as one all the same.

"Is this a house?" Hexene asked.

"Mafaufau." He shook his head slightly enough that Hexene might have missed it had she not known him so well.

"All right," she said.

She slunk through the door with Mafaufau right behind. He opened it a little wider than it had been, raising his lantern high. A long tunnel extended into the dark. The walls were squared off here, sloping slightly inward as they inclined. It looked to Hexene like a loading bay, though she couldn't imagine any vehicle that could have navigated the maze behind her. The flat floor was soothing under her battered feet.

It was a bit of a walk before they started to see doors. Mafaufau shrugged, and gestured around them. "Mafaufau."

"This way," Hexene said.

"Why this way?" Amir asked.

She didn't answer because she didn't quite know how. The door she had picked was *right*. It wasn't the buzz of magic against her skin; that was the manacles, and those were growing more uncomfortable by the minute. It was simply the right door. She went through it, and was moving into the room beyond before Mafaufau poked his head and lantern in to show that the whole place was filled with shelves of books and dusty old artifacts. The buzz was stronger now, breaking past the baffling field coming off the manacles. They were a simple enchantment, after all. Make something work better; it was what witches had done for thousands of years. This stuff retained the cobwebs of magic, from so long ago it was unlikely anyone remembered what or why.

"These items are potentially valuable," said Technika.

"Indeed," Amir said thoughtfully. "I would give them up for another drink."

"You finally finished it."

"My dear, every drink must eventually end, and we are all the poorer for it."

Hexene ignored them for the moment, snaking through the shelves. The trapdoor was nearly invisible, covered in a thick layer of dust. "Mafaufau?" she said.

"Mafaufau," he told her. He moved past and lifted up the trapdoor. The dust came off in a plume like the beginning of a sandstorm. Then it took an about-face and fell back onto the door and everything around it. Hexene appreciated the subtle spell—someone wanted this place covered in that layer of dust.

She took a step onto the ladder that she could barely see.

"Be careful," Amir said. "You have not the use of your hands."

She smiled to herself. The ladder was more solid than anything around her. She didn't feel as if she could fall off it if she tried. She wasn't going to test that particular feeling, but she would heed it. She descended and stepped onto a stone floor she knew would be there well before she could see anything. Mafaufau followed with the light. Amir took the ladder with ease, and finally Technika moved stiffly down the steps.

This tunnel wasn't chiseled. The walls were as smooth as a lava tube, and just as irregular. Hexene felt the air around her as a tangible thing, crackling like the onset of a storm. She moved quickly into the dark as her friends followed on her heels. She still didn't know where she was heading, but she knew it was in the right direction. It was the place she was supposed to be going all this time.

Ahead, she saw light. At first, she thought it must be a trick, or perhaps a reflection of the lantern Mafaufau was holding. The light grew brighter, dancing with orange and red. Then she stepped into view. A fire burned brightly in a hearth, a cauldron suspended over it. The scent billowing from it wasn't pleasant; it was magic. Hexene wasn't certain what that potion would be doing, but it would do it well. And pungently.

The rest of the chamber was almost a living room. A bearskin rug took up most of the floor, with a bone chair—really almost a throne—sitting by it. A table that looked to be made from a single giant toadstool sat in the center. All around were collections of bottles, piles of books, and other pieces of magic. She couldn't see the far wall, but the more she hunted for it, the more she had the impression it wasn't there at all.

"Where are we?" whispered Amir.

"A better question might be, 'How will you ever escape?'" The voice was like a rock coming free from a mountain: old and cracked, but booming and ultimately deadly. She spoke Spanish with an accent that was almost, but not quite, Russian in the way that a woolly mammoth is almost, but not quite, an elephant.

The speaker stepped from a shadow far too small to hold her. The woman was the size of an ogre, though when Hexene looked from the corner of her eye, she was almost as small as Hexene herself. She was a crone, with a hunchback, long nose, and a face covered in warts. Her hair was as gray as iron and hung in greasy reeds. She was dressed in a patchwork combination of skins with musky fur at her rounded shoulders. When she spoke, she revealed a mouth full of teeth that had been filed to points. She walked with the aid of a thick staff that was almost the shape of a rook chess piece, though it wasn't a staff. Hexene realized what it was a little later. Behind this crone, this hag, *something* gibbered softly in the dark.

"Who are you?" Hexene breathed.

"Hadn't you guessed, little morsel? I am Baba Yaga."

Thirty-Four

Mafaufau," Mafaufau said with the appropriate amount of wonder in his voice.

"Yes, I'm still alive," Baba Yaga said, moving a bit closer. Though her mode of locomotion could best be described as limping, that word didn't properly convey the amount of menace the Great Hag managed to imbue it with. She struck Hexene like a wounded lion who was all the more dangerous for her injury.

"You can understand him?" Amir asked.

Baba Yaga turned her antediluvian attention onto the balam. "Of course I can."

"But how?"

"I am Baba Yaga."

"That does not answer my question."

"Foolish boy. That answers *every* question." Baba Yaga looked from face to face. "No balam found me. No, no. I'm not here to talk to him. I'm here to talk to you." She leveled a gnarled finger tipped in a thorny talon. "Hexene Candlemas."

Hexene almost asked how the Great Hag knew her name, but then remembered that Baba Yaga had already answered that. "I didn't know we were going to find you," she said lamely.

"What did you think you were going to find?"

Hexene shrugged. "Somewhere to hide."

A laugh hit Baba Yaga suddenly, and she nodded in time with the unexpected sound. "That's what I was looking for, too. Well, come on, then, you and your little menagerie." She shuffled to the throne and settled into it with a faint grunt. The fire made her looming shadow dance and jump. She regarded them. "Well, come on now. I don't bite. Well, I do, but right now I'm interested enough in you not to. Bore me and you'll wind up in the pot."

The four of them, unwitch, zombie, robot, and balam, approached cautiously. Amir sat down on the bearskin rug and soon was lounging upon it. Something was wrong with the rug; it was far too big and the bear's snout was queerly short. Technika knelt by the side of the table farthest from the fire. Mafaufau simply stood. Here, in the presence of the hag, he no longer looked so gigantic.

"You haven't once addressed me as 'Great Hag'," said Baba Yaga. "Haven't kowtowed or prostrated yourself, either."

"Oh!" said Hexene, and was about to do it when she realized she couldn't. The manacles didn't stop her; she just had no idea how one could be obsequious, even to someone she admired as thoroughly as the hag herself. "I'm sorry."

"Don't be. If you had, you wouldn't be the witch I thought you were."

"I'm not a witch," Hexene said. "Not anymore."

Something large and wet moved in the darkness behind the hag. "There will be no eating now," Baba Yaga said to the dark. She turned her attention back to Hexene. "Because you lost your familiar. Yes, that can be traumatic. The connection to the Many-Faced Goddess. I suppose you're waiting for me to tell you that you don't need a familiar and the power was in you the whole time."

"That would be nice."

"No. Doesn't work that way. Familiars bridge the gap between us and her, and..." she slipped into Theban. "Don't think your friends need to

Unwitch Hunt

hear this. They might be trustworthy, but this is for witches and witches alone."

"Could you get these manacles off me?" Hexene turned halfway and jingled the chain between her bound wrists.

Baba Yaga cocked her head. "Gift from the Barrenderas, I expect. No. You can get those off yourself."

"They're enchanted."

"Of course they are."

"I told you, I don't have my magic."

Baba Yaga snorted. "I may be old, but my memory's just fine."

"How am I supposed to break the enchantment, then?"

"Making a lot of assumptions. It sounds to me like you need some motivation. How about this: get the manacles off yourself, or I'll throw you in the pot. I am hungry, and not in the habit of wasting a morsel, even if there's barely any meat on you. Might be a couple good soup bones in there. Let me see your leg."

Hexene ignored the hag with some difficulty and thought it over.

"What is going on?" Technika asked.

"She gave me a riddle…" Hexene said, trailing off. The light of the fire touched an apothecary table, and it glinted off a long silver stirring rod. Hexene went to it, then turned around and knelt. She felt around and soon had the rod in hand. With great difficulty, she maneuvered it into the lock.

"Do you require assistance?" Technika asked after a half-hour or so.

"No, I think I have it." And she did. The manacles clattered to the floor. Hexene brought her hands around to her front, massaging her wrists and circling her shoulders. "The riddle was that I don't need magic when the mundane will do."

"You could have let the robot pick it," Baba Yaga said. "She's bound to be good for something."

"Tried that earlier," Hexene said. She picked up the manacles, frowning at them. They still buzzed with the traces of their hex, most strongly where the symbols had been etched into the iron. Back when she'd had her magic, she would have scoffed at what a simple hex this was. Now it was out of reach.

"Can we stay here?" she asked Baba Yaga.

"Wouldn't stay too long. Might get hungry."

"Just for a little while."

"I suppose you would have to. I can see in your eyes, you have more questions for me. It might be nice to have someone else to talk to, but I'm out of the habit." The Great Hag gestured to the rug in front of her. "It's warm enough by the fire, so sleep there. Best not wander around in the dark too much. There's *things* out there, you know."

"Thank you," Hexene said, and meant it.

THIRTY-FIVE

Living with the Great Hag of legend was an adjustment. The group did as she asked, and stayed relatively close to the fire. Soon, Hexene learned why: the chamber got positively arctic the farther off into darkness one went. Day and night were impossible to determine underground; and Hexene had the sneaking suspicion, fueled by the constant hum of magic in her ears and the scent of not-yet-shed lightning in the air, that 'day' and 'night' might be concepts she should probably not think a great deal about while she was here. Much like 'cannibalism'.

That first night—or whatever it was—Baba Yaga lumbered off into the clammy darkness with a "Sleep well!" that ensured no one who heard it ever would. All except one person. Technika, kneeling at the edge of the bearskin rug, said, "I am going to shut down. It would behoove me to save as much energy as I can. Ironically, I do not think our erstwhile savior will be as accommodating when it comes to my battery."

"We'll turn you back on before we go," Hexene reassured her. In response, the green light in the robot's eyes faded into the dark.

"Would that I could do that, too," Amir sighed.

"I never thought turning a balam off would be a problem," Hexene remarked.

Amir laughed. "It is a strange world we find for ourselves, no? Now, I must find a way to be comfortable on this bear—" a snore obliterated the rest of the thought.

"Just you and me," Hexene said to Mafaufau. The zombie's cherubic features were shadowed in the firelight.

"Mafaufau," he said softly, and touched her shoulder. Hexene curled up on the rug. The smell was as thick as the bear, but Hexene barely noticed it. When she opened her eyes, the only way to tell that she had been sleeping at all was that she wasn't tired, and the aches and pains of her imprisonment and rescue were on the wane.

"Slept long enough," said Baba Yaga. The Great Hag sat on her throne, staring at Hexene with eyes that sparkled gold.

"How long have you been watching me?"

"Long enough to throw you in the pot were I so inclined."

"Suppose that's the only unit of time I should be thinking about."

The Great Hag cackled. "Now you're getting it. Come here. Let me show you."

The lessons began. Nothing formal, of course. The Great Hag wasn't going to move her through the process of witchcraft like some suburban crone, and Hexene wasn't some fresh maiden who didn't know a hex from a hexagram. Baba Yaga was going to do what she was going to do, and occasionally drop a nugget of wisdom—in between all the threats to eat Hexene, of course. Without the month Hexene had spent in her fruitless hunt in the library, she wouldn't have understood a single thing the Great Hag was trying to teach her. Even with that, she was certain she was only getting a small fraction of the knowledge Baba Yaga seeded through her rambling lectures and riddles.

There were times that Hexene felt they were in the dark together for years, others when she was certain it had only been a few days. She periodically had to remind herself that sort of thing didn't matter. All that did was whether the Great Hag got hungry.

"Where is the rest of your coven?" Hexene asked.

Baba Yaga was seasoning the pot, tasting poison after poison before sprinkling a shake or two in. Hexene would swear that the rising smoke moaned like a restless ghost. "Probably assume I ate them, don't you?"

"The thought had crossed my mind."

"Reasonable. Witch is a good meal."

"When I read about you in the library—"

"You read about me in the library?" The Great Hag was amused. "Thought you were here to get a new familiar."

Hexene shrugged. "I read about you. In some of the stories, it sounded like there was more than one of you. Like there used to be a coven that you were a part of."

Baba Yaga snorted. "I can barely stand to be around myself. Can't imagine what it would be like with more than one of me."

"So? What happened to them?"

"Never had a coven."

"How is that possible?" Hexene remembered the title then, the Heqatun, the Three-In-One.

"Witches didn't used to need covens. Just something that started later. Makes a certain amount of sense, safety in numbers and all that, but it's never been part of any plan."

"The Many-Faced Goddess?"

Baba Yaga shrugged. "Call it what you like."

"The roles, though—they matter."

"Why?"

Hexene realized she had no idea. "I..."

"Ever wonder why witches divide themselves up the way men see us? Maiden, mother, crone, as if that's all we are. Here." She pointed into the dark, and even though it was nearly black, Hexene knew the hag's talon was gesturing at her friends. "That one, the zombie. To the witches up there, he's a vagrant. A derelict. Is that what you would call him?"

"Of course not."

"No, I'd expect not. And her, your robot, she was a plaything, wasn't she? Taken apart like a toy. That what she is?

"How did you...right. No, Technika is more than that."

"And him, a drunken cad." Baba Yaga sucked a tooth. "Actually, sometimes one *can* judge a book by its cover. That's what a cover is for, after all."

"So you took a new word. Not maiden, or mother, or crone."

"I am no crone," said Baba Yaga, "I am a hag. There is power in words." She stirred the poison and tasted. "Needs meat."

"Like a name," Hexene said.

"You picked the one you have now, more or less."

"I've had others. Maria Foley was the one my parents gave me. Canela was the name the other kids gave me."

Baba Yaga nodded. "It matters what you call yourself, but it matters even more what you make others call you."

In the dark, the massive shape shifted and whispered slushy sounds that were uncomfortably close to words. Throughout her time in the lair of the hag, she never got a good look at the shape. It was always lurking out of the firelight, giving only the impression of being large and having more limbs than any one thing should. Half of her was disappointed, the other half relieved.

It was another day, or possibly in the middle of the night, when Hexene followed Baba Yaga beyond the fire. As she walked, Hexene began to get the impression that she wasn't quite inside anymore. In the dark, she fancied she saw the trunks of trees. Then she felt the kiss of wind, and heard the soft hooting of animals. Overhead, she could swear she saw a starry sky. The Great Hag still leaned heavily on her staff, which Hexene finally recognized as a large pestle. The mortar would be around here somewhere, if the legends were true. A candle flame burned in the air just above Baba Yaga's forehead. Between that and her sharp teeth, she reminded Hexene of an anglerfish.

"Revenge," the Great Hag muttered.

"What about it?"

"You're going to take it? On that maiden who wronged you? Arcane."

Thoughts of Angelique still hurt. She had been a friend, worming her way into Hexene's confidences. "Yes. I think I have to."

"Good."

"Does the Many-Faced Goddess care about that sort of thing?" Hexene asked.

"I don't know that the Many-Faced Goddess wants things the way we can. Don't even know what it is. We gave it all those faces simply because it's easier to look something in the eye. I said 'good' because you can't move ahead with that kind of debt weighing you down. Repay unkindness with unkindness, else brace for more."

"Wish I knew how."

"That's not my problem." Baba Yaga shrugged. "You're standing over a huge reservoir. It's not hard to kill a witch, if you really want to." Hexene scratched at her scars, pushing the sleeve of her dress up and over them. Red streaks ran down her forearm. "Those are beauties," the Great Hag said.

Hexene stared at them. "Anyone ever use water on you?"

"Many, many times."

"What did you do?"

"Revenge."

"Killing her isn't the revenge," Hexene said.

Baba Yaga's mouth stretched into a smile, revealing her razor-sharp teeth. "Now *that* is what I like to hear."

"I know what she wants. I know what she's going to do next." Hexene shrugged. "She might have already done it. I don't know how long we've been down here."

"I wouldn't worry about that. When you're ready, you go to the surface. You'll find that it's the right time. Take the next step then."

"Or you'll eat me?"

"Goes without saying," Baba Yaga huffed. Then: "Maybe I'll eat your balam first. He has a bit more meat on the bone than you."

Hexene found herself giggling. Baba Yaga smirked. Hexene still had the impression of standing deep in the woods, though she never saw anything that would confirm the suspicion. She huddled in her dress against the cold, her battered feet felt like icicles.

"Here we are." It was so dark, Hexene couldn't see much more than shadows. The Great Hag cleared her throat. "I said, 'Here we are.'"

Something big moved in front of them, sounding a bit like an avalanche in reverse. Footfalls came next, followed by the scratch of claws on stone. The thing stepping into the light was, in retrospect, something Hexene should have expected: a small hut walking with massive chicken legs on either side. It looked a bit like a Tyrannosaurus that could use some renovation.

"Now sit down," Baba Yaga told her hut. It obeyed, settling inches from the Great Hag. Hexene flinched without meaning to.

"You wanted to show me your hut?" Hexene asked. She approached carefully, putting a hand on the dried mud wall. It was warm and a little soft, like skin.

"Show it to you? No, you're here, you earn your keep. I want you to clean it up. Still smells like a chicken I cut up in there years ago."

The door of the hut opened for Hexene. She fought the trepidation and forced herself through the doorway. This was Baba Yaga's hut, one of the parts of the Great Hag's legend. As she stepped in, candles spontaneously lit in every corner. The hut itself looked fairly normal, though it was definitely bigger inside than out—Hexene imagined that it had to be bigger somewhere, and that was the wise choice. Other than that, it was fairly mundane in the sense that it was a hut in dire need of cleaning. That Baba Yaga would have a dirty hut made her less like a legend and more like any old witch who accumulated dust and mold like phantoms gathered murder charges.

Hexene located a broom and a few herbal concoctions that would help get the hut in the kind of condition that would allow Baba Yaga to entertain, were she so inclined. She cleaned as thoroughly as she was able, doing a better job on the Great Hag's hut than she ever did for Hechalé and Hermosa. That guilt was never going to go away entirely, especially after what she'd said to the mother. The only way she could even come close to balancing those scales would be revenge. She let the plans recede as she concentrated on the mindless task of cleaning.

In a windowless room, beneath a sagging shelf, she found a copse of mushrooms. They were velvety and dark, with shining spots, like a night sky in fungus form. Magic or no, Hexene was still enough of a witch that any unusual fungus was coming home with her. She picked a few carefully, and when she was too exhausted to continue, she carried them back to the fire in her dress.

As she approached the hearth, the Great Hag was stirring soup. Amir and Mafaufau sat not far away, both watching her warily.

"Done?" asked Baba Yaga.

"I'll finish after I sleep."

"If you're going to steal my mushrooms, you're going to need something to carry them in."

"I...I didn't—"

"Don't start begging, and don't you say you're sorry when you're not. Any witch worth her hexes would have taken those mushrooms. Any who didn't would be fit for the pot. So you're going to need to carry them, I expect." Baba Yaga nodded to a satchel sitting on the table. "Take that."

Hexene picked up the bag. It was supple leather, and looked distinctly meaty in the firelight. The bag featured innumerable pockets, all waiting for some part of a witch's toolkit. "Thank you," she said.

"Enh, it was collecting dust. Might as well give it to you."

Hexene put the starry mushrooms into a pocket, and one of the caps scraped along the edges. The gill exhaled a small cloud.

"What was that?" Technika asked. The robot hadn't spoken in a good deal of time, but she was just suddenly *on*, her eyes glowing with activity.

"You scared me," Hexene scolded.

"*You* scared *me*," Technika said. "I was not active, but I saw a star fall, and I awakened."

"You saw that?" Hexene pulled one of the mushrooms from her new satchel and ran her thumb over the gills like she was strumming a guitar.

If she looked closely, she could see momentary sparkles that faded.

"What is that?" Technika asked. "It looks like fireworks. I can barely stand to look at it."

"A mushroom I found," said Hexene, and her mind was turning and turning at the edges of a plan.

Hexene had slept several more times—she couldn't in good conscience call whatever happened down here 'nights'—before the rest fell into place. The hut had long since been cleaned, and she had assisted Baba Yaga at her potions so many times, she knew the recipes by heart. She and the Great Hag were sitting out beyond the fire, where she felt the edges of the forest were just out of sight.

"I'm not going to get my magic back here," Hexene said into the silence.

Baba Yaga cackled. "Is that what you thought we were doing? That you would find what you seek here?"

"No, I guess not."

The Great Hag shook her head. "Have you ever heard the saying about digging two graves when you seek revenge?"

"Of course. You dig one for the person you're taking revenge on and you dig one for yourself, because you're going to die too."

"True, but they don't mean literally. It's like the Death card in your tarot. It's not a literal death, but a figurative one. Take revenge on someone and you're not the same person who set out to do it. That's the way of things."

Hexene was about to protest, but then the final bit of the plan slammed into place right in front of her. It was the zombies Angelique had used to kill. They were the key to everything.

That night, Hexene pulled several long, curly hairs from her head and got to work.

"What are you doing?" Amir asked.

"I'm making a hex doll of myself."

THIRTY-SIX

The disguise must have weighed twenty pounds.

"No, no. Make her look older. *Older*," Amir said, gesturing expansively with motions that he must have imagined conveyed age.

"Mafaufau," Mafaufau said with annoyance. He went back to applying the makeup, darkening great circles under Hexene's eyes. He had already fashioned a pair of jowls with some mud that the Great Hag didn't mind parting with. The wig was mostly wool, coming from a sheep carcass Hexene had found in the hut with chicken legs. The meat had long ago rotted away, and she thought the pervasive stink would keep people from getting too close. The most impressive bit, though, was a false hunchback Mafaufau had fashioned out of a wooden frame, some old straw, and a burlap sack.

Mafaufau leaned back. "Mafaufau?"

"If I did not know her, I would not know her."

"Mafaufau," said the zombie, shaking his head.

"I just need to not look like the unwitch they're chasing around."

"True. You are the only one they have described; the rest of us are invisible by virtue of what we are," Amir said.

"We could put stitches on Mafaufau, but I doubt they'll look that close."

Amir nodded soberly. "And any disguise placed upon me would be an insult to the concept of handsomeness."

"Mafaufau," said the zombie, placing a hand on her shoulder. She put her hand over his.

"All right. Let's get going."

She touched the gill of a mushroom and Technika came to life. "It is time?" the robot asked.

Hexene nodded. "Baba Yaga?"

The Great Hag limped out from the shadows, leaning on her pestle. "Leaving finally? Good. One more day and I'd have eaten you all."

"Thank you for your help."

"Help? I gave you nothing, little morsel. Go quickly, before I change my mind."

Hexene smiled. "Let's go," she said to her friends.

"Mafaufau."

The massive zombie once again served as their guide, leading them back the way they came into Baba Yaga's lair. They surfaced through the same trapdoor, but instead of going back to the door into the Catacombs, he led them to another set of stairs, these going up. Lanterns started to appear, hanging from hooks set into the rock walls. None were lit. Mafaufau still carried the one he had taken from the Catacombs, lit with an ember from Baba Yaga's own fire.

"This city never fails to amaze," Amir said, sipping from a flagon fashioned from a human skull.

"Where did you get that?" Hexene asked.

"The Hag gave it to me," Amir said. "She said it was made from the skull of someone named Alyosha Popovich. It imparts the most delicious flavor to her concoctions."

"Is there anything you won't drink?"

"That is a question worth investigation."

The walls here had been squared off, and the staircases were wide, with even steps. Hexene thanked that little bit of luck; the disguise was ungainly at best, and she already felt a persistent ache in her lower back. At the first door, Mafaufau stopped and gestured. "Mafaufau."

"You did a lot of exploring."

"Mafaufau."

Hexene gave her friend a smile, but wasn't sure he would see it under the makeup. "Mafaufau," she told him, and went through the door, her companions following.

She probably shouldn't have been surprised, but she was anyway. The door opened up into a room where racks of scrolls hung from the ceiling, and lit lanterns hung every few meters. After the stygian darkness below, Hexene found herself squinting. Mafaufau, in his desperation to find the one place they could hide safely, had chosen the perfect spot: beneath the Baba Yaga Memorial Library of Spells and Hexes. Hexene wondered what they would think of the fact that the building's namesake lived in a chamber below. For how long, Hexene had no idea, and wasn't even certain Baba Yaga knew. The Great Hag seemed content to let time pass overhead.

The group shuffled out of the chamber and to the front of the building. A few witches looked up at the group as they moved, but none of them got up. Maybe they didn't expect any non-witches to be inside, and so made assumptions. Regardless, Hexene wasn't going to linger long enough to let anyone think through it.

They hobbled past the front desk and emerged into Grandmother Square. The statue of Baba Yaga loomed large here, though with some amusement, Hexene noted that it didn't quite look like the Hag. The teeth weren't sharp enough, the nose was too small, and the eyes didn't follow you around. Hexene took a deep breath; they had a long walk ahead of them.

However long she had been underground with the Great Hag hadn't been long enough. Now, posters with her face were pinned up next to the ones of Malleus. The likeness was good, even if it was a drawing. It said, "often in the presence of a zombie, a robot, and a balam," though as expected, no further description of any of them. She noted she was wanted dead or alive, and the reward was 100 philts, offered by the Moirai. She wasn't sure what that meant exactly, but it seemed high. *So I'm on the wrong side of the Moirai,* she thought to herself. *Moving up in the world.*

It was night by the time they made it to Le Chaperon Rouge, and that was exactly as she wanted. The zombie doorman was back, and a few more zombies loitered outside, their cheeks puffy with hex scrolls. Seemed like her pursuit had let the city's zombies off the hook at least for the moment. She could be a bit grateful for that, even if she would have preferred a different path there. Mafaufau joined them, as concealed as someone his size could be. Amir and Technika made their way into the deep shadows on the other side of the building.

Hexene tottered inside the club, drawing looks from the boisterous maidens all around, but none of those looks lingered. It was a brush, a scowl, and then ignoring her. Crones weren't supposed to frequent this place, and so these maidens were just going to pretend she wasn't there at all. Suited Hexene fine.

She scanned the crowd and was relieved to find that Angelique and her friends hadn't yet arrived. She left, turning the corner and limping up the stairs to the landing pad. Racks of brooms stood to one side, accompanied by a few other, more exotic conveyances. She smiled at the pestle and mortar—probably a fan of Baba Yaga who would have a heart attack if she knew her idol was nearby. Peaked rooftops surrounded the landing pad, and Hexene found a shadowy place to crouch that was more or less hidden from the air. If she was caught, she'd pretend to be one of those crones who had refused to move beyond until well after her faculties gave up to pave the way on their own.

Her hiding place was a small eave that looked like it should hold a window for an attic, but was merely blank. She pressed up and inside the cool shadows and waited, watching the skies. A witch landed on broomstick shortly after Hexene settled in. She peered from the dark, but quickly made out a mane of bright red hair. It wasn't the one she was looking for. Neither were the next two maidens who alighted on the surface and stowed their brooms.

UNWITCH HUNT

The third one, *that* was her. Hexene recognized her as soon as she landed, taking a few running steps as she came to a stop. That was the mark of a maiden: the older witches always learned that they could stop on a dime and didn't bother with the more athletic landings. It was the other witch's face, which Hexene thought had a cowlike quality, that identified her as the maiden Angelique had been spending her time with. She placed her broom on the rack and went down into the club.

Hexene crept out from under the eave. From time to time, she saw a shadow zip by overhead and fought the urge to flinch. Admit she was out of place for a second and she would be caught. She clambered up onto the platform and was heading for the brooms when she heard the telltale whisper of a landing witch and the click of bootheels on stone. Hexene turned without thinking and held her breath.

It was Petunia Pendulum. The mother had landed and was staring hard at Hexene. "Are you lost, crone?" she asked imperiously. Hexene froze, certain the other witch would see right through the disguise. Petunia *hmph*ed. "Crones. Hope *I'm* not like that. Hope *I've* got the good sense to do my duty and then go before..." She placed her broom on the rack and turned back to Hexene. This time, she spoke loudly and slowly. "Hello! Are! You! Lost! This! Is! Le! Chaperon! Rouge! A! *Maiden*! Bar!" Petunia followed that up with a theatrical smile and a happy nod.

Hexene thought fast. "Once I ate so much porridge it came out of my nose." She didn't think *that* fast.

"Right," Petunia muttered. "Well, don't fall off the roof."

Petunia disappeared down the stairs and Hexene took a deep breath. She went to the rack of brooms and found the one the maiden had ridden in on. She pulled one of the starry mushrooms from her new satchel and ran her thumb over the gills as she passed it over the broom's bristles. The resulting cloud fluoresced for a split second like tiny stars, then went dark. She tapped the broom against the stone a few times, making certain the mushroom's spores were deep within the bristles.

She took her hiding place once again, and was there when Angelique

Arcane landed. The rage that gripped Hexene was a physical thing, commanding her to burst out and do something. Had she obeyed, she probably would have been hexed into oblivion, or worse, captured and turned over to the Barrenderas again. Instead, she watched and contented herself with the idea that revenge, much like ice cream, was best served cold. The other maiden showed not a single trace of guilt after murdering four other witches. It hit Hexene that Angelique didn't feel any guilt because she didn't think she had done anything wrong. She was getting even for an eternity spent as a maiden. Even as the butcher's bill added names, she would justify it to herself. It would always be Serafina and Evangeline's faults.

Hexene waited for the rest of the night in her hiding place. Her eyelids grew heavier and heavier, but every time she found herself ready to drift off, she grabbed hold of her anger. White hot, it woke her right up. Just before dawn, Angelique, Petunia, and their maiden stepped up onto the rooftop. They exchanged hugs, and Angelique held the maiden's shoulder while staring into her eyes and saying a few forceful words. The maiden nodded. Then they got on their broomsticks and rode.

Hexene waited until they were well and truly in the sky before climbing back onto the landing pad and sprinting—or coming as close as her disguise would allow—down the front stairs. Technika and Mafaufau waited for her in the shadows.

"Where's Amir?" she hissed.

Mafaufau pointed to the door of the club. "Mafaufau."

Hexene let out a frustrated groan. "Technika, can you see the spores?"

The robot raised her glowing eyes to the sky. "Dimly," she said. "We should leave now."

Amir burst from the club, new liquid sloshing out of the top of the skull cup in his hand. "Hexene! You will never guess who I just saw."

"Think I can. Let's go."

Technika, her head craned up the short distance her neck would allow, began to navigate through the alleys. Because this was Las Brujas, though, the route twisted and turned many times, dipping into other Quarters, returning to this one. As with most walks in this city, it should have been a short jaunt, but ended up being a frustrating ramble through a serpentine maze. They ended up in the Kurdish Quarter, a place Hexene had never been before. The neighborhood had the stretched-taffy look of most of the buildings in Las Brujas and featured an abundance of graceful arches and slim, conical structures crowning the rooftops. The building Technika indicated as the end of the spores was modestly sized, far smaller than the sprawling mansion of the Arcane Adepts.

"We have to be quick," Hexene said. "The way they were acting...I think tonight is the night." She thought about what Baba Yaga said, that they would emerge at the right time. The Great Hag hadn't been kidding.

The stone wall surrounding the house was low, and Amir reflexively hopped up atop it. That he did so without spilling his drink was the impressive part. "I admit, the thought of a daring rescue has its appeal."

Hexene stepped through the gate and shrugged off the heavy parts of her disguise. Now she only had to deal with the clinging makeup. She jogged up the wide steps to the front door and paused at the top, trying to decide what to do.

Fortunately, her decision was made when the whole thing exploded.

Thirty-Seven

Hexene saw the night sky first. It was as expansive as it always was over the relatively dark Las Brujas. She watched meteors streaking upward, black stones with tails of incandescent fire slipping earth's bonds and...well, as it turned out, they were just making an arc and crashing into the walls, alleys, and neighboring houses. But for a moment there, it really was beautiful.

She didn't remember how she ended up on the ground. There had been a sizzle, and a bright flash, and as she craned her aching neck up and back to follow the pathways of the meteors, she saw the unmistakable lines of a gremlin flivver. A familiar one, as it turned out, that looked like a secondhand pulp rocket ship, its cannon smoking. Even if she hadn't already identified it, the surprise would have been gone when the hatch over the top turret banged open and Slick poked his misshapen head out. Slick hissed something, but Hexene couldn't hear anything over the pounding in her head.

She sat up, immediately regretting the rash decision as her body complained and her head swam. The front door of the house was gone, replaced with a smoking hole, the rim of which was glowing red hot. Two witches Hexene had never seen, but she guessed were the mother and crone belonging to Angelique's maiden friend, poked their heads into view from either side of the hole, staring at the sizzling edges in horrified confusion.

Hexene felt a hand close over her upper arm and pull her to her feet. It was Mafaufau, lifting her bodily out of the firing line. The disguise, what was still on her, sloughed off. She glimpsed Amir in the zombie's other hand, the balam completely unconscious, but still somehow clutching his skull-flagon. The zombie shouted something Hexene couldn't hear, but she had a fair guess as to what it was. She managed to get her feet under her and shook herself out of Mafaufau's grasp. She swooned once, but kept her feet.

"Technika! Where's Technika?" she shouted. She heard *that*, barely.

The two witches stepped through the hole, and the mother was shouting angrily at the gremlin. Hexene heard it as though she were underwater, but at least she was hearing it. The crone was in the midst of working up a hex, likely something to make Slick think twice about forcibly remodeling any other witch's house with his cannon. She had a hex bag clutched in one gnarled hand, and was sprinkling dust into it with the other while chanting in Theban. Behind her, two zombies emerged from the wreckage of the house, holding buckets. Hexene had seen one of the zombies before, when he was busy killing her coven and chasing her through Cogtown.

Hexene grabbed Mafaufau and pointed. The zombie dropped Amir and started to run, Hexene right behind him. It entered her mind, somewhere, that she was now running between a cannon that had just turned a foyer into an open-air porch and two zombies armed with water. She wouldn't call it heroism when desperation fit just as well.

The zombie she didn't know, a woman with a blank expression even for a zombie and a hex scroll poking through the papery flesh of one cheek, stepped up behind the crone. She brought up the bucket, and Hexene already knew she was too slow to do anything about it. The zombie flung the water, and Hexene got to watch as it washed over the crone, turning the witch into screaming smoke. The mother shrieked, the gremlin with the cannon suddenly forgotten. She didn't see the other zombie—Hexene recognized him, and it could only be Fallow Graves—shambling behind her, clutching another sloshing bucket.

"Behind you!" Hexene called out in Theban. Even her words felt sluggish.

Thunder came from behind Hexene. She threw herself to the ground, her bruised body too tired even to protest. The cannon had gone off again, but this time, it blew a hole in the wall surrounding the property, terminating in a molten crater in the middle of the street. Technika was only a few steps from the flivver, and Slick was maneuvering it away, cursing at her the whole time. His vehicle maneuvered on jets of fire, and where he went, the basalt of the street glowed dull red for a few moments before darkening again.

Hexene swore. On one side, the hexed Graves was staggered from the blast, but he was recovering and getting ready to kill the mother. On the other, Technika was dancing with a gremlin's custom tank.

"Mafaufau," said the zombie, laying one massive hand on her arm. He was speaking softly, but somehow Hexene heard him. She *really* heard him, more than she ever had before. Maybe the cannon had shaken something loose in her head, but she knew precisely what he meant, and he was right.

She nodded to him and each bolted in opposite directions. Mafaufau ran for the zombie and the water. Hexene ran for Slick and the flivver. The zombie was slow at first but picking up speed with locomotive momentum. Hexene, despite her fatigued and bruised body, darted like a fox. She jumped over the fallen Amir as she ran; he was stirring but had yet to come to. Hexene wasn't sure what she was going to do about the tank, but she figured she'd think of something.

Technika's solution was more prosaic than anything Hexene could come up with: she punched the fire-engine-red hide of the vehicle. Her fist dimpled the metal and the flivver rocked up on its side, the jets flinging it along the stone garden. The cannon went off, but whether that was Slick's intention or not was impossible to say. Hexene hit the deck again, but the shot didn't come close to her. Instead, it thudded through another section of wall.

Unwitch Hunt

Hexene scrambled to her feet and sprinted for the flivver. The cuts on her feet burned, but she could ignore the pain for now. To her left, she heard an awful shriek and resisted the urge to look. She knew what she was going to see anyway. Mafaufau hadn't been fast enough and the mother was dead. Hexene didn't hold it against him. She wouldn't have done any better and probably would have had at least one more scar to show for it, if not worse.

The gremlin righted his flivver. It drifted over the air like a boat over water, leaving streaks of red on the stone. Slick's reptilian features were curled in a snarl, but Hexene saw the fear in his crimson eyes. Technika advanced and only now could Hexene hear that the robot was talking. She was speaking German, so even if all she was doing was reciting a recipe for strudel, it sounded terrifying.

The problem was, the flivver was faster than Technika, who never moved quicker than an inexorable stroll. Give Slick some room, or some altitude, and he would have the robot dead to rights. Hexene didn't bother thinking anymore. She simply charged the flivver as it retreated. She tried to pretend she was still on her broomstick. Pinpoint maneuvering had been her stock in trade. She had slalomed between palm trees, dipped low into traffic; she had been what some people called a daredevil and what Hechalé had called suicidal. Piloting a broom was one part muscle to three parts will, and jumping was the exact opposite arrangement.

She gathered herself and leapt. She almost made it, too. She was going to blame sleeping on the floor for however long it had been and almost getting blown up by a cannon. Not that she had much time to think about it, merely a muttered curse as her foot slammed into the side of the flivver and she nearly flipped over. Instead, she landed on the roof, hard, and her breath went out of her in a gust. Slick turned around from his place in the flivver's cupola and hissed, "Die, witch!"

The cannon rotated around. Hexene was below it, but she had no illusions about what would happen if the gun went off that close to her. She tried to move, but found she couldn't. She had no breath and every part of her felt like it had been dipped in water and was dissolving. Her fingers curled over a vent in the flivver's side, and that was all that kept her from going sprawling into the witches' stone garden.

The gremlin chortled, rubbing his talons together. The flivver stopped its drift, but the cannon kept up its rotation. The barrel settled right over Hexene's prostrate form. Letting go didn't seem like the best option either; he could aim properly then and she would be treated like the erstwhile bodyguard, assuming he didn't just roast her with the vehicle's incandescent jets.

Salvation stalked forward. Behind them, momentarily forgotten as Slick found a new plaything, Technika moved toward the flivver. It had stopped where it was, and if it stayed that way, Hexene would have a chance. She inhaled, and felt her body catch fire.

"You can't kill me," she rasped at Slick.

Slick laughed. "Talk, talk," he said to her. "Die, die!"

"You have to answer one question, first."

Slick smirked. "Ask, ask."

"Do you like to be called Slick or Baron Sweettooth?"

"What?" Slick asked. It was the last word he would ever conclusively say; he would make some noises, sure, but calling them words would be overly charitable. Technika lifted him out of the cupola of his vehicle, and he started in on those very noises.

"Du wolltest mein Herz? Ich werde deins nehmen," she said to him. Her left hand gripping his neck, she drove the steely fingers of her right into his slimy chest. Slick's hisses turned to screams, and then choked off as she pulled the hand from his thorax, clutching his gory heart. That, presumably, was the last thing Slick ever saw, and Sweettooth Confections abruptly had a job opening at the very top. Both gremlin and heart were discarded to thump wetly against the basalt. Hexene wanted to look away, but found it impossible.

"Hexene, are you functional?"

"Yeah," Hexene said, sliding off the flivver. The wash of its engines sent her stumbling back. The flivver's engines cut and it fell to the ground with a clang.

"Your assistance was invaluable," Technika said, dropping both body and excised organ. Hexene nodded, trying to catch a bit more of her breath. Her chest felt like it was only inflating halfway or so.

"Mafaufau," said the zombie. He held a limp shape over his shoulder.

"You have Graves," Technika said. "I believe I owe everyone an apology..."

"Nonsense," said Amir, finally awake. "It is my understanding he was an unwanted suitor. It was his sin, not yours." The balam squinted at Technika's hand, still gloved in green gremlin gore. "And from the looks of it, you dealt with him."

"Mafaufau."

"He's right," Hexene said. "Las Barrenderas will be on the way. We need to leave."

"We cannot get back to the library," Technika said. "I do not believe we have the time, nor have I the reserve in my batteries. Not after that fight."

Hexene looked around, and she saw it, blazing with electrical light, not far from where they stood. "There," she pointed. "Can you get us there?"

"Mafaufau," said the zombie, lumbering as quickly as he could out to the alley. Other witches were emerging from their homes, some standing on rooftops, others taking to the air. They hadn't yet identified Hexene, or at least weren't shouting and waving her wanted poster, but that wouldn't last long. Hexene and the others followed Mafaufau. She turned around once and saw Angelique's friend, the maiden, standing in the wreckage of her front yard, staring at the smudges that had once been her coven. Hexene wondered if the maiden cried at all, if she felt any remorse for what had been done. Or if she was like Angelique, only reflecting on what the crime had purchased. It probably didn't matter one way or the other.

Thirty-Eight

All told, the right house was easy to find. For one, it was the only house in the Sushen Quarter that looked anything like a 17th-century French castle. For another, it was the only building in Las Brujas outside of Cogtown with electrical light blooming from the windows. It was also the only place even vaguely close enough that Hexene regarded as remotely safe. *It's an embassy, right? Those are supposed to have sovereign rights,* she figured. She tried to ignore the fact that the laws in Las Brujas were precisely as elastic as those in charge wanted them to be, and everyone knew it. Made it one of the more honest communities in the world.

Château Rocheverte-La-Lucé was situated on a hill, with the swooping rooftops and red lanterns of the Sushen Quarter all around. It had been precisely designed, too; there was no sense it had been pulled from the ground and imperfectly cast from a mould. This had been *built*, out of sandy bricks, with a tiled roof and everything. It was an actual building in the ways that the structures created by the witches never really were. It was also symmetrical, with two squarish wings coming on either side of a domed roof topped with an elegant minaret. Hexene wasn't used to castles, but she was used to beautiful movie houses, and she could imagine seeing the latest *Vampiro* picture in this place.

Witches zipped about overhead like angry bees. The exit from the Catacombs hadn't been far from this place, and Hexene and her friends made quick, furtive sprints—or as close as they could come to those in the case of Technika and Mafaufau—from shadow to shadow and overhang to overhang. Being caught was inevitable if they stayed out under the steadily brightening sky.

Hexene was the first up the terraces leading to the castle's front door, followed closely by Amir. The front door was big, though not what she thought of as castle-big. She pounded on it. Amir came up next to her and paused to sip from the skull.

"It would be something if no one was home, eh?" he said.

She shot him a glare. "How is there still liquid in there?"

"You must savor your drinks, as you would savor a new lover."

A panel set in the door at knee level slid back before Hexene could respond to another of Amir's lascivious statements. A high voice with a thick French accent demanded in Spanish, "What do you want?"

Hexene dropped to her hands and knees. On the other side of the panel she found a tiny face looking back at her with annoyed suspicion. The face had features similar to Count Inflamel's, though with a definite demonic cast. This had to be the homunculus she had seen at that first Sabbat. "I need to speak with Count Inflamel," she said. "It's urgent."

"I will be the judge of what is urgent," sneered the homunculus. "Who may I tell his lordship is calling?"

"Hexene Candlemas," she hissed.

"The murderess?"

"No! Well, yes. I didn't—" she stopped talking because the homunculus had slammed the panel shut. The witches overhead were circling like vultures; one of them must have spotted her, or else the robot and zombie who were now making their way up the terraces to the front door.

A clank turned Hexene's attention back to the door, which swept open to reveal a great hall that looked to run the length of the central structure. An intricate carpet in golds and greens extended down the center, with frescoes decorating the walls on either side. The ceiling was vaulted, with chandeliers at even intervals, showing off mural work in the elegant arches on either side. The homunculus perched on a nearby end table, painted gold and covered in rococo curlicues. Bat wings folded on his back, and his bare feet sported talons that hung onto his perch. He looked like a cross between Count Inflamel and a gargoyle, and was dressed in 17th-century finery. A pointed tail coiled around his legs.

"Welcome to Château Rocheverte-La-Lucé, home of His Excellency the Count Inflamel, official ambassador from the Conjecture of Atomstadt," the homunculus said prissily, with a gesture that was more sarcastic than expansive.

"Thank you," Hexene said. She waved her friends inside, and the door shut by itself behind them. From this side, she could see the gears and springs that operated it. The massive thing locked like a bank vault and gave off a barely audible hum. "We didn't think you would let us in..."

"Because of the diplomatic incident it would cause," Amir helpfully supplied.

"Understandable," squeaked the homunculus. "If you would wait in the sitting room there, I will see if the Count will receive you. Otherwise, it's back out onto the streets."

"If you do that, we'll likely be arrested," Hexene said.

"Killed is more likely," Technika corrected.

The homunculus nodded thoughtfully. "I agree. So sad. I suppose you should hope that he will see you, then." The little creature gestured with one of his three-fingered talons at a doorway a little ways down the hall. "If you would wait in there, you may help yourself to refreshments. I shall return shortly."

He hopped off the end table and threw his wings wide. With a few awkward flaps, he glided down the hall. Soon, he was tiny against the vastness of the castle. Hexene saw him alight on a doorway at the far end of the corridor and slip through a transom that opened for him.

Amir poked his head into the room the homunculus indicated. "It's a lovely space," he said, "and look at that, a full wet bar. I suppose waiting would be the least we could do."

"We're not waiting," Hexene said, stalking purposefully down the hall.

"Or I suppose we could just barge in," said Amir cheerfully, falling into step with the other three.

They followed the path of the homunculus. Hexene had to admit, the place *was* lovely. Frescoes depicting heroic male figures bringing light to adoring people, usually with gods impotently wrathful in the background, decorated every wall. The house made Hexene feel like at any moment a mob with a portable guillotine would be knocking on the door, ready to settle accounts. She supposed that wasn't all that far off base at the moment, actually.

The hallway terminated in a pair of double doors, above which was the small portal the homunculus had used. She flung them wide. The contents of the room shocked her to silence.

The orrery was enormous, each heavenly body designed to resemble a god. Earth and the moon were sculpted in familiar Greek lines, Earth a zaftig green woman half in and half out of a blue toga, while the moon was a silver pixieish girl armed with a bow. The farther from Earth the bodies were, the more inhuman their appearance. The less said about Pluto the better, but it reminded Hexene of what she thought Baba Yaga's familiar might look like. The solar system was still now, though the central pillar to which all the bodies were attached showed the joints and gears that would set the heavens spinning.

Statues in suits of armor from all over the world, looking like something between knights and giant beetles, stood at attention in alcoves all around the room. Glass windows looked out over the back of the estate, where a geometric maze wound into the dark.

Hexene recognized Count Inflamel from his appearance at the Sabbat. He was a middle-aged man with wild, chin-length hair. He wore a billowy shirt rolled to the elbows, a green waistcoat embroidered in a geometric pattern, tight breeches, and boots, with a grease-covered apron around his waist. He looked to be tinkering with one of the bodies from the orrery, and that's when Hexene noted that there were far more objects in the orrery than ones she was aware of in the solar system.

The homunculus flitted over and alighted on Infamel's shoulder. "And here they are."

"I see that." Inflamel wiped his greasy hands on a rag, but that didn't seem to do much other than dye the rag blacker. "Is there a reason you declined to await me in my sitting room? Were the accommodations not to your liking?"

"On the contrary, your Excellency," Amir said. "Miss Candlemas merely thought that it was imperative we speak to you."

"Miss Candlemas!" Inflamel's eyes brightened and Amir deflated as he was promptly forgotten. "I can assume that you are she?"

"I am," Hexene said. She didn't know whether or not to curtsey and she decided she would hate herself if she did, so she didn't.

"You have the entire world of Las Brujas in a bit of a snit," said the alchemist. "The first witch to escape the clutches of Las Barrenderas! It's wonderfully exciting. And that you have accumulated this motley band of servants about you!"

"Thank you? They're not—"

"I should thank *you*! I would not call my life boring, but truth be told, I would rather be in Atomstadt. It is difficult to collaborate on experiments via the radio or the post." He shook his head. "I thought my people were bad with the mail, but yours could lose a letter that was glued to them. Now, please introduce me to your companions, Miss Candlemas."

Hexene did, with her customary utter lack of fanfare. "Mafaufau. Technika. Amir."

"Amir *Noire*, and I am pleased—"

"And who is the gentleman presently riding on...Mafaufau, is it?"

"Mafaufau."

"...Mafaufau's back there," he finished.

"Fallow Graves. He's been hexed, so he's a little dangerous. Do you have a dungeon?"

"Do I have a dungeon? My dear, I am French." He held up a hand. "But not so fast. It would probably be in the best interests of future relations between witches and mad scientists if I were to turn you over to the Barrenderas Ward from which you escaped, or perhaps to the Moirai themselves. And perhaps I will! But first I want to know what you are doing here."

Hexene shrugged. "Desperation."

Inflamel burst out laughing. "Did you hear that?" he said to the homunculus.

The little creature held his ear in annoyance. "How could I not?" he muttered.

"Perhaps you should tell me everything," Inflamel said. He held up a hand as Hexene started to do just that. "Not here. I imagine you're hungry, and Madam Technika's eyes are flickering dangerously. You do not come to a count's household and not expect hospitality, do you?"

He clapped his hands, and the armored statues standing around the room sprang to life. Hexene tensed—surrounded by potential enemies and she never suspected. They stepped from their alcoves, spun to face the same direction with military precision, and with the grinding of gears, they marched clockwise from the room. Two halted at the last moment and came to parade rest.

"Excuse my staff," Inflamel said. "They need to prepare proper foodstuffs. Please, follow Percy, freshen up, and he will escort you to my table. Mafaufau, you may hand Mr. Graves over to Hector there."

Mafaufau handed the unconscious zombie to a suit of Spartan armor, its limbs naked gears, pipes, and cables.

"Very good," Inflamel said. A booming sound echoed through the castle. He held a finger up. "Seems I have other visitors. I shall once again explain to them the particulars of the treaty between Las Brujas and Atomstadt."

Hexene and the others followed a dented suit of plate mail to a guest suite while Inflamel went to his door. The castle continued to be grand, though after all she had seen in Las Brujas, its mundanity was shocking. A good reminder that Count Inflamel didn't truly belong in the city in which he lived.

The suite the statue escorted them to was decorated in 17th-century finery just like everything else here, and in between taking turns in the washroom, they lounged on fainting couches. When it was her turn, Hexene found a staggering array of oils and several strigils waiting for her. She washed her face and hands and did end up feeling a little better. Then she cleaned her feet, removing a thick layer of dirt that had been accumulating since her escape, and navigating around the various fresh and half-healed cuts that bedeviled her since her barefoot arrest.

Amir took by far the longest of them, and emerged wearing nothing but a towel. Mafaufau came out with wet hair and a mildly contented look on his cherubic face. Technika returned to the lounge holding a bottle of what looked like machine oil.

"What is that?" Hexene asked.

"Machine oil," said Technika.

"Oh."

"Lemon scented."

"Oh?"

When the group of them were finished and Amir had reluctantly donned his half-undone tuxedo, Percy the automaton led them down several hallways and a flight of stairs found to an baroque dining room. A long table was flanked with fussy-looking chairs, the wood painted gold, with a bright chandelier twinkling overhead. The china was ornate, the goblets were crystal, and the silverware was actually silver. This place looked to have entertained more aristocrats than werewolves.

Inflamel was already sitting at the head of the table. He gestured to the chairs around him. "Please, have a seat. Gale? The first course, please?" A huge automaton in green knight's armor clanked from the room, candlelight flickering on its emerald fixtures.

"First course?" Hexene asked.

"I apologize for the simplicity of the meal," Inflamel said. "I did the best I could under short notice, and of course used some of my own techniques to aid in the swiftness of the preparation. I can only hope it satisfies."

"What happened with the witches at the door?"

Inflamel waved the question away. "I informed them that you had passed through and continued on your way. They did not believe my subterfuge, but they did not wish to create an incident either. I believe they'll be waiting outside."

"Oh toil and trouble," Hexene muttered. Then, louder, "Thank you for taking us in."

"I have not yet decided what to do with you, but I am also not in the habit of turning away those in desperate straits."

Five of the automatons emerged from the door behind the count, each carrying a plate. Hexene found a salad placed in front of her. The greens were glowing slightly, but otherwise it looked quite normal. The machines placed a small plate of cheese in front of Inflamel, while Amir received a plate of delicately sliced and bleeding meats. Mafaufau got a plate of dumplings, and the automatons gave Technika a small copper sphere, green lights winking from it at even intervals.

"I should have mentioned that I'm a vegetarian..." Hexene said awkwardly, though she hadn't been sure what she ate in Baba Yaga's domain and had thought better of asking.

"Enough of your people are that I took the liberty of assuming," said Inflamel, eating his cheese with a tiny knife and fork.

"Is this kidney?" Amir asked, sampling one of the bits.

"Kidney, heart, a little lung, some liver, pancreas."

"Oh, your Excellency, you are a wonderful host."

"I try. Now, Hexene. Please tell me your story. From the beginning, if you please."

Inflamel listened carefully to everything that had happened, and then to what Hexene needed out of him. The only part of her story she omitted was Baba Yaga, claiming instead to have hidden in the Catacombs for what she learned was the bulk of a month. As she thought on it, she realized she had far more memories than would be contained in a single month, even though it had barely felt like a week while she had been down there.

"That is quite the tale," Inflamel mused when she had finished. "I confess, I find myself spellbound, if you will forgive the pun. What do you hope to accomplish now?"

Hexene took a deep breath, and looked at the faces of her companions in turn. Then she told Inflamel what she had planned.

"Now that is interesting," said the count, leaning forward. His green eyes sparkled, and for a moment Hexene thought she saw the glint of madness. It was gone just as quickly, and he was once again the genteel aristocrat he had been. I suppose we should speak with Mr. Graves now, since he is such an important part of your plan." The count rose from his table, setting his napkin aside. "Please, right this way."

Two of the automatons joined them. As much as Inflamel presented himself as an ally, he was not about to go without a bodyguard. Hexene couldn't blame him; she was a wanted killer, and her companions certainly looked formidable. The count led them through several more rooms, each one straddling the line between opulent and ostentatious, until they reached a large staircase leading into the depths of the castle.

The dungeon, as he called it, was actually fairly pleasant as dungeons went. Electric lights, doing a decent job of imitating the gold glow of open flame, kept the place illuminated. Inflamel had three cells, each furnished with a cot, a sink, a toilet, and what Hexene later learned was a radio with decent range. Sure, the floor was stone, but the arid atmosphere of the Atacama Desert had made certain it didn't have the kind of dank that usually went with dungeons. Graves lay unconscious on the floor of one of the cells.

Hexene had the opportunity to stare into the face of the zombie who had nearly killed her. He was fairly unremarkable, with dry, papery skin rotted away in lacy patches. He had a gaunt, saturnine expression, as though he were just as depressed when he was sleeping as awake. His mouth was no longer sewn shut, but he retained small raw patches where the thread had passed through his lips. He was dressed simply in a ragged shirt and pants, with old sandals on his decaying feet. His crow collar lay against his bony chest. As Hexene took him in, a horrible red rage boiled inside her. She wanted to hurt this man. But she forced herself to remember that he was as much a victim as the murdered witches. He had been used and discarded the same as the rest of the dead.

"What did you do to him?" Inflamel asked.

"Mafaufau," Mafaufau said.

"I see. Miss Candlemas, would you care to answer the question?"

"I think the appropriate word would be 'clobbered'. Mafaufau clobbered him," she said.

"How was he not killed?"

"Mafaufau."

"Mafaufau clobbered him *precisely*," Hexene interpreted.

Inflamel nodded with new appreciation. "You have excellent taste in manservants, Miss Candlemas."

"Mafaufau isn't my servant."

"A useful obfuscation," Inflamel said. "I would ask Mafaufau to unclobber him, but I don't think that is technically a word in any language for good reason. Gustav?"

The homunculus, who had been mimicking his master's pose from his perch on his master's head, said, "Yes?"

"Fetch the smelling salts, please." The homunculus flitted off.

"Mafaufau!"

"Not literal salt, I assure you," Inflamel said without looking directly at the zombie. "Merely an alchemical recipe of my own design. You would be astonished at how much of a call there is to raise your people from a state of unconsciousness in this city. Or perhaps not."

"Before you do, would you open the cell? There's something I want," Hexene said.

"As you wish," said the count, plucking a ring of keys from the wall and fitting one of them into the door. Hexene went inside and knelt beside the zombie. Her hands trembled. She made fists, telling herself again that Graves wouldn't do anything. Couldn't. When she relaxed her hands, the shivers were gone. She opened his mouth and pulled the scroll from between his lips. It was damp and smelled like mildew. She stood up, stepped out of the cell, and nodded to Inflamel. The count locked the door once again.

The homunculus returned, clutching a glass bottle to his chest. He landed on Inflamel's shoulders and dropped it into the alchemist's waiting hands. Inflamel pulled the cork out with his teeth, shook a small quantity of the greenish powder onto his fingers, reached through the bars, and held the substance under Graves's nose.

Graves started and opened his milky eyes. They kept opening and opening as he saw the group standing over him, and he backed away from the bars with a frightened "Brains!" He had an accent that sounded vaguely English to Hexene.

"Yes, it's me," Hexene said.

Graves shook his head. "Brains. Brains!"

"I know you didn't mean to do it," she said stiffly, unable to put any warmth into her tone. "You were just a weapon."

"Brains." His shoulders relaxed, but he remained on guard.

"And you understand him?" Inflamel asked. Hexene nodded. "Remarkable."

She supposed it was. She hadn't thought about it. The zombies around her, starting with Mafaufau, had started to make more sense since her time with Baba Yaga. It was more about paying attention to the context of the word and the zombie's attitude, but each response from Graves or Mafaufau put an image in her head the same as a more complicated sentence from anyone else. She merely had to accept it.

"Brains," insisted Graves.

"The Yana Sabbat is tonight at midnight," Hexene told the zombie.

"Every witch will be there. If you're willing to come with us and identify the witch that hexed you, we'll survive. All of us."

"Brains."

"Yes, she will be there," Hexene said. "We'll protect you. From her, or anyone else."

"Brains."

"Trust us."

"Brains?"

"We'll be able to get in, with his help." She glanced at Inflamel.

Inflamel smiled. "Miss Candlemas, I am only too pleased to assist."

THIRTY-NINE

It was nearly midnight, and by the Theban calendar, the month of Ettu was giving way to Yana. The Sabbat marking the change was that night. Hexene, Mafaufau, Technika, Amir, and Graves were all crammed in the belly of Inflamel's clockwork dragon. It wasn't the most comfortable of places to be, especially considering Mafaufau's size and Technika's lack of flexibility, but it enabled them to slip past the witches staking out the Château Rocheverte-La-Lucé. Hexene was grateful that she was small, Graves was skin and bones, and Amir's skeleton seemed to be made of liquid when he poured himself into the compartment. Hexene was going to have to get used to breathing shallowly, and felt lucky that two of the people with her in there only breathed recreationally, and one didn't even fake it.

Inflamel closed the compartment with a grin, one echoed on the face of his homunculus. "I do believe this will be the most exciting Sabbat in ages!" was the last thing he said. Then, in the dark of the container, Hexene was surrounded by the whirring of gears and the clicking of levers as the artificial dragon came to life. She felt the dragon take to the air, a sudden lurch she used to relish, and that was when she started to wonder if this wasn't a terrible idea.

She was heading into the amphitheater at the center of the Stone Forest, the heart of Las Brujas, and she was the most wanted criminal in recent history. She had a single witness—who could only say a single word—and still couldn't use her magic. It was a terrible plan that didn't stand a vampire's chance at a nude beach on Palm Sunday.

Fortunately, she didn't have long to dwell. The flight from the small landing pad at the back of Château Rocheverte-La-Lucé was so short it felt less like a flight and more like one long jump. The dragon landed with a clank, and Hexene's heart decided that it was time to remind her that it was there and none too confident about the present course of action. Outside, she heard muffled talking and remained quiet, resisting the urge to suck in air that just wasn't there. The witches were scolding Inflamel for arriving at the Yana Sabbat—he wasn't scheduled to be there. He apologized to them and promised that he had only to wind up his dragon and he would be on his way. After several years, the witches agreed, and the panel opened up.

"You have but a short time," Inflamel hissed. "Exit, quickly!"

Hexene clambered out and dropped down behind the clockwork dragon, then gasped as she almost fell over the sheer side of the amphitheater. Inflamel had landed on the narrow lip that ran around the back side of the structure and plunged into the Stone Forest below. Hexene realized that he hadn't had a lot of places to choose from, but she wouldn't have minded a warning. The distance to the ground seemed to stretch and spiral. While the fear paralyzed her, the disgust was worst. Acrophobia was unnatural in a witch. She grabbed the flagpole next to her and held on with white knuckles. At the top, a flag, decorated with a stylized raven, flapped in the night breeze.

Amir crawled out and alighted on the edge, holding his skull cup. "Oh my. We are high up." With disturbing confidence, he leaned way over to peer into the Stone Forest. He couldn't have seen much. The full moon was bright and the shadows were deep. Hexene pointed at the open panel of the dragon and raised a questioning eyebrow. "I would be pleased."

Inflamel paused in his theatrical winding of the dragon, smiling and waving to the witches below. Out of the side of his mouth, he muttered, "If you would hurry? While I have been granted leave to pause, I believe your sisters would like to continue with their business without one of my kind listening in."

Amir hauled Graves out and the zombie's eyes bugged from his skull as he beheld the drop into the Stone Garden. "Brains!" he protested. Hexene took his hand and guided him next to her, where they could both lean against the clockwork dragon's foreleg. He clutched at her, trembling, desperately trying not to look over to their deaths.

"Now, my big fellow. Hold steady." Amir gripped Mafaufau's forearm, and the zombie held the balam's. When Mafaufau saw the lip he had to stand on, he shot Inflamel a withering glare. Inflamel never noticed, making a show of winding the dragon and mopping his brow at how allegedly difficult the act was. Technika was last from the compartment, with Mafaufau hauling her bodily into the night air and setting her next to him. She beeped when she saw their precarious perch.

"All finished?" Inflamel asked the five figures variously poised on the edge of the amphitheater. "Excellent. I will take to the air, and hopefully when this turns violent, I won't be too distant to enjoy the spectacle."

Hexene nodded, and only barely rolled her eyes at him. He grinned at her and mounted the clockwork dragon. As soon as the artificial beast moved, they would all be visible to the entire Sabbat. There was no time to regret the plan. The dragon jumped into the sky, air filling the canvas webs of its wings. Hexene stood, and noted that more than a few witches were staring at the five figures on the amphitheater wall, squinting as they attempted to make out features. Some of the nearer ones could, and the murmuring spread from witch to witch as more turned to look at the fugitive who decided to just march into the Sabbat. Hexene hoped they were at least an interesting sight, perched on the edge of death.

The Crow Sisterhood were onstage, each holding a ledger, but they had been silent at least since Hexene squirmed out of the dragon. Perhaps they were friendly, or perhaps Hexene imagined the small smile on Cora's face. The Moirai watched Hexene's group with faint interest, and Hexene did her best to block them out. She wasn't going to be intimidated.

Angelique Arcane was staring as well, in utter disbelief, Petunia Pendulum and the recently orphaned maiden by her side. Hexene watched the wheels turn behind Angelique's eyes, trying to understand Hexene's play. The confusion and panic in her eyes was delicious, but Hexene couldn't savor it. She hadn't earned it yet. Angelique's eyes narrowed, she took a deep breath, and right as she opened her mouth, Hexene nodded to Technika.

The robot's speakers were far louder than Hexene could ever hope to be, though that was not why they used them now. "My name is Hexene Candlemas," said the recorded message coming from Technika. "You're looking for me."

Several witches, all wearing cloaks from various Wards, started to move in her direction like a pack of wolves cornering a sick deer. They were murmuring, though whether it was to one another or the beginnings of hexes, Hexene couldn't tell. She chewed on the object in her mouth nervously, once again thinking that maybe this plan was the stupidest thing she had ever done.

"I didn't kill anyone. You didn't believe me at my trial, but I didn't have evidence then. I have it now," the recording went. Hexene placed a hand on Graves's back. The zombie was trembling, and for the first time, Hexene felt the stab of guilt for dragging him into this. She would like to tell herself he had to clear his name as much as hers, but that was a lie. The witches didn't care about one zombie more than any of the others; he and his kind had never been more than convenient excuses. She tamped the guilt down; she was going to have to be cold if she was going to survive. "This is Fallow Graves. He is one of several zombies that were hexed in order to carry out a series of murders: the rest of my coven, the bulk of the Arcane Adepts, and two more that I'm sure I've been blamed for already."

The advancing Barrenderas paused on the stairs. Whatever spells they had been working were momentarily forgotten. Angelique, though, was charging up the steps, pushing witches aside, and cursing the whole way.

Petunia and the maiden were behind her, Petunia leaning heavily on her cane and the maiden following timidly behind.

"Who did it, then?" shouted one of the Barrenderas, and soon others were calling out for the identification.

"Angelique Arcane is the guilty party," the recording said, and Hexene pointed at the sputtering maiden. While Hexene hoped the identification would stun her, Angelique never stopped moving, and even picked up desperate speed as she charged. Some of the witches were close enough to see Hexene wasn't speaking, and more than one was frowning in confusion. The recording went on, filling in the story Hexene had put together: "She met a man and fell in love. She wanted a family. She wanted to move from maidenhood to motherhood. Except her coven wouldn't allow her to. So Angelique decided to do something about it, and the perfect scapegoat had just fallen into her lap. After all, everybody knows an unwitch will do anything at all."

"She lies!" screeched Angelique. Her familiar had risen up, hissing, his fangs unsheathed. She was close enough that Hexene could almost smell her.

"I have a witness," said the recording, and Hexene patted Graves on the back. He quailed from Angelique, who hadn't stopped her headlong rush forward.

"A zombie?" Angelique demanded, pausing only momentarily. Behind her, Petunia and the other maiden leaned against each other, breathing hard. "It's bad enough we allow an unwitch into our Sabbat, but now we're going to let anyone speak at all?" Some of the witches murmured in agreement.

"Hear him out!" That came from Cora Crow, her voice amplified by her place onstage. Soon, others were calling for the same, while others called for the troublemakers to be removed and Hexene to be arrested. The Moirai never spoke and never changed expression, remaining detached from the shouted argument. They watched as though two anthills had started a debate on the finer points of Jacobin politics.

Graves stopped shaking. Hexene squeezed his dry, rotted shoulder gently, trying to lend him a little bit of strength. Angelique was almost on top of them, and she had begun to mix a hex on the fly. Hexene didn't want to find out what it did.

"Mr. Graves," the recording boomed, "Is the witch who turned you into a murder weapon with a hex here now?"

"Brains," said the zombie. Then, louder, with a nod, "Brains!"

"Point her out."

Angelique said a few words in the scratching syllables of Theban, and Hexene knew exactly what she was casting. Hexene loved that particular hex. It was a classic. And an excellent choice, considering where they had been forced to land. Angelique held out her palm and blew the powder into Graves's face.

He stepped forward, raising his arm to finger her as the true killer, and promptly slipped like Buster Keaton finding a banana peel, toppling off the top of the amphitheater. Hexene held her breath in disbelief. *Maybe he'll be okay?* she thought madly. Then the splat echoed up from the Stone Forest and everyone present had to come to terms with the deadly bit of slapstick that had just unfolded.

"Where's your witness now, unwitch?" Angelique demanded with a triumphant smirk.

Hexene figured she should stop fighting her natural inclinations. Sometimes the old ways really were the best. She clenched her fist the way Canela had been taught and punched Angelique right in the face.

Forty

For the glorious duration of several heartbeats, it went really well. No witch expects to just get socked in the nose. That's not how magical duels go. They didn't have referees, because if they had, one would have thrown a flag as soon as Hexene's knuckles squashed soft cartilage and struck oil. Angelique had clearly expected Hexene to abide by the unspoken laws of decorum, but Angelique wasn't being punched by Hexene. Maria Foley balled up that fist. Canela swung it.

Angelique was so shocked by the reckless violation of etiquette that she absorbed several that would have made Anthony Foley proud. Blows that would have shown Angelique the error of addressing little Maria Foley as Canela. She flattened Angelique with the first hit, and fell to the floor after her, splitting skin and drawing blood. Angelique got to learn the same lesson that Gordo and every other bully learned the moment they thought they had Maria Foley dead to rights. Never back Hexene Candlemas or Maria Foley or Canela into a corner. If you're lucky, you'll live to regret it.

Surprise could only last so long, though, and Hexene was vastly outnumbered. Hands hooked under her armpits, hauling her off her fallen opponent. Angelique got the breathing room she needed to skitter away on her back, her nose and mouth like the drain at a slaughterhouse. Hexene whirled and the owners of the hands—Petunia and the maiden—backed off with frightened screams. Las Barrenderas had her entirely hemmed in, closing around her.

Amir stepped in front of her. Hexene couldn't hear what he was saying over the blood pounding in her ears, but it didn't stop a single witch from their angry advance. Mafaufau pushed Petunia and the maiden away from Hexene, but because it was Mafaufau, a shove had the force of a catapult, and to a gathering of witches, nothing looked worse than a giant zombie manhandling a mother with a cane and a maiden who couldn't be more than fifteen. The expressions of abject horror were almost funny. After witches murdered and zombies enslaved, it was a simple shove that shocked them.

The problem with witches was that they didn't even riot like humans, or like zombies. Witches maintained a collective rage that could only be spent with precisely measured curses designed to inflict the troublemaker's sins upon her sevenfold. They could still be played like lesser creatures, though, and Angelique Arcane was doing just that. She had risen to her feet, crimson now smeared over her face likely by the swipe of a sleeve, turning her face into a bloody shirt to wave. "You see? She comes to our holy place! She brings zombies to attack us! She's a murderer! She's no witch! She's not one of us! Unwitch! Unwitch! Unwitch!"

The chant started with her, and anyone who wasn't wrapping liquid Theban syllables around a hex was using it on Hexene. Hands darted out to tear hair from her head and swatches from her dress. Most awful were the faces. The expressions of rage, sure, but it was what was behind them. A sense that had Hexene not been there as an outlet, that same rage would be laying in wait for some trigger to explode. They wanted to tear her apart, but it wasn't personal, and that was the worst part. Familiars hissed, barked, snarled, squawked, and made a thousand other sounds giving voice to the boiling anger inside every witch.

Angelique leaned in out of the chaos and whispered into Hexene's ear: "It was supposed to be you. I gave you a chance, but you said no."

The hexes flew. Witches cast bones at Hexene's feet, blew clouds of powder into her face, spat frogs and bugs onto her skirts. She felt the curses wrapping around her body and soul, slimy and caustic. Magical claws fought for purchase on her spirit, looked for a place to burrow into the thing called *Hexene Candlemas*. They hunted the places she should be but found nothing, their howls echoing soundlessly in the void. Because Hexene Candlemas somehow did not exist. Standing there, flesh and blood, nothing.

The hexes slid off her, one by one, like rain that would never fall in this arid place. Hexene stood as the magic battered against her, and the assembled witches looked on in horror as hexes that could kick like an elephant gun landed like spitballs.

She smiled without teeth, reached into her bag, and removed the hex doll. The witches stared, brows furrowing as their minds told them what they were seeing, but what couldn't possibly be true. The doll's head was crowned with a mop of red curls. A dress like a patchwork quilt covered its skinny body. Crimson thread, worked into the doll's bare feet, mapped the cuts and scars Hexene had acquired during her fugitive state. She held it up, so her assailants could see, so they would know for a fact that she was a madwoman. The hexes petered out as witch after witch realized what she was looking at, her anger melting into confusion. A witch, an unwitch, immune from hexes, was now brandishing a hex doll of herself. This was the purest insanity, and yet it was undeniably happening.

Hexene watched it sink in on all the rage-filled faces around her. Then, with a contemptuous flick of her wrist, she tossed the doll to Angelique. The other maiden caught it, staring in confusion. *You wanted Hexene in your coven. Here you go*, Hexene thought. She almost wished she had recorded that statement for Technika to blast over the Stone Forest.

She gestured to the Sabbat. *Keep them coming*, the taunt commanded, and some of the witches obeyed, even as others tried to understand the riddle of the hex doll. Others didn't care; they wanted to crush the unwitch who had the audacity to think she belonged, who put herself in a Sabbat, in a city, that never wanted her. The caustic tendrils of magic went not to Hexene, but gathered instead on the hex doll. It *was* her, after all. Yet the hexes did not reach from that to her. They couldn't. Something kept that bridge broken.

"What *are* you?" Angelique whispered. Only Hexene was close enough to hear it, and certainly the only one who would see the horror on the witch's face.

Hexene stepped closer. Danbala the serpent hissed, but he didn't strike. Angelique recoiled, but her feet were nailed to the spot. Hexene was the viper now, hypnotizing her prey with sheer force of presence. Then she opened her mouth, and the scroll unrolled on her tongue like she was tasting the air. Angelique stared at it in mute incomprehension, and then, piece by piece, she realized what it was. She probably recognized her own writing on the yellow surface, and she knew that, magically speaking, it wasn't Hexene standing before her.

It was *her*.

Angelique's eyes first widened with comprehension, then narrowed as she realized the power Hexene had handed her. That scroll had come from the mouth of Fallow Graves, and it placed Hexene entirely under Angelique's control. Made her little more than a weapon, an automaton who would do anything. Angelique had only to issue an order.

Hexene snatched the doll from Angelique's hands and popped the head from its shoulders, casting both away. The doll was broken, no longer echoing Hexene's form. And all the curses that had been intended for Hexene had to continue their journey. Hexene still did not technically exist, as her will was bound by another. So the curses of an entire Sabbat could only converge around the one who held her on a magical leash.

Hexene watched the assembled magic wrap Angelique up like the coils of a snake and *squeeze*. The hexes consumed her, piece by screaming piece. Hexene thought of the screams of Angelique's victims. They weren't that far off.

She watched the agony tell its story on Angelique's face as the witch's flesh turned to smoke and dust. Hexene had seen several familiars die, and

Angelique was following their example. Embers, like fireflies, began at her feet and floated upward in a swirling cloud, taking her body with it. But Angelique's mere death was not all Hexene wanted. There was one bit of business that had drawn her to this city of witches.

Hexene reached into the hex itself, grabbing hold of the twining magic of the witches of Las Brujas. Hexene touched a cold so profound that it burned her with its absence. The agony in her head was deeper than anything she had ever felt, had ever imagined was possible, but she held on. The magic writhed like a viper in her grip, and the flesh of her hand withered, turned black, and fell from the bone. She stared at it, and instead of looking on in horror, her eyes held only a faint acceptance.

Her hand, now little more than a bony claw, clutched at the tangled curses of the Sabbat, even as the awful braided serpent of torture tore Angelique apart. Hexes slithered over the ruined hand like hungry centipedes. With the owner of Hexene's will gone, the magic wheeled about at its intended target. But it had been weakened and confused, and Hexene had learned at the feet of the Great Hag herself. Though her mind burned with the touch of these caustic magics, Hexene grappled with them, and she began to sculpt, forcing her will over those of the curses. She was Hexene Candlemas, Maria Foley, and Canela. She was three, but also one. She knew each name and where it resided in her heart. In this moment, pushed past the thresholds of pain, madness had taken over. That would explain the form her familiar chose—at the time, it seemed perfectly logical. She clasped the hexes even as they dissolved her, body and soul, and she forced them to become a body of their own.

In her mind's eye, she saw the familiar before her turn to solid light, and the light inverted to a blinding dark. What was a plane became a passage, and through it, she felt the Many-Faced Goddess both distant and uncomfortably near. Hexene would never know how she did what she did. She wasn't truly herself. *Something* was in her, working perhaps its will, perhaps hers. She saw things through the scintillating colors of the passage, and felt her new familiar's many arms around her in a wet embrace. She gripped the last remaining threads of the curses on her soul and pulled them free. They were like thorny vines, tearing bits of her as they went.

She cracked the curses like a whip, and she was back in the Sabbat, near the apex of the amphitheater as the last few bits of burning smoke that were Angelique Arcane vanished forever, leaving only her pointed hat sitting on the black stone.

Hexene cradled the eldritch monstrosity she had incarnated against her breast, raising up her ruined right hand, displaying the cost of her power to the Sabbat and the will she had displayed to take it. Most of the flesh was gone, leaving behind gray bones and funeral wrap of ragged flesh. She spat the hex scroll from her mouth, and it turned to embers before it hit the ground. Hexene picked up Angelique's hat and set it on her own head, sweeping the Sabbat with a challenging stare.

"I am Hexene Candlemas!" she boomed, this time with her own voice. "The unwitch! The Heqatun! Angelique Arcane murdered my coven. Murdered her coven. And I collected the debt a murderer owes! What says the Sabbat?"

The Moirai rose as one and regarded Hexene. She no longer saw contempt there, but respect, and perhaps a tiny bit of fear. The rest of the Sabbat stared in horror at Hexene's hand, or the blasphemous thing she held like a baby. "The matter is settled. We no longer seek the execution of Hexene Candlemas," said Morta.

Hexene once again swept the rest of the Sabbat with her gaze to see if anyone else thought they might like to avenge one of the dead, paying particular attention to the two witches who were almost in Angelique's coven. They clutched each other, staring at her in stark terror.

"Good. The matter is settled," she said.

She looked down at her familiar and grinned. He was the most hideous thing she had ever seen, somewhere between an octopus, and a bat, and maybe a bit of spider monkey if the thing had been rotting in a sinkhole for a good six months. Her new familiar. Hers.

Then he said the most lovely thing she had ever heard. "Bubububub."

Forty-One

The Arcane house was quiet. The Adepts were all dead and Evangeline's family had left for Haiti to stay with family. Maybe with Evangeline no longer keeping them in a state of arrested development, they could finally grow up. She hoped Little Raoul might find someone he could love. Hexene's responsibilities, such that they were, belonged with Hechalé's family, though she had no idea what she would tell them.

No one had cared when she had, in essence, taken over the Adept home and moved her companions in as well. Technically robots and balam weren't allowed to reside outside of Cogtown, but no one was going to say Hexene Candlemas the Heqatun couldn't live with whoever or whatever she pleased. The other witches could barely look at her familiar, little Bub, without screaming, anyway.

Hexene had survived the battle, but it hadn't been without some scars. She still sported the streaks down her left arm, and they itched from time to time. Her right hand never recovered from the flensing administered by the Sabbat. It hurt constantly, and no drug or poultice would make the pain go away entirely. She hid it beneath a green silk glove that had been a congratulatory gift from Count Inflamel—and, Hexene thought, a signal to the population of Las Brujas that he was friendly with the Heqatun.

She had a pair of black snakeskin boots made as well, in the granny style favored by some witches, as a warning to others. She didn't know if they understood the implicit threat, but she liked the boots.

After a week of quiet, the covens started turning up at her front door, or bothering her when she landed in Grandmother Square. Each one promised Hexene that she could be their maiden, or mother or crone. Any slot in the coven was open. She had only to say the word. She turned every one of them down.

"At least you are one of them again," Amir observed.

"No, she is not," said Technika.

"Mafaufau."

"What do you mean?" Amir asked. "Technika, not you, Mafaufau."

"She is of them, but she did something none of them could do, and they are frightened. They are opening the door, under the belief that a monster at their side is better than one at their back. She is still an outsider."

Hexene nodded. "They don't believe I'm innocent. They only believe that I'm powerful enough that innocence doesn't really matter. I can do what I did because no one has the guts to say otherwise. That's the only law here in Las Brujas."

Amir grinned. "In my experience, it is the only true law anywhere. Most places, they will dress it up with words, but in the end, it is only this."

Hexene was finally able to fly again, and so experience the city as it was supposed to be. It was beautiful in its way, but it wasn't for her. Hard to accept, but Las Brujas was a city of witches, and she was something else. She returned to the library to thank Baba Yaga, but the door they had gone through wasn't there and didn't look like it had ever been. She went through the Catacombs with Mafaufau's help and found that the trapdoor in the storeroom was gone as well. Hexene imagined Baba Yaga already knew she was grateful.

It was the last day of Kala when Hexene heard a knock at the door. She should have known it was bad luck then; nothing good ever happened in Kala, and this Kala was exceptionally short. Bad luck had to work extra hard this year. But it had been some time since her adventure, and she was getting bored. She opened the door to find Count Inflamel, his clockwork dragon on the walk behind him, and she invited him in. Mafaufau was considerate enough to bring him some tea; Hexene never would have thought of it. She escorted the count to the dining room and sat down at the table that was far too large for just the pair of them.

"Now, what can I do for you, Count?"

He grinned. "I have a favor to ask of you."

Considering the favors Inflamel had done her, she couldn't say no. "Is there some witch bothering you? Some introduction you want made?"

"Nothing like that," said Inflamel. "In fact, nothing *here*. Tell me, what do you know of Atomstadt?"

THE END

Acknowledgments

First and foremost, I want to thank Candlemark & Gleam. I will always be grateful for and faintly mystified by their unflagging support of me. As I've expanded the world and told different kinds of stories in the City of Devils universe, C&G remains an enthusiastic partner that I am lucky to have.

I also want to thank Team T-rex, my wife and daughter, for their support. Okay, the kid isn't so much supportive as funny, but I'll take it.

And of course I need to thank the fans of this series. Presumably that's you, holding this very book. You don't have to look around. I'm not watching. I'm not El Mirón. It's been incredible to find so many people on the same wavelength as I am. I hope you enjoy this new chapter of the story, seeing as it's the biggest departure so far. I'd been planning this at least since the outlining phase of the second book, and it's a relief to get it out there. It started life as a novella, but as I got more interested in the unique culture of the witches...it got bigger.

Don't worry, we'll be getting back to Nick soon. He's sweatily waiting in Los Angeles for his next call to adventure. In the meantime, know that every moment I work on City of Devils, I think of all of you. You're awesome. Thank you.

ABOUT THE AUTHOR

Much like film noir, Justin Robinson was born and raised in Los Angeles. He splits his time between writing and taking care of a small human. Degrees in Anthropology and History prepared him for unemployment, but an obsession with horror fiction and a laundry list of phobias provided a more attractive option. He is the author of more than 15 novels in a variety of genres including noir, humor, fantasy, science fiction, and horror. Most of them are pretty good.

FOLLOW THE AUTHOR ONLINE

Website: http://www.weirdnoirmaster.com
Twitter, Instagram, Patreon: weirdnoirmaster
Facebook: facebook.com/weirdnoirmaster

The ADVENTURE CONTINUES ONLINE!

Visit the Candlemark & Gleam website to

Find out about new releases

Read free sample chapters

Catch up on the latest news and author events

Buy books! All purchases on the Candlemark & Gleam site are DRM-free and paperbacks come with a free digital version!

Meet flying monkey-creatures from beyond the stars!*

www.candlemarkandgleam.com

*Space monkeys may not be available in your area. Some restrictions may apply. This offer is only available for a limited time and is in fact a complete lie.

CPSIA information can be obtained
at www.ICGtesting.com
Printed in the USA
LVHW042055120322
713212LV00005B/416